For homicide detectiv ................ good year. Having Tony to go home to makes him a better cop and a better person. For Tony, it's been hard being in love with a man he can't touch in public. Evasions and outright lying to friends and family take a little of the shine off his relationship with Mac, but Tony is determined to make it work.

As the Minneapolis Police Department moves into a hot, humid summer, Mac is faced with a different challenge. A killer has murdered two blond women, and the police have no real clues. Mac hates to think that another murder may be the only way they'll make progress with the case. But when that murder happens, it hits close to home for Tony. And suddenly Mac faces an ultimatum: come out into the sunlight and stand beside Tony as his lover, or walk away and live without a piece of his heart.

Featuring a roll call of some of the best writers of gay erotica and mysteries today!

| | | |
|---|---|---|
| Derek Adams | M. Jules Aedin | Maura Anderson |
| Victor J. Banis | Jeanne Barrack | Laura Baumbach |
| Alex Beecroft | Sarah Black | Ally Blue |
| J.P. Bowie | Barry Brennessel | Michael Breyette |
| Nowell Briscoe | P.A. Brown | Brenda Bryce |
| Jade Buchanan | James Buchanan | Charlie Cochrane |
| Karenna Colcroft | Jamie Craig | Kirby Crow |
| Dick D. | Ethan Day | Diana DeRicc |
| Jason Edding | Theo Fenraven | Angela Fiddler |
| Dakota Flint | S.J. Frost | Kimberly Gardner |
| Roland Graeme | Storm Grant | Amber Green |
| LB Gregg | Drewey Wayne Gunn | Kaje Harper |
| Jan Irving | David Juhren | Samantha Kane |
| Kiernan Kelly | M. King | Matthew Lang |
| J.L. Langley | Josh Lanyon | Anna Lee |
| Elizabeth Lister | Clare London | William Maltese |
| Gary Martine | Z.A. Maxfield | Timothy McGivney |
| Lloyd A. Meeker | Patric Michael | AKM Miles |
| Reiko Morgan | Jet Mykles | William Neale |
| Willa Okati | L. Picaro | Neil S. Plakcy |
| Jordan Castillo Price | Luisa Prieto | Rick R. Reed |
| A.M. Riley | George Seaton | Jardonn Smith |
| Caro Soles | JoAnne Soper-Cook | Richard Stevenson |
| Liz Strange | Marshall Thornton | Lex Valentine |
| Maggie Veness | Haley Walsh | Missy Welsh |
| Stevie Woods | Lance Zarimba | |

*Check out titles, both available and forthcoming, at*
*www.mlrpress.com*

# Breaking Cover

# Cover

*Life Lessons Book 2*

# Kaje Harper

**mlr**press

*www.mlrpress.com*

Copyright 2011 by Kaje Harper

Published by
MLR Press, LLC
3052 Gaines Waterport Rd.
Albion, NY 14411

Visit ManLoveRomance Press, LLC on the Internet:
www.mlrpress.com

Cover Art by Winterheart Designs
Editing by Amanda Faris

Print Format ISBN# 978-1-60820-409-0
ebook format ISBN# 978-1-60820-410-6

Issued 2011

A thin-sounding version of the theme from Dragnet woke Jared MacLean out of a sound sleep. With a reflex now becoming practiced, he reached for his cell phone in the charger on the nightstand with one hand and put the other hand over his bed partner's mouth. His lover said a muffled "Mmph?" against his palm, while MacLean flipped the phone open.

"Hey, Mac, you awake?" Oliver's voice said in his ear, much too alertly for whatever damned hour of morning it was.

"Am now," Mac muttered. He glanced over at where Tony lay, eyes now open and shining in the faint light from the clock radio. Tony nodded slightly and Mac withdrew his hand.

"Well, drag yourself out of bed and tell her you have to go," Oliver's voice ordered him. "We've got a dead one."

"Tell who what?" Mac asked. It was too early for what passed as his police partner's sense of humor.

"The gal you've been banging. The one who has you coming in with a smile on your face lately. Tell her there's no rest for homicide detectives and get your butt in gear."

"There's no girl in my fucking bed," Mac grumbled. "No fucking girl in my bed either." Not that there was no fucking in his bed, but he was not about to admit that to his partner.

"If you say so. Here's the address." Oliver reeled off a street location. Mac recognized the area as one of the rougher Minneapolis neighborhoods. "Second floor, apartment twenty-two. Female victim, related to something we've worked on. That's all I have so far. I'll see you there."

Mac shut his phone and stretched, wincing at the tightness in his shoulders. His muscles were stiff from a few too many laps in the community pool yesterday. There were reasons he hadn't wanted to get out of the water. As long as he was waist-deep, no one would notice where his, um, interests lay. Swim trunks could only hide so much.

The cause of his reluctance sat up in bed next to him. The faint light outlined a very nice, bare, twenty-five-year-old body. A body that had looked much too good in a pair of swim trunks yesterday. Tony's dark hair was cut shorter for summer, but those black curls were still sleep-tousled above steady blue eyes. If Mac turned on the light, he would see the blush of too much sun on Tony's fair skin. And that soft, full mouth... Mac glanced away.

"That was your work calling," Tony said. It wasn't a question. They knew each other's personalized ring tones by now.

"Yep. Oliver says we've got a case. I have to go."

Tony glanced at the clock. "Three AM. No chance you'll be back this morning then. Will I see you tonight?"

"If not, I'll call," Mac promised. "I'll probably be pretty late." He leaned over and kissed Tony softly, opening his mouth a little. Tony slid his arms around Mac's neck and leaned pliantly against him. The lightly-muscled body that Mac enjoyed was warm and willing. But when Mac pulled back, Tony let go immediately. So far he'd been pretty understanding about the demands of Mac's job. So far.

"Stay safe," Tony told him.

Mac kissed him again, hard and fast. "Go back to sleep." He rolled out of bed before his body could think about how nice it would be to lie back down.

Mac took the fastest shower on record, just enough to wash the smell of last night's sex off his skin. Oliver had started bugging him for details of his love life. No point in giving him ammunition. Ten minutes later he was dressed and out the door, hair still wet. The water dripping on his neck felt good in the muggy heat of Minneapolis in July, especially since he had to wear a regular shirt over his T-shirt to cover his holster. People associated Minnesota with frigid cold, and there was no doubt that January could freeze your breath on your face. What people didn't realize was that the summer could rival the southern states for heat and humidity. Even in the early morning darkness, the air on his skin was steamy. This place did four seasons with a vengeance. Oh well, it kept down the tourists.

His car was parked on the street, a couple of blocks down. He made a practice of moving it around, staying out of the building parking lot. Not that he expected to ever get noticed, but still. It was no one's business where he spent his nights.

The car was a junker, but it started smoothly. What money he did put into it went into engine maintenance.   Dents were irrelevant. Starting immediately in all kinds of weather was what counted. He pulled out onto the dark, quiet street.

The building Mac was looking for turned out to be a run-down wooden house, tucked back behind another larger firetrap of a building. GPS on his phone got him in the ballpark, and then he was clued in by the patrol cars on the street. None of the buildings in this neighborhood seemed to have visible street numbers.

He badged himself past the uniformed cop manning the perimeter and entered the front door. Like many of these old houses, the place had seen better days. The design of the entry showed that at some recent date it had been divided into apartments. He went up the stairs and followed the sound of his partner's voice. Oliver was chewing someone out in a tight, irritated tone. When Mac showed his face at the door, Oliver broke it off and came over to him.

"What have we got?" Mac asked.

"Woman by the name of Terri Brand, twenty-six, found in her bed by that girl," Oliver pointed at a sobbing blonde sitting on the floor, "Who has not spoken a word of sense since she called 911. Body is in the next room. At a guess, strangled and then stabbed in the chest sometime during the evening, but we're still waiting for the ME to get here and give us an official word on that."

"Strangled *and* stabbed?" Mac said.

"Yeah." Oliver ran a hand over his face. "Sounds familiar, right? That's why you and I got the call."

Mac nodded silently. A month earlier they had caught a case like that; a young woman strangled, the mark of brutal hands around her neck, then stabbed in the chest after she was dead. That case had been stone cold from the start. The woman was known to be promiscuous and frequently brought men home. The body wasn't found for days. They had semen from that case and a DNA match would be a lock, but they never had even a hint of a suspect to make a comparison to. Physical evidence was great for a conviction, but it was almost no help in telling you where to look. They had enough to know they were looking for someone male and probably Caucasian, who did not have DNA already in the system. Which left about a million suspects in this city alone.

"Does this look the same?" Mac asked.

"Yep. Down to the body being naked and posed."

"Fuck," Mac said succinctly. Unless the two victims knew each other somehow, everyone would be thinking serial killer. And everyone just might be right. Not what they needed in a city tense and irritable from a week of extreme heat.

"You talk to her," Oliver ordered, pointing at the blonde. "I've got the scene." He stalked towards the bedroom.

Mac walked over and stood looking at the crying girl. She could be anywhere from sixteen to twenty. She was probably fairly pretty when her face wasn't red and tear-streaked. Her blond hair was long and clean, but whatever style there might have been was erased by the tug of her clenched hands. She was dressed in something sequined and skimpy. Nowadays, though, that didn't mean hooker. Mac had seen twelve-year-old school kids wearing clothes that would have been over-the-top on a streetwalker ten years ago. At least this girl was maybe legal age.

She sniffled and moaned, and unclenched one of her hands from her hair to rub the back of it over her nose. Mac reached into his pocket, pulled out a clean tissue, and passed it over.

"Here," he said in his best soothe-the-witness voice. "Why don't we go somewhere more comfortable and have a talk."

"I've got no place else to go," the girl sobbed, wiping at her eyes. "I got nothing else." She wrapped her arms around her middle and rocked convulsively back and forth.

"Okay. It's okay. We can talk right here. Why don't you tell me your name."

"Lacey," she whispered. "Lacey Henderson."

"Okay, Lacey." He sat on the floor so he wasn't looming over her. "Why don't you just tell me what happened tonight."

"I don't *know* what happened!" she wailed. "I don't know. It can't be…she can't be…"

"Hush, easy now. I just want to know your story. You came over here and found her, and called 911. That was good. That was the right thing to do. Why were you here?"

"I live here," Lacey moaned. "At least I did. Terri was letting me crash with her, you know."

"Why were you coming home so late?"

The girl's face got even redder. "I was at a party. There was this guy. But then he said I couldn't stay, so I came home. But the busses don't run much at night, so it took forever, and now she's dead!" She snorted loudly into the tissue. Mac began to have a little sympathy for his partner's frustration, but kept it out of his voice.

"What time did you leave the party?"

"I don't know. Maybe one-thirty? Maybe one. I can't remember."

"And what time did you get home?"

"About two? Maybe two-thirty." She sniffled. "You guys should know. I called right away. I mean, her door was open, and she was just there naked, and she never would do that, and I could see she was dead and all. God, I just freaked! I screamed and screamed. Joan came over from next door, but she made me call 911 and then she left! She left me alone with that! And there's blood and, oh, God!"

"It's okay," Mac repeated. "You're doing fine. Did you touch Terri at all, or go in her room?"

"God, no. Why would I do that?"

"Well, to see if she was really dead, or..."

"No!" the girl whimpered. "No, no, no, no, no. I didn't go near her. I couldn't."

"Did you see anyone leaving the apartment or the building as you were coming in?"

"No, nobody."

"How about earlier?" Mac asked. "Did you talk to Terri about her plans for the evening? Did she say who she was going to be with?"

"She was going out to a bar," Lacey said. "I don't know which one. I told her I was going to be home late because of the party and she told me that was good, because she was hoping to get lucky. Oh, God, she told *me* to be careful!"

"You don't know who she was seeing?"

"No. I mean, I don't think she had someone particular in mind, you know. She liked to go out and meet guys. She was so friendly, and, you know. She liked a good time."

"How often did she bring a strange guy home?"

"I don't know. Sometimes." Lacey rubbed at her nose with the back of her hand again. "Maybe once a week or so. She wasn't a slut you know. She just liked men. They went away friendly, mostly."

"Did she have a boyfriend? Someone she was seeing more than once?"

"I don't think so. I've only known her, like, a month, but I never saw anyone. She used to say she liked a hot dick in bed, but not some slob farting up the place around the breakfast table. I think maybe someone was bad to her once. But she didn't talk about it. Oh, God! She didn't..."

Mac waited out another burst of sobbing. When she subsided,

he went on, "When did you see her last, to talk to?"

"After work, around six. We were getting ready to go out. She loaned me this shirt, and helped with my hair. Oh, God, it was like she was my big sister and now she's dead. Oh, God. Oh, Jesus." The girl broke down crying again.

Mac straightened up and walked over to a female officer standing by the door to the apartment. "You take charge of the roommate," he told her, dumping the sobbing witness on the uniform without regret. "Make sure she has a place to stay, and get the address and her phone number, because we'll need to talk to her again. While you're at it, check her driver's license and make sure she's eighteen. If she's a minor, we'll need to handle it differently." Mac left the unfortunate officer crouched down beside Lacey, trying to deal with her.

Mac headed for the bedroom, steeling himself inwardly. He knew his thoughts didn't show. He'd learned to make sure of that. But even though he could walk onto the bloodiest scene without seeming to turn a hair, he never quite got used to it. He couldn't lose his awareness that the cooling, abused flesh was someone's mother, sister, child, lover; was so recently a living person with thoughts and dreams and hopes for the future.

The murdered dead were his responsibility. Sometimes he almost felt them hovering at his elbow, waiting for whatever he could give them. Justice perhaps. Meaning, redemption. The reassurance that although they had died, the killer was caught and would never hurt anyone else. That in some small way their death was not in vain. That was his job, and he was good at it.

Of course, no matter how good you were—and he and Oliver were damned good—you couldn't solve them all. Or worse, you might know who was guilty and fail to prove it. Those ghosts hovered too, maybe fading over time as hope of justice faded. At occasional moments, their weight was heavy. Mac wondered, as he stepped into the small, stuffy bedroom, what kind of case Terri Brand would turn out to be.

Oliver had his sketchpad out, drawing the scene. They would have the official photographs and diagrams, but Oliver liked to have his own interpretation. He had an uncanny ability to focus in on the relevant details in the most chaotic scene.

Which this was not. Nothing in the room looked out of place. Clothes were folded neatly on a chair. The body of the victim lay on the bed, naked but composed. Her arms were outstretched, her feet together, almost in a crucifixion pose. Purple-red mottling on her neck, bloodshot eyes, and the color of her face made the cause of death clear. A small patch of blood on her naked chest, at the top of her left breast, presumably marked the stab wound.

Mac went over to look more closely. There wasn't much blood. The previous victim had been stabbed well after her death too. Without a beating heart, bleeding stops.

"Did you get anything out of that hysterical girl?" Oliver asked without turning.

"Victim was planning to go out to a bar," Mac reported. "She liked to bring men home. Last seen alive here around six. No known boyfriends."

"Like the other one."

"Yeah."

"Shit." Oliver muttered.

"Yeah."

"I'm guessing we'll have DNA here too. Should be simple to match, if it really is the same guy."

"And if it is the last guy they fucked that killed them," Mac added.

"Stands to reason."

"We'll be in trouble once the press gets hold of this, if there is a match," Mac pointed out.

"So the more we get done first, the better. You take the neighbors. Wake 'em up. If that girl was this loud when she found the body, there's probably not one of them actually slept through it anyway. The walls in this place are paper. Maybe someone heard something useful. As soon as the damned techs get here and do their thing I'll start on the victim's papers. Workplace, address book, maybe we'll get lucky and find someone who was out with her tonight and saw the guy."

Mac began canvassing on the ground floor, reasoning that anyone who tried to leave to avoid questioning would have to come past him. The apartment below the victim's was occupied by a newly immigrated family from the Sudan. Between the parents' poor grasp of English, and their obvious terror of the police, Mac got nothing. He made a note to send a black officer with an interpreter next day, although the chance they would learn anything useful even then was slim.

The west ground floor unit yielded an elderly man with a hearing aid, and a wealth of opinions that poured out over the top of Mac's own words. Either the old fart had his hearing aid off, or he just wasn't interested in anything but the sound of his own voice. Mac made a few attempts to ask questions, then gave up and let the man rant. The man described the victim as an empty-headed slut and finally admitted to having slept through the relevant time frame without hearing anything. Mac backed away from his querulous demands that the police do something and moved on to the next door.

The east room was inhabited by a woman Mac decided actually *was* a pro. She was distressed by the idea that a killer had been in her building, but seemed more worried for her own safety than helpful. She claimed to have been watching a video with headphones on. When Mac asked why she was still up at that hour, she gave him a knowing grin and quipped, "There ain't no rest for the wicked." Any further questions only seemed to result in her making a pass at him. He left her door before the touch of her hand became something he would have to take notice of.

Back on the second floor, the east door was closed, and no one answered even Mac's loudest knock. As he was making a note to try again later, the west door opened.

"You'd better come in before you break something." The speaker was a tall, thin woman in baggy shorts and a brief red terrycloth robe, standing in the open doorway "There's no one in there tonight. They're out of town for the weekend."

Mac nodded. "I'm Detective MacLean with the Minneapolis PD." He showed his shield. "I'd like to ask you a few questions."

"I know who you are," the woman replied. "I've been watching. I don't just invite a strange man into my room, unlike Terri." A fleeting look of embarrassment crossed her face. "I guess that's a petty thing to say, under the circumstances."

"What do you know about the circumstances?"

"I was with Lacey when she called the cops. I saw Terri's body. Actually, I checked her for a pulse, just to be sure, since all that air-headed blonde could do was stand there and scream. But she was dead and cooling already."

"You seem pretty calm about this."

"Only by comparison," the woman returned. "Come on in. I'm not standing around in the hallway in my nightclothes."

Mac thought she was pretty well covered, all things considered, but he followed her in and let her close the door. Her apartment was the mirror image of the victim's, but much more tidy and sparsely furnished. There were lots of books and a couple of tasteful prints. For a woman's place, there were remarkably few rugs, no throw pillows, no froufrou. A simple futon and chair made up the bulk of the furnishings. The woman waved Mac to the futon and perched on the edge of the chair. Mac got out his notebook and pencil.

"Your name?"

"Joan Peters."

"You live here alone?"

"Yes," the woman said, more tartly than he thought his question deserved. "I do."

"Tell me about tonight," Mac invited. "Start about six PM. Where were you?"

"I was in the library studying. Until about seven. I got home around seven-thirty. I didn't see Terri, or anyone else for that matter, when I got home. I made dinner and then settled in with my books. Around ten or so, I heard Terri come home. I assumed she was with a man, from her giggles, but if so his voice was quiet. It was only an inference, you understand. She was a lot louder and more bubbly with a man around."

"You never saw the man or heard his voice?"

"I don't even know for sure that there *was* a man," Joan said firmly. "Like I said, it was a guess. I didn't actually hear anyone else come or go. I went to bed about eleven, and woke up at two-thirty-six, when Lacey began screaming."

"You're certain of the time?" Mac asked.

"Oh, yes. I looked at my alarm in disbelief. But then I decided there was something…serious about her voice so I went to look."

"What did you see?"

"Terri's front door was open, Lacey was having hysterics in the living room and Terri was lying naked in her bedroom, bruised up and staring."

"But you went in anyway?" Mac asked.

"Of course. She might have still been alive. I know CPR. But she wasn't."

"Did you touch anything other than her body?"

"I don't think so," Joan said. "The door was wide open. I can't guarantee I didn't touch the bed somewhere but I don't think so. So I made Lacey call 911."

"You didn't stay with her." Mac let his voice make that a question.

"No," Joan admitted, coloring a little. "I'm no good with people, especially hysterical people. And she wanted to cling onto me and weep. I figured you would come talk to me eventually."

"Do you think Lacey was in Terri's room before you came?"

"You couldn't have gotten her into that room if Terri was bleeding to death before her eyes," Joan said. "Silly cow."

"You don't like her."

"I don't really have anything against her. Except that she's the kind of helpless clinging female that gives women a bad name. She wants someone to take care of her, so she doesn't have to grow up. Terri let her move in temporarily a month ago, and it would have taken a team of wild horses, or maybe a rich boyfriend, to get her back out."

"So you don't think she would have had anything to do with killing Terri?"

"Never," Joan said definitely. "Not only did she practically faint at the sight of blood, but Terri was her meal ticket. Lacey was paying a few bucks rent, but doing precious little else in return for sleeping on the couch every night and eating Terri's food."

"It sounds like you liked Terri," Mac commented.

"Better than Lacey," Joan said begrudgingly. "Terri was all right. She wasn't very smart, and she had no self esteem, but she was good natured. Liked to believe the best of everyone."

"Would it have been unusual for her to bring a man home with her?"

"No. Pretty standard for a Saturday night."

"Did she ever talk to you about the men, who they were or where she went to meet them?"

"Sometimes," Joan said. "I can try to come up with the names of a few bars she went to. We weren't friends, though. We didn't have heart-to-heart chats or anything. Just sometimes in the hall she would say something like, 'I picked up this cute guy at The Caboose last night, but he was a flop in the sack.' And I would nod and get out of there fast before she felt compelled to tell me more."

"Did she say where she was going last night?"

"Not to me."

"How about before last night," Mac asked. "Did she mention any boyfriends? Anyone who might have wanted to see her more than once, or who had been angry with her?"

"I don't know any names. I think there was a guy about a year ago, around when I first moved in. She said something about dumping a guy. How he was cheating on her and was no good. She didn't seem scared, though. I don't remember. I wasn't interested and I didn't even know her then. I haven't seen anyone more than once recently."

"Can you think of anything else that might help me?"

"No," Joan said flatly. "I have no idea who would have done this. I assume she picked up the wrong man. It was always a risk, with the way she lived."

Mac asked her to write out the names of any bars she had heard mentioned, and she came up with a list of four. As he tucked it into his notebook, he said, "I have to ask. Why are you living here? You don't seem to fit the neighborhood profile."

"I'm a student. Temporarily no money, and I got a deal on this place through a friend."

"What are you studying?"

Joan stood up and opened the door for him, her color a little high. "Mortuary science at the U," she said. "Which makes me unlikely to get hysterical over a dead body. Good night, detective."

Mac stared at the closed door. A bigger contrast to Lacey was hard to imagine. Women were sometimes like a foreign species, he thought. They had more range than men. However, tonight he was looking for a man.

*You're always looking for a man*, his inner voice quipped.

*Not anymore*, Mac told it. *I've found one.* He started up the stairs to the third floor, thinking about Tony warm and asleep in his bed. And about how it was somehow becoming *their* bed. Both of them in the past had played pick-up roulette, bringing men they hardly knew back to a room. Tony claimed to have done so rarely, but it had been Mac's style for ten years, until now. The risks had been there, especially for Tony, who wasn't six-two and two hundred pounds. *No more*, Mac thought. Tony was safe with him. But how many women out there were at risk, if he didn't solve this one? He hoped for a miracle on the third floor, but didn't get one.

CHAPTER 2

Late the next evening, Tony woke to the touch of warm feet against his own. He rolled over and moved into Mac's arms. "You weren't kidding about being late. Is it a bad one?" He slid a gentle hand to Mac's neck, fingertips brushing the ends of the man's straight brown hair.

"Could be," Mac said. His broad hands roamed slowly down Tony's back, "Yeah. I'm worried. I think this might tie into another case I had a month ago. Two women now, both killed the same way. I'm hoping it's not the same guy, because if it is, it has a hint of the crazies about it."

"How crazy?"

"Like he might do it again."

"Serial killer crazies?" Tony asked, slowing his touch.

"Maybe."

"I thought that was rare."

"Hard to say, actually. The cold cases, the ones with no suspect or motive from day one, who knows how many of those are serials, with just not enough evidence to link them up. It may be more common than we think. But the truly whack-job serial killer with a pattern, yeah, those are rare."

"But you think maybe this one…?"

"They were both stabbed well after they were dead, and there's other links. So I'm worried. That's not for the general public though, okay."

"Never," Tony said comfortably. One of his private joys over the past year was the way Mac had begun trusting him with the details of his job, trusting him both to keep confidence and to give Mac the kind of support he needed. Tony didn't know how any cops made it through alone. They saw humanity at its worst, day after day. Maybe some of them were the kind of person who could shrug that off. But most were on the job because they cared.

Tony provided Mac with a sympathetic ear, a hot meal, cold brew or a warm body, as best he could. Sometimes Mac wanted to talk things out. Other times he just wanted to lose himself for a while. From the motion of his big hands over Tony's ass, this was one of those times. Tony grinned in the dark. His favorite.

He moved his mouth to Mac's neck and jaw, feeling the stubble of beard rasp against his lips. Pushing away a little, he slipped lower, trailing his tongue down muscular shoulders and pecs, to find the hard nubs of Mac's nipples waiting for his touch. Mac groaned under the nip of his teeth around those sensitive points, and brought his hands up to clutch in Tony's hair. Tony licked and bit Mac's chest, hard enough to leave faint marks. He moved down, faster and more urgently. Mac's skin was familiar; the fine rasp of hair under his mouth, the musky warm scent of his lover's body. As Tony paused to tongue Mac's navel, the wet silken caress of Mac's big cock rose against Tony's cheek. Tony turned his head and took Mac in, suddenly and deep. Mac moaned and pushed Tony's head down further. Tony held that depth, tonguing hard until he had to come up gasping.

"Do you want…?" Mac's voice was rough.

"This is what I want," Tony told him. "Let me…"

He licked slowly up Mac's shaft, root to tip, and swirled around the broad flared head. Mac's pulse was pounding under Tony's fingers, his cock jerking in time. Tony took the base in his fist and swallowed until his mouth met his hand. He couldn't deep-throat Mac. The man was too big. But this was close, this was good. He drove Mac's breathing with the rhythm of his mouth, fast bobs then slow, barely licking at the slit. He held his fist loose at first then began closing his hand in time with the plunging motion of his lips and tongue. He felt the first twitch of climax and backed off, holding his hand closed hard and tight around the base of Mac's cock, watching Mac just barely come back from the edge.

"Jesus, Tony, baby," Mac groaned. "Don't stop."

"Never," Tony whispered against his skin. He nuzzled into the groove of hip and groin. "Not stopping. Just want to..." He urged Mac's legs apart with his hands and lowered his mouth to the soft band between balls and ass, licking slowly. His tongue moved gradually upward, wrapping around the big, firm orbs as he sucked first one testicle and then the other into his mouth.

Mac was whimpering urgently by the time Tony released his balls and found that hard shaft again, slick with his saliva. He licked toward the crown. Mac's hands fisted in Tony's hair. Tony's mouth closed on him and Mac thrust up urgently with his hips. Tony let his lover drive into his mouth, controlling the depth with his hand. Mac's motion was fast and hard, his hands tight against Tony's scalp. Tony worked his tongue, sucking tightly, tasting the seep of pre-come in his mouth.

"Oh, God," Mac moaned. "Oh, God, Tony. Now! Please!"

Tony slid his hand down, a firm stroke on silken skin, and relaxed his throat to take Mac deep. Mac shot hard in his mouth, pulsing and groaning. Tony swallowed the thick cream, milking each jet with fist and tongue. After a minute he slowly pulled off. Delicately, lingeringly, he sucked and licked the last drops, feeling Mac softening. He stopped and let go when Mac shuddered, knowing the signs when his lover became temporarily too sensitive for more touch.

Tony pillowed his head on Mac's firm stomach and sighed. He slowly traced the muscled hint of a six-pack with the tip of one finger. *I love you,* he thought. He didn't say it. *Not again. Not until I might hear it back.*

He was certain that Mac was as deeply in this relationship as he was. No one else had ever been a part of Tony like this, wrapped around his heart. It had to be mutual. But no one else had ever denied his existence outside of the bedroom like this either. He had vowed to himself not to push Mac, not to ask for more than he was willing to give. But it got harder, as he saw no sign that Mac was even thinking about cracking open his closet door.

Mac's warm hands wrapped under Tony's arms and pulled

him up into a kiss. "Mmm," Mac said. "I love it when you taste of me. You have a magic mouth."

*Almost enough.* Tony kissed him back willingly. He loved it too. They had taken the tests for the final time four months ago, and they were both healthy, negative. He had breathed a sigh of relief for Mac, who had been way more into the bar scene. Now they could love any way they wanted to. No risk to the pleasure of skin on skin, to drinking Mac down. The trust had never been an issue, just the past.

Tony deepened the kiss, opening his lips for Mac's tongue, slowly exploring. Mac's dark brown eyes stared into his own. Tony ran a finger down over those angular cheekbones as he gave himself to the kiss. This was almost better than the sex, the long slow times they spent just being together, touching. Mac traced Tony's mouth with lips and tongue, with a delight that somehow never stopped. Tony had expected they would take each other for granted eventually, but still every time, his heart ached a little at the wonder of this man in his arms, in his bed. Mac's mouth and hands moved lower, became more purposeful. Ahhh, yes. Kissing was only *almost* better than the sex. Tony gave himself to the climbing heat of Mac's skilled mouth.

Mac dragged himself out of bed when the alarm went off. On the other side of the bed, Tony made a grumbling noise and burrowed back under the covers. During the school year, they got up at the same time, the early start of the high school day matching Mac's shift. But July was the middle of a teacher's vacation. If Tony didn't have somewhere to be, he indulged in late mornings like a teenager.

Mac smacked that rounded ass through the bedclothes. "Come on, lazybones. Are you going to make me have breakfast by myself?"

Tony pulled the covers down to expose one bleary blue eye. "Do we have time to play in the shower?"

Mac glanced at the clock. "Nope."

"Then yeah," Tony mumbled, sliding back into his pillow. "Have a nice day." The covers rose back into place, leaving a few strands of tousled black curls visible.

Mac laughed and headed for the bathroom. He allowed himself a really hot shower. One of the perks of spending nights with Tony at his place was avoiding the lukewarm torture-chamber that was the tiny shower at his own apartment. Mac soaped up under the hot spray, and winced a little as he brushed over his nipples. The faint marks of Tony's teeth were still visible. Mac smiled. Unlimited hot water was only *one* of the perks.

After a quick breakfast of toast and coffee, Mac let himself out into the already-steamy morning. His car was like a sauna. The ancient air conditioning strained to produce any effect. He turned it off and opened the windows as he drove. At least the sun was still low, flashing between the buildings but not yet beating down on the roof. He liked the early morning light and the sense of starting a new day. Especially when there was useful work to be done.

They had spent the previous day trying to track Terri Brand's movements. Mac had showed her picture to the bartenders at a dozen local bars. Half of them recognized her face, but none of them could remember her being there the previous night. She had been a semi-regular at several places. She was remembered for fairly heavy drinking and her interest in men. As one bartender put it, "She usually went home smashed, happy, and not alone."

None of those bartenders recognized the photo of their first victim, Cindy Kowalski. And the detective who went back to canvass Kowalski's known drinking spots reported a similar lack of recognition for Terri. The women were both young, blond, slim and tall, with a liking for drink and men. Other than that, they appeared to have little in common. They were four years apart in age, lived in different parts of the city, had different jobs, different school backgrounds, different clothing styles and favorite shops, different hairstylists, different social circles.

Cindy had been a student at the U, in her last year of chemistry studies. Mac had hoped there might be a link to Terri through

Joan or Lacey, but both women looked at Cindy's photo without recognition. Terri had been a sales clerk at a Hot Topic store in a mall, but Cindy's friends claimed she never shopped in that mall and never dressed in those styles.

Everyone on Oliver's team was hoping to find a connection somewhere. They needed *something,* some point of intersection, to start looking for a man who had known both victims. By the end of the first day, everyone knew it wasn't going to be easy.

Mac pulled in at the county morgue and parked. His turn for autopsy duty. This was one of his least favorite parts of the job. He wasn't squeamish, but he hated seeing what was once a living person reduced to meat on a slab. Somehow, the invasion of privacy of the body was worse than the inevitable invasion of the privacy of their life. But it was necessary.

When he made his way to the autopsy room, he was glad to see they had drawn Phil Bresco for this case. The man was neat and thorough, and worked with a respect for the body that seemed to be lacking in some of the younger staff. Black humor was part of the job. You couldn't survive days spent around the dead without it. But there was a line Mac was uncomfortable crossing, and Bresco never exceeded it.

Terri Brand's body was already laid out naked on the steel table, but Bresco was just setting up his tools when Mac entered. The medical examiner waved him over to the containers of masks and gowns by the door. Mac covered up and adjusted a paper mask over his face. Breathing through the mask in the already heavy atmosphere of the room was annoying, but regulations were strictly enforced in these days of SARS and H1N1 and who knew what other lethal germs.

Mac moved to a good vantage point near the coroner. Bresco turned on his recorder, switched on the table lights, and bent over the body. He hesitated a second then turned to glance at Mac. "This looks familiar."

"You tell me."

Bresco nodded and turned back to his work. "The body is a

Caucasian woman in her mid-twenties, of slightly underweight body condition…" he began.

Mac listened as Bresco went through his exam. Terri had been manually strangled, by a person whose hands were of average size for a man. Both hands were used. The hyoid bone was fractured and the larynx crushed, suggesting a significant amount of hand strength. There was evidence of sexual activity. Bresco collected samples.

"Do you think she was raped?" Mac asked.

"Nothing points that way," Bresco reported. "There's no tearing or bruising present. Can't rule it out, but if I had to guess, I would say the sex was consensual."

He pointed out bruising on the woman's arms. "That was ante-mortem, but not by much. There's no skin under the nails, no sign she clawed at her attacker. It's just a guess, but I'm speculating he kneeled on her arms while he strangled her, to pin her down."

Mac shook his head to get rid of the picture that created. Bresco finished his external exam and began to cut. Mac made himself watch and listen.

"The stab wound is unusual," Bresco said eventually, when he reached the chest. "The blow was definitely after death, probably by about five to ten minutes. The heart had stopped, but there was still some liquid blood released into the chest. The victim was stabbed once, cleanly, with no redirection or movement of the weapon. The blade is triangular, about one centimeter each side at the base, tapering to a point that is not very sharp. More like a spike than a knife, but there is the imprint of a narrow hilt on the skin at the point of entry. Total length, about thirteen centimeters, or five inches. It was long enough to penetrate the left atrium of the heart. The blow would have been fatal, if the victim had not already been dead."

"I don't know if you remember…" Mac began.

"I did the autopsy on Kowalski," Bresco interrupted. "I remember it very well. You'll get your DNA on the semen here too, but if it doesn't match it just means the guy she had sex with wasn't the killer, because everything else matches. Same blade, same blow, the strangulation, same hand position. Kowalski didn't have the bruises on the arms, but her blood-alcohol level was so high I speculated she was unconscious when she was killed. I'd swear in court this was the same guy. I'll tell you something else. I think you should look really hard for similar priors, because I don't think you'd get a match this perfect without practice. Maybe this guy has been stabbing his knife into cadavers, but I'm betting Kowalski wasn't the first time he's done this."

*Shit.* Mac didn't say it aloud, didn't need to. Bresco turned back to his work.

CHAPTER 3

Tony straightened up from bending over the table in the teen center for LGBT youth and stretched out his back. The boy he was tutoring took the opportunity to push his book away and yawn loudly.

"Am I boring you, Justin?" Tony asked.

"No, Mr. Hart," the boy asserted, eyes wide and innocent. "I'm just a little tired. And this *Animal Farm* book is whacked, you know. I mean talking pigs! What is with this guy?"

Tony thought about trying to defend the genius of George Orwell, and gave it up as a lost cause. "Whacked or not, it's on your summer-school reading list," he said tartly. "So you can read it with my help or without. It's all the same to me."

"No, I need the help," Justin insisted. "I just didn't get much sleep. I'll listen better."

Tony eyed the boy sideways. He did look tired, with purple circles under his eyes. Orwell could wait. He was here for mentoring as much as tutoring, after all. "Why the sleep deprivation, Justin?" Probably just too much video gaming, but...

Justin gave him a minimal shrug and looked away.

Okay, so maybe not gaming. Tony knew he couldn't push these kids, but if he made himself available they would sometimes talk.

"Our little boy got himself tossed out of the house," Carter drawled from across the room. "Guess he's not sleeping so good."

Tony could feel the attention of the other boys on him, waiting for his response.

"That true?" he asked Justin mildly. Another one-shouldered twitch did not deny it. "Where are you staying then?"

"Around. With friends."

"What do you want me to do? I can try to talk to your folks."

"No," Justin said quickly. "Don't."

"You're under eighteen," Tony pointed out. In fact, probably under sixteen. "They can't just kick you out."

"They'll let me back eventually. They did before. My mom will work on my dad and eventually he'll figure something out, like maybe he'll let me back if I ditch the nail polish." The boy eyed the chipped black of his fingernails reflectively. "Then I'll be okay for a while."

"He kicked you out for your nail polish?"

"Nah, he came home early and caught me on the phone with my boyfriend." Justin shook his head. "It was his own fault. If he hadn't taken away my cell phone I wouldn't have been saying *those things* on his precious phone line."

Tony nodded. "Are you safe right now? Wherever you're staying?"

"Yes. Just my friend was away for the weekend and the guy I went to hang with wouldn't let me stay the night, so I hung out at a Wal-Mart. But I had to keep moving around, 'cause they watch you on the cameras and kick you out if it doesn't look like you're shopping, so I couldn't sleep."

"A Wal-Mart?" Tony repeated.

"Yeah. Twenty-four hour air-conditioned comfort." Justin grinned. "Complete with MacDonald's." As he turned to glance at the other boys, the sleeve of his shirt rode up to reveal a purpling bruise below his elbow. Tony put a hand on the boy's wrist and took a closer look.

"Did your dad do that?"

"No," Justin said, jerking his arm free. "Don't worry. It's cool. That was just my brother. He was frustrated and he got a little rough, but he didn't mean it."

"You're sure?"

"Oh, yeah." Justin laughed humorlessly. "It's pretty stupid, you know. My dad tells my brother to teach me to wrestle 'cause he's on the team. Like it will make me less of a fag, you know.

He's clueless. There's more queers on the wrestling team than any other sport in high school. Hell, my boyfriend used to wrestle. My brother hates being put in between like that, you know. But he didn't mean to hurt me. He's a good guy. He's the one who knows where I am, for when my dad cools down."

"Okay. I guess that's okay. But if you get stranded like that again, without a place to sleep, call the hotline. They'll find you something." Tony sighed, looking around the room at the young kids sprawled in chairs and on the battered couch. His heart ached for all of them. "Maybe you should let your brother teach you to wrestle after all. A little self-protection might be good. Save you from worse bruises."

"Wrestling's not much use when they punch you in the head," Carter said.

"Or when there's three of them," Cody added.

"Damn," Tony said. "This has to stop. I mean, who in here has been beat up badly enough to leave major bruises?" He raised his hand and looked around the room with a raised eyebrow. Carter laughed and raised both arms. With Carter's approval on the question, almost all the boys, and one of the four girls on the couch, raised their hands.

"If I found someone," Tony said, "to teach us self-defense moves, would you guys come to a class?"

"Seems futile," Carter drawled. "You fight back, you get beat worse. Most of us have learned that."

"Maybe not. Maybe if we knew how to fight back effectively we could avoid some pain. And then…there are times when they don't just want to rough you up, you know. Some of those guys are crazy. I have a friend who had his ribs broken and got a punctured lung. He almost died. I want to find a way for us to be safer."

"Sure, Mr. H," Carter said. "You find us a ninja, willing to turn us all into little black belts."

"If I find someone willing to teach us," Tony repeated, "Will you come? Girls too. You should all know something about keeping safe."

"I guess," Cody muttered. "If the guy's willing to teach a bunch of queers."

"Anyone I find had better be."

Carter shrugged, "Maybe I'd be there. And maybe I wouldn't." Tony took that for approval.

When his tutoring time ended, he hung around for a while chatting with the kids. By the time he started picking up the books, the group had thinned out. Two boys worked the pool table, Justin was sleeping on the couch, and a couple of boys sat on the floor in the corner by the door. One of them stood as Tony headed past.

"Mr. H," he said. "Did you mean it about the self-defense classes?"

"Yes, of course. I know a couple of people I can ask."

"That's good," the boy said. "That would be good."

"Are you okay, David?"

"I'm fine." The boy's gaze strayed to his friend, who was sitting against the wall with his head turned away. Tony lowered his bag and squatted down.

"How about you, Pete?" he asked.

For a moment the boy didn't respond. Then he turned toward Tony. "I'm just peachy," he said, glaring at Tony through an eye almost swollen shut. "Go away."

Tony worked hard to give no visible reaction to the swelling and bruising on the boy's face. "Uh huh," he said after a moment. "I can see how fine you are."

"It's no big deal."

"No double vision, nausea, dizziness, tunnel vision?"

"Nah."

"Are you hurt anyplace else?" Tony asked as calmly as he could.

"Just bruises." Pete rubbed his hands up and down his arms, covered by a jean jacket despite the heat of the day.

Tony looked the boy over for a moment. He sat hunched, but not with the kind of stiffness that suggested broken ribs. His color was okay, although the faint patina of dirt on his skin suggested he wasn't washing often. Tony suspected some of the boys who came into the teen center were living on the streets, and probably working them. Pete was one of those.

"Other kids, or a trick?" he asked.

Pete colored and didn't answer. David waited for a moment then said, "It was a trick. Fancy guy in a fancy car. Some of them like it rough, and you can't always tell."

"Do you need a doctor?" Tony asked gently. "If you're bleeding or something, you should get seen. I'll cover it."

"No, I'm okay," Pete muttered. "I just blew him and he smacked me around a bit. No big."

Tony bit his lip. He wanted to say the kid should report it, get the guy arrested for assault. He knew that was a fantasy. It would never happen. "Well, at least warn the other guys about him," he suggested helplessly. "No reason to give the bastard a chance to do it again with a friend of yours. And here." He pulled out his wallet and extracted forty dollars. "Get a lightweight shirt if you want to cover those bruises, so you don't die of heatstroke in that jacket. And some ibuprophen and an ice pack, huh?" Except the kid probably didn't have a refrigerator to chill an ice pack. Shit. "Or a bag of ice. Whatever you need. And if you feel worse you see a doctor, all right?"

Pete looked at him from his one good eye for a moment, and then reached out stiffly to take the money. "Okay, Mr. H. Thanks."

Tony picked up his bag and headed out to his nice safe apartment with his paying job and his good friends and his wonderful closeted boyfriend. While this gay kid would head back out onto the street. Something had to change.

❖ ❖ ❖

Mac stared at Tony, pacing agitatedly around the living room, and tried to come up with a diplomatic way to say no. He had come home from a long futile day of questioning and canvassing that had brought him no closer to his killer, to find Tony well launched on another crusade.

Tony was an idealist. It was one of the things Mac liked about him, that he wanted to make the world a better place. It was just that Mac had nine more years of living in the real world. It gave him a more realistic picture of what could actually be done.

The summer holidays had given Tony a chance to volunteer for some of his favorite causes. The Habitat for Humanity builds were good, although the Jesus tinge to the rhetoric made Mac a little leery. Still, Tony went two or three times a week and no one gave him problems. And the sun and exercise were doing no harm at all to his body. Mac had even volunteered a couple of times, when days off coincided with a build day. Although Tony had been lying when he said the job site was full of cute guys in jeans and tool belts, Mac had still enjoyed working with the wide array of volunteers. There was satisfaction in building something worthwhile. And Tony in jeans and a tool belt made other eye candy unnecessary.

The teen center made Mac nervous in a different way. Tony was right. There was a real need for mentors for gay youth, guys who could say, "Look at me, I survived being a gay teen and I'm doing fine, and you can too." Mac just was not going to be one of those guys. And he had worried all along that somehow, as Tony got involved with the kids, he would want to drag Mac into it. Tony had said no, he had promised no, and now here it was.

"You don't have to tell them you're gay," Tony said. "I won't even look at you while you're there. I just need you to teach these guys how to keep themselves safe."

"I can't do it," Mac said, trying for a reasonable tone. "Right now I don't have time. Every spare minute is going into this case. You know that. But even if I had the time, I'm not the right guy for this."

"Why?" Tony demanded. "Because you don't want to be seen around us queers, in case someone gets the right idea?"

"No, it's not that. But my work is what's important right now."

"Yeah, I get it. You have to put all your time into going out protecting the lives of heterosexual blond girls. They're so much more important than a few gay kids getting beaten up."

"Two women are dead," Mac snapped. "It's not a contest. If a gay kid is dead, he gets all my time too. That's what I do. I don't give self-defense classes."

"Preventing murders before they happen doesn't appeal to you, huh?" Tony snarled. "Wait until someone gets killed. Then Detective MacLean will have time for you."

"What is your problem?" Mac demanded. "There are good self-defense instructors out there. Hire one. I'll even chip in for the cost." He would find money in his stretched-to-screaming budget if it would make Tony happy.

"That's right. You'd rather give us money you don't have than show up where someone might discover your deep dark secret. I promised those kids I'd find someone who won't treat them like lepers for being gay. How many gay-friendly self-defense instructors do you know?"

"Look." Mac took a deep breath. "You're not understanding what I'm saying. I'm the wrong person to teach those kids. I'm betting very few of them are my size. I've never had a real problem with personal safety, and if I did, the moves I would use would not be the ones that would work for those kids. I haven't had any formal training beyond what you get at the Academy. I don't know enough."

Tony stared at him, breathing hard, then rubbed at his face tiredly. "Okay. I get that."

"Listen," Mac said. "I know a woman detective on the squad. She sometimes teaches women's self-defense classes. Not formal martial arts or anything, but like rape defense moves and personal safety. I'll talk to her. Maybe she would be willing to work with your kids, or knows someone who would."

Tony nodded. He didn't look as pleased as Mac expected. "You'll give me her number or you'll actually ask her in person?"

"I'll ask her myself," Mac promised. He wasn't looking forward to going up to Mary Liu and asking her to teach a class at a gay teen center, but he could present it as a favor for a friend. It should be fine.

"And will you come to the class and help her demonstrate?"

Mac was taken aback. Tony usually understood a no when he heard it and didn't make Mac repeat it. "I'll probably be too busy," he said cautiously.

"Uh huh. Probably."

They looked at each other. Mac was tired, and all he wanted was to go to bed, spoon up against Tony's warm body and get some sleep. But there was a tension in Tony that told him they weren't done yet.

"It really bothers you that I don't want to volunteer at the center," Mac said finally.

"Yeah, it does. These kids are in desperate need of role models. People who can tell them it's okay to be gay. And I feel like a hypocrite when my own boyfriend feels it's so *not* okay to be gay that he won't even be seen with me."

"You know why I'm not out." They'd had this discussion. He couldn't believe Tony needed to rehash this again, at this hour of night. "You know I can't afford…"

"Yeah, yeah. I know all your reasons. In my head, I can see why you won't risk it. But in my gut it's starting to feel like a cop-out. It makes me feel that there's something wrong with me. And I spent a fucking long time since I came out at fifteen convincing myself that there's nothing wrong with being who I am."

"There's nothing wrong with you, Tony," Mac said softly, reaching for him. "You are amazingly right."

Tony dodged his touch. "As long as I'm behind closed doors."

Mac dropped his hand and sat there, searching for something to say. It was Tony who finally blew out his breath and said, "I'm going to have a shower before bed. I'll try not to wake you."

"You…don't want me to leave, do you?" Mac asked. They'd never had a real fight about this before. Mac realized he had always set the limits, and Tony had accepted them, with no more than a little wheedling or pouting. But this teen center thing was clearly different from not going out to a movie or a show.

Tony looked at him and there was love and exasperation in equal measure in those blue eyes. "No, I don't want you to leave. Go to bed and get some sleep, sweetie. Midnight is the wrong time to be rehashing this."

"I'm sorry," Mac tried.

"Yeah, I know you are, babe," Tony said. "I'm just not sure that will always be good enough."

Mac wanted to say he would change, he would open up for Tony. He couldn't even begin to say the words. "Is this going to break us up?"

"Not right now. God, I hope never. But if anything could…I *hate* being in the closet."

Mac watched with an ache in his chest as Tony walked away and shut himself in the bathroom. Things had been working fine. All this time, Tony had said he was willing to live with Mac's limits. Damn the man for changing the rules on him now. He couldn't lose Tony. It would just about kill him. But coming out wasn't any more of an option now than when this…thing they had going started. If Tony couldn't accept that, couldn't live with that…

Mac went to the bedroom and undressed for sleep, slowly and carefully, folding each item in precise shapes to give his hands no opportunity to tear and break things as they ached to do. He slid in between the sheets on his side of the bed, put his phone in the charger, and folded back the covers on Tony's side. The sounds of running water came dimly from the bathroom and he turned out the reading lamp on his nightstand. The room was softly lit by the single remaining bulb. The pillow was cool against his cheek. This was his haven, this and the man at the center of it, and he couldn't lose it.

Mac tracked down Detective Liu at her desk, late in the afternoon. From the look on her face, her day had been no more productive than his own. She pounded on her computer keyboard as if it offended her. Mac really didn't want to do this.

"Hey, Liu," he said. "Can I have a word with you?"

She looked up and shook her thick black hair out of her face. "Why not? Everyone else has."

"Um."

Liu laughed. "Relax, MacLean. I won't bite. Hey, you're looking good. I hear you have a new girl. When do we get to meet her?"

"What?" Mac said, thrown off course. "Who says that?"

"Oliver, who else," Liu grinned. "For someone who claims to be antisocial, he gets all the gossip first. I shouldn't tell you, but there's a pool going for who will see this elusive woman first. You could introduce me to her. It would pay for the new muffler on my car."

"I don't…" Mac began. "Damn Oliver. He can't resist getting on my case. There is no new girlfriend. Anyway it's none of his business."

Liu stretched her toned arms overhead and stood, leaning one hip on the corner of her desk. She was a small, compact woman and even that position barely put her head at Mac's chest level. "Hey, chill out, big guy. I was just asking. So what can I do for you?"

Mac had to take a second to reorganize his practiced request. "Do you still do that course? The women's self-defense thing you used to teach?"

"Occasionally. I got a couple of other instructors who are

trained and we take it in turns. I get pretty busy these days. Why?"

"There's a friend of mine," Mac said cautiously. "His kid plays with my daughter, Anna. Anyway, we were talking and he was telling me about this place he volunteers at. It's a teen center for gay and lesbian kids here in the city. He says some of the kids have real problems with getting roughed up, and he wanted to know if I would come teach them some self-defense. I told him I wasn't the right person for the job, but I thought of you. These kids are sort of like the women you teach. They're smaller and often weaker than the people beating on them. Your techniques could help."

"I don't know," Liu said slowly. "What I teach is aimed at getting women to fight back in dangerous situations. You don't want some kid putting out another kid's eye with his keys because he's getting shoved around a little."

"Not every situation is life and death for the women either. You must talk to them about appropriate levels of response. A stomp on some bully's instep might go a long way at the right time. And as for dangerous situations, some of these kids, boys as well as girls, are probably more at risk of rape than some of the women are. Tony tells me at least a couple of them are tricking, and one boy got badly beaten by a john. He made it out of the guy's car intact, but he might not be so lucky the next time."

"I guess. But will they come to a class and listen and take it seriously?"

"Tony thinks they will."

"Would you charge them a class fee?" Liu asked.

"What do you do at the Y?"

"There's a charge for the class. People pay more attention if they've put some money into it. I usually try to arrange a couple of free slots for women who really don't have the cash. They're often the ones who need it most."

"Maybe we could do the same. Some of these kids have money, some don't."

"I suppose I could try to arrange it," Liu said. "You can come along and be my attacker."

"Actually, I bet Tony would be up for that," Mac suggested.

"How big is Tony?"

"How big? Um…" *Mind out of the gutter, you idiot.* "He's five-ten, about one-fifty. Why?"

"'Cause you would be better," she said. "It makes a good impression when they see a five-three woman take down a two-hundred pound guy."

"Um," Mac hedged. "I don't know if I'd be available. I've got a couple of tough cases on my plate."

"If I can find time, you can," Liu told him firmly. "I won't hurt you too badly." As he still hesitated, she frowned. "Or what, does the idea of being around a bunch of gay teens make you nervous?"

"No," Mac said quickly. "I'll do it, if you think it would help." *Damn it.* "I just really can't predict my schedule."

"So if you're not available, I'll fall back on your Tony."

"He's not *my* Tony. I barely know the guy," Mac said, and tried to take back the words as they left his mouth. *Wrong thing to say, for so many reasons.* "Um, I'll tell him you might be able to do it."

"Give him my number," Liu said, looking at him oddly. "Here, take a card for him." She pinched a business card out of her drawer with two fingers and held it out to him. "Have him call me and we'll talk about dates. I usually do at least one hour a week for three weeks. It takes time just to get over the inhibitions against actually hurting someone. That alone usually needs a couple of lessons to sink in."

"Thanks, Liu," Mac said. "I really appreciate it." The woman sat back down at her laptop, giving him a vague wave with her hand. Mac beat a retreat and found himself in the second floor men's room with his head against the wall.

This was so fucked up. He was committed to going to the teen center, and Tony would be there, around people whose gaydar was probably pretty acute. There was a betting pool encouraging everyone in the building to snoop into his private affairs even more than they otherwise would.

*I said he's not my Tony.*

That was the worst. Echoes of his childhood Lutheran upbringing whispered, *Three times will deny me.* Stupid, he told himself. He wasn't Peter, and Tony certainly wasn't Jesus. It had been a dumb thing to say because it was suspicious, not because saying it would make it true. Being in the closet meant telling lies sometimes. That's how it worked. He was all right with that. He was.

The door opened and Oliver came in. He offered a breezy, "Hey, partner," and then looked more closely. "Are you okay?"

Mac wondered what had changed from Liu's "looking great" to now.

"I'm fine," he said curtly.

"She didn't dump you, did she?" Oliver asked.

"No," Mac said loudly. "She didn't fucking dump me! What is with you? Why do you suddenly need to know everything about me? You want details about my love life? Okay, details; average height, slim build, dark hair, blue eyes and none of your goddamned, fucking business!"

"Hey, calm down. There's no reason to go postal on me."

"Just drop it, okay?" Mac demanded.

"Okay, okay." Oliver pointed a thumb at his own chest. "Detective, you know. I just like to find out stuff, hate secrets. It's why I like the job." He peered at Mac. "Is she married?"

Mac sighed. "What part of none of your goddamned, fucking business wasn't clear?"

"She is." Oliver whistled. "Okay, that's tough, sorry."

Mac stared at him. Now it would be all over the station that he was dating a married blue-eyed dark-haired woman. *Which is better than the truth, right?* Suddenly he just wanted to go home.

"I'm done," Mac said. *Done with work, done with this conversation, done.* "I'm already on overtime that there's no money for. I'll see you in the morning."

❖ ❖ ❖

When he got back to the apartment, Tony was sitting on the couch, watching a video. He looked up at the sound of the door and gave Mac that sweet smile. "You're home early. I like this."

Mac kicked off his shoes, dumped the contents of his pockets on the counter, and locked his weapon in the gun safe he'd installed under the sink. Tony watched him without comment. Mac walked over to the couch and lay down curled up on the free end, with his head in Tony's lap.

"Hey, sweetie," Tony said, twining his fingers in Mac's hair. "Tough day?"

"Kind of." The feeling of those long fingers stroking him, the firm heat of Tony's leg under his cheek, eased something tight in his chest. "I did find you a self-defense instructor for the kids."

"That's great! Thanks, babe."

"I volunteered to go along and let her kick my ass around the room," he added glumly.

"Are you okay with that?"

"Yeah, it'll be okay."

"I won't out you, I promise. I won't even look at you. And you'll like the kids."

"It's okay," Mac repeated, "I can do this." He turned his face deeper into Tony's lap and closed his eyes. The motion of Tony's fingers through his hair was soothing. The sound from the video was a muted background.

"So what do you want to do?" Tony asked eventually. "Are you hungry?"

"We could go to Iowa and get married," Mac mumbled.

Tony's fingers stilled. "Was that a proposal?"

Mac wasn't sure. His mouth was *way* out in front of his brain.

"I guess so."

"How romantic." Tony's tone did not match the words. "Why?"

"Why what?"

"Why do you want to marry me?"

Mac choked on it. *I love you. I want to be with you.* He couldn't get the words out. "I'm scared I'm going to lose you," he said eventually.

"Huh. That's honest, at least."

Mac waited, and waited, while Tony's fingers resumed their slow circles in his hair. Was there a little tugging that was not there before? Was Tony angry? Happy? "Was that a yes?" he had to ask at last.

"No." Tony pulled his hands away and urged Mac to sit up so their eyes could meet. "I love you, Mac," he said slowly. "You know that. I've said it before. But when I say, 'until death do us part,' I want to be sure I can keep that promise. I'm not sure now."

"Because of me or because of the job?"

"Both. Neither. Because of how things are between us right now." Tony reached out and touched a fingertip to Mac's mouth. Mac turned a little to return the gesture as a kiss on his finger.

"Listen, sweetie," Tony said. "What we have that is good is really good. I've never felt like this about anyone before. But I'm not ready to get married. I'm not sure I ever want to get married if it's not only unofficial but also has to be a secret. It *would* have to be a secret, right?"

"Yeah," Mac admitted. "I guess. Maybe you could tell one friend…"

"Nope. Not going there. We're doing okay the way we are right now. We don't need to rock the boat. Someday something will push us, either together or apart. Right now I'm just going to enjoy having the hottest detective in the MPD in my bed and in my life."

"You haven't seen Mary Liu," Mac quipped. "She's smoking. Every guy in the place would be after her if they didn't know that she could break them in half."

"Not my type," Tony said. "Come on." He got up off the couch and headed for the kitchen. "I haven't eaten and I'm betting you haven't either. There's a pizza in the freezer, and French bread and some salad. Dinner in ten minutes."

Mac found it reassuringly familiar to sit across from Tony with a slice of pizza and a brew, picking the tomatoes out of his share of the salad. He hadn't scared Tony off, apparently. He also hadn't locked him in safely. Not that Mac really wanted to be married either. But for just a moment there, after he said it and before he thought about it, it had sounded nice. He had been relieved Tony said no, of course he was. But it hadn't made him feel more secure, either.

He told Tony about the case, as frustratingly stalled out as the one before. "We're trying to track down the weapon," he said. "I've got someone browsing the online knife sellers, looking for it. It's weird, to have something that blunt and triangular, and then apparently have a knife-hilt on it. With the first victim we thought it was a spike of some sort, but Bresco says this time there's the clear print of a simple narrow crosspiece hilt."

"Sounds like a bodice dagger," Tony mumbled through his pizza.

"A what?"

"A bodice dagger," Tony repeated more clearly. "You can get them at RenFest. Sabrina bought one last year."

"She bought one where? A weapon like this?" Mac said urgently.

"RenFest. The Renaissance Festival. In Shakopee. You know, it's open August through October every year. They usually have at least one sword-maker because you know, Renaissance, swords. Last year there was a booth with really beautiful stuff, knives and swords so sharp they could shave a piece of paper in layers."

"This thing isn't sharp at all."

"Yeah, I know," Tony told him. "Their stuff is all pretty expensive, but the cheapest pieces they had were these bodice daggers. At least, that's what they called them. They were triangular, about yay-long." He held his hand stretched about six inches. "They weren't sharp, and they tapered to a blunt point. The guy at the booth was promoting them as a woman's self-defense weapon. Legal to carry, because it's not really a sharp blade, but stiff and pointed enough to be a lot better than a bunch of keys in your hand in a dark parking lot. Sabrina bought one and she keeps it in her purse. They came in several different styles, some with notched or twisted blades, and different handles, but they all had a hilt with a narrow crosspiece."

"That sounds right," Mac said. "That describes it. But the Festival isn't open in July, right? And definitely not in June when he did the first one. Do you think he could have bought it online?"

"Probably. Or last year. If your computer guy hasn't spotted a source online, tell him to look under sword makers. Although," he hesitated, "It's kind of an odd choice for a man to buy."

"Why?" Mac asked.

"Well, it was the cheapest thing they had, but it was still about two hundred and fifty dollars. For just twenty or thirty more, you could start to get their real knives with the gorgeous sharp blades. And it's a woman's defensive weapon. If you were going to spend that kind of money for a knife to kill people with, why not get a better blade?"

"Maybe it had some special significance for him, or he doesn't like sharp blades."

"Or maybe he got it from a woman," Tony speculated. "Maybe he stole it, or some woman he went after tried to use it to protect herself and he took it from her."

"There's a thought. And if it's that valuable it might have been reported lost or stolen. Unless he killed the woman he got it from." They sat in glum silence for a moment. "Well, it opens up some avenues anyway. Maybe we can get lists of purchasers and work backwards too." Mac stood and bent over to kiss Tony.

"Thanks, Tony. I'm always surprised by the things you know."

"A Renaissance man," Tony laughed. "You should see me in tights and a cod-piece."

Mac kissed him again, more deeply. "I think I would pay to see that."

"It's free for you," Tony breathed, pulling his head down.

Mac opened his mouth for Tony's searching tongue and slid a hand into the short dark curls. This was good, this was what he needed. He tugged Tony up out of his seat and pulled him in tight, a hand on the small of his back.

"Oh, yeah," Tony murmured against his mouth. "Dessert."

Mac laughed softly and kissed him hard, and harder, filling that soft wet mouth, feeling Tony getting stiff against him.

"Do we have to do dishes first?" Mac asked eventually.

"Fuck the dishes." Tony shoved his plate out from under as Mac pressed him back against the table.

"Not what I had in mind to fuck." Mac unbuttoned Tony's jeans and slid his hands down inside the denim in back to cup that firm ass. Tony moaned softly and pressed back into his hands. Mac dug his fingers in and used his wrists to work the fabric down. Tony reached down and fumbled with his own zipper, releasing himself and shoving the jeans toward the floor. Mac knelt to strip them off, and took advantage of the position to nuzzle in, filling his senses with the smell of Tony's skin. His hands made quick work of the briefs underneath. Then Tony was bare and hard, the hot silk of his dick against Mac's cheek. Mac turned his face to lick and kiss, running his tongue along the full shaft, tracing the pattern of the veins, drawing little sounds from his lover.

Tony's fingers plunged into his hair again, tugging hard this time. Mac arched into the pull on his scalp and took Tony's flared cock-head into his mouth. The slit already tasted wet and salty, and Tony moaned for him. Mac sucked deep and then pulled off.

"Turn around, babe," Mac told him.

Tony turned, bracing his hands on the table. Mac spread Tony's legs apart with his hands, kissing the inside of his thighs. He circled in with a wet mouth, biting, licking at that hot ass until his tongue touched its goal.

"Oh, God," Tony moaned. "Oh, yeah, baby, rim me."

Mac breathed in the musky scent as he licked and stroked. His cock was like iron in his jeans, but he waited, giving Tony his hands and mouth and full attention, until Tony whimpered and shoved back against him. Mac replaced his mouth with a finger, stroking him open. *No lube.* The bathroom was only twenty feet away, but...

He fumbled for the butter on the table, stabbing his fingers into it. Tony gave a choked laugh. "We're going to smell like cookies."

"Cookies are good," Mac growled, stroking the butter onto Tony then taking a lick. "I eat cookies."

"Oh, God." The rest of Tony's comeback was lost in his panting breath. Mac slicked him up, fingers sliding in the creamy butter and plunging deep into Tony. He found Tony's prostate and rubbed over it, enjoying the moaning sounds the motion dragged from Tony's mouth. Finally, finally, he yanked down his own zipper and shorts, and let himself free. A handful of butter slathered over his length lubed him up too, and then he pressed against Tony.

"Ready, babe?"

"Oh, yeah," Tony moaned. "God, yeah. Now, please, hard."

Mac held the younger man's hips firmly and pushed forward. Firm muscle resisted for a moment then gave way, and he sank into that beloved tight heat. Tony whimpered at the penetration, but he was already shoving back, pumping rhythmically.

"Easy, easy, Tony," Mac panted, trying to hold Tony still. "I'm not going to last if you do that."

"I don't care. I don't care. Do me now, baby."

Mac stopped resisting and took up the rhythm, sliding deeper and deeper into Tony with each thrust. *So good, so good!* Heat flooded up and down his thighs, centered in his groin. No other man had ever felt like this. None of them took over his senses, his very breath, until there was nothing but the heat around him, the skin under him, the sound of his lover's voice. Mac breathed in rough gasps and his blood drummed in his ears.

"Close, baby," Tony moaned. "So close."

Mac reached one butter-slicked hand around to close on Tony's erect cock. With each slam of his hips, he drove the younger man forward into his fist. Tony whimpered, faster and faster, shaking under him. Then he heard Tony groan, deep and hard, and felt the cum spilling hot and wet between his fingers. Mac stroked him a moment longer, reveling in the way Tony's body arched and shook as he came. Then Mac let go of Tony's cock and set both hands firmly on those narrow hips. He shoved himself in hard. Once, twice, and he exploded. At a distance he heard his own voice chanting, "Oh God, oh God, oh God, Tony!" His knees were trembling as he spilled himself deep inside his lover's body. Tony pressed back firmly against him, taking all of him.

When he could breathe again, Tony was collapsed on the table under him, sweat-damp back against Mac's chest. Mac slid his elbows up to take a little of his weight off the other man. He didn't think he could move further yet. He kissed Tony's shoulder through the damp T-shirt.

"Wow." Tony's voice was breathless. "Keeps getting better."

"Yeah, me too." Mac kissed him again and licked the salt sweat off his neck with the tip of his tongue. Slowly he pulled back and out, watching the slow drip of his cum slide down Tony's thigh. It was so sweet, being able to come raw and deep, knowing that Tony was walking around with a little bit of Mac inside him all day. Mac straightened and turned Tony around. He pulled him into a tight hug, their bodies pressed together, slippery and sticky and wet. Mac kissed Tony under his ear. *I love you.* He wanted to say it, but his voice was missing. He kissed the man again slowly instead, mouth to mouth, warm and sweet.

Eventually Tony looked over at the table. "That's one stick of butter that is not going back in the refrigerator."

"Worth it," Mac told him.

"You're not the one who does the grocery shopping," Tony teased, but when Mac opened his mouth to apologize, Tony stopped him with a kiss. "More than worth it," he whispered.

"We need a shower." Mac reached down to pull up his pants, and was stopped by Tony's hand on his arm.

"Anything you touch is going to have permanent grease stains," Tony pointed out. "And as the one who also does most of the laundry lately, I don't like that idea. Hobble over to the sink and wash up while I start the shower."

Mac shuffled over to the kitchen sink with his pants down around his ankles and soaped up in the warm water. From the bathroom he caught the sound of the shower starting and the hint of Tony singing softly over the water. He smiled, drying his hands on the towel. A long, slow, hot shower with Tony would be perfect. Knowing Tony, they might even get around to playtime in the water. He was full and content right now, sated with loving. But Tony had a magic touch. He kind of thought that, in ten or fifteen minutes, there might be a reason to bring the regular lube along, for comparison. Mac pulled up his pants but didn't bother to fasten them as he headed for the bathroom. Pants were definitely optional when Tony was around.

CHAPTER 4

Mac was surprised at the number of people who showed up for the MPD picnic the next Sunday. His own team was very busy with several cases, which were getting nowhere with each passing day, but most of his co-workers were there despite the workload and the oppressively hot weather. He squinted skyward. The blue sky was streaked with clouds, but the muggy haze did not promise actual rain.

Of course, Captain Severs had made this sound like a command performance. The man had a burr up his ass about improving teamwork and…what was his word? Oh, yes, department cohesiveness. Almost worthy of Tony, that word, using four syllables where one would do. Cohesiveness. Like this would help. At least the food was free, and it gave him time to spend with his little daughter. And if truth be told, to show her off. He shouldn't enjoy the attention she drew, but he had to admit that he did.

Right now, Anna was over on the baseball field, getting gentle lessons on catching a ball from Ann Carson in Family Violence. Anna was missing far more than she was catching, partly because the glove was so big she had to work it with both hands, but she looked delighted with her attempts. With her long silky black hair and fair skin, she looked like a fragile doll, but appearances were deceiving. Mac bet Anna's catching attempts would outlast Carson's throwing.

A couple of the younger men were playing a real game of catch with Oliver's teenage sons, out in the outfield. Attempts to get a baseball game going had died in the heat. Mac was quite content to sit back on the bench, digest his burger, and watch.

"She's very beautiful, your daughter," a voice said from behind him. Mac turned to squint up into the sun and recognized Linda Ramsey, a recent transfer to Homicide. He grunted, "Thanks." Ramsey sat beside him despite that less than welcoming response.

"How old is she?"

"Five. She takes after her mother, thank God."

Ramsey looked at him searchingly, from under strawberry blond curls going limp in the heat. "I heard you're a widower?"

"Yeah."

"I'm sorry."

"It's been a while," he said dismissively. He still missed Mai, but their marriage had been a sham right from the start. He was uncomfortable accepting the sympathy people felt he deserved. They had helped each other out in a difficult situation, he providing a green card for Mai and a father for her child, she providing him with a cover family. She had been brave and smart, and her child was the center of his heart, but they had never been lovers. "It's been almost five years," he realized.

"Then you raised the girl alone," Ramsey said. "That's impressive. She's very bright. I spoke with her earlier and I was impressed."

"Thank you, although I had help." *Of a sort.* His cousin Brenda had taken the girl in, when the hours of his career made single parenting impossible. He paid for childcare and gave Anna every moment he could get free, and Anna had thrived. But more and more he found himself clashing with Brenda's ultra-religious worldview. He was starting to worry about Anna as she got older, getting caught between himself and Brenda. There was no easy answer. And if he came out with Tony, there would be no Brenda, and no child care. That was one of the painful realities of his situation. He realized Ramsey had said something.

"Sorry," he said. "I missed that."

"I said there are lots of us cops here, but not as many families as I would have expected. When I was in uniform, the family events always had scads of kids running around."

"This group's a little older," Mac pointed out, "And we've been on the job longer. It tends to be hard on the wives, and husbands I guess. And you're catching us at kind of a low point."

"How so?" Ramsey asked, leaning toward him a little.

Mac didn't usually gossip, since he hated his own private life speculated about, but a little information might keep this pretty young woman's foot out of her mouth around her co-workers. "Well, Severs just got divorced," Mac told her. "His wife took the kids and headed for Maine." *Smart woman.* "Oliver's been divorced for three years. Those two boys in the outfield are his, but his ex isn't here. Johansson's wife is away. Terrance just broke up with his girlfriend and isn't rebounding yet. Loes's wife left somewhere back in the Cretaceous era, although he still says they're just separated. And Hanson tries to make up for it by always having at least three girlfriends on a string at any time, but he usually doesn't bring them around the rest of us grunts. And working Family Violence or Sex Crimes is even worse on relationships than Homicide, so not many families there. There may be some happy couples over in Robbery." Mac huffed a breath. He hadn't realized just how short of family his teammates were. He was better off than most of them. *Better off than any of them, even if he had to keep it hidden.*

"God. That sounds pretty dire."

"Well, I guess the right spouse can make it work," Mac said, thinking it through. "We cops tend to be short-tempered and morose when we come up against the bad stuff, and we work unpredictable hours, and we're selfish."

"Selfish? I can't see you as selfish somehow."

"Oh, yes," Mac told her. "You have to be. We're out there in hairy situations with guns and violence. If we're sleep-deprived and angry and distracted, people could get hurt or killed. A cop has to do what it takes to keep an even keel, if he can, for the public's sake as much as his own." He sighed. "If you have a strong spouse, that's best of all. Too many of us are alone with a bottle or some other remedy that doesn't do the job right."

"You must really miss your wife," Ramsey said softly.

Mac glanced at her, startled, then said, "Yes, I guess so." He hadn't been thinking of Mai. He suddenly wondered just what demands he had been putting on Tony. Somehow the man seemed to know what to do when Mac was stressed, when to be quiet and listen, when to distract him. He had never felt as relaxed and centered in his work as he had the last few months. Did that make him too selfish? He wondered if he was giving back to Tony anything like what he was getting.

He did listen to Tony's day-to-day problems. *And how often have you thought they were trivial relative to your own?* Although he had helped with the kid who was getting abused. He'd spent a fair bit of time working with Child Protection to find a safe solution the teenager would accept. And he wouldn't have had nearly as much patience with the angry rebellious boy if it hadn't been so important to Tony.

*I took care of Tony when he had the flu. I helped save his life.* The flu thing was actually more telling. He would have helped anyone who was in danger from a killer with a gun. And in fact Tony had halfway rescued himself. But there was only one other person in the world he would voluntarily clean up puke for, and she was five years old.

Tony was happy. That was the best he could come up with for now. That smile Mac got when he came in the door was worth everything. *But how long will he be happy kept out of the rest of your life?*

He couldn't imagine bringing Tony to a family event like this. *This is my boyfriend and his kid.* Not happening. Although Anna had wanted to bring them. She really liked Tony and Ben, the boy Tony was all but father to.

They had spent that morning with the pair of them, at Minnehaha Park. They'd all walked back to Minnehaha Falls and watched the spill and play of the water. The kids coaxed them into getting as close to the falls as possible. A wisp of spray caught a breeze and drifted their way. And then Tony casually pulled off his sweat-dampened T-shirt and tucked it in his belt, seeking relief from the oppressive heat. Mac's tongue glued to the roof of his mouth. As the children chattered to Tony, Mac took one step backward, eyes averted from Tony's bare chest, searching for control. Until his silence drew Tony's questioning gaze. A small smile, equal parts teasing and affection, quirked Tony's mouth. Then he'd obediently shaken out the damp shirt and pulled it back on. Mac found his family-outing mode again and relaxed, tucking the smallest sliver of regret away out of mind.

They had spent a quiet hour wandering along the creek in the relative cool of the shade beside the water. He and Tony had talked lightly about nothing in particular, while Ben and Anna explored. Ben had spotted a half-grown gosling, and the kids had fed it crackers.

Ben was great, smart and sweet, but scarily independent. Having an inattentive mother made Ben likely to do stuff without asking for help, or permission. Mac still had vivid memories of the day they had taken both kids out to a park, and he looked up from a moment's inattention to see Ben trying to stop traffic on a busy street to let a suicidal mother mallard and her ducklings cross unharmed. He bet Tony still had nightmares about the little boy stepping off the curb, waving his arms at the oncoming cars.

That morning, when he pulled Anna away from their feathered friend to remind her of the picnic, she had asked, "Can we bring Ben 'n Tony? I bet they'd like to come."

Tony had met his eyes ruefully over the kids' heads. "You know, Anna," he said. "They're serving food at this picnic, and they're not expecting extra people. It's kind of rude to just show up for a meal when you're not invited. Maybe another time, Mac can check first and see if there will be extras and you can bring Ben, at least."

Anna had been okay with that, although her first comment when she saw the laden tables alongside the barbeque grills was, "There would've been plenty enough for Ben and Tony." Which had never been the point.

Ramsey moved even closer to Mac on the bench. "What about two cops together?" she asked. "Do you think that would work better?"

Mac realized belatedly that she was flirting with him a little.

"Probably a disaster," he said firmly, and truthfully. "Especially if you're in the same department. You'd both be stressed at the same time. And imagine if you had kids. Nope." He turned to look at her, moving their bodies further apart. "So if Hanson starts suggesting he needs a girl in the department to match the ones he has outside it, you be firm and resist, okay?"

"Who are you slandering, Mac?" Hanson said over his shoulder. He turned his blindingly handsome grin on Ramsey. "Don't listen to a word this guy says. It's just sour grapes because he doesn't have his girlfriend here. I can't tell you why because it's a secret." He winked at Mac, who cursed Oliver and the grapevine silently. *It's better than the truth*, he reminded himself.

Hanson extended a hand to Ramsey. "Come on, I'll introduce you to some of the gang you haven't met yet. I know everyone. I won't bite." Ramsey looked over at Mac, but when he gazed back impassively, she rose and let Hanson lead her away toward the picnic tables. Mac sighed and wondered when his life got so complicated.

Tony sat in the passenger seat of the car, watching Minneapolis go by. Mac was driving silently, as if it took his whole concentration. Each attempt at starting a conversation had fallen flatter than a pancake, and they were definitely not touching.

Tony tried to remember the last time the two of them had been alone in a car together. After he had been hurt in the hit-and-run last fall Mac had given him a lift a few times, until he got off the heavy pain meds. Since then, nothing. They only shared the front seat if there were two pint-sized chaperones in the backseat. Like when they took Ben and Anna together to the pool or the zoo.

Tony turned his head a little to include Mac's unrevealing profile in the periphery of his vision. Mac had wanted him here. Tony had suggested separate cars, but Mac had muttered something about the cost of gas, and held the door open for him. Since then he hadn't said a word. Sometimes Tony thought he would never understand the man. As they approached the teen center he gave Mac monosyllabic directions.

He knew Mac was frustrated about the serial killer case. He had borrowed Sabrina's dagger for a comparison, and Mac reported that it was a good match, although hers had an extra decorative spiral at the base that the killer's did not. Tracking down the knife-maker and getting customer lists proved fairly simple, but there were no daggers reported lost or stolen. Quite a few of the weapons had been untraceable cash purchases. There were lots of possibilities open.

Mac continued to put long hours in on the case, despite the new cases that had crossed his desk in the last two weeks. He had submitted a request to do DNA matching with samples from several other rapes and murders over the past two years. He had even cajoled other Twin Cities police forces to submit any possibilities from their cases, which he told Tony took a combination of humble begging and tap dancing. But the request was stuck in the budget-crunched backlog. Mac said they might see the results in a few weeks.

In the dark hours of morning, Mac admitted that he was both fearing and hoping there would be another body. Because much as he didn't want another death, he was sure that without one, they were not going to catch this guy. So his mood had been dark lately. But this sullen silence was closed-down even for Mac.

Mac found parking on the street near the center and pulled into the space. Tony checked the meter as he got out.

"In force until ten PM," he noted, fishing for quarters in his pocket. Mac came up behind him and fed two dollars worth into the slot. He glanced around.

"Not a great neighborhood."

"Hey," Tony said cheerfully. "At least with this car you don't have to worry about it being stolen."

Mac hesitated and turned to Tony, probably to defend his ride, then gave it up as hopeless. "Lead the way."

The common room of the center was almost deserted. Only

three teenage boys were around, desultorily watching TV. At least Carter was one of them, which meant this class had the seal of approval. Tony hoped some of the other kids would show up. He had badgered and persuaded about ten of them to sign up ahead of time, paying for three out of his own pocket. He had been impressed by Mary Liu when they met to discuss the details. *These kids had better take advantage of this.*

He put the boys and Mac to work moving the couch and chairs into the hallway, and the TV completely out of harm's way in another room. The space they cleared would be a little cramped, but it was the biggest open area the center possessed. By the time the moving was done, other kids were beginning to straggle in. Attendance was looking up.

Mary Liu strode in just before seven. For a small woman, she took up a lot of psychological space. She spotted Mac and came over.

"Hey there, victim," she said. "Hope you're wearing a jock strap."

"I borrowed some hockey pads. They're out in the car."

"Good. You're going to need them." She turned to Tony. "If you can draft a crew to help carry stuff, I brought some floor mats. They're in my car trunk out front."

It was the work of a few minutes to bring in the mats and set them up on the floor. The kids paid more attention as the padding slapped down on the tiles.

"Okay," Mary said in a voice that wasn't loud, but cut through the conversations. "Let's get this show on the road." She nodded to Tony.

Tony stood up in front of the group. Eight boys and five girls had showed up. Better than he'd expected. They eyed him warily.

"These people are Detectives Liu and MacLean," Tony said. "They're here to teach you how to be safer, in dangerous situations. At least, Detective Liu is here to teach you, and MacLean is here to show you how even a big guy can be stopped if you have the right moves. So listen up and learn something." He nodded to

Mary and took a place in the audience. Mary moved to the front of the room.

"I'm Mary Liu. I teach this class other places, as Personal Safety 101, or rape prevention, or whatever the program wants to call it. It's the same class, and there are three basic things I want you to walk away with at the end of the course. First, what moves you can use to protect yourself against an attacker. Second, how to anticipate and decide if a situation is really dangerous. And last but not least, the idea that you have the right to protect yourself.

"That last bit may seem obvious, but I've found it's perhaps the most difficult part of all." Her voice became a little more reminiscent. "I came into this the long way round. You see I was brought up to be good and respectful and polite. And when I was a nineteen-year-old sophomore in college I was raped." She paused and looked around at the kids. Tony noticed one of the girls staring fixedly at the floor, slowly shaking her head.

Liu went on, "My attacker was a guy I knew slightly. I'd turned him down for a date. There were no weapons involved, and he was drunk, but he was bigger than me, and I couldn't do enough to stop him. And afterward, I was so ashamed."

Liu nodded to her audience. "How backward is that? *He* hurt *me*, and *I* was ashamed. I thought it must be my fault. I must have done something wrong, must have given the wrong signals. I figured I was young, ignorant, stupid, female. I must have deserved it somehow. I wondered if I had some invisible target on my back that made him pick me. It wasn't until I dropped out of school a year later, and entered the police academy, that I started thinking straighter.

"I realized that there were other girls he had asked on dates. He might have raped any one of them if they'd happened to be in the wrong place at the wrong time. And if I didn't believe that girl would have deserved it, then neither had I. I learned enough in combat classes to realize I probably could have stopped that guy if I had been willing to use enough force. If I had given myself permission to hurt that man I could have gotten away. But I was too civilized, and I didn't think I had that right."

Liu frowned, looking slowly at each of the kids. "I see thirteen teenagers in this room," she said. "Odds are, at least one or two of you have been sexually abused, perhaps even raped, already. Some of you have been hit or beaten. And probably none of you reported it. Maybe you thought no one would listen. I'm not going to be a Pollyanna here. In some cases, you may have been right. But anyone who wants to talk to me about an assault can get hold of me after class, and I *will* listen.

"The other problem is that you may have been thinking the way I did after the rape. You're thinking, I'm small, female, Goth, gay, a nerd, a lesbian, a geek, weird, stupid, and that's why these things happen to me. Well you're wrong," she said fiercely. "Violence is about the attacker, not the victim. If you weren't there, your attacker would have chosen some other victim. You are all real, good, and valuable people and you are entitled to be safe. And you are allowed to fight back, run, scream, get help or do whatever it takes to be safe."

Liu paused for a moment and then repeated, "You are allowed to do whatever it takes to keep yourself safe. I want everyone to repeat after me, 'I am a good person and I have the right to be safe.'"

The chorus of responses was almost inaudible.

"You don't sound like you believe it. Again. 'I am a good person and I have the right to be safe.'"

The kids were a little louder. After a moment Pete said, "But what if you're not a good person?"

Liu replied, "I don't mean good like going to church or not breaking laws. If, in your heart, you try to get through the day without hurting other people, then you are a good person and no one has the right to hurt you."

She sighed. "Sometimes that's the thing that takes the longest, letting go of the idea that somehow you deserve it or it's your own fault, giving yourself permission to fight back.

"Right now I'm going to move on. We're going to discuss how to decide how dangerous a situation is. If the worst that a guy is going to do is bruise your arm, you don't want to put out his eye to stop him. If he is going to rape you, cut you, or break your ribs, you need to give yourself permission to really hurt him if that's what it takes to get away.

"Eventually I'll show you some moves you can use when someone, like our large detective friend over there, tries to grab you. So while Detective MacLean goes and puts on a little padding for protection, we're going to talk about the first step, which is preventing violence before it happens. Something as simple as walking confidently and briskly down a dark street can discourage an attacker who's looking for a victim…"

An hour and a half later, Tony pushed sweaty hair out of his face. The techniques Mary Liu had worked on were not hard exercise, but Tony had been kept hopping as attacker number two. Although the kids had pulled their blows at his unpadded self, he thought he would have a few bruises. But it was worth it to see them gain confidence. Even with well-protected Mac, some of the kids were still very hesitant about striking back. But others took to the training with relish.

"How sore are you going to be?" Tony asked Mac out of the corner of his mouth as they began picking up Mary's mats.

"I'll know tomorrow. I'm dreaming of a hot shower right now."

"I bet," Tony said sympathetically, biting back his first response. "It was worth it though, don't you think? She's really good."

"Yeah," Mac agreed. "This was a good thing. Although next class *you* get the hockey padding. I think I may be busy at work."

"Wimp," Tony snorted.

Mac said, "I've been thinking about enrolling Anna in some kind of martial arts class. Do you think Ben would like to do that too?"

"I'm sure he'd love it. Although neither of those wild kids has much problem with being inhibited and lacking confidence."

"No, I just..." Mac sighed. "I want her to be safe, you know. And there's no way I can make certain of that. But it would help a little if I knew she at least wouldn't hesitate to fight back, and knew how to do it."

"She's just a kid," Tony began, but he knew that wasn't the point. "Sure," he said. "Find a class and I'll pay for Ben to join too, if Sandy lets him, and I'll do the transportation for both kids." Because he too couldn't help thinking of the child he considered his own when he heard about a kid getting hurt. One in four girls, one in six boys, they said. Ben and Anna wouldn't be the ones, if he could do anything to prevent it.

CHAPTER 5

Mac sometimes loathed the squad room. This morning he felt stifled. The air conditioning and heating seemed designed to keep things at a sauna level nine months of the year, the phones were shrill, the odor of stale pizza constant, his desk chair creaked… He sighed. The litany of complaints was a poor excuse for putting off the report he had to write.

There was something to be said for a murderer so stupid that he stayed in his victim's house, drinking his beer, until the police arrived. The guy actually thought that catching his friend stealing his good pool cue made it justifiable homicide. A blood alcohol level higher than his IQ was probably part of the explanation. Case solved, but Mac was getting really tired of stupid violence.

Oliver appeared at his elbow before he could dig into the forms. "Hey, partner," he said, excitement evident in his voice. "We may have victim number three for our dagger man."

Mac gladly signed out of his computer and followed Oliver out to the car. "Another young blonde, strangled and stabbed to death," Oliver reported as he tooled the car out of the lot and turned on the flashers. Mac grabbed the dash in anticipation of his partner's driving style. "Just found this morning, twenty minutes ago," Oliver continued. "Last seen alive last night, so it's a recent scene. Maybe we'll get lucky. God knows it's about time we got a break."

The new victim's apartment was in a large, dilapidated tenement. A handful of neighbors hung out on the steps, goggling at the patrol cars pulled up to the curb in front. Mac ignored their calls of enquiry as he headed up the steps. He followed Oliver to the third floor into a small, dingy apartment. The uniformed officer at the door let them past. Another officer came towards them.

"The victim's name is Alexandra Thompson," she reported. "You can see the driver's license in the stuff that spilled out of the purse." She pointed to the counter where a small purse lay on its side, contents trailing out. "I haven't touched it, and I only checked a carotid pulse on the victim, left side. Face matches the ID."

"Who called it in?" Oliver asked.

"A neighbor. Came over to meet the victim for a trip out to the hairdresser, couldn't get an answer at the door. It wasn't locked, so she let herself in and found the victim on the bed. She called 911 and then went back to her own apartment. I have another officer with her, anytime you want to question her. I've kept the scene locked down."

"Good work." Oliver turned and headed for the bedroom. Mac followed behind. Something was nagging at him, like that tip-of-the-tongue thing, something that wasn't right about the scene. He glanced over Oliver's shoulder at the victim, who certainly was blond, naked, posed, and stabbed. His gaze slid around the room. *Not in here. There was something wrong out there.*

Leaving Oliver to the bedroom, he went out again into the tiny living room. *Two other doors.* Putting on gloves, he reached behind the door handle to avoid smudging prints and opened the first remaining door. *Bathroom.* That wasn't it. He tried the second. It opened into what was obviously a young boy's room. The empty bed was lined with stuffed animals, a baseball poster hung on the wall. Nothing there, but it still nagged at him. He went back to the living room.

"Where's the boy?" he asked the officer. "With a neighbor?"

"I don't know. He wasn't here when we got here."

"I don't like it." Mac took a slow look around the room. On one shelf, a set of photographs in cheap frames caught his eye. A moment later he was plunging back into the boy's room.

"Ben!" he shouted. "Ben, can you hear me?" Nothing under the bed. A pile of dirty laundry in the closet, but no child. "*Ben!*"

Oliver came running and stared at him from the doorway. "What the fuck?"

"She has a boy," Mac said urgently. "Six years old. His name is Ben Serrano. His photo is out in the living room. She sometimes has him stay with a neighbor, but I don't know which one."

"You know her?" Oliver said. "Oh God, Mac, she's not your girlfriend!"

"No, not like that," Mac snapped impatiently. "I've never met her, but the boy plays with my daughter Anna. I know Ben."

The female officer stepped out, but after a few minutes she returned. "Talked to the neighbor," she said. "The woman says Gonzales in 310 has the boy most mornings in the summer, while Thompson works, but I checked and the boy's not there this morning. She doesn't know where he would be."

"Damn," Mac cursed, wheeling around to look at the apartment. *Were there hiding places for a small boy in here? Dear God, don't let him be taken, or dead.*

"Ben," he called loudly and clearly. "It's Mac. You're safe now, but I need you to come out. Ben, come out for Mac please."

For a minute there was no response, but as he was turning to take the search out into the building, he heard a sound from the boy's room. Six quick strides and he was standing at the open closet door. Ben's pale face looked up from under the pile of dirty clothes.

"Thank God," Mac whispered, and crouched and held out his arms. Ben flew into them and clung around his neck with a strangle hold. Mac could feel the boy's small body shaking. He stood, lifting the boy, and Ben's legs wrapped around his waist like a limpet. Mac murmured in his ear, "You're safe. I've got you. You're safe now." Gradually Ben's hold softened a little, until Mac could shift him into a more workable seat on his hip. The boy hid his face on Mac's shoulder.

"Listen, Ben," Mac said. "Are you hurt?"

The boy shook his head mutely against Mac's shirt.

"You're sure."

An equally silent nod.

"Okay," Mac told him. "I'm going to take you out of here. Just hang on."

"I want Ted," Ben whimpered.

"Who?"

"Ted." The boy fisted one hand in Mac's collar to reach out with the other toward the bed. Mac looked over and saw a battered stuffed bear on the pillow. He didn't want to disturb a crime scene, but surely... He dipped to one side, just close enough for the small hand to snag the bear and reel it in. With boy and bear, he headed out into the living room.

Ben's head came up off Mac's shoulder as they went through the door and he looked towards his mother's room. Mac was unutterably glad that the body was not visible from that angle. "Mom?" Ben's voice was thin.

"Your mom can't be with you right now," Mac said. *How do you tell a six-year-old his mother is dead?*

"I want Tony," Ben whispered.

"Yes. As soon as he can get here." Mac looked over at Oliver. "I'm going to take the kid down to the car and call his guardian. I'll stay with him until then and see if I can ask a few questions."

"Okay," Oliver agreed. "When you're free, the neighbor is all yours too."

"Right." Mac shifted Ben's weight to one arm and pulled out his cell phone as he headed down the stairs. Tony's number rang through to voice mail. *Answer, damn it.* Mac remembered that Tony was at a Habitat build. Maybe his hands were full. He dialed again, and a third time, and a fourth.

Finally Tony picked up on the other end. "Sorry, paint on my hands," he said. "What's the problem? Are you okay?"

"I'm fine," Mac said. "I need you at Sandy's, right away."

"Is Ben...?" Tony began in alarm.

"Ben's fine too," Mac told him. "But Sandy's not. Ben needs you here."

"As fast as I can clean up and get out of here. Maybe twenty minutes with the drive. Wait, are you there…officially?"

"Yes," Mac told him.

"Oh. Oh, shit. Okay, I'll be there. You'll take care of Ben until I arrive?"

"Of course," Mac assured him. "We'll be in an unmarked car on the street, a grey Taurus." He pocketed the phone and squinted at the glare as they stepped out onto the street.

The inside of the car was like an oven. Mac sat sideways in the driver's seat to start the engine and turn on the AC. He held Ben awkwardly on his lap, since the boy would not release his death grip. The sweat ran down Mac's skin where the small, hot body pressed against him but he held Ben firmly and waited.

After a few minutes, the air from the vents turned cool. He lifted the boy, transferred them both to the backseat, and closed the doors. For a while he just sat, rubbing the boy's back gently. Eventually he turned a little and slid Ben over so he could see the boy's face.

"Was someone with your mom last night, Ben?" he asked quietly.

Ben nodded.

"A man or a woman?"

"Man," Ben whispered.

"Did you see him?"

"No. I stayed in my room. I was always in my room." Ben's voice began climbing.

"Hush," Mac soothed him. "It's okay. It's good that you were safe in your room. Did you hear the man's voice?"

"A little bit. I don't remember." Ben shook his head. "I don't remember."

"Did your mom say the man's name?"

"I don't think so. She was laughing. I don't remember!"

"Okay, that's okay." As long as they weren't going to get an immediate ID out of the boy, the rest of his story could wait until he was safe with Tony. Mac settled Ben against his shoulder again. "I called Tony. He'll be here soon."

After a long pause, Ben whispered, "Is my mom hurt bad?"

Mac swallowed, but evading the truth would only be worse in the long run. "Ben. Your mom is dead."

Ben nodded against his shoulder. "Like my dad."

It was more statement than question, but Mac said, "Yes, like your dad." He waited, letting the boy steer this conversation. Ben sat still, barely breathing, not crying. Eventually he said, "I don't have a mom or a dad now."

"No. But you have Tony and you have me, and we'll take care of you. You're not alone."

"Mom said…" Ben's voice trailed off.

"What?" Mac asked.

Ben just shook his head, and sat there, still and tense. Mac suppressed the instinct to ask questions, push for answers. *He's so small, to be alone.* Mac ran his hand over the soft brown curls, rubbing the boy's neck. *Why isn't he crying?*

Eventually Ben said, "I'm kind of tired, but I need to pee really bad 'cause there's no bathroom in my room."

"Got it," Mac slid out of the car, leaving it running, and carried the boy in to the superintendent's apartment. She opened to his knock reluctantly, but Mac didn't give her a chance to say no.

"I'm with the police," he told her. "The boy just needs to use your bathroom for a moment." He pushed past her and set Ben on his feet by the open bathroom door. "Do you need help?" he asked.

"I'm six," Ben said disgustedly, hurrying in and closing the door. Mac leaned against it. The superintendent sidled over to him. "I heard a woman was stabbed to death and she was naked," she whispered loudly.

"Shush!" Mac was glad the flush of the toilet had probably drowned out the words. "That's her boy there, so keep quiet, you hear me?"

The woman backed off, muttering. Mac ignored her, taking Ben's hand as he came out and leading him back out to the car. The interior had cooled down and Ben curled up against him on the backseat. Mac looked at his watch and settled in to wait.

Then Tony appeared, opening the car door, and Ben dove sobbing into the younger man's arms. *He wasn't crying because he didn't quite trust you enough to let go,* Mac realized. He was vastly relieved to have Tony there too. He slid over to the other side of the seat.

"Come on in and shut the door so we don't melt," he suggested softly. Tony struggled awkwardly onto the seat with his armful of crying boy, and looked at Mac over Ben's head. Mac shook his head in return. "Sandy's dead," he said quietly.

Tony bent over the boy, murmuring and soothing, until Ben's wild sobs wound down into hiccoughing breaths.

"I've got Ben," Tony said to Mac eventually, "If you need to go."

"I'd like to talk to Ben a little more, if he's willing. If not, then it can wait."

Tony looked like he might protest, but then tilted Ben's face up to his own. "How about it, Benny boy? Can you answer a few questions for Mac?"

"Okay," Ben whispered. "I guess."

"Did your mom go out last night?" Mac asked him.

Ben opened his mouth to answer, and then looked up at Tony again. "Mom said not to tell Tony about it."

"Ben," Mac said softly. "The only thing that can help your mom now is if you tell me the truth. Tony is going to take care of you. I'm sure your mom would say it was okay now to tell."

Ben thought about it for a moment, sobbed once, and then said, "Yeah, she went out."

"What time?"

"I don't know."

"Well, um, what did you do before she left? Did you have dinner?"

"Yes," Ben told him. "She made spaghetti and chicken. It was good. And I brushed my teeth and got ready for bed and everything, 'cause after she goes out then I stay in my room until morning."

"She's gone out in the evening before?"

"Yes, sometimes." Ben frowned. "She said not ever to tell."

"It's okay to tell now. We're not mad." *At least not mad at you.* "What happened after that?"

"She came back and I wasn't sleeping. She was laughing, and I heard someone else, so I went into the closet."

"You went in the closet because you heard someone?"

"There was a man, and mom says to stay in my room, but I got scared because one time there was this man who came in my room and…and so I went into my closet under the laundry, 'cause it's safe there. It's hot though."

Mac met Tony's startled angry eyes. *One time there was a man who…what?* Sometime they would have to pursue that, but not now.

"So you stayed in the closet all night?"

"I guess."

"Did you sleep in there?"

"Yes," Ben said. "And then I waked up, and there was light outside, so I knew it was morning, but Mom didn't come get me. And she didn't come, and then someone was screaming and I got scared, so I went under the laundry some more but I left Ted on the bed. I was scared. But then I heard you, so I came out."

"And I got you and you got Ted."

"Yeah." The boy hugged his stuffed animal tightly in his arm.

"But my mom is dead." He looked up at Tony. "Is it really real?"

Tony snuggled him closer. "Yes, sweetie, really. But I'm here, and Mac, and Ted."

"Where will I sleep?" Ben asked.

Tony looked over at Mac. "I have guardianship of Ben in Sandy's will. It was part of a deal… anyway it's down on paper. He should be with me, but I don't want to screw anything up by just walking off with him."

"I'll tell Child Protection of Hennepin County where he is," Mac promised. "They should be able to make it official. Probably best you take him home now." He glanced over at the front door of the building. He'd bet reporters would be arriving any minute. The medical examiner had gone in a while ago. Mac didn't want Ben to see the body bag come out.

Tony followed his eyes, and nodded. "Come on, sweetie," he said to Ben. "My car is just down the road. We'll go back to my place for a while."

"What about my stuff?" Ben asked.

"The police need to look at it for a bit," Mac told him, "But pretty soon you'll be able to have it back. I'll call Tony and let him know when."

"Can I see my mom?" Ben whispered.

"I don't think that's a good idea, baby," Tony said. "People look a little different when they're dead. Your mom would want you to remember what she looked like when she was alive."

"Okay." Ben looked down at his feet. "Can we go now?"

"Sure." Tony climbed out of the car and took Ben's hand as he emerged. He looked back at Mac over the car roof. "Will you come by my place later, and talk to us?"

Mac opened his mouth to say of course, and caught the hidden emphasis on *talk*. Ouch, ouch, this was bad. Tony's small one-bedroom apartment was going to be full of six-year-old. Talking was all they would be doing, for who knows how long. *God, MacLean, the kid lost his mother and you're bitching because you're not going to get laid tonight.* But this was going to change things. Mac didn't want to think about how much. *First things first, you have a murder to investigate.*

"Sure," he said. "I'll come by, but probably pretty late."

"Good. I'll see you then. Stay safe." Tony turned and led the boy up the sidewalk. Mac watched them go. Tony headed across the street, the boy's hand held securely in his own. In the heat shimmer off the pavement, Mac's view of their backs seemed to waver and fade, like a mirage in the desert. Surely they hadn't walked that far, to seem so small and distant. Tony put the boy in the backseat as usual, because of the front airbag, and leaned in to fasten his seatbelt. For a moment the two dark heads were close together, talking seriously. Then the front door of the blue Prius shut behind Tony, and they pulled out into the flow of traffic and were gone. Mac stood for a moment, staring after them, before the pull of duty turned him back to the building behind him.

It was nearly three AM when Tony heard his front door open from where he lay stretched out on his couch. He swung his feet down and got up, stretching painfully. The couch was just long enough for him, but boy, did it need new cushions. He thought he had a permanent spring-print on his hip.

Mac closed the door behind himself and just stood there in the entry, looking uncertain. Tony went to him and pulled his mouth down for a long kiss. He felt some of the tension go out of his lover as their tongues touched softly.

"Hey, baby," he said softly. "Come on in and sit. Do you need food?"

"Grabbed Arby's at work," Mac whispered. "Where's the boy?"

"I put him in my room for now. I think he's finally asleep. I'm going to need a bigger place, though."

"Did Child Protection get hold of you? I had to leave a

message."

"Yeah, they came by," Tony said. "Luckily I have copies of Sandy's will and all. The lady wrinkled her nose at the size of this place, and promised a more complete home visit to come, but at least they left Ben with me for now."

"How's he doing?" Mac asked.

"Sad, scared, confused. About what you'd expect. I talked to him a little bit. He says Sandy has been going out in the evening for months and leaving him alone for an hour or two. Not every night, but a couple of nights a week in addition to regular Saturdays when he stays with Mrs. Gonzales. She usually comes home drunk and she'd brought a man home with her a few times before. Damn!" He couldn't believe he had missed the signs, even if Ben had been forbidden to talk to him. "I knew she was drinking more over the past year, but I thought she was just keeping booze in the house again. I never thought she would leave Ben home alone."

"Not your fault, Tony. You've been looking out for Ben a lot but you couldn't be there twenty-four/seven."

"I should have seen something," Tony insisted. "And you know what's worse?" This was the thing that had kept him far from sleep the last few hours. "I didn't warn Sandy. About the killer. Even without this weekday thing, I knew she brought strange men home on Saturdays when Ben was safely out of the apartment. I knew there was this guy going around killing women, and I even gave Sabrina a little warning, although she's short and brunette. But I never thought of Sandy!"

"It's not your fault," Mac repeated. "We didn't warn the public either. My boss said that two cases wasn't enough justification for a panic. When the media failed to link them, because they had one as a strangulation and one as a stabbing, the decision was made not to publicize. That's on me and my department, even more than on you. I asked you not to discuss it."

"But I should have…" Tony sighed. *Not like Sandy would have taken this warning more seriously than any of the other times he had cautioned her over the years.* Her lifestyle had always held that risk. She never took advice from him, especially when she was drinking. But he wished he had tried. "Come on," he told Mac. "Sit down for a bit and tell me how close you are to catching this bastard. Did losing Sandy at least give you a good lead?"

Mac followed him to the couch and sat heavily. Tony leaned up against him, glad of his solid bulk. Mac's arm came around him automatically. "I wish. But no, not really. It's early yet. We may find someone who saw them at a bar together. With Sandy, we did at least find out where she was drinking last night. She's a regular at the place closest to her apartment. But so far, all we have is some brown hair caught in her fingers. So the guy has short brown hair, not dyed. Which is a baby step forward, not a real help. We got DNA, and fingerprints off her skin, but nothing we didn't have from Brand. If we catch this guy, we'll have the evidence to put him away for life, but first we have to find him."

"What's next?" Tony asked.

"Canvassing the bar again. We're trying to find someone who saw a man with Sandy. I'm trying to persuade my boss to go to the media and ask the public for help. A 'Did you see this woman?' appeal. Three cases is a serial by everyone's definition, and the media aren't likely to miss it again."

"I hope I can keep Ben clear of it. Losing his mother is bad enough without him seeing the details on tabloids at the supermarket."

Mac kissed Tony's forehead. "You'll be a good dad." After a long moment he added, "You are going to keep the boy, right?"

"Yes, of course. If they let me. Even with Sandy's will choosing me, I'm male, single and not related, and let's not forget gay. There's a chance someone will have objections."

"You're employed, sober, and squeaky-clean," Mac said. "With how backed up the foster system is, I can't believe they won't approve you, to avoid having one more kid to place. Only…where does that leave us?"

"I don't know," Tony admitted. He had been avoiding thinking about it, burying that concern under all the others. "I don't think I can deal with that tonight."

"No, of course not," Mac agreed. "I'm not pushing, I just… we'll have to discuss it sometime."

"Yeah." Tony yawned. Suddenly, in the familiar comfort of Mac's arms, he was exhausted. Mac must be too. "You should go, before we fall asleep. No way this couch is made for two." Not that they had never fallen asleep on it together before, but never with a six-year-old in the bedroom.

"Right," Mac said without moving. "I'm getting up now."

Tony pulled out of his hold and poked him in the ribs. "Make that true, big boy. But drive carefully, okay?"

"Always." Mac turned to kiss him, and hesitated with a glance at the bedroom door. Tony made the kiss quick and light, and stood to brace his lover off the couch.

"Call me tomorrow?" he said. It felt odd. It had been months since they had spent a night apart unless Mac was working. From the expression on Mac's face, he wasn't happy either.

"Definitely. And you tell me if I can help with Child Protection, if you need a reference or something."

Tony nodded. "See you." He closed the door behind Mac and threw the deadbolt. The click was final in the early morning silence. He couldn't hear Mac's footsteps in the hall.

Tony was still standing, staring blankly at the closed door, when he heard a whimper from the bedroom. He turned and went in. Ben was curled up in a tight ball on the bed, eyes wide and scared in the low light of the lamp. Tony went over and sat on the bed beside him.

"Hey, sport," he said softly. "Bad dream?"

"I heard voices…"

"Sure. That was Mac. He came by to make sure we were okay."

"Is he going to stay with us?" Ben asked hopefully.

"Nope," Tony said cheerfully. "One bed, one couch, and three people just doesn't work."

"You could stay here on the bed with me," Ben suggested, "And Mac could have the couch."

"Mac's too tall for the couch. And he has his own apartment. But we'll see him soon, and he'll always come if we need him. You know that." He couldn't resist asking, "You like having Mac around?"

"Yeah." Ben's voice was fading. "He's big and strong and it feels real good and safe when he's with us." The boy's eyes closed, long lashes fluttering against his cheeks. Tony looked down at the small, thin body curled up tightly, battered bear clutched to his chest. He ran a hand lightly over those soft curls, cleaner now after a good bath.

"Yeah," he whispered to the sleeping child. "It does feel good."

The give of the bed under him was far more inviting than the couch out in the other room. Tony swung his legs up and lay down on the pillow a careful distance from the boy. To hell with what people would think if Ben told someone they shared a bed for the night. He still didn't know why a man's voice in the other room brought that look of terror to Ben's face, but he wanted to be in reach, just in case he was needed.

CHAPTER 6

Mac knocked on his cousin Brenda's door firmly. He had a childcare agreement with his cousin. Although she didn't want him in her house, he still had the right to see his daughter whenever he chose. His work schedule was erratic enough to make that a necessity. And this morning he really wanted to be with Anna for a while, before the rest of the day dumped on him.

Brenda had been uncharacteristically hostile when he phoned to let her know he was coming. Not that she ever approved of him, but it was usually a cool distance, not active anger. Well, it didn't matter. She would hold to her agreement, since the money he paid her was most of her income. He thumped the door more loudly.

When it finally opened, Brenda's expression was dour. "And how long will the child be out with you?" she demanded instead of a greeting.

Mac gave her a cool stare. "Probably not long." After all, he really only had a half hour of free time before he had to be at work. He tried not to think about what was waiting for him at work. "I'll let you know," he added, mostly to jerk Brenda's chain. She glared at him, but held open the door enough to allow his small daughter to squeeze through.

"Daddy!" Anna leapt into his arms, secure in the certainty that he would catch her. He hugged her, breathing in the clean child scent of her hair, then set her on her feet.

"How about we walk to the park?" he suggested, pointing to the little space of grass and benches half a block away.

"Sure." Anna took his hand confidingly and skipped along beside him. "How did you know I wanted you to come this morning specially?" she asked.

"I didn't," Mac admitted, "But I'm happy if you're glad to see me."

"Yep. And if you stay long enough it will be too late to go to church."

"Church on a Wednesday morning?" Mac asked.

Anna nodded solemnly. "Aunt Brenda is real sad, and she says going to church will make things better."

"Why is she sad?" Mac usually didn't believe in quizzing his daughter about the details of Brenda's life, but if it was affecting their routines, he wanted to understand.

"I don't know." Anna hopped up on one of the benches and swung her feet. "She was watching TV last night, and she got all mad and sad, like she does. She was talking about sin in the world and God's rat. I told her I liked your God better, 'cause you said he loves us and doesn't get angry with us, and she got madder. She said I shouldn't listen to you about God, 'cause you're a forminator, and we should go to church today so I'd learn better. Daddy, what's a forminator?"

Mac had just translated God's rat into wrath, and cursed his cousin silently for making him try and explain things like this to a five-year-old. "Did she maybe say fornicator?" he asked, stalling for time.

"I guess," Anna said doubtfully. "What *is* a formicator, though? I want to know. Is it something bad? Aunt Brenda makes it sound bad, but you're good."

"Um, a fornicator is…a grownup who…it's complicated to explain," Mac hedged. "It's really not a big deal to most people. As long as no one's feelings are hurt, I don't think it's bad at all. But to people who are—" *obsessed with* "—strongly concerned with the Bible, it seems like more of a bad thing."

"Is Tony a formicator too?" Anna asked. "Or Miss Lindsay?"

"I don't know about your teacher," Mac said. "But yeah, Tony is just like me, and you could say the same about and lots and lots of other people."

"Then it can't be bad," Anna said decisively, with a small nod of her head, "'Cause Tony's really good."

*Especially at fornication.* "I don't want you to worry about it. You know Aunt Brenda doesn't approve of me because I don't do the church things she wants me to. This is just more of the same thing."

"Okay. So can I stay with you today and not go to church?"

"I'm sorry, Anna," Mac said regretfully. "I have to go to work soon."

"Could I maybe play with Cindy, or Ben 'n Tony?"

Mac was about to say no, then reconsidered. "Maybe," he said. "Why don't you go take a turn on the swing while I call Tony?"

Anna skipped off to the small swing set and climbed on, pumping herself expertly into motion. Mac pulled out his phone and dialed.

"Hey, you." Tony's voice was soft in his ear.

"Hey," Mac returned. "How are you two?"

"Doing okay. Ben's pretty quiet, doesn't say much. I was wondering, could we go by Sandy's place and pick up some of his stuff? Is it cleared yet?"

"Um, yeah, the crime scene team is done with it. But it might not be smart to go there yet."

"Why not?"

"I guess you didn't catch the news last night. They didn't miss the connection this time. The press was camped out around Sandy's place last night, spinning the serial killer story for all it's worth. A neighbor spilled the beans about Ben being in the apartment at the time, and some of the reporters really latched onto the image of a little boy asleep in the other room while his mother was killed. I wouldn't take the chance of getting Ben within a mile of that circus."

"Well, thanks for telling me last night," Tony said acidly.

"I wasn't thinking," Mac admitted. "I'm telling you now."

"Okay."

"If you get Ben to make a list of what he really wants I could try to pick it up for him," Mac offered. "Another cop going in and out of there won't attract much attention."

"I'll do that."

"So listen," Mac said. "The main reason I was calling you was to ask if you think it would be good for Ben to have Anna around today, as a kind of distraction maybe."

"Uh, maybe. Yeah, actually, I think it might be good. He's too quiet and thinking too much. But don't you have to work?"

"I have to go in and do the press conference on this case in half an hour," Mac admitted. "I'm the sacrificial goat, since Oliver won't do it and Captain Severs isn't sure this will be good enough publicity to put his face on it."

"Poor baby," Tony teased. "All those lights and cameras and microphones."

"It's more a question of finding a way to say we don't know dick without the department looking bad."

"You'll manage. After all, you do know dick."

Mac choked, and hoped no one happened to be listening in. "Don't let Ben see the broadcast," he cautioned.

"I'm not stupid. I think the TV will be broken except for videos for a while."

"So," Mac continued, "I thought I could bring Anna over to you, if you can cope with both kids for the day." They'd always taken the kids out together in the past, but there was no one he would rather trust with Anna. "You'd have to take her back home to Brenda's, though."

"No problem. Hang on." Off the phone he could be heard asking Ben if he would like to play with Anna. "He says yes please," Tony reported.

"Fifteen minutes," Mac said.

"See you then."

Mac pocketed his phone and waved to Anna. She leapt from the swing, at a height that put his heart in his mouth even as she landed safely, and ran over.

"Ben would like to see you," Mac told her. "So I'll take you to Tony's place, if you promise to be good for Tony."

"I've never seen Tony's place," Anna said. Mac wondered belatedly if she would recognize any of his stuff, stashed away among Tony's. Hopefully the issue wouldn't arise.

"I know. Listen, Anna, you need to know something important. Ben is pretty sad today, because his mom died yesterday. He wants to play with you, but he may be feeling bad. You need to be really nice to him."

"Dead like my mom?" Anna asked, her eyes big.

"Yes, except your mom's been dead for a while, and you've had a chance to get sort of used to it. For Ben, it's really hard right now."

"Then he needs presents and hugs," Anna said decidedly. "You should come, 'cause you do better hugs than anyone."

"I wish I could," Mac said, realizing how true that was. "But he has you and Tony to hug him. You can help him play at things and not think about it too much."

"Okay. Ben doesn't have a daddy though, so who's he going to live with? Does he have an aunt?"

"He's going to live with Tony," Mac told her.

"Oh, good." Anna skipped ahead of him towards his car. Mac followed, making a quick call to Brenda to tell her that Anna would be with a friend for the day. He cut off her complaints rudely. He just didn't have time for it, although he might be sorry later. As he leaned in to buckle Anna into her booster seat she looked up at him. "Was Ben's mom a formicator too?"

Mac choked. But one of his personal rules was to tell Anna as much truth as possible. "Um, I don't think that's any of our business. I told you, most people don't worry about that or even think about it. Ben wouldn't know what you mean, and you shouldn't talk to him about it."

"Okay, I won't." Anna agreed.

Tony and Ben were waiting in the parking lot of his building when they pulled up. Mac barely had time to hand Anna over safely and pull back out. In his rearview mirror he saw Anna giving Ben a hug, and then tugging him by the hand toward the building. *God*, he thought with a catch in his throat, *sometimes she is so much like her mother.*

The press people were setting up in the biggest conference room when he arrived at police headquarters. He managed to sneak past them unspotted and make his way up to Homicide. Oliver and Severs were waiting for him in the captain's office.

"About time," Severs said, urging him inside. "Is that the best suit you have? You're representing the department, you know. And you should straighten your tie."

Mac tugged his tie straighter and ignored the rest. This was the *only* suit he had, and it was too frigging hot for a suit anyway. He could feel the sweat trickling down under his shirt. He ran a finger under his collar, but resisted loosening it while the captain was staring at him.

Oliver handed him the case folder they had put together for this purpose. "The reporters all have copies of the relevant photos. They're waiting for you."

Mac glanced at his watch. "You know this really isn't my job," he said plaintively. "Either of you would be a better choice."

"Go on, you wuss," Oliver said unsympathetically.

"Now remember," Severs added as he followed Mac out the door. "You want to stick to the truth, but they should believe that we're going to solve this case soon. I mean, we want the public's help, but we don't want to alarm them. You should sound confident, you know, and…"

Mac let the stairwell door cut Severs off in mid spiel as he headed down. If he was doing this, then he wasn't going to take any backseat driving from someone unwilling to put his own face out there. On the first floor he found the conference room filled to capacity with reporters and lights and cords. They surged forward with questions as he entered, but he ignored them all until he reached the podium with its bristling array of microphones. He stepped behind it, scanned around the room once, then banged down with his hand. The reporters quieted.

"Okay," he said clearly. "Here's how this is going to work. I'll give you a brief statement and then you'll have the opportunity to ask questions. Raise your hands and I'll call on you, just like in school. If you all start yelling at me, I'm going to walk out and go back to my real job, which is catching this guy. Is that clear?" A look around the room suggested it was.

"I'm Detective MacLean of the Minneapolis Police homicide division," he began. "As you know by now, three young women have been killed in the last two months, and we believe the killer was the same man in each case." He went on to give some of the details of each death, knowing that the networks would be superimposing photos of the victims over his words. He left out some details, like the fact that the stab wounds occurred well after death, and that the women were naked and posed. He described the size of the knife fairly closely, but left out the fact that it was not sharp, and that the blade was triangular. The goal was to prevent copycats, and weed out true leads from false later on.

"We can use the public's help," he concluded. "If you saw any of these three women on the dates in question, especially if you saw Alexandra Thompson the evening before last, we want to hear from you at the hotline number you see on the screen." He had been assured that they would run the number visually, but he recited it aloud anyway. "If you once owned a dagger of the type described and it was lost or stolen, or if you know someone who has such a dagger, please contact us. And stay safe. The young women who fell victim to this killer made the mistake of bringing a stranger home from a bar and spending time with him alone. All young women out there should be very careful about who they invite into their homes. We don't want any more killings. If you had an experience with a date who tried to strangle you or had a knife, and you got away from him, we want to hear from you too. We have evidence which we hope will lead us to this killer. With your help, we may catch him sooner."

Mac stopped there, and began taking questions.

"Is it true that the bodies were mutilated after death?"

*Jesus, he hoped Tony was successful in keeping Ben away from TVs.* "There was no mutilation," he said.

"Do you have any suspects?"

"We are pursuing several leads but we do not yet have a single prime suspect," *or secondary suspect, or tertiary suspect…*

"Is it true that Alexandra Thompson's son witnessed the murder?"

"Her son was present in the apartment," Mac confirmed, since it was established beyond doubt anyway, "But the boy was asleep."

"Where is the boy now?"

"He's being well taken care of." Mac let his voice sharpen. "That six-year-old kid just lost his mother and he has no information for you. Common decency says you'd better leave him alone."

"Is it true that all the victims were highly promiscuous?"

"They all had slept with more than one man in the past. But there is no evidence that this made them more likely to be chosen as victims, except for increasing the chance they would say yes to a stranger."

"What are you doing to keep the women of this city safe in their beds?"

"I'm trying to catch the killer," Mac said acidly. "They can also help keep themselves safe by not bringing anyone they don't know well home with them."

"Is it true that the police were aware that a serial killer was stalking the city even before Alexandra Thompson was murdered, and they failed to pass on the warning?"

Mac sighed. "By definition, a serial killer has killed three or more people," he said. "Alexandra was number three." He stepped back from the podium. The information they wanted was out there. Time to pull the plug. "Now, if you folks will excuse me, I'm going to go back and do my job."

He ignored the questions now being shouted at him as he worked his way through the jostling reporters and out of the room. A couple of uniformed officers were on crowd duty, seeing that the media people stayed where they belonged. He passed between them and entered the stairwell with relief.

Oliver slapped him on the back as he came out into the homicide bullpen. "We caught you on the live news. Good job."

"Yeah, well, the next news conference is someone else's fucking job," Mac retorted, taking off his jacket. "Jesus, I'm soaked. Those lights are even hotter than outdoors."

"You looked fine," Oliver said. "In fact, I bet some of those women out there call the hotline just to chat with the handsome detective."

Mac glared at him. "Good thing I won't be the one answering the line, then."

They had set up a team of people to answer the phone and do the initial weeding out of the cranks, the curious, and the ignorant. Anyone with a possible lead would be passed along to the detectives to pursue further. A public appeal always ended up being a huge mess. Most of the information would turn out to be useless or downright misleading, but sometimes a kernel of truth snuck in there. On this case, they needed any lead they could get.

Mac spent a couple of hours at his desk, writing up reports from the notes of yesterday's interviews. Two people he had questioned in the bar Wednesday night, in addition to the bartender, remembered seeing Sandy in there on Tuesday. All three said she had been chatting with a man, but the descriptions were widely different. Either they were poor observers, or she was chatting up more than one guy. Which, given her history, was quite possible. She almost certainly didn't leave before ten PM, but none of the witnesses remembered her much after that. The bartender had tried to make a list of Tuesday night regulars who had been in, and promised to have them contact the police.

The man knew very few names, so they were dependent on his recognizing faces as people came in again. They would send a detective to the bar again tonight, to show pictures around and do more interviews.

The neighbors had plenty to say about Sandy's habits and lifestyle, but nothing useful about the night in question. Their comments made Mac even more concerned for Ben. Although most said grudgingly that Sandy was a loving mother, they also described escalating drinking and neglect that Sandy had apparently hidden from Tony. One neighbor who sometimes babysat reported feeding the boy breakfast a couple of times, when he admitted his mother had forgotten as she staggered out to work in the morning after an evening binge. Mac was almost glad Tony didn't have to confront Sandy over it. That would have been the conversation from hell, with the little boy caught in the middle.

The phone team was receiving lots of calls, and a few were passed on to the detectives. Hanson and Loes were doing most of the follow-up. When his reports were done, Mac went over to hang around their desks and harass them about their progress.

Hanson rolled an eye at him. "Go away, MacLean, unless you're offering to take over the job of talking to the crazies out there. The last one I had was a woman who sounded rational, claimed to have seen Alexandra Thompson walking down the street Tuesday night. So I'm asking about where and what time, and then she starts describing how Thompson was all misty, and pale, and she could see blood trickling down her body from all the stab wounds. I hung up before she got to the details about what the ghost was wailing. Or did you want that information?"

Mac aimed a swipe at the back of Hanson's head. "Sounds right up your alley," he teased. "You crazies know how to talk to each other. I'm sure she would never have opened up to me."

"Lucky you," Hanson muttered, picking up the next sheet of information and beginning to dial.

"Hey, Mac," Loes called from his seat. "Might have something for you here." He switched the phone to speaker. "Go ahead."

"Yeah," said the female voice on the other end. "Like I said, I picked up this guy a couple of months ago. He seemed nice at first, but …well, it's a long story, but eventually he pulled this knife and started stabbing at me. I got away, just ran out of the room and got clear. I didn't get a good look at the knife, but it was sort of like the one they were describing on TV. I mean it was long and very narrow, but this one wasn't very sharp, you know. I had more like punctures than cuts on my arms."

Mac glanced quickly at Loes. "We're very interested in your story, ma'am," he said into the speaker. "If you would be willing to come here and give us the details. Or you could give us your address and we'd gladly come and speak with you there."

The caller gave an odd laugh. "Why don't you come here?" She gave them an address. "I'll be around for a couple of hours, anyway."

Loes palmed his callback duties off on Linda Ramsey, who was a newbie and had to take what she was given. He left her with a stack of possible leads and Mac followed him out to his car.

The address in question was an apartment in a fringe area, between the rough parts of downtown and the suburbanized edges. The building was ugly yellow brick, but solid enough. Loes pushed the buzzer for the second-floor apartment, caught the return buzz, and led them up.

The apartment door was opened by a tall blond woman with strong features. She asked to see ID, then stood back to let them in. Mac glanced around the room as he entered. It was tidy and pleasant, neatly furnished, and cool. The sunlight filtered in through sheer curtains. The room matched the woman, well put together and stylish without being fussy. The woman herself was more attractive than pretty, but she moved well and had a good figure. She turned to face them.

"Hey," she said in a breathy voice, giving him an appreciative once-over. "You're that detective from TV. You look even better in person."

Mac flushed, glad he had Loes along, despite the amused look on the older man's face. "Thank you," he muttered, pulling out his notebook. "If we could get your information as clearly as possible, that would be great. Your name again?"

The woman hesitated a second then said, "Lulu Sinclair."

"Okay, Miss Sinclair, would you tell us about this man who attacked you. When was it exactly?"

"Wouldn't you like to come and sit down?" she asked, gesturing at the small living room. "I have coffee or water, if you'd like."

Mac wanted to hurry this along. Something about the looks she was giving him made him uncomfortable. But witnesses talked best when they were relaxed. "Sure," he agreed, heading for a chair. "Water would be good."

"For me too," Loes agreed. "It's hot out there again. Thank you." He gave the woman a warm smile.

Lulu went into the kitchen and came back with three bottles of water, which she passed around. She seated herself on the couch, arranged her skirt around her legs, and looked up.

"I thought it might be useful," she said, "So I looked back at my records, because I had to get a tetanus shot and some antibiotics afterward. It was the night of June sixth."

Mac made a note. That was about two weeks before Kowalski's murder. "How did you meet this man?"

"Well, I was in a bar. Barney's, on Tenth. It's not my usual kind of place, but I was supposed to meet someone there. Anyway, he stood me up, and I was feeling dumped, you know, so I started drinking a little more than I usually do. Okay, maybe a lot more, because I really thought…well, it doesn't matter now." She paused, looking sad.

"About what time?"

"I got there about seven, left about ten."

"The man approached you?" Mac asked.

"He sat down at my table. We started talking, about nothing, like you do with a stranger. Isn't it warm for so early in the summer, and did you hear about the truck that spilled chemicals on I-94 last week. Stuff like that. He was pleasant. He bought me a drink. Eventually I decided I needed to cut myself off and go home. He said he was worried about me and would walk me home. I don't usually let men pick me up but…anyway, as we're heading out he's obviously coming on to me, and I was feeling lonely, but I never let men in my place. So I…"

"You what?" Mac said when the silence began to stretch out.

"I suggested a motel," she admitted. "He had a car and we drove to the Super-8 on Washington. He asked me to rent the room while he stayed in the car. I figured he might be married or something."

"So he didn't sign the paperwork or give his license or anything?"

"Unfortunately, no." Lulu sighed. "We went to the room, and he started kissing me, and already I was thinking about what a bad idea this was. So I figured I'd give him a fast blowjob and get out of there. Because I wasn't quite as drunk as I had been and he kept trying to unbutton my shirt."

"And?"

"So I'm on my knees going down on him, and he's liking it, but he keeps asking me to undress, which I don't want to do. And eventually he reaches down and rips my shirt off, and then he went crazy. He pulled this knife out of his boot and he started stabbing at me, just wild. He hit my arms a couple of times but it didn't cut me, just bruised. But when I put my hand up to protect myself, the damned thing punctured right through it." She held out her hand to show a small irregular scar in the center of her palm. "Luckily I was closer to the door than he was, and I didn't have pants down around my ankles, so I ran. He came after me, but I headed for the motel office and when he saw I was going to get there safely, he turned and ran to his car and drove away."

"Did you call the police from the motel?" Mac asked.

"Um," Lulu looked down. "I didn't report it."

"Why the hell not?" Loes demanded. "This guy stabbed you bad enough to leave a scar."

"Yeah. But I went with him to the motel voluntarily, and I was drunk. I didn't have his name or even his license number. I figured I'd get a few 'It's your own fault, you slut' kind of looks and not much action."

Mac said, "We take violence against women seriously. Being drunk or having sex does not give some guy the right to hurt you."

"Yeah," she sighed. "You take violence against women seriously. There's only one problem." She reached up and pulled off her long blond wig. Her voice dropped an octave. "I'm not a woman." Without the hair, the strong-featured woman transformed into a slightly-built man with a dark crew-cut, wearing a dress.

Loes muttered, "Shit!" Mac struggled to keep any reaction off his face and out of his voice.

"That explains why he went crazy when he undressed you," he commented blandly. "He was expecting something different, since you're so convincing as a woman."

Lulu, or whatever her…his name was, gave Mac a blinding smile. "I knew I liked you. Exactly right. Which is why the whole idea was so bad from the start. If I hadn't been totally smashed, I never would have gone for a straight guy in a conservative bar."

"I have to say," Mac told him, "That your man sounds like a possible candidate for our killer. You may have been more lucky than you realized to get away with only a cut or two. The women he dated have ended up dead."

"You really think it could be your guy?" the man said worriedly. "He didn't try to strangle me."

"I think he didn't get far enough before your big surprise," Mac said. "I definitely want any information you can give us. Can you describe him for me?"

"Tall. Maybe six-one or six-two. Dark hair cut short back then, and *not* at a good salon. Medium complexion, clean shaven, some muscle but not heavy, more of the beanpole type. Not rich. His clothes were definitely off the rack, a polo shirt and jeans, with old cowboy boots. That was one of the things I liked about him, actually, that his jeans and boots were worn a bit. Like he wore his regular clothes, not some get-dressed-to-pick-up-women outfit."

"Could you work with a sketch artist to get us a picture of him?"

Lulu sighed. "I can sure as hell try, but I have to tell you, honey, as intense as it was, it was two months ago, the light was never bright and I was smashed out of my little gourd. I'll do my best but I wouldn't want you to put too much faith in it."

"Would you recognize him in a line-up?"

"Maybe," he said slowly. "Especially if you had him speak. We talked for a while, and I have a pretty good ear for voices. But I'm not certain."

"I understand. Can you describe the knife?"

"It happened pretty fast. It wasn't shiny, and the handle was small, almost hidden in his hand. I'd say the blade was about six inches long. It was weird. The doctor who fixed up my hand said it looked like I'd impaled myself on a spike. Which was lucky, because I didn't have any cut tendons. It just hurt like shit for a while."

"What about the car?"

"It was dark, blue or green, maybe black, a four-door sedan, not new or fancy, cloth seats." He shook his head. "Really, I wasn't paying much attention."

"Surely you took a look at the car when the guy who stabbed you was driving away in it," Loes said acidly.

"Honey, I was booking for that motel office as hard as I could. I heard him go, but I didn't look back until he was almost out of sight."

"You're being a big help," Mac said. "I'm going to have a sketch artist come out just as soon as possible to work with you.

Can you think of anything else that would help us?"

The man considered, head cocked to one side. "He was probably from the Midwest, or at least he's been here for a while. He had the accent and the turns of phrase. He mentioned football a lot, and seemed pretty ignorant about movies." He paused, thinking, and then shook his head. "I really don't remember our conversation well, just the football, because I got bored with it, and the movies because that's my favorite conversation topic. If I remember anything else, I'll let you know. I'd been trying to forget it, not remember."

"We appreciate anything you come up with," Mac said. He looked down at his notebook. "Do you have a legal name I should add to this?"

The man sighed. "Walter, I'm Walter Sinclair." He batted his eyelashes at Mac. "Don't I look like a Walt to you?"

Mac smiled. "Not exactly." At least not with the makeup and the dress. It was odd how the combination made Mac's perception float back and forth between man and woman. "What's your day job?"

"I'm an actor," the man said. "For four months a year I work for H&R Block doing tax returns, and I have a few accounting clients to keep the wolf from the door, but acting is my real profession. I'm starting a new part at the Guthrie right now."

"Congratulations," Mac said. "That's a great theater." He stood. "I'll have the artist call you and set up a time to get that sketch. The sooner the better. We may be back with other questions, if they come up."

Loes preceded them to the door and let himself out. Walter/ Lulu put a hand on Mac's arm to detain him. "That guy has his nose in the air like I smell bad," he whispered, with a nod toward Loes. "If you have other questions, come alone." He smiled warmly. "You're welcome anytime, honey. For anything you like."

"I may be back to talk to you," Mac returned in the same low voice, "But I'm afraid you're not my type." He held up his wedding ring.

The man sighed. "What a waste."

Loes was waiting impatiently for Mac at the bottom of the front stairs. "Can you believe that?" he burst out. "Here I'm thinking what a pretty woman she is and then boom, she's really a fag! No wonder the guy pulled out a knife when he saw she was a fake."

"He's a transvestite," Mac pointed out, "And given that the guy was getting a blow job at the time, his reaction seems a little extreme."

"I don't know," Loes said. "Wouldn't you freak out, finding out you were getting sucked off by a guy?"

*Not exactly.* "Either way, the knife sounds promising," Mac said. "How many guys can we have out there picking up pretty blondes in bars, and using a dull pointed knife on them? I'm betting there's a connection."

"I hope so," Loes grumbled as he got in the car. "Because otherwise we've got shit. But if anyone has to talk to that faggot guy again, you're elected. He gives me the creeps. I can't believe I couldn't tell from the beginning. No one's just straight and normal anymore."

Mac realized that their suspect wasn't the only one freaked out by having been attracted to a guy. Loes was shaking his head.

"Fucking weirdoes," Loes muttered, putting the car in gear. "The world is overrun with fucking weirdoes and I seem to get stuck with most of them."

The fucking weirdo in the passenger seat took a deep breath, and pulled out his phone to call the sketch artist.

CHAPTER 7

Tony's apartment showed evidence of a day spent with kids. He wiped a remnant of Kraft dinner off the counter and dumped half a glass of juice down the sink. It was late, and Ben was finally sleeping quietly, but Tony was restless.

He stuffed yet another empty plastic Target bag into a drawer and pushed it shut. With Ben's own belongings unavailable, the afternoon had turned into a shopping trip. Which Anna had enjoyed much more than he and Ben did. He wondered idly whether there was a shopping gene attached to the X chromosome. Why would a cloistered five-year-old be a better shopper than an adult man?

At least Ben had enjoyed the toy section. Tony's bank account was going to be scraping bottom, but the new Wii setup would keep the kid distracted. And it had made him smile. Worth digging into the rainy-day reserve for. He glanced around his small living room. There was a puzzle on the coffee table, a truck garaged under the TV stand, and a Nerf ball on the couch. He felt like a dad. A scared-shitless dad.

He had never been allowed to have Ben for more than a day at a time. Sandy had been too jealous of their closeness. She had kept his time with Ben to the minimum she had agreed to, back when he paid her hospital bills. He had never taken care of the little boy when he was really sick, never handled nightmares or chosen daily meals. He had done what he could to be there for Ben. He had listened to the boy, taken him for outings, and bought him those new sneakers he needed. But Sandy, for all her flaws, had been his real parent. Now Tony was the sole support for a traumatized, hurting little boy. He was so scared he was going to screw it up.

Mac's key in the door was a welcome distraction. Tony looked up with a smile. Mac came over to him and bent to kiss him, but Tony made it fast, with one eye on the bedroom door.

"Not even a real kiss?" Mac asked, only half teasing.

"Ben's been waking up a lot. I'm not going to kiss you where he might see, if it's something he'll have to keep secret. That's not fair for a kid."

"I guess." Mac sighed. "I've missed you."

Tony felt warm at that admission. It was unlike his self-sufficient Mac.

"I've missed you too. At least we can sit and talk for a bit. Tell me about the case."

"Ah," Mac said, dropping heavily onto the couch. "Now there we may have a break. Once the story broke on all the networks, Severs decided we could appeal for public help. We got a witness who may have seen our man." Mac gave him an odd smile. "She came on to me when I interviewed her."

"I don't blame her," Tony said easily. "You're pretty hot."

"She turned out to be a transvestite," Mac told him. "Made an amazingly convincing woman, but her name is Walter."

"And she still came on to you? Do I need to be worried?"

"Never." Mac leaned toward him, then remembered and pulled back. "She's not my type, and he's definitely not. I flashed my wedding ring." Tony realized his expression must have changed, because Mac asked, "What's wrong?"

"Nothing," Tony made himself say. How could he explain to Mac that he hated having Mai still be the public face of Mac's love life, like Tony didn't even exist? "I'm glad if you scare off the other boys."

"Mm." Mac still looked doubtful. "Well, we got a lot of good information, although the guy didn't have much confidence in his ID sketch. It had been a while since the incident. We have a couple of people who may have seen our victims with a man, too. We're trying to match descriptions and get a better picture of the guy."

"So that's progress."

"Yeah. Not like a name and address, but moving forward." Mac settled into the couch. "So how was your day?"

"Busy. I got Ben some clothes and toys to replace his old stuff. Anna was great with the clothes shopping. She has some pretty definite ideas. I think Ben just gave up and went along with whatever she chose. I dropped her off at about six. Brenda doesn't like me, pulled Anna inside like I was going to molest her on the doorstep."

"Brenda doesn't like anyone much, except Anna, and maybe her minister." Mac sighed heavily. Tony turned to him with concern.

"Are you still having problems with her taking Anna to church all the time?"

"Some. She was scheduled to go this morning when I sent her out with you heathens to do shopping instead. I wish Brenda had something else to fixate on." He snorted. "She told Anna I don't understand God because I'm a fornicator. Try explaining that to a five-year-old."

"What did you tell her?"

"Basically that Brenda was overreacting and it wasn't anything Anna needed to worry about."

"And she was okay with that?"

"So far." Mac gave him a warm smile. "She asked if you were a forminator too, and I said yes. Just so you know."

"Only with you, babe," Tony said, leaning back beside Mac so their bodies touched. "I only forminate with you."

Mac was silent for a long time. Finally he whispered, "What are we going to do, Tony?"

"One day at a time," Tony told him. It was the only way he was getting through this. "Let me take care of Ben and do the custody thing, you go catch your killer, and when we can both breathe again, we'll see where we stand."

"Loes was really freaked by the transvestite," Mac said. "He thought our killer was justified pulling a knife on the guy."

"Really?" Tony felt a little sick.

"Well, maybe not justified. But that it was understandable."

"What did you say?"

"I guess not much. Just that violence is violence, you know. We need to catch this guy."

"Wow," Tony said sarcastically. "That will really help the next gay man Loes has to deal with."

"What do you want from me?" Mac snapped back. "Trust me, this was not a *teachable moment*. With Loes, there's never going to be a good time to speak up for LGBT people everywhere."

"So you let it slide, like you agree with him, rather than take any chance he might tar you with the same brush?"

"That's not..." Mac shook his head. "You don't get it. Loes..."

"Oh, I think I get it," Tony began heatedly.

A whimper from the bedroom, followed by a loud cry, distracted them both. Mac followed Tony as he hurried in. Ben was sitting up in bed.

"Problem, sport?" Tony asked, sitting beside him.

The boy knuckled at his eyes and shook his head. The new pajamas were a little big on him, and his hair stood up in a sweaty cowlick, making him look younger than his years.

"Hey, Ben," Mac said softly, sitting down on the other side of the bed. "It's good to see you."

Ben gave Mac a watery smile. "Hey, are you going to get my stuff?"

"Sure," Mac said. "Did you make a list?"

"Yep." Ben scrambled out of bed and went to the dresser, coming back with a piece of paper written in crayon. He handed it to Mac.

"Stuffed cat," Mac deciphered. "Baseball glove, new sneakers, um, gamble?" He looked a little closer at the big messy writing.

"That's a Y," Ben said pointing. Tony felt proud. The kid was way ahead of his age group in reading and writing.

"Game Boy." Mac realized.

"Yeah."

"And this word?"

"There's a picture on my dresser, of my mom and my dad, when I was in her tummy. It's a good picture."

"I'll find it," Mac promised. "Anything else?"

"I got kind of tired writing it," Ben said, leaning sleepily against Mac. Mac's big arm went around him, pulling him in close. Tony, watching, felt an odd little pain under his heart.

"What else did you want, son?" Mac asked.

"My fire truck, and the book about dragons, and I like my team jacket from T-ball but I guess it's hot so I don't really need it."

"I think that can be arranged. And maybe some other clothes?"

"I guess." Clothes were obviously not high on Ben's want list, but Tony would appreciate not having to do more shopping.

Mac eased the boy back into bed. "You go back to sleep now. I'll get this stuff for you tomorrow. It's after bedtime."

"Will you stay till I fall asleep? You an' Tony?" Ben asked muzzily.

"Sure," Mac said. "If you want me to."

They sat quietly on either side of the bed until the boy's breathing slowed. Tony pulled the covers up over him a little more, then led the way out. Mac pulled a pen out of his pocket and made a few notes on the paper.

"I'll try to get this stuff for him tomorrow," he whispered. "May not be till afternoon, though. What kind of clothes does he need?"

"Everything. Just grab an assortment of warm-weather stuff.

Is it really still too soon for us to go back there?"

"I'm betting at least one of the neighbors has been paid to call if Ben shows up, so some reporter can get him on camera. You might be okay with a quick in and out, but this is better." Mac put his arm around Tony in turn, and Tony leaned into him. "You look pretty ragged. Are you doing okay?"

"Just tired. Ben's up a lot. But no more beat than you are, working all hours. I guess I'm scared I'm not doing the right things for Ben. Maybe he should see a therapist. I haven't even touched on what frightened him enough to make him sleep in the closet."

"Give it time," Mac suggested. "He's safe right now. You're great with him."

"Thanks." Tony turned in against Mac, rubbing his face into the cloth over that broad chest. *Can't, shouldn't.* Just the smell of Mac's skin was home. Reluctantly, he pushed himself away. "Get out of here, before I do something I'll regret."

"I was kind of hoping maybe we could both do something you'd regret," Mac said. "There's the bathroom."

"Ben could wake up any time."

"I can name that tune in five minutes. I bet I can take you over too."

Tony wanted to. *God, did he want to.* His whole body was hard and aching at the thought. He could lose himself in being with Mac. He wouldn't. "Not tonight, sweetie," he said reluctantly. "It doesn't feel right."

"Okay," Mac said quietly. "Listen, it sounds petty, but so much of my stuff is over here...I need to pick up a few things."

"Sure. Of course. Do you need a bag?" He opened the kitchen drawer. "It just happens I accumulated quite a collection today."

Mac pulled one out and headed to the bathroom. Tony stood in the kitchen, hearing his lover fumble through the drawers and the medicine cabinet. Eventually he came out with a bag of stuff.

"What about clothes?" Tony asked carefully.

Mac glanced at the bedroom door. "I'm okay for a few more days. Maybe sometime, if you're going out with Ben, you can call me and I'll come by for my stuff."

"I'll do that." Tony's voice was barely a whisper. He hadn't meant for it to be.

Mac nodded. "I'll call you when I have Ben's things for him."

Tony walked him to the door and pulled him down for a quick kiss. He cleared his throat. "Get out of here, hot stuff, and stay away from the other boys," he said with an effort at lightness. "Stay safe."

The door closed softly behind Mac, and Tony was alone with his kid.

Tony dozed on his couch mid-morning while Ben played with the Wii on the bedroom TV. Another night of interrupted sleep had left Tony a little groggy, although Ben seemed more chipper. He'd always sneered at parents who used electronics to babysit their kids, but after playing with the boy for three hours, the opportunity to close his eyes for a few minutes had become appealing. The beep and whoosh through the bedroom door made a soothing background at this distance.

The buzzer for the outer lobby door interrupted his drifting. He got up and responded to the intercom.

"Sheila Burns from Hennepin County Child Protection," the voice said. "Can I come up?"

"Of course." Tony triggered the door for her and glanced frantically around the apartment. It was clean enough. The breakfast dishes were done, thank God. Toys left out probably wouldn't be a down check. He picked up a towel off the bathroom floor, used it to wipe out the sink, and hung it on the rail. Not perfect, but hopefully good enough.

The woman's knock sounded on the door. Tony opened it and held out his hand.

"Hi, I'm Tony Hart. Come in."

The woman shook his hand with an almost imperceptible delay. "Sheila Burns."

"Are you here for the home visit?" Tony asked. "I was told there would have to be one or two more. You should know this place is only temporary. I'm looking for a bigger apartment right now."

"Where is Ben?" the woman enquired.

Tony gestured to the bedroom door. "He's in there killing aliens. After he wiped the floor with me half a dozen times he decided it would be fun to try playing against the computer." He paused. "Not that I'll let him be on the screen too long…" He let his voice trail off as the expression on the woman's face registered. "What's wrong?"

Sheila Burns sighed. "I'm here to pick Ben up."

"You're what?"

"There was a complaint," she said, pulling out a form. "The boy's maternal grandparents are applying for custody, on the grounds that living with you will expose the boy to a, quote, 'neglectful, promiscuous, and deviant lifestyle that will be unhealthy for him,' end quote. The department has to take complaints like that seriously."

"But…" Tony couldn't grasp it. "I'm not promiscuous, and how would they know since they see me about once a year? Anyway, where are they if they're so concerned about Ben? They haven't come by or even called to see how he's doing. And I know they have my number."

"Look," Burns said in a calming voice. "I'm just doing my job. I'm not in a position to make any decisions. If there is the possibility of harm to the child, we have to take steps. Since you are not an approved foster parent or a relative and don't have legal custody, it's my job to be sure Ben is somewhere safe until a judge can make a ruling."

"Jesus," Tony breathed. "The boy just lost his mother, he's scared, he's not sleeping well, and you want to place him with strangers, just on someone's baseless complaint?"

"I want him somewhere I know is safe," Burns said flatly. "That's the first priority. I'll let you fight it out in front of the judge."

"Can he at least stay with the Thompsons?" Tony asked. "I mean, I don't like them much, but they are his family and he at least knows them. It would be marginally less traumatic for him."

"That's not possible. As I understand it, the mother's will specifically says the boy should not live with her parents. In fact, she alleges that she was emotionally abused and neglected in that home as a teenager. A judge will have to make a ruling, and Ben needs to be somewhere approved until then."

"Okay," Tony said. "Okay. No way around it. Do you have to take him now?"

He thought she looked a little sympathetic when she said, "Yes."

"Let me tell him about this," Tony asked. "He's going to be scared, but he trusts me."

"Bring him out here and we'll talk to him together."

Tony nodded and headed for the bedroom. For a moment after he opened the door he just watched the boy play with his game, putting body English into the controller. Then Ben looked up and spotted him.

"Hey, Tony," he called eagerly. "Look how good I'm doing!"

"That's great. But I have to talk to you out here. Could you save your game?"

"I guess," Ben agreed, turning back to the screen. After a moment he put down his controller and came to the door. Tony walked the boy out with a hand on his shoulder.

"Ben," he said. "This is Sheila Burns from Child Protection. They're the people who take care of kids that are in a bad situation." Ben turned to look up at Tony, and he could feel the small shoulders tense but the boy said nothing.

"Come and sit down, Ben," the woman urged softly. Ben didn't move until Tony gave him a little push. Then he perched on the couch as far from her as possible. Tony knelt beside Ben.

"Listen, Benny boy," Tony said. "You know I want to have you with me forever, and that's what your mom wanted too." *Or at least what I got her to put in writing.* In fairness, Sandy had always wanted what was best for Ben. "But I'm not your family and I'm not approved to take care of a little boy yet. Miss Burns says the law requires her to make sure you are safe while they check me out to see if I'm a good person to take care of you."

"But I'm safe with you," Ben said thinly.

"You know that and I know that," Tony agreed. "But they don't know me. The Child Protection people need to check me out, to be sure I don't break laws, or keep dangerous stuff like drugs in the house, or drink too much."

"Like Mom and Grandma sometimes?"

"Yeah, like that. They want to be sure I'm the best person to take care of you."

"You are the best," Ben said. "Mac's a cop. He could tell them so."

Tony turned to the woman. "Mac is a friend of ours. He works Homicide." He turned back to Ben. "If I need someone to give me a good report, I might ask Mac, but we still have to follow the rules. And that means you have to go stay with someone else for a little while, while they check me out."

"I don't want to," Ben whined. "I want to stay here."

"I know, sweetie. But it won't be for long and then hopefully you'll be back here with me forever."

"The foster family has a dog," Burns put in hopefully. "And a couple of other boys you can play with."

"I don't care!" Ben wailed. Tony hugged him firmly and set him back in his place. Ben knuckled his eyes.

"You can do this," Tony said. "You're a strong kid. It won't be long."

"Why can't I just stay here while they do the checking stuff?"

Ben demanded.

"Because if I was a bad person I might hurt you before they found out about me. They want you with someone they already know."

"But you're not a bad person."

Tony sighed. "Ben. It's the rules. We have to follow the rules."

"I bet Mac would make them stop."

Tony winced. He wasn't sure whether to be glad or worried that Ben looked on Mac as their protector. "Mac has to follow the laws too, even though he's a cop. He'll help us all he can, but we have to do this right."

"You'll like the foster parents," Burns said. "They're very nice."

"I don't care," Ben repeated mulishly, holding the edge of the couch cushion with both hands.

Sheila Burns turned to Tony. "Why don't you pack up Ben's stuff while I talk to him?"

Tony didn't want to. He *really* didn't want to. He made himself get up and pulled his favorite backpack out of the closet. In the bedroom he carefully packed the new shirts and shorts and underwear in it, the toy racing car, the books, the stuffed dog. He could hear the woman's voice, low and coaxing, in the other room, but nothing from Ben. He hefted the backpack and grabbed Ted in his free hand. On the way to the bathroom, past the couch, he stuffed Ted into Ben's arms. The boy didn't look at him.

Toothbrush, toothpaste, comb, hand towel with the fire truck on it...he felt like he was erasing the little boy from his bathroom. The water toys, the toothbrush holder shaped like a truck, it couldn't all go along. How had Ben become so firmly rooted in here in just a day?

When the backpack was full he lugged it back to the living room. There was space for the Nerf ball if he compressed it. He tugged the zipper shut. Burns stood, took the bag from him and held out her hand to Ben.

"Come on, honey," she said.

Ben shook his head silently.

"Come on. We don't have any choice."

Ben clutched his teddy bear to his chest and hid his face in it.

Tony held out his own hand. "Ben. Come here, son."

Ben looked up at him, his face streaked with silent tears. Then the little boy took a deep breath and came to him, and took his hand.

"I'll walk you down to the car," Tony said firmly. They followed Burns out of the apartment. Tony didn't let go of Ben's hand to lock the door. What did it matter? Everything that was precious to him was right here. Hallway, elevator, lobby, front steps; the woman's car was parked in a visitor's spot. She had a low booster seat in the back, and Tony buckled the silent child into it securely, even though Ben was growing past the point of needing one. Burns got in the front and turned to him. "We'll be in touch, Mr. Hart."

Tony barely heard her. He squatted down beside the open car door and put a hand on Ben's arm. "Ben." The boy stared blankly ahead. "Benny boy." A tear rolled down the child's cheek and Tony wiped it away with his thumb. Ben wouldn't look at him.

"Listen." Tony suddenly fumbled in his pocket and pulled out a pen. "Hold out your arm." Startled, Ben did as he was told. Tony stood and reoriented himself, then wrote in pen on the child's skin, just below the elbow in the direction for Ben to be able to read it.

"That's my cell phone number, with the T in front," he said, "And the other one with the M is Mac's. If you really need us, if you are really scared or hurt, you can call and we'll be there."

"The children are not allowed to make phone calls," Burns interrupted from the front seat.

"I know," Tony said. "You hear her, Ben. If you call us, you're breaking the rules, and if we come get you, we are breaking the rules too. If we have to do that we may get in big trouble. But if you really need help I don't care about rules. I love you, Ben, and if you need me I'll be there. Okay?"

Ben nodded silently and folded his arm in against his chest. Tony stood, stepped back. "I'll see you soon, son. I promise." He shut the door and moved out of the way. The light blue Honda pulled carefully out of the lot, flashed blinkers for a left turn, hovered what seemed like forever waiting for the traffic to clear, and then pulled away. Tony stared hard at the rear window, but Ben did not look back.

Up in his apartment, Tony wandered around, almost dazed, picking things up and putting them down. The big fire truck was still under the TV, the aborted sounds of the Wii game hummed from the bedroom. The empty space echoed.

Tony sat at the kitchen table and pulled out paper. *A list, make a list of what to do next.* The paper stayed blank. He pulled out his phone.

Mac's number went to voice mail. He could call back three more times, if it was an emergency, and Mac had promised to always answer. It wasn't an emergency. He let Mac's voice get to the end of the voice mail message and said simply, "Call me."

Sabrina's cell went to voice mail too. "Hey, Bree, it's Tony. I know it's not your field, but I need all the information you can get on applying to foster or adopt a child who is an orphan but has grandparents. Please call me."

He picked up the pen again and began writing some of the things the first CPHC caseworker had mentioned: health report, police record, home visit, finances. Did he need to prove the grandparents unfit, or only himself fit? Sabrina was a lawyer. He hoped she could find out.

He looked around the apartment. A home visit was the most problematic thing. He knew his paperwork was in order; it was just a matter of getting copies. But there was no denying the apartment was too small, and not pristine, and if they started digging around, there were men's clothes here that were not his own size.

He got up and pulled paper shopping bags out of the closet, and began. It was amazing how much of Mac's stuff had migrated to his place over the months. Or perhaps not amazing, considering that Mac's own apartment could give closets a bad name. He packed shirts and socks, sweats, jeans, slacks, shampoo, an MPD mug, a photo of Mai and Anna from the bedside drawer. He hesitated over condoms and lube. Would it look better for a single guy to have the tools for safe sex, or not to have them? In the end he threw the half-used tube and open box into the trash, and put new unopened ones from the bathroom in their place. There, prepared but not in use. A couple of his old sex toys, the butt plug and dildo, he tossed in with Mac's stuff. They hadn't been into the toys much. Mac alone filled his senses, beyond the need for other aids.

He hesitated over a T-shirt retrieved from under the bed. It was dusty, but held a faint scent of Mac's skin. He pressed the fabric to his face. Could he keep just one, or should he toss it in the laundry? Oh God, the laundry. The hamper was full of their commingled stuff, chinos and button shirts tangled with skinny jeans and briefs.

He hauled the whole thing down to the basement laundry room and started a load. At the last moment he pulled out the T-shirt before the water touched more than the hem. He could put it under the counter like a rag. No one was going to try the size on him. He rubbed it against his cheek, the cotton musky with sweat and lime shampoo and male skin. It came with him back upstairs.

When every trace of Mac's presence was in bags by the door, he began cleaning. The bathroom hadn't been really cleaned in a while, and oops, there was open lube in the shower rack. The grout needed scrubbing. He used his old toothbrush then got out a new clean one for the holder. Eventually the smell of Lysol drove him out into the kitchen. There were crumbs in the bottom of the toaster. There was dust under the refrigerator. He was struggling to pull it out from the wall when his phone rang. The theme from Perry Mason, not Hawaii Five-O. He flipped it open.

"Hey, Sabrina."

"Long time no call," her smooth soprano responded on the other end. "What's up, boy? That was a pretty cryptic message."

"You remember Ben?" Tony said. "Well, his mother just died."

"That *was* Sandy on the TV?" Sabrina said. "I thought it was the right name, but you didn't call me and… God, that poor little boy."

"Yeah, it's been rough," Tony agreed. "He's been staying with me, and I'm named as his guardian in Sandy's will, but apparently the grandparents are contesting it. Child Protection just came and got him."

"Jesus. Did they accuse you of something?"

"No," Tony said. "Not that bad. Just that I would be an unfit parent due to my promiscuous and deviant lifestyle."

"Ouch," Sabrina said sympathetically. "Although if they think you're promiscuous, they don't know you. You're practically a monk. You haven't had a date in a year."

*You don't know me either, anymore.* "I need to know how to get him back," Tony said. "What do I have to do to meet their standards, do I have to prove I'm fitter than the grandparents, stuff like that."

"Shouldn't that be easy?" Sabrina asked. "I thought you said the grandmother was a lush."

"Emphasis on the 'was,'" Tony said bitterly. "She's in AA right now, and sober for at least a year. It's ironic, you could tell how sober Arlene was by how drunk Sandy was. Her mother would get clean, start twelve-stepping with a vengeance, and Sandy would go out and start two-stepping with a glass in her fist. Oil and water."

"So the grandmother's relapsed before?"

"Yeah, but right now she's clean."

"Still might be worth having evidence that she's fallen off the wagon before," Bree suggested.

"I guess."

"I'll call up some people, find you an expert on custody," Sabrina offered. "It might take a couple of days. What were you planning to do about your apartment? It's got to be too small."

"Yeah, I was looking for bigger," Tony told her. "I called the company that manages this building, but all they had right now is a big three-bedroom. It would be a stretch for my budget."

"Maybe you should do it anyway. Show good faith. I'm a lawyer now, not a struggling student. If you get short of cash, I'll float you a loan."

"I hate to take your money."

"Hey, if it's something important, I hope you'll always take my money. Not like you've never helped me out."

"You're right," Tony admitted. "It is important. Thank you." He suddenly missed her urgently. He had pulled back from their former intimacy, because he would never have been able to keep Mac a secret. They had met now and then, between her crazy schedule as a new lawyer trying to accumulate billing hours, and his preoccupation with Mac. But the conversations were more superficial these days. Not the way it had been when they were both in school. It had been so sweet, to have someone he could talk to, without sexual tension or hurt feelings. Right now, when he was losing Mac, or losing Ben, or God forbid, both, he could use her sane perspective. "I miss talking to you," he said softly. "Thanks for calling me back."

"We've both been too busy. We should get together. I'll call you when I have some information."

Tony closed his phone, then thought again and checked for messages or missed calls. Nothing. Mac must be busy with his important police business. He guessed the dead trumped the living again. Tony looked down at the kitchen floor. The linoleum could use scrubbing.

CHAPTER 8

Mac stepped through the doors into the parking area behind the headquarters building. With the sun dipping toward the horizon, the air outside was slightly less humid and oppressive than the air inside the building. Sometimes he wondered cynically who had skimmed off the budget for heating and cooling, 'cause the department surely didn't intend to deliberately parboil its employees. He unbuttoned his shirt and let the faint breeze loosen the fabric from his back. Maybe it was a hint of cooler weather coming at last.

He flipped his phone open, checking for messages on his backlit screen. Nothing new. There had been the one call from Tony in the morning. He had been out with Loes at the time, interviewing. No way was he going to call Tony back around that guy, even for a cryptic conversation. Loes was as nosy as he was bigoted. And since then he had been busy. Now he was eager to hear Tony's voice. Maybe they could take Ben out for a late dinner, if Tony hadn't already fed him. Which could lead into a quiet evening and then the kid would go to bed, and maybe the boy would be sleeping better now.

Tony picked up on the first ring. "Busy day, huh?"

Somehow the tone of his voice made Mac defensive. "Yeah, we're firming up the sketch we have, trying to see if it's worth putting out on the air, you know." So far no one who hadn't originally contributed to the sketch had claimed to remember seeing the guy in any of the bars. Which might mean they hadn't noticed him, or might mean the picture just wasn't accurate enough. Witness memories were the least reliable type of evidence.

"I had a kind of busy day, too," Tony said. That definitely wasn't his usual voice. "I need you to do something for me."

"Sure, Tony," Mac said. "What do you need?"

"Do you still have the number of that woman you worked

with in Child Protection before, Sarah what's-her-name?"

"Sarah Jefferson," Mac recalled. "Yeah, I probably have it in my phone."

"I need you to call her for me."

"Um, Tony," Mac said. "It's almost seven. She'll be gone for the day. I could try tomorrow."

"I know what fucking time it is," Tony snapped. "But Child Protection came this morning and hauled Ben off to a foster home and I really, *really* need to know that it's an okay place so I can sleep tonight."

"They did what?" Mac said, startled.

"They decided that Ben would be safer somewhere else, until they determine if I'm fit to keep him."

"God, Tony, I'm sorry. Why didn't you..." He swallowed the end of that. Tony *had* called him. He just hadn't called back. Which he would have if Tony had made it sound urgent. Why hadn't Tony given him a clue?

"You have that woman's home number," Tony said. "Could you call her there?"

"I don't know if..." Mac stopped again. "Sure I can try. But she doesn't owe me any favors. More the other way around."

"You could pick up Ben's stuff," Tony suggested. "I assume you haven't done that already."

"No," Mac said quietly. "I haven't."

"So tell her that he left his place without his stuff and you want to get it to him. Maybe she might even let you bring it yourself and see him, since you're a cop and not some promiscuous faggot."

"Tony..."

"Could you just do it?" Tony said urgently. "Before it gets any later. At least, ask her about this foster family, if they're any good."

"What's their name?"

"I don't know. Why would they tell me something like that? The caseworker this morning was a Sheila Burns. She would know."

"Okay," Mac said soothingly. He could hear the ragged edge of pain in Tony's voice. "Okay, I'll make the calls and pick up Ben's stuff and call you."

"Just come back to your place. I'll wait for you there."

Mac called Sarah's work number and got the expected answering machine, and left a request for a call back. Important but not critical; in his and Sarah's work, critical was a little worse than a child in an approved foster situation, however worried Tony might be.

Sarah answered her home number and was gratifyingly pleased to hear Mac's voice. They had hit it off well before. Sarah listened as Mac laid out the problem for her. At first, she was reluctant to pursue the matter tonight, but Mac laid it on thick about the traumatized boy leaving his home without any of his clothes or familiar belongings, and she finally agreed to contact Burns, whom she fortunately knew, and ask after Ben. With that promise, Mac signed out Sandy's key and made the trip out to her apartment.

The tenement building was no more inviting in the growing dusk than it had been in the daylight. Mac imagined Sandy coming back here, laughing and drunk, with the man who would kill her. Did she think about the danger? Did she worry at all about the little boy sleeping in the other room? Or did the lubricating effect of the alcohol fade it all into a mellow haze? If they didn't get lucky, some other woman would be in this spot in a few weeks, or a month. Mac was damned if he would let that happen on his watch. That was what his job was really about. That was why it was so important.

Upstairs, the crime scene tape over the door was still intact. Mac loosened one side, applied the key, and stepped inside. The apartment smelled stale, a faint odor of shit and urine, layered over musty heat-baked neglect. A tang in the kitchen suggested moldering food somewhere, although the refrigerator still ran. At least there had been very little blood.

He glanced around. There was fingerprint powder everywhere, and evidence of the methodical police search, but no sign that thieves or scavengers had been here yet. Perhaps the intense police and media attention had made them nervous, but the apartment was known to be empty. It wouldn't be long before someone broke in to see what they could steal.

Mac had brought his duffle bag, and he found an old battered suitcase in the entry closet. First things first. He started with Ben's room. The requested items went in the bottom of the duffle. He took a moment to look at the picture. Ray Serrano had been tall, dark, and well-built with a handsome smile. He wondered if Tony had ever felt more for the guy than just friendship. The man looked happy, with his arm around his pregnant wife. A month later he would be dead. Mac wrapped the photo in one of Ben's T-shirts and placed it carefully in a smaller pocket in the front of the bag. Once the toys were in place, he added clothes, holding things up to get the biggest sizes. Kids outgrew stuff before you could turn around.

Out in the living room, he glanced around. No way to keep the place safe. Sarah hadn't called him back yet. For Ben's sake, he should take the good stuff before it vanished. Not that there was much good stuff.

A couple of pictures in small silver frames stood on the bookcase: Sandy's wedding picture and an early shot of baby Ben, his hair sticking straight up in a comical curl. While he was at it, Mac picked up the photo albums. One was from Sandy's younger days, no other faces recognizable as he flipped through it. The other was all Ben; Ben at the playground, Ben crawling on the rug. The pictures were coming loose from the cheap magic-cling pages, and as Mac flipped through it, a couple fluttered to the floor. He picked up Ben on a tricycle, and then saw the next one. A younger Ben sat perched on the shoulders of a younger Tony. The little boy's legs were held securely, his tiny hands fisted in the man's hair. Both wore identical grins of sheer joy. No comment on the back of when or where, but you could tell they had been having a great time. Mac hesitated, and then slipped the photo in his own shirt pocket.

There was little else worth taking. The cheap electronics would be a good riddance, the jewelry in Sandy's box was all costume stuff as far as Mac could tell. He packed a couple of pieces where he wasn't certain. He took the videos that had child-appropriate content, the picture books from the shelf, anything that looked like it might be Ben's. A couple of files of bills, medical records, and letters were worth preserving. The remains of Ben's life almost fit into one duffle and the suitcase.

His phone rang as he debated about a poster on Ben's wall. Sarah had come through for him. She gave him the name and address of the foster family that had Ben.

"Only because you're law enforcement," she said, "And I know you. You can bring the boy his stuff. And don't worry. Sheila told me this is a good placement. They do a lot of the short-term, traumatic-situation kids."

"I really appreciate it," Mac told her gratefully.

"Now you owe me big time, cop man," Sarah returned. "Don't think I won't call in that marker sometime."

"Worth it."

He locked the door behind him and smoothed the tape back over the frame as well as possible. It might keep the vultures out a little longer.

The foster home was a twenty-minute drive. It was getting dark as Mac pulled up in the driveway. The house wasn't big, but there was a nice old tree in the yard, and a safe chain-link fence, with a sandbox and toys visible. The woman who answered the door looked a little wary. Mac guessed that taking in other people's kids might make you a little worried about a big man showing up on your doorstep in the dark. He quickly flashed his badge.

"Detective MacLean with Homicide," he said. "I brought Ben Serrano's stuff from his mother's apartment."

"I can take that for him. Thank you," the woman said, reaching for the duffle.

Mac held onto it. "Actually I have a couple of other questions for him," he hedged. "It won't take long, and I can give him the bag as an excuse."

The woman looked cautiously at him. "It's late and the boy is tired. I don't want him upset."

"Ben knows me already," Mac said as ingratiatingly as he knew how. "I'll be quick and I won't upset him. I promise."

"I have to be there," she said doubtfully.

"Of course."

The woman finally nodded. "Come on in. I'll get Ben."

Mac stepped into the tiled entryway. A big kitchen off to the left looked fairly clean and still smelled of something appetizing. Mac's stomach growled, reminding him he hadn't eaten yet. To the right, the living room contained a modest TV, which held the attention of two pre-teen boys. They had both given Mac one wary glance when he came in, but then turned back to the screen as if hypnotized.

Running feet pulled Mac's attention to the hallway ahead. He barely had time to brace himself before the Ben torpedo hit him. He staggered a little, and hugged the boy close.

"Mac!" Ben said softly. "You came. I knew you would come. Can I go home now?"

The foster mother was frowning at Mac. "I thought you said this was about the case."

"It is," Mac assured her, unwinding Ben from around his waist. "But I've known Ben longer than that, so of course he's glad to see me." He sat on the floor where he was and pulled Ben into his lap, to hide the fact that he had not gotten his shirt free from one small fist.

"Hey, Ben," he said calmly. "I'm glad to see you too. I brought you the things from your mother's apartment that you wanted." He gestured at the duffle bag.

Ben glanced over, some of the animation leaving his face. "You're not taking me home?"

"Not yet. Tony wants me to say he loves you, and you both need to be good and patient a little longer. You need to stay here for a while."

"I don't want to," Ben said plaintively.

"I know. We all have to do stuff we don't want to. It's not that bad here though, is it?" He smiled. "It smells like Mrs. Wilson is a good cook."

"I guess." Ben lowered his voice to a whisper. "But Aaron pinches me and the closet is too small."

Mac blinked, interpreting that. "You should tell Mrs. Wilson if Aaron is being mean to you," he directed, with a glance at her. "Maybe he's had a bad day too. And you don't need the closet to be big. I'm sure you have a nice bed."

Ben gave a small shrug that was not quite agreement.

Time to cover his visit, and who knew, maybe he'd get some information. Mac reached into his pocket and pulled out a copy of the composite sketch. "Did you ever see anyone who looks like this with your mom or around your building?"

Ben looked at the sketch. "It doesn't look much like a real person, like a picture."

"It's just a drawing of the guy. It's okay to say no."

Ben shook his head.

*Oh well, it was a long shot anyway.*

"Did your mom ever talk to men on the phone?" Mac asked. They were tracking down Sandy's phone contacts.

"No," Ben said. "She talked to Grandma, 'n Mrs. Gonzales, 'n Lisa, 'n Shayna, and some other women people, but I don't think men."

Mac nodded. "Okay, son. That's all the questions I had right now. Maybe you can get some help to take your bag up to your room." He stood and boosted the boy onto his feet. Reluctantly,

Ben's fist opened and let him go.

"Mac," Ben said, staring intensely into his eyes. "When can I go home?"

"I don't know, Ben," Mac had to tell him. "It will be as soon as we can make it. Hang tough until then, okay?"

Ben's nod was just barely visible, but it was a nod.

"Hey, Jason," Mrs. Wilson called to the bigger of the two TV-watching boys. "I've got a heavy bag here. Do you think you can carry it up the stairs for Ben?"

"Do I have to?" the boy whined.

"Yes." Her voice was firm, and the boy rose reluctantly and schlepped the duffle up the steps. Mrs. Wilson turned to Ben. "You go with him and tell him where you want it."

Ben turned to Mac.

"Go on," Mac told him. He ruffled the boy's hair. "I'll see you soon and we'll get you back with Tony in no time." Ben ducked his head and turned away, climbing the stairs one reluctant step at a time.

Mrs. Wilson smiled at Mac. "He'll be fine. He seems like a good kid, just real quiet right now."

"He's a great kid," Mac said emphatically. "He's been through a lot. That bit with the closet…he used to sleep in the closet if his mom brought a man home. If he's missing out of his bed in the night, you might look there before you panic."

"That's good to know," she agreed, heading for the door. "That drawing, was that a suspect in his mother's case?"

"Yes." Mac hesitated and then passed her the picture. What could it hurt? "We don't know if that's even close to accurate. But if you see someone like that around, call me." He handed her his card. "Call me if the boy needs anything, okay. Or if the media find him. This case is like a feeding frenzy, and they won't care if they upset him."

"He's safe here," she assured him, holding the door open.

"Good night, Detective."

When Mac arrived at his apartment, he found Tony sitting on his front steps with an array of paper and plastic bags around him. Tony stood up tensely as he approached.

"I saw Ben," Mac said immediately. "He's fine, he's safe. The foster home seems nice enough and Sarah says it's one of the good ones."

Tony sighed, and some of the tension visibly left him. Mac gestured at the array of containers. "What's all this?"

"Your stuff. I think I found it all."

Mac swallowed a protest and surveyed the piles. "I didn't even realize I owned this much stuff. I don't know if it will fit back in my place."

"I'll help you carry it up," Tony told him, hefting a group of bags. Mac held the outer door with his foot while they slung the bags and the heavy box with free weights through onto the bottom of the stairs. Then he let the door shut behind them and they were alone in the dim of the enclosed stairway. He turned and folded Tony into his arms.

"You look like hell, babe," he whispered. This Tony looked a lifetime older than the one in the photo in his pocket. For a minute, Tony stood stiffly in his arms, but then he melted into a hard hug, his head falling against Mac's shoulder. Mac kissed his hair. "Come on, babe," he said. "Let's get this stuff upstairs and I'll tell you about your boy."

They brought the stuff up into his dark apartment, stowing it in the low space where the rafters came down to meet the floor. The row of bags were no more trashy-looking than the rest of the place, Mac decided. He pushed Tony into one of the two chairs at the table, tossed his own outer shirt on the floor, put away his weapon, and hauled a cold beer out of the refrigerator for each of them. The windows were open and the first cool breeze in a long time was clearing some of the oppressive heat.

The previous two nights had been almost unbearable, after the air-conditioned cool of Tony's place.

Mac described the foster home for Tony, and detailed his visit. For good measure, he showed Tony the sketch, but the younger man just shrugged after a long look.

"So you have the foster family's name and address?" Tony asked.

"Yes. But I promised not to tell anyone else. The CPHC folks are pretty serious about keeping the kids out of reach for their safety."

"I'm not a threat to Ben. You know that!"

"I know," Mac agreed. "But I gave my word. And it would be bad if you accidentally revealed that you'd been stalking the kid."

"It's not stalking! Jesus!" Tony snapped. "I just need to know that he's safe."

"Calm down. I didn't mean that. I'm just saying how it might look. You need to be squeaky-clean if you want him back."

"I know." Tony deflated, lowering his face to his hands. "What am I going to do, Mac? His grandparents are petitioning for custody. He hardly knows them, they see him a few times a year, but how do I compete with straight, white, middle-class heterosexual close-relatives in a stable marriage? Hell, *I* probably wouldn't give me a kid instead of them either."

"I don't know," Mac said, his heart aching for Tony and Ben. "We have to hope that the judge wants what's best for the boy enough to look beyond the obvious."

"My friend Sabrina found me a lawyer who does a lot of divorce custody cases. I'm going to meet with them tomorrow, find out what the judges are influenced by, what kind of testimonials and things might be useful."

"What can I do?" Mac asked.

"Keep an eye on Ben for me, if you can. But…" He hesitated. "I hate to say it, babe, but the best thing you can do for me now is stay away."

"What?"

Tony looked up and caught his gaze. "I'm going to have home visits and interviews and all that shit. That's why I cleared your stuff out of my place." He opened his mouth to say more, but Mac leaned over and kissed him quickly. Bad news was coming. Mac could feel it like a sword over his head. He didn't want to hear it, didn't want to know. As long as he could keep Tony otherwise occupied, he wouldn't say it.

He moved toward Tony, cupping the other man's cheekbones in his hands and sucking on his lower lip. Tony stopped pulling back and gave a soft moan. Mac leaned in, dropping to one knee beside his chair, deepening the kiss. He tongued Tony's mouth gently, touching the softness of his cheek, the smoothness of his teeth. Tony opened to his exploration, and he took it deeper, filling his lover's mouth. Mac's hands slid to caress the back of Tony's neck, fingers working up into his hair. Then he took one hand lower, across firm muscled shoulders, and the faint ridges of scarring under the soft T-shirt, and down to the sweet hollow where Tony's back flared to that fine ass.

Tony pulled his mouth free to whisper, "We really shouldn't."

"No, babe. We really should. You're here, I'm here, there's nothing else either one of us can do about anything tonight. I want to make love to you. I want to do it right, slow like you taught me. Please, baby." He was begging. That wasn't his style, but he knew it wasn't just tonight he was asking for. "I want to play in bed with you, like we used to. It's been so hard lately. Please, let me take you to bed and just make love to you."

Tony gazed back at him, their eyes inches apart. Mac couldn't interpret what he saw in those blue depths, but finally Tony smiled. "You are so bad," he said softly. "How do I say no to that?"

"You don't," Mac told him, feeling better. "Come on." He led Tony over to where his pile of mattresses made a low wide bed, and pushed the younger man down on them. "Just let me do it." He knelt to pull off Tony's sneakers and took each slender pale foot in turn, kissing at the arch to make Tony wiggle, and then licking slowly from toe to ankle. He loved Tony's feet. He was crazy about every part of this man. He massaged slowly, flexing each foot up towards the knee as he rubbed. Tony gave a little purr of contentment.

"You give the best foot rubs," he said.

Mac kissed him again, and sucked lightly on one toe. "That's not all I give." He slid his hands up under Tony's shirt, avoiding the sensitive bits, and pulled it over the younger man's head. "Roll over," he directed. Tony eyed him for a moment then obeyed, burying his face in the pillows. Mac ran his hands over the lovely planes of Tony's back, digging in gently with his fingers. He could feel the knots of tension loosening as he pummeled and rubbed. Half of Tony's back was rough and ridged with scar tissue, the legacy of a near-fatal hit-and-run almost a year ago. The skin was finally healed, and Tony said the pain was gone, but it would never be the same. Mac didn't care, except that it bothered Tony when people stared at the pool or on a beach. He bent and kissed the rough spots, running tongue and teeth over the ridges. Tony said the sensitivity there was odd, but he seemed to like the feel of Mac playing with it. Mac played while his hands massaged contented groans out of Tony.

"Other side," he directed eventually.

Tony sighed. "You are so good at that."

"Yeah, you're getting too relaxed," Mac told him. "That's not what I'm looking for. Roll over."

Tony complied with a wicked smile that was explained when Mac looked down at the denim straining to contain Tony's cock. "Okay, maybe not too relaxed."

"Can I come out and play?" Tony asked.

"Not yet." Mac began at the top again, kissing Tony's neck and shoulders. He ran tongue and teeth down Tony's neck, and dipped into the hollow at his throat. Tony's hands closed in his hair, pushing him lower, but he resisted, teasing, circling nipples without touching, licking towards Tony's navel and then rising again without reaching his goal.

"You are such a fucking tease," Tony groaned.

"Foreplay is the biggest difference between fucking and making love," Mac intoned, aiming for something like Tony's light voice.

"I'm a pompous ass. Don't listen to anything I've said."

"I like your ass." Mac latched onto a nipple at last, sucking hard, feeling the soft disc tighten and the nub rise under his lips. Tony hissed softly. Mac moved to the other side, dividing his attention back and forth, moving enough to interfere with Tony's effort to pull Mac's T-shirt off in turn. Tony groaned and yanked hard enough to make the cotton tear. Mac laughed, pulled the remains over his head, and sent it flying to land on top of his overshirt on the floor.

"You want me to strip for you?" he asked. "You don't have to destroy the clothes." He got up and stood by the bed, in Tony's view. Tony lay back, eyes a little wide, and watched. Mac considered music, but with his luck he'd turn on the radio and get the chicken dance or something. He ran his hands up and down his thighs, tightening the fabric across his crotch, as if it wasn't already tightly tented. He could do this. He'd worked Sex Crimes, he'd seen strippers.

He began moving, just a little, subtle rotation of his hips, as he slowly unbuckled his belt. The metal tongue came free, and he flipped it with his finger before pulling the leather through the belt loops, inch by inch. He snapped the belt once, with a soft pop, and then dangled the end to run the metal buckle over the soft belly skin above Tony's denims. Tony reached for his own zipper, but Mac shook his head. "Nope," he said. He bent and pressed Tony's hands down on the bed. "You lie there and watch, and then if you're good, maybe we'll let you out to play."

Tony's laugh was half disbelief, but he obediently put his hands down on the sheets. Mac took up his motions again, popping the button on his slacks, and then sliding the zipper, an inch at a time, letting the motion of his hand rub across his cock, getting harder by the minute. He pushed the slacks down at last, over his hips, leaving his cotton boxers barely containing him. A half turn, showing his ass to Tony as he bent, pushing the pants down his legs and off, then a turn back. The head of his cock rose past the elastic of his boxers as he moved, letting the fabric rub across him.

"Mmm," Tony said. "Looks tasty."

Mac stretched upward, flexing. He lifted weights; he knew Tony liked the shoulders and biceps it produced. He posed a little, licking his lips. Then with his eyes fixed on Tony's, he pushed his boxers down and stepped out of them, standing naked before his lover. He ran his hands slowly down his own thighs and up, cupping his balls, rubbing lightly. His cock jerked as he touched himself, but he was watching the heat in Tony's eyes.

"If you don't come here now and get these fucking jeans off me, something is going to break," Tony warned him breathlessly. Mac smiled slowly and knelt beside him. With mouth and teeth he fumbled at the button of Tony's pants, and then took the tab in his teeth, fighting to pull the zipper down. It was harder than usual, as the tightness of the denim stiffened the zip. Tony was laughing in need and frustration before Mac had him free.

Mac pantsed him expertly, lifting him high in the air with the fabric so his butt hit the mattresses with a thump as his feet came free. Before Tony could move, Mac lunged to splay naked across him, kissing him, bodies pressed together at a hundred points. Tony moaned, probing Mac's mouth with his tongue, humping up against him while his hands clamped on Mac's ass. They pressed together harder, kissing frantically, moving against each other. Then Mac wrenched himself free.

"You know," he said, aiming at conversational tones with a voice that was trying to pant. "I liked the butter thing a lot. I don't have any butter in my fridge, but I do have a bottle of chocolate sauce."

"Jesus," Tony gasped. "I'm begging to be fucked here and you want to play with food."

"Uh huh," Mac said. "You and chocolate. Sounds perfect."

Aware of Tony watching him, he walked naked and iron hard

to the kitchen, found the chocolate sauce, and, way in the back of a cabinet, a bottle of hazelnut oil that had been a gift from some deluded co-worker who thought Mac actually cooked. Mac figured he'd found the perfect use. He walked back to Tony and looked down at that beautiful body splayed across his bed. "Chocolate first, I think," he said.

Shaking and warming the bottle with his hands, he upended it and drizzled a fine streak of dark brown across Tony's flat stomach. Tony gasped, "Hey, that's cold."

"Let me warm it up." He knelt to lick at it, smearing the color like a streaky tan across Tony's skin, then rasping it clean slowly.

"Lower," Tony urged.

He let a line of chocolate drip across Tony's hip, and then over the tip of his cock, and slowly down the shaft. Tony shuddered at the cold liquid, then shuddered differently as Mac followed the food with his tongue. Mac licked and sucked, tasting Tony and chocolate commingled on his tongue. He rose up to kiss Tony deeply, sharing the flavors. Tony ran his tongue over Mac's lower lip. "Getting messy here."

"Yeah," Mac said happily. "Grab your knees."

He urged Tony's legs up and out, and Tony took hold under his own knees to open and spread his body for Mac. Mac stopped and just looked. He never tired of the sight of Tony like this, ready and begging for his touch. For a long time they hadn't been able to do this, as Tony's back was painful and slow to heal. Two surgeries, grafting, it had been months before he had put Tony on his back in a bed. The sight hit him as hard now as it had then.

"God, baby," he whispered. "You are so beautiful."

He bent to lick and kiss around Tony's balls, and then upended the chocolate sauce again. "It'll be all over your sheets," Tony protested, although he only moved to open himself up more.

"Do I care?" Mac whispered. He drizzled the thick brown liquid over Tony's ass and leaned in. The musky nutty taste of Tony and the dense richness of chocolate were a heady combination as he licked and sucked, working with his tongue. Tony moaned and writhed, curling his back to lift himself higher into Mac's face. His hard cock left smears of shiny pre-cum across his stomach as he moved.

"Please, Mac." Tony's moans were becoming words. "Please, baby, now. I need you."

Mac reached for the oil. "Not more foreplay!" Tony groaned. "Baby, I'm gonna explode before you ever get inside me."

"Chocolate sauce is sticky," Mac growled. "This isn't." A silky trail of oil drizzled from the bottle across Tony's cock and ass and across Mac. He stroked a finger through the slick mixture and sucked it slowly. Then he wiped a dab across Tony's full lower lip. Tony licked it off, eyes scorching Mac. *Enough.* He leaned forward, sliding his shaft against Tony's body, smearing the slick oil over them both. Tony moaned and pushed back, intensifying the motion. Mac reached down, changed his aim, and sank deep into Tony's body.

Tony gasped and arched for a second, and Mac froze, giving his lover time to get used to being filled. When he felt Tony begin to relax he leaned forward again, slowly letting his weight drive him into Tony, deeper and deeper. Tony's eyes opened, staring intensely into his, as their bodies merged. Hilt-sunk in that sweet tight ass, Mac bent over and kissed Tony's mouth.

Softly, not moving much, they played with the tips of their tongues, just touching, licking lips and teeth. Mac held still, afraid to move as he hovered on the brink. Tony let go of his knees and wrapped his legs around Mac, raising his hands to Mac's hair. They kissed, carefully, gently, and then Mac began moving, just a little. Tony gasped at the first slow slide of Mac's body, and he stopped again, breathing against his lover's mouth.

"God, don't stop, baby," Tony whispered urgently. "Slow is nice, but I'm gonna go in two seconds. I want it hard."

Mac moaned and arched his back, slamming his hips forward, released by Tony's words. No time for slow, no time for thought, just the urgent rhythm of two bodies straining together, trying to become one. Now, and now, and now, and holy fucking shit!

"Tony!" His body arched and spasmed, everything inside him trying to empty itself out into his lover. There were sparkles in front of his eyes, and his whole awareness condensed down to heat and connection. Tony whimpered his name under him, shaking around him. The beloved soft tight heat clasped Mac, milking him empty. He eased down into Tony's loving grasp, and let go.

They drifted in silence afterward, still connected, sticky and slick and sloppy together, skin and cum and oil and chocolate. The mingled scents were better than Christmas. Mac slid a little sideways to take his weight off Tony's chest, and felt himself slip free. Tony made that soft sad little sound he sometimes uttered when Mac left him, and then snuggled in against Mac's shoulder. Mac let himself drift off.

It could have been minutes or hours later when Tony moved under him and woke him. He whimpered in involuntary protest, but opened his eyes.

"We need to clean up, sweetie," Tony said.

Mac couldn't argue with that. The bed was a mess. "You get first shower," he offered. At his place, showering together just wasn't an option.

Tony slid out from under him and stood, stretching. Mac watched his body's long lines from hand to hip flex and curve. Tony found his clothes, scattered across the floor, and headed silently for the bathroom. Mac watched him go. The anxiety that sex had temporarily buried was coming back.

He got himself up and bundled the sheets in a ball, taking the opportunity to wipe himself off as he did so. The fabric couldn't get dirtier at this point. He had one spare set of sheets, and he remade the bed, listening to the anemic trickle of water in the shower. Eventually it shut off. Tony came out in jeans and T-shirt, toweling his hair. Mac's fears ramped up a notch. Jeans were not spending-the-night wear.

"I left you some hot water," Tony said. "At least, I think I did."

Mac nodded and retreated to the bathroom with a clean pair of boxers. He stared at himself in the mirror as he peed and prepared to shower. Thirty-four years old, a few more lines in his face than he'd had ten years ago. He still had the body and the muscles, women hit on him a lot, but Tony was nine years younger and ten times prettier. Mac's face was okay, hair still free of grey, but really, what did he have to offer Tony that he couldn't get elsewhere?

He showered slowly, soaping and rinsing carefully. He was still a little sensitive, as he sometimes was after the best sex with Tony. Not necessarily the roughest sex, although sometimes they took biting and hard play to the edge, but after the times that emptied him out. Like his body knew there was nothing more to give.

He let the water run cold, until his shivers finally drove him out. Then he dried himself and rubbed his hair with the towel. He pulled on his boxers, stopped to trim his fingernails, knowing he was stalling, not able to move forward. *You've faced men with guns, for God's sake,* he told himself. *Get your ass out there.*

Tony was sitting at the table, sipping at a beer. A second bottle stood in front of the second chair in invitation. Mac walked over slowly and sat, wrapping his hands around the cold sweating glass. He waited.

"That was kind of a mistake," Tony began.

"No, it wasn't."

Tony shook his head. "You know what I mean. Mac, I love you more than breath, but I can't be with you this way anymore."

"What way?" Mac's voice was thin.

"The only way we've had so far. Hiding it and only being together in the dark. Lying to people."

Mac couldn't believe this was happening so fast, all the rules changing without warning. "It's none of their business," he said harshly.

"Perhaps not in the past," Tony agreed. "I could live with

that. But now it is. I'm going to be asked if I have boyfriends, if I'm sexually active, if I bring people home. They have a right to ask me, and I want to tell the truth. If we break up now," he paused, his breath catching. "If we're not together anymore, then I can make this slide past. I'm not active *at present*. I don't have a boyfriend *right now*. You can disappear out of the story. I may have to bend the truth, but not break it. And I won't have to lie to Ben either."

"What do you want me to say?" Mac whispered.

"What do I want?" Tony looked at him. "I want the moon. I want you and me and Ben and Anna, and a little house, and a fucking white picket fence, and me bitching to the kids because you're late for dinner again. I want you standing up for the next poor tranny who gets a knife waved in his face, and no one wondering why. I want to leave the kids with a sitter and go to a movie with you, and kiss the shit out of you on the street after the show because it was just so romantic. I want everything." He paused.

Mac sat silent. He should say something. He could feel it slipping through his fingers. He could picture Loes staring at him as he defended some transvestite hooker. He could feel the stares, the hatred, as he kissed his gay lover on the street. He could feel the warmth of a little house with his kids and Tony in it, and the firestorm of anger from his homophobic relatives falling upon them. He said nothing.

After a moment, Tony sighed. "But if I can't have that I want Ben. I want that kid to live with me, and feel safe, and grow and learn, and become the best person he is capable of being. I want him to know he is loved for whoever he turns out to be. And I will do whatever it takes to make that happen."

Tony was good with words, better than Mac. Mac couldn't explain what he felt, not and make it sound right. If he opened his mouth now, God only knew what would come out of it. In fact he pressed a fist against his lips, to keep it inside.

Tony was looking at him with gentle eyes, but he was getting up and going to the door. He was going to walk out. Mac let up the pressure on his mouth enough to say, "Don't." He tasted blood from his lips on his teeth.

"Baby," Tony said softly. "If I don't leave now, I won't be able to."

"So don't leave." The words tumbled over themselves out of Mac's throat. How had they gone from okay to ultimatum just like that? He wasn't ready for this, couldn't wrap his mind around it. "Stay. At least for tonight. There must be a way. We can figure this out."

"I can't do this," Tony said. "I can't hide and I can't lie. If you come out now, I'm yours. But I won't compromise anymore."

Mac wanted desperately to say something else, anything else. His throat closed and he was silent.

Tony shook his head. Mac imagined there was pity in the gesture.

"Well, if you're going to fuck and run," Mac spat out, "Then you should go now. Wouldn't want to miss a night's sleep. I have to say, you were the best lay I've ever had."

Tony looked startled, then hurt, then something else Mac couldn't identify. "I'll let you know how it works out with Ben," he said, opening the door. "I have your e-mail."

"I could come to the hearing," Mac offered, his anger impossible to maintain. "If you need a reference or…"

"Don't," Tony said sharply. "Just don't. This is fucking ripping me in two and don't pretend you don't know that. I can't be friends and I can't be around you anymore. Maybe one day you can take both of the kids out somewhere, or I can, so they don't lose each other too. But I don't want to see you and I don't want to hear your voice, and I don't fucking want to have you stand up and tell a judge what a good person I am when you can't even say you love me in private. And I hope someday you find someone worth coming out of your closet for, and I'm sorry as hell that it wasn't me." He sighed. "Stay safe, Mac. Don't do anything stupid, okay?" He stepped out and closed the door behind him. Mac froze, staring at it.

*Go after him, get him back, promise anything.*

Slowly, with control, Mac crossed the room to the front window and pushed the curtain aside. On the pavement below, Tony emerged from the building, indistinct in the darkness, and crossed the street. That stupid blue Prius was parked a few doors down. The light came on inside it in response to the remote. Tony got in and closed the door. The car sat for a moment without moving. *Go to him. It's not too late.* Mac's feet were nailed to the floor. After a minute, the Prius started, its electric engine silent on the empty street, and Tony drove away.

Mac let the curtain fall back. The shabby apartment looked back at him, bags piled under the rafters, dirty sheets in a heap, the scent of nuts and chocolate and sex still heavy in the air. A gust of wind blew in and stirred the smells, overlaying them with a hint of rain to come. Soon the smell of the night would clean the stale air.

Mac closed the windows tightly and grabbed the wadded sheets. He curled up in a ball on his bed, pressing the lump of cloth to his stomach like a heating pad to a wound. Chocolate and Tony surrounded him again. It was hours later before he stopped shaking.

CHAPTER 9

Tony let his end of the couch down with a sigh and looked around the new apartment. It was bigger, brighter, and airier than his old one. His furniture was almost lost in the full-sized living room. Daniel, on the other end of the couch, grinned at him.

"I think your stuff is embarrassed to be seen in here, Tony. You seriously need to invest in something new."

Tony shook his head with a smile. "Not in this pay period, my friend. Which lasts until the middle of September, when I'll actually get a paycheck." His budget was stretched to the limit for this. He had broken down and borrowed first and last month, and the security deposit, from Sabrina. It allowed his bank statement to still look marginally healthy on paper. The landlord had been more than happy to have him move in right away, with his lease back-dated to August first, once he had the money in hand. He would have to sublet his old place soon. He couldn't afford to pay two rents through till December.

It was worth it, Tony told himself. He had a CPHC home visit scheduled for Monday, and he would show them this big three-bedroom, with a bedroom and a playroom for Ben, instead of the old place. No one could claim this wasn't a fit place to raise a child. Tony looked around again in satisfaction. Heading for the elevator, he passed Jack and Martin with his table. Daniel, coming behind him, stopped to help them maneuver it through the doorway.

Up in the old apartment, Rick and Sabrina had made a start on the kitchen, packing the smaller stuff into boxes.

"I must say," Sabrina called as he came in, "This is easier than your past moves. We don't even need to seal the boxes."

"Yeah, and I'm moving up in size," Tony agreed. "So you can just pack everything. There's plenty of space."

Rick was rummaging in the lower cupboards. "How about

this?" he asked, pulling out a rag. "Keep it down here for cleanup after we finish?" He was tossing it into a corner when the faded blue color caught Tony's eye.

"Wait a second," he said urgently.

Rick raised an eyebrow. "Not a rag?" He shook out the shirt and looked at it. "Ooh, XXL. Not Luke's then. He never had shoulders that big. Who is he, and if you're done with him will you introduce us?"

Tony walked over and took the shirt. It wasn't close to new. In fact, there was a little hole starting in the fabric at the back of the neck. Mac always cut out the tags if they itched him and failed to fix the stitches. Tony had mended half a dozen of those, but not this one. He put an index finger through the hole. It stretched a little for him. In fact, the other index finger fit too. He took hold and pulled. The shirt split neatly, right down the back until it reached the hem. He tugged again sideways, and the tear arced around, separating the sleeve from the back. The piece flapped forlornly. Tony tossed the whole thing into the corner. "I guess it's a rag now."

"Whoa," Rick muttered. "I take it I don't want to meet this guy."

"Luke wasn't my only mistake," Tony said. Then, covering for Mac, like always, he added, "Just my most recent." *Because Mac was a disaster, but not a mistake.*

Sabrina's expression suggested she wasn't buying it, just letting him get away with it. He needed a distraction.

"So do either of you know where I can get a cheap bed for Ben? Because I was thinking about bringing his own bed from Sandy's place. But then I thought about roaches." He gave an exaggerated shudder. "But I hate to shop IKEA. It's such a cliché." The resulting conversation took time, drew in his other friends as they came to collect the kitchen chairs, and led the subject well into safe territory.

It took most of the afternoon to move his stuff and set it back up. At least his frenzy of cleaning had put his own apartment in good enough shape that only a little touch-up was needed to guarantee his security deposit back. Or it would be once he got to the end of the lease. He took a last look around the place and sighed. He was attached to that kitchen counter, and the shower, and there was a place on the wall by the front door that he was surprised didn't show the indented print of his hands. This had been a world, small and confining, but so sweet.

He closed the door firmly behind him and dropped the keys in his pocket. Home was one floor down now.

Mac got off the elevator at the fourth floor quietly, out of respect for the early morning hour. He wasn't sure what he was doing. The door opened to his key, just like always. The quality of silence warned him, even before he reached for the switch, that Tony wasn't home. He still blinked when the light came on.

The apartment was deserted. The marks on the carpet spoke to him of couch and table, chair, bookcase, bookcase, bookcase. The kitchen was cleaner than he had ever seen it, the cabinets open and empty. The curtains were pulled across the windows. Tony was gone.

For a long time, he stood there. Tony had said he needed to move, would need more space once he had a boy to raise. Mac had just not pictured it happening this fast. This place had always been here for him, with that man in it. Even these past few days, as he threw himself headlong into his work, he had kept that image like a talisman in the back of his mind. It was here for him, if he dared to grasp it. Except it wasn't anymore. And Tony hadn't even called to let him know.

*Maybe he doesn't want you to find him.*

Except that was paranoid. Tony knew Mac could find anyone he was looking for. Tony had mentioned there were bigger units in the same building, even. Mac pulled the door shut and made his way back down to the mailboxes in the lobby. Sure enough, the old box was now unmarked, but one row down and two over, at number 305, was the name "Hart, A."

Mac ran a finger over the name. He could let himself back in the lobby door, go up to the new place, knock on the door. Tony would open up for him. Probably. And then what? Nothing had really changed since that night in his apartment, had it? *Why are you here, you fool?* Was he really offering Tony anything different than before, or just wishing he could? He had driven here on autopilot, sleep-deprived and aching, not thinking beyond seeing Tony again. Now he was here, this seemed like a really bad idea.

He pulled those two keys out of his pocket and turned them around in his hand, bending the rubber automobile fob back and forth. The mail slot was a little narrow. Mac had to wiggle the ring around to fit first one and then the other key through the new mailbox. For a moment they got hung up at the fob. Then it slipped through and they fell with a muted clink into the box. Mac had a moment's hesitation. Maybe he should add a note, explain. *What's to explain?* He headed back out into the early morning darkness.

He sat in his car for a couple of hours, dozing and startling awake over and over, until the sun was up and it was a reasonable time to knock on Brenda's door. She complained that Anna hadn't yet had time for breakfast, but Mac overrode her, promising to take the child out and feed her.

"Something full of fat and sugar, no doubt," Brenda grumbled, but she gave the girl a pat on the shoulder and told her to be good for her father.

Mac led a bubbly Anna to his car, got the booster seat out of the trunk, and strapped her in. His car was so old it didn't have a passenger airbag. Mac considered that a bonus feature, because it meant Anna could safely sit beside him. He took her request for breakfast, which was IHOP, and headed out.

Anna was telling him about the kitten her friend Cindy had just bought. The kitten's name was either Whiskey or Whiskers; Anna appeared unsure which. Mac assumed the latter. He had met Cindy's parents, and they were a bland couple who met even Brenda's grudging approval. Not the type to name a cat after the demon rum.

Anna was very taken by the kitten. Apparently it was totally cute, asleep or awake. "If you're going to ask for a kitten, don't bother," Mac warned her. "Aunt Brenda would not go for that."

"I know," Anna said sadly. "I wasn't asking. It would just be nice."

The waitress seated them at a booth, with a booster seat and child menu for Anna. She looked at the pictures in the menu carefully, making her selection.

"You love Aunt Brenda, don't you?" Mac asked her, once orders for strawberry pancakes had been placed.

"Oh, yes," Anna said. "She's my aunt and she loves me too. But I wish she wouldn't be so sad."

"Is she sad?"

"Mostly," Anna said, coloring industriously with her crayons. "You're mostly happy, and Tony's happy, and Cindy's mom sings a lot when she cooks. But Aunt Brenda is mostly sad. I try to make her happier, but it doesn't work so well now that I'm older."

"What doesn't, Anna?"

"Anything." Anna looked up and wrinkled her nose. "She worries about me more now. I'm supposed to be becoming a lady, but I don't think I know how."

"Uh-huh," Mac encouraged.

Anna contemplated her drawing, head tilted to one side, and then picked up the green crayon. "Ladies don't run and climb things, and they're polite and say please and thank you and stuff, and they don't yell or swing on stuff. But I keep forgetting."

"Well, being polite is a good thing," Mac said cautiously, "And you should be learning to say please and thank you. But I don't think you're old enough to have to give up running and climbing. In fact, some ladies are just as good at running and climbing as some boys are."

"Aunt Brenda says those aren't real ladies," Anna pointed out doubtfully. "I'm starting kinnergarden soon."

"So you are," Mac agreed. *Where had the time gone?* "I'll tell you what. When you go to kindergarten, you can ask your teacher how much running and climbing is okay at school, and then you'll know."

"That would work," Anna said happily. "You're smart, Daddy."

Mac smiled a little sheepishly. *Flattered by a five-year-old and liking it.* He didn't like this feeling of being in the middle again, trying to bend Brenda's rigid rules to fit the rest of the world Anna lived in. Anna was looking at him sympathetically.

"You're sad a lot too today, Daddy. Is it because we can't be with Ben and Tony today, even though it's a Sunday?"

"I guess so," Mac admitted. "I'm a little worried about Ben. He's visiting with some nice people until Tony's new place is ready and approved for him. I hope he'll be back with Tony again soon."

"Me too," Anna agreed. "I want to go to the zoo, and the rides are always funner if Ben comes along. And Tony knows everything about the animals."

Mac wondered if he should warn her that things had changed, but bit back the words at the last moment. Why spoil her day? If Tony didn't get custody of Ben, things would change even more. Sufficient until the day. He devoted himself to entertaining her, enjoying her responses, until he was replete with affection and pancakes. He took her to the playground. Then, when it got warmer, to the beach at Lake Calhoun to watch the sailboats flit across the water. By the time he dropped her off at the house, hot, happy, and tired, he could tell himself that his life was back to normal.

Climbing the stairs to his apartment, entering his small dusty kitchen, noticing the bags of his stuff still packed where they were dumped along the walls, he had to wonder when normal became so fucking empty.

❖ ❖ ❖

Tony pulled his gaze back from staring into space to look at Sabrina. She sat across the café table, her coffee cup cradled between her palms. She was leaning earnestly toward him. He tried to remember what she'd just said.

It was good, this should be good, getting together with his BFF like he used to do. He'd missed spending time with Sabrina. Back when they were both struggling students, they'd spent hours talking about men and life and ambitions. Sabrina had been in law school, looking for the light at the end of a very long educational tunnel. He'd been in the education program, wondering if a gay man could get a job teaching school in this city. They'd been tight.

It wasn't her fault that Sundays had come to mean going out somewhere with Mac, and Ben and Anna, and getting a taste of the future he had wanted so badly. And it wasn't her fault that, as much as he loved her, she couldn't compare. And he still couldn't remember what she'd said. She was waiting for an answer.

"Sorry," he admitted. "Missed that."

"Tony, focus," she said firmly. "This is important stuff. Why did I go to the trouble of consulting an expert in custody battles, off the record and at a reduced cost, I might add, if you're not going to listen?"

"I'm listening," he said, giving himself a mental shake. This *was* important.

He took careful notes as she went through the advice. Apparently he'd lucked out with the judge whom Ben had drawn for this hearing. She was known for creative and humane decisions. He tried to be optimistic.

Sabrina finished and closed her portfolio. "So. A bottle of wine now? This may be your last chance to get sloshed if you're going to become a single daddy."

"Sure," Tony said, going along with her mood. "It'll be like old times."

"Not quite," Sabrina said, collaring the waiter and putting in the order. "Because I now have money and because you seem to have stopped talking."

"Huh?"

"Tony, I've hung out with you in good times and bad, and you've never run out of things to say. This is the first time I've had to completely carry the conversation. Are you really that scared of losing Ben? Or are you that scared of having to take care of him?"

"There's no *having to*. I want Ben. Yeah, I'm scared he'll end up with his grandparents, or in foster care if the judge doesn't like either of us. Sandy ran away from her parents multiple times, starting before she was twelve. I don't trust them to do right by Ben."

"Hopefully they won't have to." Sabrina took a sip of the offered wine and gestured at the server to fill both glasses. "You know I'm with you on this. You can use me as a reference, offer me as a source of female influence in Ben's life if he lives with you, whatever helps."

"I know. Thank you." He drank a mouthful to hide a catch in his voice. At least he still had Bree on his side.

"So talk to me," she said. "Tell me what's been going on with you. It's been ages since we got together."

*I've been falling in love with a guy in a closet so tight he has mothballs coming out his ears. And I got dumped in favor of that closet.* "I've been volunteering at the Lambda House shelter downtown," he said, because it was something he could talk about. The ups and downs of the shelter and the kids took them through a bottle of Shiraz, with Tony downing more than his share.

"Do you ever hear about how the police are doing with their search for Sandy's murderer?" Bree asked eventually. "Do they have any idea who did it?"

"I don't think they have a suspect yet," Tony said carefully. Mac wouldn't want anything he'd said in confidence to get spread around.

"You have to wonder if they're even trying," Bree said

acidly. "After all, three women are dead, but they were all cheap promiscuous sluts, so it serves them right."

"The cops don't think like that," Tony protested. "Or at least most of them don't." *Loes might.* "I'd bet that the detectives on this case are pretty frustrated right now, and would do almost anything for a good lead." Mac would be pacing the floor, and not sleeping much even when he was home. He'd be trying to figure out some other angle, some other possible source of information. He'd be getting those dark shadows under his eyes that he developed when a case was stalled out. Even a hot shower and screaming sex would only take him down for a few hours, and then he'd be at it again. If anything, he cared too much.

Bree raised her eyebrows at him. "You, taking the side of the cops? After some of the stuff you told me in college?"

"I've gotten to know a few," he said defensively. "After that mess last fall. They're mostly doing the best they can. You couldn't pay me enough to do their job. A few of them may be bigoted assholes, but we'd be in trouble without them."

"Wow. Next you'll be wearing a suit and getting a buzz cut."

"Hardly." *Mac liked fisting his hands in the length of Tony's hair.* He drank deeply again. He was getting drunk, he decided, and he was going to let himself. Just this once. "Tell me about your boyfriend, Harley. Are you still sending him home at night?"

Bree sighed. "I'm thinking about breaking up with him. I mean, the sex is awesome, but afterward I just look at him and think, *what am I doing with this jerk?* He's so corporate, he would get up in the middle of fucking to take a business call. In fact, he has."

"Ouch," Tony sympathized.

"I mean, I work for a law firm. I know how hard it is to get ahead. But if I'm going to be serious about a guy, I want to be certain I come ahead of his career."

*That would be nice,* Tony thought wistfully. He'd never been sure with Mac. The man's career and his daughter and whatever other fears kept him in the closet had all blended together in one insurmountable mess. For just a moment, as Tony walked out of that tiny third-floor apartment, he had thought Mac would stop him. He'd heard the man shift, the floor creak, something, behind him. His heart had leapt inside him, for just that instant. One shining moment of believing that Mac would change his mind. But there had been only silence, until he closed the door with Mac still inside.

He was never falling in love again, he thought. It hurt too much. It sucked the energy and breath out of you, until everything else you were doing was just dust. He could learn to live without it. He would raise a little boy, and volunteer his time, and teach. He could have a good life without Mac. He *would* have a good life.

Bree was looking at him again, oddly.

"Huh?"

"You're not listening to me, are you? Are you going to tell me what's wrong?"

"Probably not." He drained his glass.

"Is it what happened last fall? Marty dying and you being held hostage and all? Because you've never really wanted to talk about that. You've been so quiet, like you're shutting me out. I figured you would talk to me about it some day, if I gave you time. But you really haven't. And…I worry about you."

"I'm just fine."

"Tony, your best friend died. You don't have to be fine about it. It's just… I thought this winter you were starting to seem happier. And now, with all this new stuff happening, it just seems like you're worse again."

"Big surprise," he said, because it made a good diversion and Bree's instincts were a little too acute. "It's not just the violence again. It's the press and the cops and everything starting up like before. It's feeling like I don't own my life. I just want it to be fucking over, so I can take Ben and start fresh. Maybe somewhere else. Maybe this city is cursed for me. Maybe when I have custody, and the cops don't need me and Ben for anything to do with Sandy, I'll start job-hunting in California. Or Oregon.

Somewhere temperate, where it's not this hot or this cold. Somewhere I can live a life like it's supposed to be lived, safe and out of the closet in the sunshine."

Bree frowned. "Tony, the first time I met you, you were wearing a 2Q2BSTR8 button. You've always been out of the closet."

"Yeah," he said bitterly, pushing away from the table. "I have, haven't I?" He would go walking, he thought. Walk the streets here in LynLake, where it took all kinds of people, and you could meet some of them on any corner. Walk off the wine, and the fucking tightness in his chest, without worrying who might see him. Remember what the sunshine was like.

Mac turned over again on his mattress in the dark, hunting in vain for a cooler spot on his pillow. The air in his apartment was just one degree short of an oven. Maybe not even that much. It was hard to breathe.

He was so fucking hot. He could take another shower. But then he'd just be hot and wet. *And God, he wished he hadn't thought that, because hot and wet evoked a whole different set of memories. And he'd been holding those at bay all night, from one breath to the next.*

He hadn't cleaned this place, hadn't unpacked his stuff from the bags under the eaves. He crashed here only because Oliver had ordered him not to come in until Monday, and he'd run out of other places to be. Tony had been in this place so seldom. It was unfair that every inch of it resonated with his absence. Mac could close his eyes and see the man moving through like a ghost, touching bed, counter, shower, floor, with scent and heat and movement. And now grey dust covered it all.

He had made the only possible choice. He knew that. He'd never pretended it would be different. Right from the start he'd told Tony he was never going to be out, and the other man had accepted those terms. They'd had a good run. It wasn't Mac's fault that life had conspired to pull them apart.

Life was like that. He remembered the first time he'd fully

realized how arbitrary life was, and how you had to protect yourself. He'd been eighteen and in Chicago, almost graduated from high school. He'd worked up the nerve to go out to a bar. Not a real gay bar, but one of those places where gays and straights mingled. There were couples of both kinds at the tables, and he'd watched covertly. His gaydar was for shit. He couldn't tell who was going up to whom, in the dance of contact and flirting.

After a while, he'd worked up the nerve to ask a girl to dance. He watched the men on the floor, moving to the music. He tried to imagine the nerve it would have taken to ask one of them. He couldn't picture it.

When the kid came in, Mac only noticed because of the jacket. His own school jacket, although he didn't recognize the boy. Which didn't mean the reverse would be true. Mac…he was Jared then…eased back into the crowd a little. He was on the football team, after all. People sometimes recognized him from that.

The other boy was smaller, slimmer, probably younger. His dark hair was thick and long, a little unkempt. He asked for a drink at the bar, and showed what Mac figured was fake ID, but got served anyway.

No gaydar needed here. For one thing, the clothes were a dead giveaway. For another, half the gay men in the place seemed to be checking the boy out. Young and hot was obviously at a premium here. The boy had three men proffer money to the bartender for his drink when it came.

Jared watched as the boy smiled, flirted, accepted a refill. This kid was younger than him, but he seemed so at ease. Time passed, just watching. A couple of women came up to Jared, making conversation, but they left pretty quickly when his disinterest showed. One older man hung around. His conversation started subtly and gradually got more blatant. It took Jared blatantly turning his back to make that one go away.

The boy left close to eleven, with a tall blond man. Jared slid off his stool and followed them. It wasn't stalking, he thought.

He wasn't spying on them. He was just curious. How could you do that? How could you walk into a bar, have fun with other guys, go out with a man, and survive it? And the boy was from his own school.

He hung well back. The weather was pleasant and the two men ahead of him walked slowly, window-shopping in the closed storefronts. They were heading into the gay part of town. Jared hadn't planned on venturing this far. Because around here, well, you might be straight and slumming, but there would be that assumption…if you happened to be seen.

He paused to look in the window of a bookstore. There were titles he'd never imagined. He tried to memorize authors. Maybe at the library, if he read them there and didn't check them out…

That was why he was a block behind when it happened. The boy and his blond friend had stopped, talking with their heads close together, maybe kissing, Jared would never be sure. A big man stumbled out of the door of a bar just beyond them, and took two lurching steps in their direction. As they drew apart, startled, he growled drunkenly, "Faggots. This place is full of goddamn faggots." His uneven steps jolted him up against the blond man, who shoved at him irritably. With a shout, the man turned and slammed a huge fist into the blond's face. Caught off guard, the smaller man flew backwards, tangling with the dark-haired kid. And a second punch from the drunk slammed them both through the plate glass of a storefront window.

For a moment, Jared froze as the night exploded with the sound of smashing glass and the shriek of a burglar alarm. The drunk spat in the direction of the fallen men, yanked open the door of a car parked at the curb, and squealed off down the road.

A dozen men and women streamed out of the bar, yelling and bending over the two men and the broken glass. A couple people pulled out cell phones, presumably calling 911. The blond man was pulled clear, bleeding heavily from one arm and his shoulder. The younger boy had a scalp wound that trickled red blood down his face.

Emergency services responded to the call quickly. Paramedics treated the two men while the cops listened to the bar patrons raging over the attack. There were lots of people around. They didn't need Jared to get involved.

But he stayed and listened. He heard the paramedics in the first ambulance talk about blood loss and surgery. They drove off fast, siren wailing. He heard how the cops tried to get information of any kind about the guy who attacked them, and failed to get more than, "He was big. It happened so fast." He heard them ask the kid how old he was.

"Sixteen," the boy admitted, sitting in the back of the second ambulance.

"We'll call your parents, have them meet you at the hospital."

"You can try." The boy made a face, but gave the cops a phone number. The older cop stepped away, presumably to make the call. When he came back, he looked at the kid and cleared his throat uncomfortably.

"They're not coming, are they?" the kid said bitterly.

"Um, no," the older cop said. "I spoke with your father, and he, well, he said you brought it on yourself and you would have to deal with it. I'm sorry. You know, we'll have to call children's services for you, to get permission for the doctors to treat you."

The boy leaned back on the stretcher and closed his eyes. "Whatever. I knew they wouldn't care."

Jared hung around after the ambulances pulled out. He heard the mutters in the crowd; this wasn't the first time, wouldn't be the last time. He heard the cops talk about how they would never catch the guy who did this. The older cop was angry. But as they were getting in the patrol car the younger one shrugged. "They should know better than to act like that out on the street," he said. "Christ, it figures someone's gonna get offended. If the faggots want to keep their skulls intact, they've gotta learn to keep it indoors. You can't keep regular guys from queer-bashing when they're liquored up. It's human nature."

The older cop shook his head. "No one deserves to get their face sliced open."

"Not saying that," the other man replied. "But if they want us to be able to protect them, they've got to do their part. That's all I'm saying."

The police car pulled away, roof lights off, patrolling. Slowly the crowd dispersed too. Jared was left staring at the dark patch on the sidewalk where the boy's blood had stained it.

He had wondered how you could walk with a man, out in the open, and make it work. Obviously you couldn't. Not without pain, and violence, and rejection. Not ever safely. Even the cops couldn't keep you safe, although they tried.

And he knew that night that he was never going to put himself in that position. He was never going to face gay-bashing fists, never have his father reject him with those cold words. Although with his father, a punch in the face was more likely. His mother would be the one whose voice would go cold and dead.

He wanted to be a cop himself, and this night didn't change that. But clearly there was no safety in uniform for a faggot. So in uniform, he would have to not be one.

Nothing he had seen since had changed his mind. He'd come up against violence, and hatred, and pure disdain, aimed at the open homosexuals who crossed his path in uniform. And some of it had been from other cops. He'd seen worse in Sex Crimes, and in Homicide. It wasn't safe to be out. It would never be safe. Anna and Brenda had just given him one more critical reason in a lifetime of reasons.

He should have been able to make Tony understand. Tony had been safer with Mac. He was out in the world again now. There was nothing Mac could do.

Images, memories of other people's past disasters, passed through his mind. Everything affirmed his decision. Nothing good would come of stepping one inch outside the closet.

*Nothing except Tony.*

He couldn't do it. He could face a drug addict with a knife, or a hysterical couple in a domestic dispute. He could drive at ninety miles an hour, siren blaring, through congested traffic, and pull over a suspected criminal with a gun. He could dive into the cold waters of the Mississippi in flood, after a man trying to commit suicide. In fact, he had. But even for Tony, he could not change the way he lived his life.

*He was a freaking coward.*

And the night crept on, unendingly, one sticky, hot, aching breath after another.

Mac was surprised to find Oliver waiting for him when he arrived at work Monday morning. He glanced at his watch; it was later than he thought. Lately he had been first in, last out. He wasn't sleeping much anyway. He figured he might as well get some work done. In fact he had cleared two cases neatly last week. One time he'd surprised himself by drawing a confession from the street-punk suspect. Oliver had eyed him sideways when he commented, "I'd have confessed too, to get you out of my face. Bulldogs have nothing on you lately." Still, it was satisfying to see *something* ending right.

This morning Oliver bounded up, waving a manila envelope in his face. "Look what we got for Christmas!"

Mac took the envelope and pulled out the contents. It was the list of the old case DNA cross checks he had requested from Brand's semen sample, way back when. Scanning the list showed "No match," "No match," until about halfway down, where a 99.7% sat in the comparison column. And at the bottom was another, 100%. Mac hurried to his desk, scrabbling for the list of cases that matched those file numbers. The first one was a rape and homicide in St. Paul in March, where the victim was sexually assaulted and died of head trauma. The second one… holy shit! The second one was a rape back in January, and that victim survived.

"Christmas and my birthday," he breathed. "Okay, who are you assigning to these?"

"Gather round, children," Oliver yelled. "Get your asses over here." Loes and Hanson were just arriving, heading for the coffee maker, and he got a "Hold your fucking horses," from Loes. Ramsey came over eagerly and sat on the corner of Mac's desk. Her smile at Mac was a little tentative, and he wondered if he had yelled at her lately. His temper wasn't what it should have been.

When the team was assembled, Oliver gave them the good news. "Mac, you get the rape victim. Take Ramsey with you. She may talk more to another woman. Loes and Johansson, you get the murder. Beg St. Paul nicely for the file, but don't take no for an answer. They can kibitz, but we need everything they've got. Check the evidence, get us a list of people to talk to. Hanson, you're on the computer. Background checks on these two victims, cross-referenced with the other three. There's got to be some kind of pattern here. Pull up everything you can get on the first one, the rape. He's likely to have been less careful and organized there."

"Why do I always get the sweatbox and the machine, while you all go out and talk to real people?" Hanson grumbled.

"Because, son," Oliver said, patting him on the head, "You young hot-shots are faster than us old fogeys with computers. You keep telling us so, right?" He smiled sharply. "So go prove it."

Mac looked up the information on the rape case while Ramsey hovered nearby. He wrote out numbers and addresses, and motioned with a jerk of his head that she should follow him. As they headed toward the car, she ran a couple of steps to catch up with his long-legged stride, and put a hand on his arm.

"Mac," she said. "Don't you think we should call her and set up an appointment?"

Mac glanced at her. "This is murder. She doesn't get the choice about whether to talk to us."

"This was rape," Ramsey pointed out. "If we push her too hard, she may have to sit there in our presence, but we won't get squat from her in the way of information."

Mac looked at her. She was right. Of course she was right. He was wound too tightly to go at this logically. He passed the sheet of information to her. "You're right. You call her and set something up."

Ramsey took the paper from him and made the call, her voice polite and calming, while Mac leaned against the wall. He used to be good with people, hadn't he?

Eventually Ramsey came over. "She'll see us now. We'll meet her at her apartment. She was on her way to work, but she'll turn around. She has a new address. I got directions."

They fought the rush hour traffic through the city. When they passed through the victim's old neighborhood, Mac made note of the location. It wasn't close to any of the other cases. It seemed as if the guy deliberately went hunting in a new spot each time. Maybe they could do something with that, anticipate where he might go next by eliminating where he had already been.

This woman's new apartment was in a nice high-rise with a doorman. It was a sleek, modern building, with an open lobby fronted by glass. Lights were bright, even in the daytime, and the doorman was alert and conscientious. He buzzed the woman's apartment, checked ID, and let them in. The elevator rose quickly and quietly to the seventeenth floor.

The woman who opened the door was another tall blonde, although a little older than any of the other victims. She was well dressed, fashionable and carefully put together. Her golden hair was pulled back in a tight bun. The look on her face was tight, too. They showed her their badges, and Mac let Ramsey go ahead of him into the apartment.

Ramsey wandered over to the floor-to-ceiling windows that brightened the living room. "Wow, that's a great view," she said.

"Yes, isn't it," the woman responded quietly. She sat carefully on her couch, posture erect and composed, but her hands wound themselves over and around each other in her lap.

"Look," she said abruptly. "I don't want to do small talk, or easing into this conversation. You said you had questions for me that could tie into a murder. I want you to ask your questions and then I want you to go."

"Okay," Mac said as softly as he could. He sat on the easy chair and leaned forward a little. "I'm sorry that we have to bring your attack up again. I'm sure you must find it difficult to talk about. As you know, we had enough physical evidence in your case to get DNA on the man who attacked you."

"Yes," the woman said painfully.

"Well, we matched that DNA," Mac told her, "But not to a known suspect. Miss Klein, we matched it to the unknown killer in three recent murder cases."

"Three?" Her voice was barely a thread. "Not..."

"Yes. The ones the media is calling the dagger killings. Based on the evidence, the man who attacked you is the same man who killed those three women."

Emily Klein's mouth moved silently.

"So," Mac told her, "We need to ask you some more questions, to see if there is any connection between you and those three women that might help us catch this guy."

"If I can help," she whispered.

"In the other cases, the women had been out to a bar and probably brought the killer home, but that wasn't the case with you."

"No," she said. "I was coming home from work and he was waiting for me."

"This is a much nicer building than any of the other locations," Mac commented, with a question in his voice.

"Where I was living then wasn't like this. I moved the next day; took all the savings I had and...anyway I got this place, high up with a doorman and security. When it happened, I was in a ground floor apartment in a small building."

"I see. This must feel safer."

"Yes." The expression on Emily Klein's face said she didn't feel safe anywhere.

"When was the last time you had been to a bar, before that

night?"

"Um, the weekend before. I usually went out on Saturdays with friends."

"Do you remember where you went?"

"Grumpy's. It was a goodbye thing for Lisa. She got a part in New York and we got together to see her off."

"A part? Are you an actor?"

Klein smiled tiredly. "I thought I was then, or was going to be. I'm a receptionist at a law firm now."

"Do you remember if any men came on to you at the bar, or seemed particularly interested in you?"

"Yeah, the cops asked that last time too. There were several of us, all actors. We got hit on pretty steady, all night, but we weren't interested because we were spending time with Lisa, not looking for guys. I couldn't remember anyone specific."

Mac pulled out the sketch they were circulating. "Does this guy look familiar?"

Klein took it. The paper rustled a little as her fingers shook. "Is this the man?"

"We don't know," Mac told her. "Maybe it's close."

Klein looked at the picture steadily for a minute then offered it back to Mac. "It looks a little familiar, but I'm not sure. I wasn't paying much attention to the men that night, you know."

"That's okay. We'll ask around the bar too." He leaned his elbows on his knees, to lower his head, and said softly, "Miss Klein, I hate to ask you again, and I know you've been through this too much already, but I want you to tell me anything you can about the man who attacked you. Please."

She breathed out hard and closed her eyes. "And then you'll go?"

"Yes." *For now.*

"He grabbed me from behind," she said, "And pushed me down on my face. I never saw him. I think he was tall but not fat, maybe even skinny. He whispered stuff, insults, called me a slut, said I was out looking for it and now I was going to get it." Her breath caught in a sob, but she went on steadily. "He had whiskey or rum or something on his breath. There was nothing special about his voice. When he was done, he put his hands around my neck and I passed out. By the time I came to, he was gone. After a while I made it to my neighbor's place."

Mac sighed but kept it silent. The height would fit, but there was nothing new. The drink meant he might have been at a bar, probably not too far from the scene of the attack. But he also could have had a solitary bottle in a car somewhere. They could canvass the bars.

He asked her about the places the other victims had worked, shopped, drunk and cruised for men. There was very little overlap. At most, she might have once shopped in the Hot Topic where Terri Brand had worked, but years earlier. She had spent some time around the U, but not in the right years or right departments. However the killer was choosing his victims, it wasn't through any obvious connections.

Mac showed Klein the additional photos of the other victims, pulled from framed shots and family albums. Terri Brand with her hair streaked pink and cut short, Cindy Kowalski in three-quarter profile, looking sad, Sandy holding a younger Ben. She leafed through them, her face impassive even though the pages trembled in her hand. Eventually she shook her head. "I'm pretty sure I've never met any of them, not to talk to."

"Is there anything else you can tell us?"

"He took my purse," she said eventually. "I…it was another reason I moved right away. He had my keys, my ID. Everything."

"Did you ever find out if he did come back looking for you or used your credit cards or anything else from your purse?"

She shuddered. "No. No, I cancelled everything and had a moving company pack up my stuff and I never went back."

No chance the killer was still getting cash that could be traced that way then. "You're sure all your cards were deactivated?"

"Oh, yes."

Ramsey suddenly leaned forward and said, "Did you by any chance have a…self-defense weapon in your purse at the time? Pepper spray or anything?"

"For all the good it did me?" Klein's lip twisted. "Yeah, somewhere in the bottom of my bag I had this dagger thing my boyfriend bought me the year we played travelling minstrels at the Renaissance Faire. When it…happened…I never even got the chance to open my purse, let alone grab the dagger. I carry pepper spray now that fits in my pocket."

Mac forgave Ramsey for the shit-eating grin she couldn't quite suppress. "Good catch, Linda. Can you describe the dagger, Miss Klein?"

"It was matte grey metal, triangular, dull not sharp. I was told it was legal to carry."

"Yes. Don't worry about that. How big was it?"

"I don't know. This long?" She held her hands about nine inches apart. "It was kind of pretty, well-made. It had a little hilt with leather wrapping and a clear crystal set on the end…" Her voice trailed off as she stared at Mac. "That's not what…I stay away from the news, it's too sad, I can't listen to it, but it's hard to avoid. They said those women, he stabbed them?"

"Yes."

"With…my knife?"

"It's possible," Mac said gently.

"No. God, no." She put her hand over her mouth. "It was just for self-defense, not meant…such a small thing. And he took it and…" Her throat worked convulsively.

They were keeping the details of the cases under wraps, but Mac said quietly, "Even if he is using your knife, it's not the thing he's killing them with. I promise you."

"You're sure?"

"Yes."

"But he may have it, use it?"

"He may."

Klein turned toward the window, staring blindly ahead. She blinked, over and over. Mac could almost see new nightmares forming. "Is there someone who could come stay with you?"

She shuddered and sat straighter, visibly pulling herself together. "I'm fine detective. I need to get to work now. Is that all you wanted to know?"

"The name of the man who originally bought you the knife?"

"Colby Masters. But I lost touch with him. I can't tell you where he is now."

"That's all right." It was probably a minor detail. "If there's anything else, can we contact you again?"

She nodded silently.

"Thank you, Miss Klein," he said finally. "I know this is difficult for you, and I appreciate your help."

"I wish I could help more," she said. "I wish you could catch this man. Maybe then I would sleep." She looked at Mac, and her grey eyes momentarily looked so tired.

"We'll get this guy," Mac promised earnestly. "Can't promise when, but we will."

"Yeah. Now that people are dead, I guess they're pulling out all the stops, huh."

"Now that we have more clues," Mac said gently, "we can make some progress. Your case was always important. Cindy Kowalski was important. Terri Brand was important. But we just aren't there yet. Every cop on the force would give his or her right arm to make the arrest now, before anyone else gets hurt or killed."

"Okay," Klein said. "Okay." She rose to show them out. At the door she looked up at Mac. "Will you tell me, when you get him?"

"I'm sure you'll know. The press is all over the murders, but yes, I will call you."

"Thank you," she said.

In the elevator down, Mac gave Ramsey a light punch in the arm. "You just might make a detective yet. Call Oliver and tell him we've got the weapon nailed. We'll get on to those sword-makers, see if we can find out exactly what one of them sold to Colby Masters."

"Why do you think he's still using her knife, instead of something better? That was months ago."

Mac tried to get into serial killer mode. They really needed to get a professional profiler in to address shit like this. Oliver had a request in with the FBI, but in the meantime they were getting by with their own half-assed guesses. "Maybe it's a kind of fuck-you to the women, like, 'you thought this would keep you safe and now I'm turning it against you.' Or maybe…maybe he just likes it. You heard how she described it. It's kind of fancy and medieval-looking. He's not killing them with it. It's more like a ritual. A blade like that might feel more appropriate for a kind of crucifixion than a kitchen knife or even a hunting knife."

Ramsey nodded slowly. "So, now we know where it came from but…it doesn't help much, does it?"

"Hey. Every piece of the puzzle is good. Maybe he's crazy about clear crystals and we'll find him that way. You never know. It was pretty sharp of you to connect the purse and the knife that fast."

Ramsey tried and failed to look humble. "You would have asked about it if I hadn't."

"Well, of course." Mac laughed. "Nah, I was a step behind you. It's a good thing I brought you along. I'm sure it helped get Klein to open up for us too."

"She seemed to talk to you just fine."

"She might not have if you hadn't been with me. She might not even have let a man alone into her apartment, cop or not." Because Emily Kline might have survived her attack, but she hadn't escaped unwounded.

Looking up the address where the rape had happened, they began searching for bars around that area. They took down addresses while they waited for the hour to get late enough for places to open. When the bars finally started opening, they began at Grumpy's. They struck out with the sketch, but the staff opening the place for the lunch crowd were not the people who worked the evening shift. Mac made a note to come back later. They gradually went down the list.

It was at the seventh place, getting far enough from the crime scene that Mac had almost passed it by, that they found a bartender who looked at the sketch and said, "Yeah, that guy looks familiar."

Mac blinked. "You know him?"

"Not sure," the man said. "Hey, Lou?" A tall, generously built woman left off cleaning tables and came over to them. The bartender passed her the sketch. "Doesn't that look like that Leonard guy that used to come in, a few months back?"

The woman glanced at the sketch, then with a slightly sheepish look at Mac, pulled a pair of reading glasses out of her apron pocket and looked again.

"Yeah," she agreed. "Looks a lot like him. There's something not right about it, though."

Mac dropped onto one of the bar stools and pulled out his notebook. "Tell me about this Leonard guy," he said urgently.

They looked at each other. "Rum drinker, not too heavy. Never saw him really drunk. He would come in by himself, evenings usually."

"He used to hit on girls," the woman said tentatively. "This was maybe five, six months back. Mid-winter. He liked the ones who drank, the ones where he thought he might get lucky."

"The women didn't object," the bartender said. "He seemed okay, decent-looking, and he'd mostly sit down and talk to them, buy them a drink. But that vibe was there. You knew what he was after. Once he got a little insistent about seeing a girl out to her car, when she didn't want to be seen. It's my bar and I want the women coming in so I warned him off her. He was unpleasant about it, and after that he stopped coming around. I don't think I've seen him since spring."

"How tall was he?" Mac asked. "How big?"

"A little over six feet maybe," the bartender said. "On the skinny side."

Mac glanced at Ramsey. He knew they were both feeling the vibe that said they had something. "How did he dress?"

"Casual," Lou said when her husband hesitated. "Khakis or jeans, basic shirt, cowboy boots. Long overcoat in the winter."

"And his name was Leonard?"

"So he said," the bartender agreed. "Probably was true, because he got mad when I called him Lenny. Said it was Leonard, no nicknames."

"You don't have a last name?" Mac held his breath.

"Nope," the bartender said. *Of course not.* "But you know." The man looked thoughtful. "One time he used a credit card to pay for his drinks. He ran out of cash after he'd bought this girl a drink, and she got pissy about him asking her to pay for it, so he put it on a card."

"When? Do you remember when that was?"

"Last winter sometime." The man gave it some thought. "It was before March, because that's when I got the new credit card machine. We didn't used to do much card business. A bar used to be cash on the table. But it's getting to be more and more plastic, so in March I got one of those faster machines with the printer. Before that, it was the slow kind that you swipe, with the carbons. I remember swiping his card."

"Would your credit card service have those records?"

The bartender shrugged. "You know, I don't know what information they save. You could ask them. I used to just run the charge over the phone line and have the customer sign the slip."

Mac leaned forward. "Please say that you saved the slips."

"If it was after January first and before March," the man replied. "I still have the January and February stuff, for next year's taxes. The charge slips from the year before, I already shredded."

Mac puffed out a breath. "Would you be willing to let us look through the slips, to see if we can find this guy?"

"I don't know. We're supposed to keep that sort of thing confidential, with identity theft and all. I could get into trouble for letting you look at it."

"What has the guy done, that you want to find him?" Lou put in curiously.

"He's a suspect in a murder case," Ramsey told them when Mac hesitated.

"Murder!" Lou looked at the bartender. "He seemed like a pretty ordinary guy."

The bartender was looking speculatively at Mac. "Murder of a woman?"

"Yes."

"Hmm," the man said. "I'm not saying I ever thought he would do something like that, but there was something kind of... intense about the way he hit on girls." He sighed. "Okay, you can look. But if anyone complains, you have to promise me it's all legal."

"I promise," Mac said. He would call in and get whatever warrant was needed, but his hands were itching for those slips.

"I could get them for you tonight, after we close."

"I don't want to wait that long!"

"Look," the guy said. "I don't keep the old stuff here. It's in my office at home, and I live twenty minutes away. And I'm open for business and I have customers. I can't just walk out for an hour. I'm the only bartender."

Mac glanced around the bar. Two tables held pairs of men, finishing the job of lunchtime lubrication. There was a solitary woman sipping a beer, and an elderly man at the bar clearly trying to eavesdrop on their conversation. Not a big crowd. "Ramsey can watch the bar for you," Mac offered recklessly, "While you get the stuff."

Ramsey choked and stared at him. "I don't know how to tend bar!" she said, her voice squeaking a little. "I can barely open a can of beer."

"You joined the department to learn new things," Mac teased her. But that would hardly be convincing to a man concerned about his business. "All right, I'll tend bar and you go with Mr…" He looked questioningly at the bartender.

"Christopher, Tom Christopher. Lou is my wife. But I don't know… Do *you* know how to tend bar?"

"I can get by," Mac said confidently. He'd been in a lot of bars, and this wasn't high-end chi-chi drink territory. How hard could it be? "I'm sure Lou can set me straight, if necessary." He aimed his very best smile at her.

"Go get the slips, Tom," the woman told her husband, smiling a little. "I can tell we're not going to get rid of this very large cop until you do."

"Um, all right," the bartender agreed reluctantly. "Can I see your ID again?"

Mac and Ramsey both passed over their ID folders and the man made a written note of the names and numbers. Mac handed him a business card with phone numbers as well. Eventually, after more fiddling around than he thought he could stand, including a tour of the back of the bar to acquaint him with the booze, the man followed Ramsey out the door. Mac called the precinct, to bring Oliver up to date and set him onto the necessary legalities, and then moved into place behind the bar.

The old man had begun beckoning impatiently, and Mac headed over to him. He provided a refill of the man's whiskey, and dodged questions about who he was and why he was there. He wasn't sure what Severs would say about his moonlighting as a bartender, but he knew how much he wanted to see those credit slips.

The post-lunchtime lull kept things from getting too hectic. Mac found that if he didn't recognize a request, a nice smile and asking the customer to help out a confused newbie mostly worked. Lou shook her head once at the volume of liquor a customer convinced him went into a gin sling. Mac pulled out his own wallet and laid a couple of twenties on the ledge under the bar to cover losses from his inexperience. She glanced at the money and let him off with a smile and a pat on the ass.

Hanson called back from headquarters after half an hour to tell him the credit card slip search had been okayed by the legal guys. Ramsey and Christopher returned after forty-five minutes with a big envelope in Ramsey's hand. Mac eagerly surrendered his position behind the bar.

"Could you look at those slips here in the building?" the bartender asked. "I'd feel better if you didn't walk off with all of them. There's a little room in back."

"Sure," Mac agreed. "Lead us to it."

The little office had a scarred desk and two old chairs, and very deficient air conditioning. The bartender swept the papers from the top of the desk into a cardboard box and left them to it. Mac and Ramsey pulled up seats and put on gloves, in case any prints might be found on the slips. Ramsey drew the rubber-banded packets of paper out of the envelope. They each seized one batch and began to flip through.

"I wish he'd pressed harder on the cards," Ramsey muttered after a minute. "Some of these are hard to read."

"Just be glad he had them," Mac told her. "And that the guy's name wasn't David or Michael."

"I guess." After ten minutes, Ramsey sat up with a yelp. "This one!" She shoved it under Mac's nose. "That says Leonard, right?"

"Looks like it," Mac agreed, controlling his own excitement. "Pull it out and put it aside, and keep looking. Leonard's not *that* rare of a name around here."

"Oh, yeah," Ramsey agreed, a little more subdued.

About an hour later they had finished with the slips and found four Leonards, and one possible, indecipherable and beginning with Le. Mac carefully returned the rest of the slips to the envelope and went up front.

It was pushing happy hour and the bar was getting busy. Mac watched Christopher execute a smooth path from one customer to another, handling drink requests and light conversation. Mac decided there was more to being a bartender than he had realized. Christopher caught sight of them and came over.

"You found something?"

"Five slips we want to pursue further," Mac told him. "Where do you want the rest?"

"Leave them on the desk." Christopher eyed the slips in his hand. "Can you give me a receipt for those? Or maybe copies? There's a print shop down the street that should be open."

Mac left Ramsey in the bar as a kind of security deposit while he made a quick run to the print shop to get copies of the slips. One he gave to the bartender with Mac's written receipt and signature on it. Another he had the bartender sign as further proof of the provenance of his evidence. This case was not going to get thrown out for any failure on his part to document evidence.

By the time they hit the car, he was revved. "Call those names in," he told Ramsey as they pulled away. "Get Hanson or someone running them down: age, height, weight, DMV photos." They had missed the five o'clock case review, but who cared if they finally had a lead. He could only hear her side of the conversation, but he could tell when the tone went from a dressing down for being late, to Oliver catching their excitement.

Oliver was hanging over Hanson's shoulder at the best computer the department had when they came in. He glanced up.

"Hey, Golden Boy. Get your ass over here."

Mac tried to see the screen over Oliver's shoulder. "Anything?"

"We've eliminated two for age," Hanson said, working the keyboard. "I'm going for the other photos now."

The first was a heavy blond middle-aged man with a crooked nose that had them all shaking their heads, the second bore a superficial resemblance to the sketch, but the third was greeted with intakes of breath, followed by profanity and high-fives. Mac stared at the screen. This was as close as you got with an ID sketch. The face was longer, the jaw less square than in the drawing, and the nose was less regular. But it was as close as a portrait drawn by a good amateur artist.

"Your cross-dressing actor was fucking golden. Name, address, all that shit." Oliver grinned. "Get it down and let's get this guy."

Hanson pulled the information up on the screen. Leonard Anderson, thirty-two, six-one, one-sixty, white, brown on brown, with an address in St. Louis Park.

"Okay," Oliver said. "We need to think this through. Probable cause. Do we have enough to arrest this guy? Where's our ID coming from?"

"The sketch came from the assault on that transvestite," Hanson said.

"He was seen around the vicinity of the connected rape," Mac continued. "Height and weight fit the description of the rapist. But no," he admitted. "We need something more solid. We can talk to the guy, but if he won't consent to come in, all we'll have done is warn him." His gut told him they were on the right track. Unfortunately that was not admissible in court.

"What about the St. Paul murder?" Oliver asked Loes. "Any help for us there?"

"Not much. The dumb asses in SPPD didn't have jack shit. They'd cold-cased it. The victim was Nicole Simmons, blond and blue, twenty-two, so she fits the profile. She wasn't a full-time hooker but word was she would put out for money. Her body wasn't found for almost two weeks so the forensics weren't great. But those SPPD guys should have given us the case as soon as we went public, because she was strangled. Their ME thinks she fought the guy and they fell, so she was actually killed by head trauma in the fall, but his hands were around her neck just before she died. And then she was stabbed. Not in the chest, but through the hands and feet. The ME said like a crucifixion. But he made a mess of the feet, did a couple of attempts and hit bone or something. They had thought he used a spike, and then took it away with him when he botched the job. But it fits our knife. You *know* the guys working that case saw the connection. They just didn't want to hand it off to us. Pair of assholes. If our captain hadn't gotten on to their captain, they would still be stonewalling us."

"But they had no leads we could tie into Anderson?"

"Not a damn thing."

"We need something solid enough to haul Anderson's ass in and hold him, whether he comes willingly or not," Mac muttered.

"So we'll get it," Oliver said. "Hanson, print copies of the photo and put together a photo line-up for it. We'll get our dress-wearing friend to confirm the ID. Get that credit slip down to the lab for prints. If we're really lucky, he put a finger on it when he signed it that we can match to one of the murders. Take copies of the photo to our witnesses who refined the sketch, and our rape victim, and out to the bars again. People didn't recognize the sketch, but it's not perfect. All we need is someone to put a victim with this guy and we can at least bring him in for questioning without him having the option to refuse."

"If Sinclair can ID the guy," Mac said, "We can arrest him on the assault, print him, and we'll have it."

"Perfect," Loes said. "You go talk to the fairy and convince him to cooperate. He likes you."

"Sinclair's yours," Oliver confirmed to Mac. "Take Ramsey." He divided up the other tasks and the detectives scattered to follow up.

Unfortunately, it was not going to be that simple. Sinclair wasn't answering his phone, either home or cell. When Mac headed down to the Guthrie Theater a performance was in progress, but he was told that Sinclair was in daytime rehearsals for the next show, not one of the current ones. No one could tell him where the man was likely to be that evening. He camped out by the man's apartment to watch. After an hour, he sent Ramsey home. At two-thirty in the morning, he gave up the vigil. It appeared Sinclair had found some other bed for the night. *Lucky man.*

On top of the witness's disappearance, the team sent to find and follow Leonard Anderson had come up empty. The address on his driver's license and car registration was now rented by a young black couple who had never met the previous tenant. The landlord, roused from a stupor in front of his TV, claimed he barely recognized the picture of Anderson. He managed a grunt about "Paid his rent on time," and had no forwarding address. The job listed on Anderson's rental application, once it was dug out of the landlord's haphazard files, had closed five months earlier in the slow economy.

Oliver called Mac to vent. He'd set Hanson on the trail of their suspect in the wide vista of the Internet. They would check with the clerks at unemployment tomorrow and see if the man had applied. They could go after his auto insurance and credit cards, looking for recent use and a new address. Without a warrant, though, some information would be unavailable, at least legally. They needed Sinclair. Who was apparently not showing up tonight.

Mac drove back to his own cruddy apartment and bounced off the walls. The place seemed to close in on him. He wanted to be out there, doing something useful, but Minneapolis's sidewalks were pretty firmly rolled up at this hour. And if he couldn't be useful, he wanted Tony.

He had come to count on having Tony there. He could vent, and Tony would sympathize, or distract him, or laugh and throw pillows at him until… Mac took his frustrations into the shower. Standing under the meager flow, hard as iron from wanting something he couldn't have, he tried to laugh at himself and failed. He let himself remember Tony. Remember that first time when Tony kissed him, all pale skin, bandages and bruises and laughing blue eyes and white-hot need. He would never have made that first move, but Tony's mouth on his was electric. And when Tony invited him, begged him… Mac stroked himself hard, lost in the vivid recall of smooth muscle and soft heat. It had never been like that before. Tony's hands, and Tony's voice, and the smell of his skin… Mac worked himself, eyes closed, until he came in his hand, spilling between his fingers. It was a relief, but it wasn't Tony.

He made himself eat, and lie down on his bed for a couple of hours, but sleep escaped him. Mac had been keeping track. Tomorrow Tony would be in court, trying to convince a judge to look beyond the obvious and do the right thing for Ben. If Tony failed then maybe, just maybe, he would be willing to step back into the closet again. Mac tried hard not to let himself hope for that. He was not going to be that damned selfish. If Tony failed to keep Ben, he would be devastated. Mac knew Ben's grandparents had always been distant, and periodically at war with Sandy. The boy would survive with them, but it would be hard on him.

Mac wondered if he should go to the hearing after all. If there was something he could have done to help Tony and Ben and he wasn't there… but Tony had told him without ambiguity to stay away. The battered suitcase with Sandy's adult possessions in it still stood by the door of Mac's place. He'd figured Ben didn't need that stuff in temporary housing. He could bring it along, as an excuse to show up. The ideas circled in Mac's brain, no more productive than his obsessing about the case.

By six AM he was back at the office to check in. There was a message from Oliver that a uniformed officer had been set to watch Sinclair's home, and call them when the man showed. The team trying to track Anderson down was having no luck so far. It didn't help that he had one of the most common surnames in Minnesota. Mac left another message on Sinclair's voice mail, and began his written report on the actions of the day before to keep his hands busy.

CHAPTER 10

Tony glanced around the courtroom as he and Sabrina entered. It was shabbier and much smaller than he had expected from exposure to TV. There was very little room for spectators. But it made sense that family court would not be the drama that a criminal court was.

The only surviving defendant of last fall's hostage disaster had taken a plea bargain, so Tony had never had to testify in court. He could have quite happily gone a lifetime that way. Even here, there was an oppressive weight to the place. The walls seemed close and high.

They followed the gesture of the bailiff directing them to a table in front of the bench. The Thompsons came in after them, moving to a second table and chairs. The judge was already seated, watching them enter. No one sat down. The bailiff announced the case and the Honorable Sharon Crowley presiding. She beckoned impatiently at them.

"Everyone approach the bench. I don't want to yell."

When they were standing in front of her, she eyed them over her glasses, and said, "I run a pretty informal court in cases like this. I expect you to answer my questions completely and avoid unnecessary comments. This is not the place to insult each other. If you waste my time you will regret it. Now, I'm going to have you introduce yourselves." She pointed first at Ben's grandparents.

"I'm Samuel Thompson, and this is my wife Arlene," the grey-haired man said. Tony eyed them, trying to keep his expression neutral. Neither one looked at him. "Ben Serrano is our grandchild, the child of our only daughter, and his place is with us, not some…stranger." He looked ready to comment further, but stopped when the judge held up her hand.

"Just introductions first," she said. She pointed at Tony. "You, sir?"

"I'm Anthony Hart," he said, "And this is Sabrina Cassidy. She's a lawyer, but she's mostly here as a friend."

"Okay," the judge agreed. "Mr. Thompson, do you have any legal representation with you?"

"No," the man said. "Didn't think we'd need one. It should be obvious. Boy's our flesh and blood. He belongs with us."

"Few things are that obvious," the judge said tartly, "Or I wouldn't need to be here. All right, let's get started. I've read the case files." She patted a pile of papers under her hand. "I like cases like this, where I'm choosing between two possible homes for a child. Sometimes I don't have this luxury. All of you seem genuine in your desire to give the boy a home and family, and the caseworker does not consider either option completely unacceptable. I do have some questions for each of you, though, about details in these files." She opened a page.

"Mrs. Thompson first." The judge ran her finger over a line and then looked sharply at Arlene Thompson. "I'm aware that you are currently attending AA meetings, and your physician and testing confirm that you have been sober for quite some time."

"Over a year," Mr. Thompson put in.

"Yes. However, your doctor also reports that over the past fifteen years you have been sober for periods ranging from a couple of months to almost three years, on four different occasions. Each time you eventually relapsed, and you have been drinking heavily for more years than you've been sober. What can you say to convince me that you will maintain sobriety this time, if I give you custody of a small boy?"

"Doctor shouldn't have told you that," Mr. Thompson muttered. "That's all long past."

"This is exactly the kind of information he is supposed to give me," the judge said sharply, "And you signed the waivers to allow it. Mrs. Thompson? Do you have any comment?"

"I've put my recovery in the Lord's hands," Arlene said softly. "This time I know what I'm doing. And having Ben would be the best thing for me. Having to do something for a child is easier than doing it just for yourself. I am never going to drink again. God and my husband will help keep me from temptation."

"Only you can keep yourself from temptation," the judge said, although her voice was kinder. "And I do note that fifteen years ago, when you apparently began drinking excessively, you had a young child in the house."

"Sandy was a rebellious girl, especially as a teenager," Samuel Thompson told her. "Difficult and wild. My wife will not be tempted the same way with Ben in the house."

"You may be underestimating the difficulties of a traumatized six-year-old," the judge told him. There was a sound from the back of the room and the judge glanced up, but then looked back at her papers. "Speaking of which, the foster parents took Ben to a doctor. You will be relieved to know that there was no medical evidence of physical or sexual abuse in the boy's past. However his behavior, particularly…" She glanced at the paper. "His tendency to sleep in the closet rather than in his bed, is suggestive of possible sexual abuse. What do you plan to do to help him?"

"He needs a decent home," Mr. Thompson replied. "Sandy was wild as a grown woman too. The boy needs a place in a decent, God-fearing home where he isn't exposed to perversion and sex, and he'll be fine." He turned a twisted glare on Tony as he spoke.

The judge gave him a flat look, and glanced over at Tony. "Mr. Hart?"

Tony had prepared for this. "I asked a friend of mine to get a list of recommended child therapists," he said. "I was worried myself, because in the two days I had him, he made a comment about a man coming into his room when his mother was drunk. I don't think Sandy would have committed or allowed regular abuse. She loved Ben. But if she was drunk, she may not have protected him. I think something happened. I found a therapist who is taking new patients and made an appointment with her for Ben for Friday. I hope that if he ends up with the Thompsons, they will still be willing to take advantage of it, since it was hard to find an opening."

The judge nodded. "Mr. Thompson?"

"If he really needs to see a doctor, we'll pick out someone ourselves," Samuel Thompson said grudgingly. "But Ben seems fine to me. He doesn't need a shrink. He just needs good care in a decent home. Which he's not going to get with that…man." He spat out the word, in obvious lieu of a worse one. "The boy is no relation of his," he added. "What kind of life would a boy have in his house, exposed to all that perversion, men going in and out, hell, half of them probably pedophiles?"

"Mr. Thompson," the judge said warningly. "I warned you about insults when we started here. My decision will be based on facts, not your opinions and innuendo." She turned to Tony. "I do have some questions for you, however."

It was Tony's turn to face her penetrating gaze. "You state that you are currently single, have no boyfriend or significant other." She focused a quick glare on Arlene Thompson for her disgusted snort at the word boyfriend, and then looked back at Tony.

"That's right," Tony said.

"You're surely not planning to stay celibate for the next twelve years," she said mildly.

"No," Tony told her. "Although I'm in no hurry to find a new relationship. Taking care of a little boy is likely to take all of my energy for quite a while. However I do hope to go out and date some day. And I will be dating men." He turned a defiant look on the Thompsons, and then ignored them. Their opinion was not what mattered here. "If I get into a serious relationship, I'm sure sex will be part of it. But it will be discrete, when Ben is sleeping or out, it will take place behind locked doors, and will involve a man I have feelings for, not a one-night-stand. In fact, it will be just like what the Thompsons would do, since I doubt Samuel is planning to be celibate for the next twelve years either."

Mr. Thompson growled, "How dare you compare your perversion with the relations of a man and woman in a marriage!"

Tony ignored him, looking back at the judge quietly. She gave a little nod and glanced down at the papers in front of her again.

"Your friends and co-workers would seem to agree," she said. "Your references were very positive. I'm not totally sanguine about giving a small boy to a single man to raise, partly because I think you may underestimate the sheer work involved in single parenting. But as a teacher you have plenty of experience with youngsters." She paused, and Tony's growing optimism was frozen by the look in her eyes.

"You list your last relationship as lasting almost a year, and ending May a year ago. Is that correct?"

Tony licked his lips and chose wording to negotiate around this without lying. *Damn Mac for putting him in this position, weaseling around the truth with his words.* "I had a relationship with another man that ended at that time, yes."

"Then explain for me," the judge said, "Why you gave me results for an HIV test taken more than ten months later, and why one of your neighbors reports that you have had a series of men entering and leaving your apartment at all hours of night this past year."

Tony froze. *Because Mrs. Travers is a sanctimonious bitch with way too much time on her hands.* He was fumbling for something to say when a thin but recognizable voice from behind him said, "Your Honor, that wasn't a series of men; that was me."

The voice caught Tony in the gut. He didn't turn, didn't look back. He felt Sabrina beside him whirl around, but he kept his own gaze fixed on the pattern of the carved wood across the judge's bench. Mac would say what he was going to say, and Tony was not going to ask for one more word or one less from him. He didn't know if this would save him, or damn them both. His pulse was loud in his ears, almost drowning out the sound of Mac's footsteps as he approached.

"I saw you come in," the judge said, "and assumed you had a role in this case, since the bailiff let you attend. This was not what I was expecting." She squinted at Mac. "You look familiar. What's your name?"

Mac had stopped beside Tony, not quite close enough to touch. Tony was electrically aware of the bulk of the big man standing there.

"I'm Jared MacLean."

"Have you come before me in the past?" the judge asked.

"As a witness, Your Honor," Mac said. His voice was less tight, easing into the deep rumble that Tony had missed. "I believe I brought cases up before you several times, when you were in traffic court and I was in uniform."

"Ah, yes. Officer MacLean. I do remember. What are you doing these days, officer?"

"I work MPD Homicide," Mac told her.

"Detective MacLean, then. And you spend time at night with this young man, who has been less than honest with me."

"That was my fault, Your Honor," Mac said urgently. "I think if you look at Tony's statements, you'll find that he never told an outright lie, even if he bent the truth sometimes to protect me."

"Protect you?"

"I have not been open," Mac said tautly. "About my sexuality. I have a job working with people who are not...who are sometimes judgmental of...non-heterosexuals. I have a childcare provider for my small daughter who is very fundamentalist in her religion. For a variety of reasons I asked Tony to keep our relationship a secret, and he did so. He...we stopped seeing each other when the issue of custody for Ben came up. I wanted to remain...unknown, and Tony promised to try to keep my name out of things."

"Apparently he did. May I ask why you're here now?"

"I know Tony and I know Ben Serrano," Mac said. "I was afraid that if you didn't have good information, you might make the wrong decision here. And I was afraid that what I was asking of Tony would end up putting him between a rock and a hard place if the subject came up. I didn't want to be the reason Tony failed to get custody of Ben."

"So you think Ben belongs with Mr. Hart?"

"I do, Your Honor," Mac said firmly. He lifted the bag he was holding and took out a thick album. "I submit as evidence Sandy's, Alexandra Thompson's, photo album. I took it from her apartment to keep it safe for her son."

The judge nodded slowly. "And?"

"If you look through this, you'll find seventeen photos of Tony with Ben, from that first day in the hospital, to last month playing in a sprinkler at the park. You'll also find thirty-six photos noted as being taken by Tony. They show Ben's first swing ride, Ben's first tooth, Ben's first time on a tricycle. There are only six photos of Ben with his grandparents, and each one is a formal posed shot with a birthday cake or Christmas tree. It's Tony who has been a part of Ben's life.

"I've known the man for a year, and there's not a week that he didn't spend time with Ben. When Ben outgrew his sneakers, Tony got him new ones. When Ben fell out of a tree and needed five stitches, Tony took him to the emergency room. Sandy only stayed around long enough to sign the forms, because she hated the sight of blood. Tony held Ben's hand while the work was done. Ben showed those stitches to everyone for a week. I'm betting his grandparents don't even know where the cut was."

The judge turned to the Thompsons with a questioning look, and received only a scowl in return.

"Tony is Ben's father in all but blood," Mac said. "That little boy has lost enough. He shouldn't have to lose Tony too."

"That's very eloquent, Detective," the judge said. "Tell me, if Tony Hart gets custody of Ben, what will your role be?"

Tony was wondering that too. He let himself turn a little, to see Mac's face more clearly. He saw Mac swallow hard. "I don't know, Your Honor."

"But you do have a relationship, a sexual relationship, with Mr. Hart?"

"I did," Mac said. "We broke up, because I didn't want to

come out, and Tony wanted to be able to tell the truth when he said he had no current, um, significant other. I don't know where we go from here."

"You didn't come here to try to get back together?"

"I came here to show you the album, and make the case for Ben and Tony," Mac said. "I think I was still hoping I wouldn't have to…out myself, like that. I wasn't thinking past this."

"Well I suggest you do some more thinking," the judge said tartly. "Both of you." She frowned at Tony. "I'm going to retire to my chambers and make a few phone calls, mainly to check you out, Detective, since you clearly are part of this situation and you failed to give us that opportunity previously. Then I'll come back with my decision." She stood and headed out, but paused for a moment to look back. "I assume they call you Mac?" she asked cryptically.

"Yes, Your Honor," Mac agreed.

"Mm," she said, and left the room.

Tony turned to look at Mac at last, but was distracted by Sabrina's hard kick on his shins. "You secretive son of a bitch," she said. "You've been holding out on me!"

"I've been holding out on everyone," Tony sighed. This was a bigger mess than he had ever imagined. He gestured indistinctly between his two friends. "Sabrina Cassidy, Jared MacLean. Mac, Bree."

Before they could shake hands, Samuel Thompson strode over and stabbed a finger into the middle of Mac's chest. "You should be ashamed of yourself," he hissed. "Call yourself a cop? You're a disgrace. You don't belong around clean, normal people. How dare you get in the middle of a family affair like this?"

"Let me handle this," Sabrina told a stunned-looking Mac. She forced herself between them. "Mr. Thompson," she said at top volume. "You are one inch away from being sued for harassment and assault. And I guarantee you will not get custody of a small boy if you go that far." Thompson glared at her, but backed off a little. Bree turned to Tony. "You two boys need to talk. Take the big hunk over in the corner while I keep an eye on Ma and Pa Kettle here."

Tony grabbed Mac's arm and towed him away toward the corner of the room. Mac came willingly, but seemed dazed. Tony stopped and turned them so that they faced away from the Thompsons. It wasn't privacy. It wasn't where he wanted to be to have this conversation, but it would have to do,

"So," Tony started, "I didn't expect to see you here."

"I didn't expect to be here," Mac said quietly.

*Undoubtedly true, but not helpful.* "You were right about the rock and the hard place," Tony told him. "I'm not sure what I was going to say."

"Hopefully you would have given me up for Ben. Like you did before."

*Was that really true, or a subtle complaint?* "I'm really glad I didn't have to. So thank you." *And don't you dare say you're welcome, you son of a bitch.*

Mac didn't say anything, which was only marginally better.

"You're not really out, you know," Tony suggested eventually. "This is a pretty small group. You can probably go back to your closet safely."

Mac shook his head wearily and didn't take the bait. "The bailiff knows me. And word will go round eventually. I'm out."

"Okay," Tony said softly. "And you're still standing. Now what?"

"I don't know," Mac admitted. He looked tired, and lost. Tony had a boatload of hurt and anger built up, but it couldn't last with Mac looking like a scared little boy. Tony wanted to put his arms around the man, but not here and now. It would just make things worse.

"Are we going to start seeing each other again?" Tony wasn't sure what he wanted to hear.

"God, I hope so," Mac said fervently. "It would make the

shit-storm that's coming worthwhile. But you have to believe that's not why I came. First you have to get Ben. Then we can see what's left for us."

"You are not less important to me than Ben," Tony felt compelled to tell him. "Only more able to survive on your own."

He got a small wry smile back at that. "Thank you for the vote of confidence."

The judge returning to the room kept Tony from having to find the next step in that conversation. She motioned them all over to the bench. Tony looked at her, trying to predict her decision from who she looked at. Unfortunately, her first look swept them all equally.

"I have learned," she said, "That the best way to predict future behavior is to look at past behavior. People change, but it's more rare than you'd think. Mrs. Thompson, your history of relapsing alcoholism concerns me. I admire the fact that you are currently sober, but I don't think having a traumatized, bereaved six-year-old in the house is likely to help you stay that way. Especially since you began to have drinking problems when you were raising a young child of your own. Alexandra's allegations in her will, accusing you and her father of emotional abuse, might be exaggerations, but they are definitely troubling to me. She ran away from you multiple times, beginning at a young age, and her situation was not handled well."

Arlene Thompson made a small inarticulate sound of protest and stopped at a wave of the judge's hand.

"I've also learned," the judge continued, "To give weight to the opinions of the child involved, when the right questions are asked. The caseworker spent some time talking to Ben."

"He's only a child," Mr. Thompson protested. "He'll want to live with whoever gave him more candy last time."

"You underestimate children," the judge told him. "I don't always do what the child wants, but I do listen. The caseworker asked Ben, if he had to go to the doctor for a scary procedure, who would he want to have with him? He said, 'Tony.' She asked, if he woke up from a nightmare, who would he feel best about telling it to? He said, 'Tony.' She asked, if he had a problem with a bully at school and he needed help figuring out what to do, who would he ask? He said, 'Tony.'

"Note that when she asked him who usually gave him the best presents at Christmas, he said, 'Grandpa.' He's not just picking the person he gets the most stuff from." She turned to look at Tony, and then at Mac. "You might also note that when she asked who would be best to protect him from something scary, he said, 'Mac.' I was going to ask you who Mac was, until that question answered itself. He says Mac keeps everyone safe."

She straightened the papers on her desk then looked at Tony. "Ben clearly thinks of you as his parent. If I don't have to worry about you having a secret sex life, I have few doubts about your suitability as a foster parent for this boy. In accordance with the terms of his mother's will I am therefore awarding temporary custody of Ben Serrano to Anthony Hart."

Tony swayed in relief, and saw Sabrina break into a grin.

"You can't!" Arlene Thompson protested. "It's not right. He's our grandson!"

"He is," the judge agreed. "And I am writing in your right to visitation in the agreement. I'm giving you two weekend days a month, which appears to be more time than you have spent with Ben over the past few years. Mr. Hart?" Tony looked up at her. "Do you agree to allow his grandparents regular access to visit with Ben?"

"Yes, Your Honor." Tony said hoarsely. "Of course. Although…I worry about what they will say to him…"

"Yes," the judge agreed. "Mr. and Mrs. Thompson, I have been aware of the comments you have made to and about Mr. Hart at this hearing, and also your statements about the boy's mother. If you want to spend time with Ben, you'll have to make an effort not to slander or insult his guardian or his mom. If Mr. Hart feels Ben is distressed by his visits to you, or if you are making Ben's life more difficult, Mr. Hart can petition to have your rights terminated."

"You mean this…person can keep us from even seeing our grandson?" Mr. Thompson demanded.

"If you make it necessary," the judge replied calmly.

"We'll just see about that," Thompson growled. "I'm going to get a good lawyer and get this changed. It's not right. No one in their right mind would choose that faggot over us." He grabbed his wife's arm. "Come along, Arlene. We'll find someone with the common decency to listen to us." He marched her out, and the bailiff, at a nod from the judge, let them through the door.

"Which is contempt of court, I guess," the judge said, "But hardly worth pursuing at this point." She looked at Tony. "You may have trouble with those two, but I would need more excuse than that to cut the boy off from his only blood relatives."

"No," Tony said. "Ben needs his grandparents, if they can live with this arrangement." He looked up at the judge. "When can I get Ben?"

She smiled at last, a warmer expression than he would have expected. "I imagine from reading the interviews that Ben is just as impatient as you are. The foster parents report he isn't sleeping well. Maybe he'll do better with you. You get the paperwork done and I'll have the caseworker bring him by your new apartment about five." She gave Tony a look that had a hint of sternness. "This is a temporary custody order, you understand. There will still be interviews and visits. If Detective MacLean moves into that big new apartment I read about, we'll need formal background checks on him as well."

"Yes, Your Honor," Tony said.

"I hope it will become permanent," she said. "Getting children into good homes is part of what I'm here for." She picked up a document from her desk, signed it, and passed a copy to Tony. "Take that to the records office on the third floor. They'll walk you through the paperwork. Now get out of my courtroom so I can tackle the next case."

"Thank you, Your Honor," Tony said intensely.

"Good luck," she told him. "To all of you. Dismissed." She waved a hand toward the door.

Tony followed Mac out, and wondered if it was his imagination or if the bailiff did step back a little from Mac as he passed through. In the hallway, he turned to Sabrina. "Wait here for me, okay Bree?"

He towed a reluctant Mac toward the nearest men's room. The restroom door closed behind them and Tony turned to Mac.

"Um, why are we in here?" Mac asked.

"Don't worry," Tony told him, wrapping his arms around his own middle so he wouldn't wrap them around Mac. "I'm not going to kiss you in a public toilet." He laughed shortly as Mac instinctively glanced around. "We're in here because it's as close to private as we're going to get, and you're wearing a totally freaked look."

"I'm not freaked," Mac said. "I'm scared shitless." He looked around the empty bathroom again. "Tony, what do I do now?"

"Relax," Tony told him. "You don't have to go back to work wearing a pink triangle. I wouldn't do anything at all. Once rumors start going around, you can just deny them, or...not. It will be plenty soon enough. Don't make a big deal out of it. It's no more their business now than it was when you were hiding it."

"People are going to wonder about Mai."

"Let them wonder. That's actually good. Some guys will be a lot more relaxed if they think you're bi than if you're gay."

Mac shook his head. "I don't know how to do this. Loes is going to kill me."

"There are always a few guys who are going to be a problem. I think you can handle Loes."

"I should tell Oliver first, though. Shouldn't I?"

Tony considered it. Oliver and Mac weren't extremely close, as partners went, but he knew they spent a lot of time together on the job, and occasionally shared a meal or evening in a bar. Oliver was as close to a real friend as Mac seemed to have.

"I guess so," he agreed. "How do you think he'll handle it?"

"No clue." Mac snorted a choked laugh. "Better than Loes."

"There is that." Tony gave Mac his best smile. Mac needed his support right now. Tony could consider killing him later. "You can come home and dump on me afterward."

Mac nodded. "And we're finally making progress on the case. Maybe everyone will be too busy to care."

"Tell me about it tonight," Tony invited. "Can you come by to welcome Ben home?"

"Not at five. I took some personal time to do this, but I've got a ton of work. I'll come by in the evening. It may be good for Ben to have time to settle down first anyway."

The door to the washroom opened and a tall, thin man came in. He looked at them blandly, and went into a stall.

"I have to get back to work," Mac said, with a glance at the closed stall door. "Good luck with the paperwork. I'll see you later."

"See you," Tony said softly at his retreating back. When Tony made it out the door, Mac was already down the hall.

"Argument?" Bree asked, tucking her arm through Tony's.

"Nope," Tony said. "He just has lots of work."

"Right," she told him. "You keep telling yourself that. Honey, that man is going to need some work himself."

Tony sighed. "Okay. Help me get Ben's paperwork filed and I'll tell you all about it." He realized suddenly, "I actually *can* tell you all about it."

"You'd better. You've been holding out on me big time. You were dating that guy. Then you broke up with him, and you've apparently been lying through your teeth for him, and now you're going to take him back, just like that? I can't believe you were willing to be on the down low in the first place."

"I didn't like it," Tony admitted. "But for Mac…I'd do most anything, for Mac."

"I gathered." Bree narrowed her eyes. "Aren't you mad at him for making you choose? For making you tell lies? You?"

"No!" Tony lied. Actually he was. He had been since he shut Mac's apartment door. Maybe a lot longer. Mad and sad and frustrated and scared and bitter, all in turns. He wasn't sure, when he got Mac alone again, if he was going to kiss him or kick him in the nuts. But one thing he was sure about. He wasn't going to let this man go, if there was any way in this wide world to keep him. He started walking again, feeling so light he might just float away. "Okay, yeah, I'm mad at him. But I'm also so in love with him it's hard to breathe sometimes. Mac has reasons, and issues, that kept him in the closet. And holy God, he just stepped out of it for me!" He felt the grin tug at the corners of his mouth. *Holy God.* "I can't wait to tell you."

"Let's get your paperwork done," Bree said. "I have to be back at the office by one. You can give me the highlights."

Tony headed for the stairs happily. He had the right to dish to Bree again, he was getting Ben, and Mac…well, he wasn't sure where he stood with Mac. But wherever it was, it was a whole hell of a lot better than that morning.

CHAPTER 11

Mac drove back to work carefully, obeying every traffic law. He watched the other drivers, noting every violation he saw. He had no intention of stopping anyone. It just kept his mind busy, kept him from looking at that place way in back of his head where he had the feeling he was panicking. What had he done? *What had he done!*

This whole morning he had been running on instinct. He'd brought the photo album to work with some vague idea of calling Tony and giving him the numbers of pictures and the idea to use it as evidence in his favor. He had checked the courthouse for information about when the hearing was. Time passed and he hadn't made the call.

When lunch break came, he'd found himself carrying the album into the courthouse, locating the room. The hearing was already in progress. He'd identified himself to the bailiff and observed from the back because he was interested…concerned. He'd heard the judge pin down Tony with that question, and stepped up. And stuff just came out of his mouth.

It was right. It was good. Ben would be safe with Tony, not suffering with the self-righteous grandparents who would probably teach him to hate his parents, and himself in the bargain. Mac had done a good thing. But he had to admit to himself, he was shit scared.

Tony said no one would probably find out. Mac knew better. The grapevine in law enforcement was second to none. That bailiff probably knew a dozen guys on the force. And then it would start. Cops who had been friends and co-workers the day before would cold-shoulder him, cross the room to avoid him, or worse. He had seen worse. And before it started he had to warn Oliver. Sometime. Soon.

The room was busy when he walked in, with the hum of a dozen different conversations. Oliver was at his own desk, talking to someone on his phone, but he waved Mac over with a circling motion as he spoke.

"Okay," he said into the phone as Mac came over. "Yeah, we're set for five o'clock." He hung up and looked up at Mac. "And where the hell have you been? We've got work to do."

"Took some personal time," Mac said blandly.

"To do what?"

He was allowed to say, *none of your business.* That's what personal time was for. But his partner was nosy and would push. He said, "I went over to the courthouse to make sure Tony Hart got custody of the boy, Ben Serrano. The grandparents were contesting it but the boy belongs with Hart."

"That's sick!" Loes' voice said from behind him.

Mac turned. "What is?" His stomach felt tight. *Was it starting already?*

"You helped some fag get custody of a small boy," Loes said angrily. "I can't believe you did that."

"Hey," Mac snapped. "Hart has been like that kid's dad since the day Ben was born."

"Who knows what he wants the kid for," Loes said.

"You're the one who's sick," Mac growled. "Hart is gay, he's not a pedophile."

"They're all weird. You never know what they're going to do. A single guy like that shouldn't be around a young boy."

"Jesus," Mac said in disgust. "That's like saying a single straight guy shouldn't be allowed to raise a young girl. You think I'm going to molest Anna?"

"No, Christ, keep your shirt on," Loes said. "That's not the same thing at all."

"It's exactly the same thing."

Oliver punched his arm. "Back off, MacLean. Loes is just being an asshole, like usual. No big deal. If you say Hart is good with the boy, I'm sure you're right."

Mac shook off the punch and bit back a retort. He couldn't fight it; there wasn't enough logic in the whole world to change the mind of guys like Loes. And he would be fighting his own battle soon enough. This was just a taste.

Oliver stood up. "Come on," he said. "The uniform who was watching Sinclair's place saw him come home a few minutes ago. If you hadn't come back I was going to bring Ramsey. Let's go get that statement signed, so we can really go after Anderson."

Mac followed him down to the car. His nerves were still vibrating from the argument with Loes, the things he had wanted to say, the fist he had wanted to put through that superior sneering face. Oliver unlocked the grey Taurus and heaved himself in. He started it, cranked the AC, and got out again, eyeing Mac over the roof of the car. They stood there waiting with the motor running, doors ajar, while the dark interior cooled down enough to sit in it.

"Mary Liu gave me a message for you," Oliver said. "She wants you to call her about rescheduling the next class at the center. She said you'd know what that meant."

"Yes." Mac was going to leave it flat like that, but then he added, "I got her to do a self-defense class for some of the teens at this center where Hart volunteers. They need all the edge they can get."

"Gay teens?" Oliver said.

"Yeah, gay, lesbian," Mac hesitated and then bit the bullet. He had to do this some time. Better now than trapped together in the car doing sixty on a freeway. "Fifteen, sixteen years old. Some of them have it pretty rough. You couldn't pay me enough to be fifteen again."

"Me either," Oliver agreed. "Although I'd take the body back. Sixteen, anyway. I got some pretty good action at sixteen."

"You weren't gay. Take all the hormones, the acne, the growth spurt, not being cool, and add gay. That's a ton of extra fear and shame on the top. And unlike black kids, or Hispanic kids, whose parents at least sympathize with them, gay kids are mainly born to straight parents. It's like living in enemy territory 24/7." He hesitated again and then made himself just say it. "It was hell on earth."

"I imagine…" Oliver said then ground to a stop, staring at Mac. "You didn't just say what I think you said."

"Um," Mac couldn't say it. Two little words, five letters, and he couldn't fit it out of his mouth. Instead he said, "When I was at the courthouse, the judge was worried that Tony might cause problems for Ben by bringing random dates home. I told her I knew he wouldn't, because most nights, he was with me."

Oliver was silent for a moment. Then he said very quietly, "You and Hart?"

"Yes."

"Shit." Oliver's voice was almost expressionless. He swung himself into the car and pulled his door shut.

Mac hesitated. Was he supposed to go away? Get in? Quietly melt into the cracks in the pavement?

"Get the hell in and stop letting out the cold air," Oliver snapped at him.

Mac sat down cautiously and pulled his own door shut. Oliver adjusted the rearview mirror, and then the side view, without looking at Mac. "This car is a piece of shit," Oliver muttered. Mac said nothing. "You're not pulling my leg?" Oliver asked eventually.

"Why the fuck would I joke about something like this?"

"You were married. You have a kid."

"Yes." *Don't excuse, don't explain.*

"Shit," Oliver said again. "Why are you telling me this?"

Mac sighed. "Because it's going to come out. I said it in court, and even if there were only six other people there, that's five too many to keep a secret. I wanted to let you know first, so you can act unsurprised when it trickles down. Or so you can, you know, ditch me now, before it rubs off on you."

"Huh." Oliver started the car and pulled out of the lot. "Fasten your fucking seatbelt."

Good advice when Oliver was driving. Mac did so.

"I don't want to ditch you," Oliver said after a while. "You're a freaking genius at getting people to talk to you. Witnesses, suspects, they all open their flapping jaws and spill for you. It's uncanny and I don't want to lose the edge."

Mac was both relieved and vaguely insulted. Was that what Oliver thought he was useful for? Better than nothing, but still.

At the traffic light, Oliver turned to him. "You're a good cop, gay or not," he said. "I've had other partners a lot worse, and we work pretty well together. I just don't know…is this going to change things?"

"Change things how?" Mac asked. "I've been gay for twenty years." *He'd said it!* He plunged on. "I think I've got the hang of it by now."

"I meant, like, working with the other guys."

"That's on them," Mac said, a little bitterly. "I haven't had a problem. But yeah, probably. Loes will be the worst, but there's several won't want to work with me, might drag their feet on a case if they can make me look bad that way." He was silent a minute, thinking back. "There's some might not back me up, if we got into a dangerous situation and I'm the one calling for help. I've heard gay murder called vermin control by cops on the job. You may be less safe with me as a partner than without."

"Shit." Oliver seemed to think for a minute. "That's just plain wrong."

Mac couldn't believe how it felt to hear that, like warm water flowing over him. His whole body relaxed a notch. "It's better now than it used to be. I'm not worried about getting scragged in the locker room."

Oliver glanced at him. "Be a brave man to take you on."

Mac shrugged. They drove for a while in silence. Then Oliver asked tentatively, "You and Hart, you been…together long?"

"Since that case," Mac said. His eyes had met Tony's for the first time in that high school hallway, with a dead man down the hall, and he had been toast. He had resisted for a little while, but not long.

"Before he got taken hostage?" Oliver asked curiously.

"Yes." *And hadn't that been a moment from hell.*

"So," Oliver said slowly, "You were negotiating with this strung out kid with a gun, and it was your…significant other tied to the radiator inside?"

"My boyfriend," Mac said. Enough PC shit. "Yeah, that's right."

"Jesus." Oliver glanced over again. "No wonder you were stressed."

"I was so far past stressed you couldn't see it from there," Mac said reminiscently.

Oliver barked a laugh. "And I never guessed. And all those times we went out to a bar, or just…you were gay all that time. And stuff I said, about women, or, um, times with the guys. That's…it's just hard to believe."

Mac shrugged one shoulder. He had been good at the closet, had it down to a science, although he had never come closer to losing it than that day with Tony held hostage. Until today.

Eventually, they pulled into the parking lot of Sinclair's apartment. Oliver cut the motor, but turned to Mac before getting out. "We're partners. I thought we were friends. Didn't you think I could keep a secret? Why didn't you tell me before?"

Mac had to laugh. "If you can't answer that question already, wait a few days. You'll find out." He shoved the door open and climbed out into the sticky heat.

Sinclair opened the apartment door for them reluctantly. He was dressed in a light cotton robe and sweatpants, his face devoid of makeup and his wig put away. In the morning light, he was a slim, tired-looking man. The woman was nowhere in evidence.

Oliver glanced at Mac with a question in his eyes, as if to ask if this was really the person they wanted.

"Can we come in for a moment?" Mac asked.

"I suppose." Sinclair stepped back to let them by. "What do you need?"

"Don't you ever check your cell phone?" Oliver said. "There must be a dozen messages on there from us."

"Oh?" Sinclair raised an eyebrow and allowed a little camp to slip into his voice. "Well then you know I was out all night, and there is nothing more rude than letting your cell phone ring when you are...otherwise engaged."

"And afterward?" Oliver insisted.

"Afterward is now. And I'm tired and I want to get a few hours of sleep. So spit it out."

"We found a suspect who might be the man who stabbed you," Mac told him. "We want you to look at a set of photos and see if you can pick the guy out from them."

"Really?" Sinclair looked more interested. "I'm surprised. But sure, I can look at a few pictures for you."

"We need to do this right," Mac told him, "So the identification isn't questioned. Can we go into the living room?"

Sinclair hesitated then led the way. Oliver set up the photos and conducted the lineup. Sinclair looked at each photo carefully. Mac's heart dropped when he passed over Anderson's face with no more attention than he gave the others, but at the end Sinclair came back and tapped Anderson's picture. "That one. Definitely. Having the picture makes it all come back clearly." He frowned at the photo. "You've been a very bad boy, my man," he told the suspect's face.

Mac breathed out. "Good. So here's what we need. I wrote out a copy of your statement, the way you told it last time we were here. I want you to read it over for errors, make any corrections, and then sign it. Once we have your complaint, we have a legitimate charge against this guy and we can go after him full bore."

Sinclair was shaking his head before Mac finished. "Sorry," he said. "I'm glad if I've been some help, but I'm not going to place a formal complaint."

"Why the hell not?" Oliver burst out angrily.

Mac kicked his partner in the shins. "Why don't you want to take the next step?" he asked more mildly.

"You wouldn't understand. This case you're on now is a media circus. If I get involved, especially if I accuse this guy of trying to stab me while I'm sucking him off in a motel, my more conservative accounting clients will definitely not be sympathetic. I can't support myself on my acting alone. I need the accounting money, and believe me, firms do not want their accountant wearing dresses and giving blowjobs to serial killers. No."

"I can see the problem," Mac said. "But you have to understand the position we're in. We're pretty sure this guy is our killer, but we have no good hard evidence yet. Without some kind of solid identification, enough for a warrant, we can't even pick him up and start getting that evidence. If you don't help us, he may walk."

"So follow him around until he messes up, and then arrest him," Sinclair suggested.

"If we try that, but then we lose him and he kills someone else, how are you going to feel?" Mac asked. He didn't think it would be productive to admit they didn't even know where Anderson was.

Sinclair eyed him sourly. "You have no idea what you're asking."

"Maybe not," Mac said, suddenly reckless. They needed this complaint. "But you're not the only one being outed by this case. You think it's hard explaining a dress to a business firm? You try explaining a boyfriend to a bunch of homicide cops."

He felt Oliver shift uncomfortably, but Sinclair's expression was a lot more open.

"You?" the man said, a little skeptically. "Bullshit. You showed me your wedding ring."

"Old history. And current camouflage." He needed to convince Sinclair to do this. He pulled out his wallet. The photo had taken a little trimming, but the main part fit. He pulled it out and passed it to Sinclair. "My boyfriend Tony," he said. "And his foster son, Ben. That was a few years ago. Ben is six now. Ben's mother was Alexandra Thompson, the most recent murder victim. And I couldn't keep Tony under wraps through all this."

Sinclair tilted the photo to the light. "He's cute." He smiled. "So's the little boy. Are the other cops giving you a hard time?"

"Not too bad yet, but it's early. I just cracked that closet door. I had to, because catching this killer, and limiting the pain and suffering he causes, are worth it. And that's why I need your statement too." When Sinclair still hesitated, Mac added, "You may not get too badly caught up in this, if we're lucky. We just need your statement to put our hands on the suspect. As soon as we have him, we can fingerprint him, and then we should be home free. We have prints and DNA and other evidence from the crime scenes. We just can't get his to compare until we have enough to arrest him in the first place."

Sinclair handed him back the photo. "All right," he said wearily. "You're right, if he kills again and I could have prevented it, I couldn't live with myself. At least H&R Block is big enough not to worry about one temporary employee having an alternative lifestyle. It's just money."

"Great," Oliver said, pulling the typed copy of the statement out of his pocket. "Thank you. Just read that, make and initial any changes, and sign where indicated."

Sinclair spread the paper out on the coffee table, smoothed it flat and read. He made a couple of changes and then added his name at the bottom. He handed the paper to Mac, but didn't let go when Mac reached to take it.

"I want something from you," he said.

"What?"

"Promise you'll keep my name out of this if at all possible.

If you have enough evidence to charge him with the murders, I want to avoid testifying."

"I can't promise. Some of that is up to the DA's office. I will do my best."

"Okay," Sinclair said. "I'll settle for that." He smiled, and in the sudden wicked grin, Mac caught a flash of the beautiful woman. "Especially if you introduce me to your cute boyfriend."

"Dream on," Mac told him, folding the precious document and handing it to Oliver. Sinclair showed them out and shut the door with a firm thump behind them. Mac took a deep breath. One more hole in the dyke he'd maintained for so long. But if he'd guilt-tripped Sinclair into this, he owed the man some solidarity.

"Did you have to do that?" Oliver asked as they got into the car.

"Do what?"

"Fucking tell him you were gay! It's one thing to tell me, but why the fuck would you go spreading it around like that? Are you going to start telling everyone we meet?"

Mac blinked. He had thought this was going too easily. "I would have told him I hump camels if it would have gotten our statement," he said, trying for humor.

"That's not the point," Oliver said irritably, pulling out. "I figured you would still be keeping it quiet. It's going to be all through the department now."

"It was anyway. I don't think this will make a difference."

"I'm your partner," Oliver snapped. "And while I don't give a damn who you are fucking, some of the guys will. You could have waited until things calm down. I'm going to be catching shit."

"*You* are?" Mac frowned at him, gripping the dashboard tightly to keep from being tossed around by Oliver's Mach 10 turns. His partner was bad enough behind the wheel on an ordinary day, but the man turned into Mario Andretti on crack when he was pissed. "You think I'm doing this just to screw with your life?"

"You know what they'll say. If your partner's gay, then you probably are too."

"So dump me," Mac said viciously. "Get another partner and keep your precious rep uncontaminated. You've probably got a few hours before everyone will know why you're bailing out."

Oliver turned to look at him.

"Watch the fucking road!" Mac yelped.

Oliver cut around the double-parked truck ahead of them, avoided the head-on collision with the oncoming Beamer, and pulled back into his lane. "I'm not dumping you," Oliver said more calmly. "I just…I wanted…damn. Shit!"

"Look," Mac tried. "I'm not going to turn flaming on you. You've known me three years. Have you ever once wondered if I was gay before?"

"No. Fuck, no."

"So, I'm not going to change now, for God's sake." Mac sighed. "This thing with the witness was a one-off, because I thought it was the quickest way to get what we needed. Yeah, there's shit coming, but I'm not going to invite one extra ounce of it."

"Loes is going to be ballistic. Terrance is going to make sure everyone in six counties knows. And Jesus, Severs!"

Mac had to laugh. "I'm the public face of this investigation. He'll have to choke on it."

"He'll have your balls in private, though." Oliver's speed had backed off to merely suicidal. "He'll try to transfer you, dump you onto someone else in another department somewhere."

"Yeah," Mac agreed. "I don't think he can, though, unless you ask to have me gone too."

"I'm not going up against Severs for you and trashing my career," Oliver told him.

"I'm not asking you to. Just, don't back him up. Remember

my case clearance rate."

"Bastard," Oliver said with a trace of humor. "You know, if you weren't so good at what you do, I'd ditch you in a minute."

Mac was surprised to realize that he didn't believe that at all.

CHAPTER 12

Five o'clock came and went. Tony paced the living room of his new apartment, pretending he was straightening things and rearranging furniture. The paperwork was done and registered. He had his temporary guardianship papers. Sabrina had hung with him long enough to be sure every i was dotted and every t was crossed. Then she'd run off to work with a demand that he tell her the whole story at the first available moment. He had come back here and shopped for groceries and a few other items. Okay, he'd made a toy store run, and stocked up on books at the library. Everything was ready, so where was Ben?

He hadn't called Mac. He had pulled out his phone a dozen times, just to touch base, to be sure the guy was okay. He didn't let himself do it. The next move had to be Mac's. Because there was still Brenda and her church, and there were still the homophobic co-workers, and who was he to give Mac advice about his life? Mac knew where to find him, if he wanted to.

The downstairs door buzzer finally sounded and Tony about sprained a finger pushing the release. He pictured front door, elevator, hallway. *How slow was the freaking elevator?* Then there was the knock on his door.

Sheila Burns stood in the hall with a duffle in one hand and her other hand on Ben's shoulder. Ben was pulled a little sideways by the knapsack over his other shoulder. His face was solemn and unsmiling.

Tony stood back. "Come on in," he said. "Ben, sweetie, I'm so glad you're here." The boy's demeanor didn't invite the hug Tony wanted to give him.

Ben walked past him into the apartment and lowered his pack to the floor. Silently, he went to the window and looked out, his back to them. Tony glanced at the caseworker, who gave him a little shrug.

"Why don't we get the paperwork done," she said, walking

over to the table. Tony put his signature on a couple more forms. She put the papers away in her purse and smiled encouragingly at him. "Give Ben a little time," she said quietly. "He's had a lot of changes in a short period. I'm not worried about the two of you. This has been one of my easier cases. You know he really wants to be with you. He just needs to feel really settled and secure again, and you can't rush that. I heard you have a therapist lined up for him?"

"Yes. Friday morning," Tony said, eyeing that rigid little back.

"Good. And don't forget to take care of yourself too. Single parenting is rewarding, but it's probably the hardest job on earth. Get yourself some support, and be ready for some rough weather at first. It helps to remember, none of what that boy has been through is your fault."

"Thanks," Tony said, holding out his hand. "I appreciate that."

Burns shook hands firmly. "I'll be back. You haven't seen the last of me. But I'm not worried. You'll do fine." She let herself out of the apartment.

Tony turned back to Ben. The boy hadn't moved or given a sign that he had been listening, although Tony was certain he had heard the conversation.

"Are you hungry, Ben?" Tony asked. "Did you have dinner?"

He got a silent headshake in return. Which meant what? *Idiot. Ask two opposite questions and you can't interpret the answer.* He tried again. "Would you like something to eat?" The headshake was more definite. All right then. "Would you like to see your room?"

"It's all different," Ben said quietly.

*The apartment? Your life? Work the obvious first.* "Yeah. I moved down a floor to this apartment, because you're going to be living with me forever, and you need a room of your own. I wanted my bed back." That was meant to be funny, but the boy didn't react. "Come on, Ben," Tony said. "I'll bring the duffel if you can get the knapsack and we'll put the things in your room. It's this one."

He led the way to the second bedroom and held the door open. For a minute Ben hesitated by the window, but eventually curiosity won and he came over to look in. Tony had made a start with the room. The bed was there, and a dresser and a bookshelf. There were baseball-themed curtains on the window. Tony had stopped himself there. Furnishing this room with Ben's own choices would make it more his own. At least he should like the bed. Tony watched Ben's expression.

Sure enough, there was a lightening of the boy's eyes as he spotted it. "It's a car," he said softly.

So it was. Tony had spotted it at Toys-R-Us, the blue plastic racing-car frame, big enough to fit a single mattress. It was so Ben, and it was different from anything in that stuffy little room in Sandy's apartment. He would have spent twice as much. The bed came up around the mattress in an enclosing way, and he had pushed it into the corner to make it more cozy.

"You like it?"

"I guess," Ben said. "I guess I could sleep in that."

"I hope so," Tony said, "Because it's a little small for me."

He got a tiny twitch of the boy's lips, and then Ben went over slowly and sat on the edge. Tony left him to it and went to fetch the knapsack. When he returned, Ben was in the corner of the headboard, feet tucked up, stroking the plastic headlights. Tony opened the bags and began putting clothes in the drawers, pausing to inspect and toss dirty stuff onto the closet floor. *Hamper; he needed to get Ben a hamper.* Although maybe a pile of dirty laundry on the floor was added security for the boy. Tony was so looking forward to having Ben talk to a professional. He was flying by the seat of his pants here.

Ted and the stuffed dog flew over to Ben on the bed. The first toss made Ben startle, but the second made him smile. Ben set the two critters in the corner, against the blue of the car. He looked at them. "I guess I am staying here," he said softly. Tony heard him and put back down the shirt he was folding. Ben looked up and met his eyes. "I guess I am staying 'cause this is a boy bed and it's too small for you."

"I got it for you," Tony told him. "This is your room. This is your home."

Ben smiled, but suddenly his face crumpled and tears poured down his cheeks. Tony tripped over the duffle bag going to him, and the hug became a tackle. Ben didn't object. His grip was just as hard as he buried his face in Tony's stomach and wailed. Tony pulled his feet up onto the bed and eased the boy into a more comfortable hold.

"Go ahead and cry," he told his boy. "You're entitled, and I'm not going anywhere. I've got you."

Tony thought he had given up hope of hearing from Mac that night, until the buzzer sounded. He realized, as he hurried over to the button, that his whole body had been tuned for the sound of a key in the door. *Mac doesn't have keys to this door. Mac doesn't have any keys anymore.* He remembered the cold feeling in his stomach when he found the old set in his new mailbox. No explanation, no note, just…final.

He opened the apartment door a crack, so that Mac wouldn't have to knock. When it swung open a little tentatively, he stayed in the kitchen, busily wiping the table. "Come on in, babe," he said casually.

Mac stepped in and shut the door behind him. Tony tossed his sponge into the sink. They looked at each other.

"Is Ben here?" Mac asked. "Is he okay?"

Tony smiled. "Come see." He led the way to Ben's room. The boy was curled up in the corner of the car bed with Ted, the plush cat, and the stuffed dog cuddled in. His face was a little flushed, but he slept easily and deeply. Tony backed out and shut the door softly.

"Two hours and he hasn't woken up yet," he said, rapping his knuckles on the wood of the doorframe, just in case.

"That's good. That's great."

And there they were, staring at each other again. Tony wasn't sure what he had expected from Mac the first time they saw each other again in private. A hug, certainly; perhaps for Mac to nearly eat him alive. *He's been through a lot of changes too,* Tony told himself. "Give it time" was always good advice.

"Have you eaten lately?" he asked. Frankly, Mac looked like hell again.

Mac blinked and seemed to think about it. "I don't recall…"

"Then it's been too long," Tony told him. "Go sit on the couch. I'll make you a sandwich." He headed for the kitchen, breaking the weird staring contest naturally, and began pulling out bread and cold-cuts. "So how was your day, after it exploded?" he asked.

Mac came into the kitchen. "Gun safe still under the sink?"

"Yeah, I brought it along."

Mac unstrapped his holster and stowed it safely, sighing as the air reached his skin where the straps had been. Tony could smell Mac's warm skin, the hint of musk, male sweat, that familiar presence at the end of a long day. Mac came over and filched a piece of salami, and Tony slapped his hand away.

"Go sit," Tony said. "I'll bring it. Talk to me."

"Um," Mac's voice was low. "I, um, came out to Oliver."

"You did?" Tony hesitated then went back to building a sandwich. "How did that go?"

"Better than I expected, actually," Mac admitted. "He says he doesn't want to ditch me. As his partner. Although he is pretty freaked and worried about what the other guys will say when they find out."

"They haven't yet?"

"Not so far." Tony heard Mac sigh heavily. Tony put the sandwich on a plate, added a beer from the fridge, and brought it out to his… *What was Mac now? His beloved; that anyway, the oblivious son-of-a-bitch.*

"Eat up," he told Mac cheerfully. "You're practically grey, and you have those raccoon circles again."

Mac took a bite, slowly, and then chowed down with a will. Tony got up to fetch cookies. Ten minutes later, the man was looking more himself.

"God," Mac said. "That was good. I actually don't remember when I ate."

"Have to keep up the nutrition, babe," Tony told him, sticking the empty plates on the end table and sitting down carefully beside him. "You can't solve a case if you're fainting from low blood sugar." He surveyed the familiar signs; Mac's face, body language. "I'm guessing you're temporarily stalled, but the case is moving. You don't have that cold-as-ice-case look."

"Yeah. We've got a good lead. Just can't find the guy."

"You have a suspect in Sandy's murder?" Tony was suddenly as interested in the case as in the man. "Who is he? Did she know him?"

"I think, if we're right, it's someone she met that night. If we're right. It's still a big if."

"You'll get him," Tony said. He believed it. "And when you do, I'm going to have to work on my disapproval of the death penalty, because I wish he was dead!" He was surprised at the wash of pure hatred he felt for this man who had casually snuffed out four women's lives, and turned theirs upside down. And left a small boy without a mother.

"No death penalty in Minnesota, Tony," Mac told him.

"I know. Usually I'm glad." He leaned back into the couch beside Mac and tried to think about what came next. His mouth opened of its own accord and said, "You don't just get to come back, you know. I'll be *damned* if I'll just let you walk in the door and into my bed like nothing happened."

"I know." Mac's voice was quiet. Tony wasn't sure if the man was contrite, or just tired. *He fucking well better be contrite.*

"You did a good thing today." Tony kept his own tones cool.

"But it doesn't mean everything is fixed."

Mac nodded slowly. "We need to talk, don't we?"

"Shit." Tony got up and paced, because it was an alternative to yelling, and he was *not* going to wake Ben up. "Yeah, talk, something…I am so mad at you I can't think straight."

Mac slumped a little. "Do you want me to leave?"

"No!" Tony bit his lip and modulated his voice. "No. I want you to do something, say something, show me you know what you did when you chose the damned closet over being with me."

"I didn't choose…" Mac's voice trailed off. "Maybe I did. I didn't mean to. I didn't think that was the choice I was making. Or maybe I didn't think I had a choice." He scrubbed his hands over his face. "I'm sorry. I'm too fucking tired to make any sense, but all I know is I didn't want to hurt you and I didn't want to wreck my life and I did both and I'm sorry I was ever born, and will you please sit down here and let me hold you for a minute, because I don't think I can make it without you."

*What do you say to that?* Tony found himself moving to the couch, to Mac's arms. He let himself slide into that space against Mac and feel the warmth flow through him, just for a moment. Mac let out a sigh that seemed to last forever. Eventually, Tony eased back a little.

"We're not done, babe," he said cautiously. "But I guess we don't have to solve everything all at once. Just so you know that there have to be changes."

"What do you want?"

"I want you to be honest with me," Tony said, moving over to sit on his own end of the couch and look Mac in the eye, feeling his way. "I want a future with you, but to be workable, to be honest around Ben, it has to be different from what we've had."

"And if I can't do that?"

"One step at a time, baby," Tony said, keeping his tone much lighter than he felt. "First step is, do you still want me?"

"Jesus," Mac breathed. "I haven't slept in a week for wanting you."

"Not just like that. Do you want to be around me, talk to me, do the stupid little everyday life things with me?"

"I'm here," Mac pointed out, "And however optimistic my dick may be, I don't really expect to get some tonight." He hesitated. "It's not the sex, Tony. Or not just the sex. You're the only person I've ever known who really sees me, who sees all of me, and who likes what he sees."

"If you come out of the closet, there will be any number of men glad to see all of you."

Mac punched Tony's thigh lightly. "I mean, you understand how I get when I'm on a case, and how I feel about Anna, and all of that. You make me feel…alive. I need you safe and close and…I want to help you, protect you. I would take a bullet for you. Hell, you're the only man I've ever met that I would stand in front of a judge and say I'm gay for."

And the man still hadn't said those three important little words, but Tony didn't think he'd heard a better definition of love. He leaned over and kissed Mac lightly on the chin. "Then the rest is time and details, babe. We'll get there somehow."

Mac caught Tony's jaw in his hand, turned and made the light kiss into something quite different. That familiar mouth was hot and sweet, and Tony opened his lips and invited Mac in. Tongues met, played, drove deep. The familiar taste and smell made Tony a little dizzy, or maybe it was the not-breathing. When he pulled back, he was splayed across Mac's body, warm with his lover's breath, with those big hands pressing his hips down against that very nice package. Tony squirmed his hips a little, to make Mac whimper, and then took up the kiss again. After a long time, he eased back and settled his head in the crook of Mac's neck. Mac's hand came up to caress his hair.

"Tony," Mac said softly, and then like a sigh, "Tony."

"But we're still not getting any tonight," Tony told him. And told himself. *God, he wanted this man.* Regular sex made it harder to take an abstinence break, not easier.

"How do we do this?" Mac asked. "Because I like talking to you, but I sure as hell do want more than that, if you'll let me."

"*When* I decide we get to do this, there's a lock on the bedroom door," Tony told him, "And on the bathroom. Once I know Ben will sleep through, we can practice not making each other scream." He kissed Mac's neck. "But only if I can kiss you in front of him, and call you my boyfriend. I want him to know I have one steady guy, and that's you. I can't have him thinking I'm like his mother, sneaking in a man whom he's not supposed to know about and making him scared that there may be others."

"I'm not sure I'm ready for that."

Tony sighed. "I know, babe. And that's why you're going home soon, before he wakes up or you fall asleep here."

"I could sleep on the couch," Mac said, not moving.

"Bad precedent."

"Tomorrow's going to be rough," Mac said ruminatively. "We're on the brink with this case. We're tracking the suspect. Severs wants another press conference if we don't make more progress soon. Put the guy's face out to the public for help and warn the women. The profiler he called in says the guy is escalating, getting closer together in his crimes. The next one could be soon."

*Yeah, move to an easier subject. Like murder.* Tony was just as glad to let their personal dilemma slide for a while. "Why don't you want a press conference?" he asked, judging by Mac's tone. "Besides the fact that Severs might make you do the talking head bit again?"

Mac chuckled sleepily. "That's part of it. Can you imagine if Severs knew who he was making the public face of the department…not worth telling him to get out of it, though. But no, I'm worried that if this guy knows we're after him he might vanish, just move on and start up again somewhere else. Publicity is a two-edged sword."

"I can see that. How sure are you about the suspect?"

"Varies," Mac mumbled. "Sometimes I'm certain. Gut feeling, you know. But the evidence is damned thin. We could be wrong…" His voice trailed off.

Tony shifted more comfortably against that broad chest, thinking about it. What a dilemma, to choose between warning the public of the risk, and warning the killer of the pursuit. He was glad all over again that this was Mac's career, not his own.

He was letting his thoughts drift when he realized that the steady rise and fall of Mac's breath had slipped into sleep. He should wake the man, chase him out to his car…and worry himself sick about the man falling asleep at the wheel. He sighed. Guys crashed on each other's couches all the time. It didn't have to mean anything. *Tell the truth, you chickenshit. You just really want to have him here, any way you can.* It was true. And he couldn't regret it.

He got up and lifted Mac's feet from the floor to the couch. Of course, the big guy was going to be sorry in the morning. Tony's couch hadn't gotten any more comfortable with the move. *It's still real sleep, which he obviously needs.* He went and fetched a blanket, and threw it over the sleeping man. Mac stirred, and whimpered something plaintive. Tony bent and kissed his cheek. "It's all right," he whispered. "Go back to sleep, sweetie." Mac gave a contented snort and turned further into the pillow. Tony smiled and took himself to his own bed. He left his door open, the better to hear if either of his men needed him in the night.

Mac woke with a crick in his neck and the conviction that someone had been performing illegal surgery on his right hip. He groaned softly and struggled up out of the awkward position he was in. The room around him was dim. The only light came from a small fixture left on in the kitchen. *Tony's place, and the damned couch.* In retrospect, the hip thing was familiar.

A dark figure standing silently nearby made him start momentarily, until he recognized the shape. "Tony?"

"I'm damned and going to hell," Tony's voice said out of the darkness, its tone more whimsical than the words suggested.

"What?" Clearly his ears and his brain had yet to reconnect.

"I've been awake for hours, and I can't stand having you out here on my couch anymore, and I guess I am damned and I don't care."

Mac puzzled that one over for a moment. "Tony?" Then he remembered, *I'm damned if I'll let you just walk back into my bed…* He felt a slow smile creeping over his face.

Tony came to him, and kissed him, and the direction of his thoughts was more than obvious.

Mac laughed softly. "I think I'm going to heaven."

Tony bit him on the neck, hard. "It's five-thirty in the morning, and Ben is fast asleep, and I have a baby monitor, and I need a shower."

"By yourself?" Mac still wondered if he was misinterpreting here.

"Only if you want to die young, you son of a bitch."

"Which bathroom?" Mac was rapidly waking up, in every way possible.

"This way." Tony opened a door for them and waited to switch on the light until the door was shut and locked. "I picked the bathroom with the walk-in shower for the adults, and left the tub for the kids."

"Kids?" Mac was confused. Then it didn't matter, because Tony was kissing him, and holy shit, the things he was doing with his hands and his tongue.

"Tony, babe," Mac whispered. "I want you out of those shorts." He fumbled with his hands to find the waistband of Tony's boxers, as the man ground hard against him.

"Shower," Tony said breathlessly. "We're going to shower." He broke away from Mac to open the shower door and turn on the water. Mac took the chance to skin out of his shirt and slacks. His boxers snagged on his erect cock, dragging him down as he tugged at them, and he grunted. Tony was standing in front of the shower, naked and ready. Mac just stopped and looked at him.

He had missed this, just the sight of this man, with the heat in his eyes to match Mac's own. Slowly, not taking his eyes off Tony, Mac pushed his shorts down and stepped out of them. Tony's grin was sinful. "Missed me, huh?"

"Get in the shower, brat," Mac growled. "I want to see you all wet with the soap running down your ass." *Yeah, he did.*

Tony opened the glass door and stepped under the water, closing his eyes and shaking his head as he ducked into the spray. Streams of water slid over his chest, slicking down around his nipples and flowing in rivulets that went south. Mac's eyes followed the water and, hey! "You shaved," he said softly.

"Thought you might like not getting hair in your mouth," Tony said without opening his eyes. Mac looked some more. He liked it, all clean and fine, the flat muscle of Tony's groin revealed, the long sleek lines pointing at his hard cock. Mac stepped in and pulled the glass door shut behind him. Tony's eyes opened, that intense blue inches from his own.

"Howdy, stranger," Tony said softly.

Mac fisted a hand in Tony's dark hair and dragged his head back to lick and bite at his throat. "I'm not a stranger," he growled, moving his mouth lower. "I'm your man and don't you forget it."

"Never." Tony's hands skimmed over Mac's back. "I haven't forgotten anything."

Mac licked the warm water from the soft skin around Tony's nipples in spirals that never reached their targets. Tony groaned a little and slid his hands up to push Mac's head. Mac resisted, licking, teasing, and then bit hard.

Tony gasped.

Mac knelt. He liked the shape of this shower stall that gave him better access than a narrow tub. He moved his mouth across Tony's flat belly, sliding his tongue over newly silky skin. Tony spread his feet apart and took hold of the safety rail. Mac explored with fingers and mouth, sucking Tony's soft sac, pulling one ball and then the other into his mouth. Everything was there for him, clean and ready. He pulled gently, stretching those firm orbs with his mouth until Tony was whimpering. He opened his lips and let the sweet flesh slide from his mouth. Tony's hard shaft bobbed against his temple, rubbing in his hair. Mac allowed himself one swift lick of salty pre-cum, gliding his tongue around that eager head, and then stood.

Tony kissed him, swift as a snake striking, with a force that mashed Mac's lips against his teeth. Water ran down over their faces, making Mac close his eyes. The heavy wet air and the scent of Tony made it hard to breathe. He licked his way into Tony's mouth, forcing his tongue deep, as Tony opened for him. Then his hands found Tony's shoulders, pushing him down.

Tony knelt willingly, eagerly, sliding his palms over the hard muscle of Mac's thighs. He looked up, blue eyes so dark they were almost black, water beading his long eyelashes.

"I'm jealous of every man who ever knelt down in front of you," he said hoarsely.

"Don't be," Mac told him, threading his fingers through the wet dark hair. "Yeah, there were a bunch of strangers I fucked, or let suck me, but not one other man that made love to me like you do. Not one that I wanted to make love with."

Tony closed his eyes and kissed Mac in the groove of his groin, fingers trailing up his thighs. He scraped his fingernails across Mac's ass as his mouth found the base of Mac's rigid cock. Then Mac had to groan when that hot mouth took him in, and Tony's fingertip penetrated him from behind. Mac leaned forward, spreading his legs, as Tony sucked and stroked, teasing sensitive flesh with mouth and tongue and fingers. Mac fought to hold back, not to plunge into that willing wetness. It was so hard, so hard, when searing heat was spreading from ass to thighs and cock and Tony's sweet mouth took him deeper.

Mac reached down and hauled Tony's lean body up against him. "Jesus, Tony," he groaned. "I want to come inside you. I want to put my cum deep in your ass so you're walking around all day tomorrow with me in there. God, I want you!"

"Oh, yes," Tony breathed, turning in his arms and bracing on the safety rail. "Please."

Mac pressed against him, running the steel of his dick up the slick hairless groove of Tony's ass. So smooth, so hot. He reached for the lube, and fumbled, panting.

"Lube, Tony, where?"

"Fuck, I pitched it for the home visit," Tony said, shoving hard back against him. "Use the aloe gel, babe." He twisted to grab the bottle off the shelf and poured a generous handful of liquid out. He took hold of Mac, gliding slick gel over Mac's length, twisting his hand around Mac's throbbing head. The clench and twist of Tony's fingers ratcheted up the heat in Mac's groin, wound him too tight for rational thought. He pushed Tony around and spread him. Tony was slick and clean, and Mac's gel-coated fingers slid in easily. He made himself wait, working his fingertips, making Tony open and groan and push back into his hand. Then he bent his knees a little, guided himself into place and pressed in.

The tight ring of Tony's ass resisted, the gel less slippery than their favorites. When Mac would have gone slow, Tony shoved back against him hard, whimpering in frustration. Mac took those lean hips between his hands and pushed. Tony opened to him with a gasp, shaking, as Mac sank into tight silky softness. Mac froze for a moment, letting Tony feel his size.

"More, baby." Tony began moving again rhythmically. "Go deep."

Mac let his lover drive them, loving the taut eagerness of Tony's body under him, slowly sinking deeper. Each thrust was a little more, and a little more, and then his balls were slapping against Tony's ass, and he was riding fast thrusts, from tip to hilt. Tony groaned and babbled. "So good, so good, so hot, yeah baby, Mac, Mac, Jesus, Mac!"

Mac felt Tony shaking, his whole body clenching under and around Mac. Tony stroked himself frantically with one hand and the hot jets of cum splashed the wall of the shower. Mac hauled him in closer, bent him over, and drove forward. *This, this was what he had needed for so long. Himself and Tony, one body, one rhythm, one flesh.* All of his need and heat and wanting poured out of him, deep inside Tony's body. He groaned between clenched teeth then bit down on Tony's shoulder as the shudders hit him again, and again, and he filled Tony's ass.

As the intensity eased, they slid toward the floor of the shower, managing just barely enough control that Mac landed sitting with Tony in his lap. His legs shook uncontrollably. Tony was laughing, as he sometimes did, in wonder and pleasure. "Oh, baby. Oh, man." Tony leaned back in Mac's arms, his head tilted onto Mac's shoulder. They shuddered in unison as aftershocks hit them with the contact of skin on skin.

Mac wrapped his arms around his man, hugging him tight, blinking through the streams of water down his face. Tony leaned his head back to look up at Mac, eyes alight.

Mac rubbed his cheek against Tony's soft dark hair and then pulled back to meet those blue eyes. And suddenly it was easy. "I love you, Tony Hart," he said.

Tony's smile was everything Mac wanted in the world. "Oh, yes," Tony breathed. "You're mine."

They sat unmoving, just rocking slightly, until water up Tony's nose made him cough. Mac unwound himself and pulled Tony to his feet. He shut off the water, hauled the man out, and wrapped him in a towel. He felt a vast tenderness, almost like with Anna, only different. He rubbed his hands up and down Tony's back and arms through the towel, drying him.

"Get your own towel on, babe," Tony told him softly. "I'm good."

Mac wrapped the terrycloth around himself and squinted at the little white plastic monitor on the counter, one indicator light glowing steady red.

"Baby monitor, huh?"

"Yeah. Just be glad he didn't wake up at the wrong moment, 'cause I promised to come if he called."

"You came for me instead," Mac teased.

"Definitely."

Mac took a closer look at the receiver, suddenly worried. "You're sure this isn't set to transmit too?"

Tony laughed. "I bought the kind that doesn't transmit both ways. I'm not taking any chances. Plus it was cheaper."

"Good." Mac kissed him. "So we had fun, and didn't wake the baby. That's good, right?"

"If all the rating I get for that is good, I'm leaving."

"It was great, it was amazing, you know what you do to me. Do I get to do it again some time?"

"I can't say no to you babe. I tried. But you know what I want."

"In this house, I'm your boyfriend," Mac told him. "In front of Ben too, if that makes it all okay. Outside this place…I still don't know how that will work."

"And in front of Anna?" Tony asked softly.

"Jesus." *He loved Tony, he really did, knew it, had even finally said it, but Jesus.* "Please don't push me, babe. Please."

"Okay." Tony leaned over and kissed Mac softly. "But think fast, because anything Ben knows, Anna is gonna know soon."

Mac shuddered. That was the truth. He was burning bridges faster than he realized they were there.

Tony's arms wrapped around him, and Mac laid his head down on Tony's shoulder for a moment. "It'll be okay," Tony whispered into his hair. "I promise, it will be okay." And Mac let himself believe it.

Tony gave him one last rub and then shoved him upright. "Get dressed, babe, and go make us some breakfast. I need to clean up a bit in here."

"Sorry," Mac said, not in the least contritely, pulling on yesterday's clothes.

"Bullshit," Tony laughed. "You love that I'm leaking your spunk all over." He administered a quick kiss. "I love it too, carrying you around with me. Now get out."

Mac took himself off to the kitchen, glancing through the refrigerator. He pulled out milk and orange juice, and bagels, being as quiet as he could. So he jumped when a hand touched his arm. He whirled around, and there was Ben, wide-eyed, the battered teddy-bear dangling from one hand.

"Hey, Ben," Mac said softly. "It's good to see you."

"I didn't know you were here."

"I got here after you were asleep," Mac told him. "I crashed on the couch for the night."

"Where's Tony?" Ben seemed calm, just curious.

"I think he's in the bathroom, finishing his shower. I'm just making breakfast, because I have to go to work early. Do you want breakfast, or do you want to go back to bed? You're lucky. You get the choice."

"Can I have breakfast and then go back to bed?" Ben asked.

"I guess. Sure. What do you want?"

Ben perched on a chair at the table and set Ted carefully on the chair next to him. "Toast 'n strawberry jam," he requested.

"Milk or juice?" It was all so ordinary, so domestic, and yet scary and new.

"Milk," Ben told him. He watched silently as Mac got out butter and jam, started the coffee brewing, and put bread and bagels in the toaster. Eventually he said, "Can you stay over lots?"

"Do you want me to?" Mac asked, startled.

"Yeah." Ben's agreement was a sigh. "'Cause it's real safe if you're here."

"We'll see," Mac said noncommittally.

Tony came into the kitchen rubbing his hair dry, and hesitated a second, before walking up to Ben and ruffling his hair. "Hey, sport. You're up early."

"I woke up," Ben said, "And Mac is here making breakfast."

"So he is," Tony agreed. "Kind of nice to have breakfast made for us, huh?"

"Uh-huh." Ben took the plate Mac gave him and bit into his toast. "Mac says he's going to stay here lots."

"He did?" Tony looked steadily at Mac.

"I said we'll see," Mac repeated, feeling pressured.

"That means you're gonna say yes," Ben explained. "Only you don't want to say it yet."

Tony laughed. "You have grown-ups figured out, don't you sport?"

"Yep." Ben took a big gulp of milk, and smiled around his white mustache.

Mac ate his breakfast in fits and starts as he alternated between deep contentment and near panic. It was like his body wanted to do both and had to take turns. When he was done, he got up to go, leaving Tony with the child and the kitchen clean-up. Tony followed him to the door.

"Bye, Tony," Mac said softly, aware of small eyes on them. "I'll call you later."

"Good luck at work," Tony told him. "Stay safe."

Mac was worried that their new agreement meant Tony would kiss him, here and now, in front of Ben, but Tony just smiled, his single dimple appearing.

"Don't worry," he said. "You're still under cover."

Mac ducked his head, gave Ben a small wave, and let himself out.

CHAPTER 13

Work was a busy place when Mac arrived. The air was practically vibrating with the hope of making progress on their most urgent case. He'd had to take a trip back to his apartment, to change and fetch his hated suit. Then a brief visit with Anna on Brenda's front steps had put Mac late despite the early start. He smiled a little. He regretted none of that; well, except the suit.

"It's coming together," Oliver said, looking up from his desk as Mac approached. "We've got positives on the photo from three witnesses. We can put Anderson in bars frequented by Klein and Kowalski, and get this: we have a witness putting Anderson with Thompson on the evening she died. Not leaving together, but in the same bar at the same time."

"It's got to be him," Mac said.

"Got to be." They looked at each other for a moment. They both knew there was still room for doubt. Witnesses were unreliable, telling you what they *thought* they remembered. And most of them had seen the sketch first.

"We need prints or DNA," Mac said. "We need to fucking find this guy."

"I've got a crime team working the place he used to live," Oliver said. "Hundreds of prints, and we're picking up hairs for testing. But that other couple has been in there for months. And the damned landlord hired a cleaning company to come in and do the place after Anderson moved out. They even put chemical cleaner down all of the drains. It's a long shot."

"How did the computer searches go?" Mac asked. He had been out with the teams who'd taken the DMV photo around the bars last night. He'd missed the progress meeting, again. *Shucks.*

"Anderson looks like he deliberately dropped out of sight," Oliver told him. "Somewhere between the Klein rape and that Nicole Simmons murder that we hadn't picked up on before, he moved out. Of course he'd lost the job about then, but the landlord and the ex-owner of the business say no one ever called for a reference. With the warrant, we got his credit card records. He pulled the limit in cash advances on both of them. Since then he hasn't used them or made payments. Credit records show no new applications, which he wouldn't get at this point anyway. He closed his bank account, pulled about two thousand in cash. No phone listing, no new bank accounts. His car insurance company says they still have his old address and he's now overdue on his payment. He hasn't sold the car, at least not legally."

"How much walking around money did he score altogether?" Mac asked.

"Near as we can tell, about five thousand," Oliver said. "That was almost six months ago. He's got to be doing something for cash soon, even if he's living on the cheap."

"He could have sold the car under the table."

"He could," Oliver agreed sourly, "Although, how much is a 2004 Honda Civic worth? Especially without the registration."

"So what's the plan?"

Oliver yawned and rubbed at his face. "We found a couple of old co-workers and one relative, a cousin. We'll go shake them down for information. We have a BOLO out on the car. If we still come up empty, Severs wants to put the photo out for the public on the five o'clock news. And it's a good thing you brought the suit, because he tapped you to do it."

Mac sighed. He'd figured that by missing the meeting he had also missed the chance to get out of being volunteered. "You couldn't convince him that this progress by his tireless team would be a feather in his cap and he should announce it himself?"

"If Anderson melts into the woodwork after the public announcement, Severs wants a degree of separation," Oliver said. "You know this is a gamble."

"Yeah. So we need to find this guy before five."

Unfortunately four-thirty found Mac changing into the suit

in the stifling men's room, cursing under his breath. No one had seen Leonard Anderson. No one had any idea where he might go. They all described a quiet guy who kept to himself but could hold up his end of a conversation. Didn't talk about himself, didn't invite people over, a little fussy about his stuff, basically nothing special. All were surprised to hear he was wanted for assault, although one co-worker said Anderson had a temper, just usually well-controlled. So Severs had decided on the dog-and-pony show. With Mac as the pony.

Walking into a room full of lights and cameras was marginally easier the second time. It probably helped that he had something productive to tell them this time. He and Oliver and Severs had spent a long time going through the evidence, deciding how much to reveal. The department lawyer had chimed in to prevent lawsuits, should Anderson prove to be innocent. The final statement was a compromise. Mac crumpled the paper in his fist as he walked up to the podium. Not like he didn't remember what it said at this point.

"Okay," he told the crowd when they had quieted for him. "You all remember me; Detective MacLean, Homicide. You're here because we have a suspect in the recent murders of three young women in Minneapolis. You have the photo. This man, Leonard Anderson, is wanted for assault with a deadly weapon, and for questioning in regard to the murders. Anderson is six foot one, one hundred sixty pounds, brown hair, brown eyes. He drives a blue 2004 Honda Civic, Minnesota license KNB 147. He may be armed and dangerous. We're asking the public not to approach this man. If you see Leonard Anderson, or know where he is currently living or working, we ask you to call the hotline number on your screen. Do not attempt to question or apprehend this man on your own." He stopped there. Shouted questions began, and then slowly quieted as he eyed them blandly without responding. When they began raising hands he gestured at a TV reporter.

"What evidence do you have against Anderson?" she asked.

"I can't comment on that at this time," Mac told her.

"Is Anderson a threat to other women?"

"If he is involved in these murders," Mac said, "Then he definitely could be a threat. I would certainly advise single women not to be alone with anyone who fits this description." *A lot of tall men with brown hair won't be scoring this week.*

"Did a witness identify Anderson for you?"

"No comment."

A woman from the back of the room shouted, "Did Alexandra Thompson's son make the identification?"

"Yeah," a man chimed in. "Did the boy see his mother's killer?"

*Jesus.* "The boy is not a witness in this case."

"But you're pretty sure this is the guy. Does Anderson have a criminal record?"

"No," Mac told them. "There is currently a warrant out on him for assault, but he has no prior convictions."

"Who is the victim in the assault?"

"No comment," Mac stated. Unfortunately, that information would be a matter of public record. Unless they caught Anderson soon, Sinclair would be in the hot seat and there would be nothing Mac could do about it.

He stepped back a little from the podium. "I want to remind you that Leonard Anderson is only a suspect in the case at this time. A woman should not feel safe with a strange man just because he does not look like Anderson. Exercise reasonable caution." It wasn't as if Anderson was the only abusive man out there, either. But alcohol, sex, and risk always went together.

He walked away from the briefing, closing his ears to the babble from the frustrated reporters. They had everything the department wanted to put out there. Now the fun with phones would begin.

Up in Homicide, the rest of the team was watching his performance on TV. Mac thought he looked like shit, but Severs gave him a slap on the back. "Good work, MacLean. Looks good."

Mac eyed the TV. "Time for the crazies to come out."

"You got the Sinclair guy from the last TV appeal," Severs told him. "It's worth a try."

Mac shrugged out of his jacket as the reporter on the screen went live to the home of Terri Brand's parents, to stick a microphone in their faces.

"How does it feel to know that the police may have found the man responsible for your daughter's death?" she asked breathlessly.

Beside Mac, Oliver muttered, "How the fuck do you think it feels?"

On the screen, the distraught parents were saying the usual things about hoping the guy is caught soon and wanting this over. Mac was going to switch off the set, when the reporter said, "Now we go live to the scene of Alexandra Thompson's murder, where her son is speaking with Lydia Brown."

"What the hell?" Mac turned up the volume.

The picture showed Ben, pressed back against Tony's legs in the hallway of the apartment building. A reporter extended a microphone at him. Tony held a duffle bag in one hand, with his other arm wrapped across Ben, and a furious look on his face.

"Did you see the man who hurt your mom?" the reporter asked Ben.

"This is totally inappropriate," Tony snapped at her, trying to guide Ben past. "He has nothing to say."

"Will you be happy if they catch the man who killed your mom?" she persisted.

Ben twisted in Tony's hold to look at her. "I want Mac to arrest him and lock him up for ever and ever," the boy said clearly.

Tony pulled him forward and out the door. The camera followed them as Tony swept Ben up one-armed and carried him to the Prius.

"Alexandra Thompson's small son expresses his wish that the police catch his mother's murderer," the reporter voice-overed. "With the information just released, there is hope that they will do just that. This is Lydia Brown, for Channel 8 News in Minneapolis."

"Shit!" Mac ground out. "How the hell did that happen?" He shut off the TV set and pulled out his phone.

Tony answered on the fourth ring.

"What happened?" Mac demanded. "Why were you at Sandy's building?"

"We're fine, thank you," Tony said acidly. "We're in the car. Wait a sec—let me pull over. I gather we made the news broadcast."

"Front and center. What the hell were you thinking going over there? You knew the press would love to put Ben on the screen."

"What?" Tony retorted. "You think I exposed Ben to that on purpose?"

"No. I know you just didn't expect...but I told you they'd be paying someone for a phone call if Ben showed up."

"Yes." Tony's voice was weary. "But I figured by now it was old news. Ben wanted to see some of his friends, and get his dad's baseball poster, and I needed his vaccination records for Friday, which weren't in the stuff you picked up. I didn't expect them to put that kind of effort into getting a photo op."

"Yeah. Sorry. Are you sure Ben's okay?"

"Ben didn't care. It was no big deal to him; he's fine, for now. It's a good thing school is still a month off though. The other kids aren't likely to cut him any slack about being a celebrity."

Mac made an effort to soften his voice. "What about you?"

"I'm just mad."

"Well, go on home. If you need something, call me. Don't answer the door."

"They're not going to follow us, surely?" Tony said. "Aren't there laws about the privacy of a minor child?"

"Yes, some. They can't use his name, stuff like that. But they can follow him by pretending they're following you. You were on TV yourself last fall, after that hostage thing."

"Yeah. My five minutes of fame that were ten minutes too many."

"So they may recognize you and track Ben down," Mac told him. "We just did the press conference about our suspect. That's why they were so hot for a sound bite. They got both Ben and Terri Brand's poor parents."

"F…freaking vultures," Tony muttered.

"You already knew that. Go home, stay away from the press, keep the TV off."

"By the way," Tony told him, "You should know that Sandy's apartment was broken into and trashed. Good thing you got stuff out early."

"Damn. Did you get what you needed?"

"Mostly." Tony sighed over the line. "I'm not taking Ben back there, that's for sure."

"You're doing the best you can. Stay tough, okay. Give Ben a hug for me and I'll see you later."

Oliver was eyeing Mac as he pocketed his phone. "The boy all right?"

"Yes," Mac said. "He's a tough kid. And Tony will take care of him."

Oliver nodded, although his expression was still thoughtful. "Okay, partner. Let's go see what crawls out of the woodwork on the hotline."

They spent the rest of the evening collecting tips and tracking them down. The response was bigger than Mac had expected. Anderson apparently had a very common face, because hundreds of people had seen him, in as many locations. He was living under a dozen aliases, each of which had to be checked out discretely.

A couple of possible leads seemed promising, but each time the man in question was long gone when they went to follow up. Anderson might have bought clothes at a downtown thrift shop last Thursday, and a motel owner was certain the man had stayed for a few nights a month earlier. Neither sighting was recent enough to be any help.

They made the rounds of other bars, especially around the thrift shop, leaving hard copies of his photo for every bartender they could find. The profiler thought he would be working up to another murder soon, although seeing his own face on TV might change things.

More tips came in, more follow-ups were done. They talked to well-meaning and mistaken people, attention-seekers, the deluded and the frankly loony. None of it got them any closer to Anderson.

The Lulu/Walter Sinclair story broke with a bang on all the media channels Wednesday night. Mac figured it had been inevitable, but he still couldn't help feeling guilty. Anything further from his promise about keeping Sinclair's name out of it than a headline screaming, "Sinclair saved from Dagger Killer by falsies" was hard to imagine.

Mac wasn't sure how almost all the details of Sinclair's complaint against Anderson got leaked. Maybe it was someone who figured a cross-dresser wasn't entitled to privacy. Or maybe Mac was being paranoid and it was just too good a story for some gossiping cop to keep to himself. Either way, the TV reporters swarmed after Sinclair and camped outside his apartment. With no other new leads, the story of how Lulu escaped from Anderson and was able to identify him and break the case got repeated airplay over the next two days.

At one point, Mac looked up at a TV in a bar he was canvassing to see video of a harried-looking Sinclair facing a crowd of cameras outside the Guthrie. Mac didn't catch much of the shouted questions and responses, but he did hear Sinclair say wryly, "I'm not sure whether I need more privacy or an agent. But if you all buy tickets to my next show, I'll tell you anything. I'm easy." Mac marveled at Sinclair's composure. Although maybe the man was just that good of an actor.

At least the photo of Anderson was getting great airplay. Even the video billboard off I-94 had his face up with the hotline phone number. Anyone who hadn't seen the picture at least ten times had to have been a TV-hating recluse or a blind man. And yet none of the recent calls they were getting seemed in the least helpful. By Friday morning they were all bleary and discouraged. Mac sat at his desk, sipping coffee that had nothing going for it except wetness and caffeine. He flipped idly through the slips of new phone calls on his desk, trying to decide if any of the rejects were worth a second look. Amazing that no one had really recognized Anderson's photo. He had to have been living somewhere. Of course all the man had to do was grow a beard, or dye his hair, and most people wouldn't make the connection. They had toyed with the idea of putting out photo-shopped versions with facial hair. Except the witness from the bar where Sandy spent her last night remembered the man as clean-shaven. And the hairs found in Sandy's hand were un-dyed. *So where was he?*

"Hey, Mac," Johansson called from his seat nearer the door. "There's someone here to see you."

Mac looked over. Lulu Sinclair, and it was definitely Lulu, stood in the doorway, a small purse over one shoulder. Mac jumped to his feet.

"Miss Sinclair. What can we do for you?"

She walked over to his desk, seated herself neatly in his own chair, and looked up at him archly. He laughed and hitched a hip on the desk. "Yeah, sorry, I don't know where the extra chairs went."

"It's okay," she replied in her husky contralto. "I won't be here long. I wanted to give you my new address. I've decided to move in with a friend out of town for a while, until the excitement dies down."

"But what about your work? And your part at the Guthrie?"

"Work travels on my computer. The part…I really regret that, but my being around the theater with all the press attention has completely disrupted rehearsals for the last two days. The management will be glad to have me out of there. In fact, they promised me a comparable part in a future production as soon as I broached the idea of leaving."

"I'm sorry," Mac said sincerely. "I was hoping we'd catch Anderson fast and the interest in you would get buried under the interest in him."

"So was I," she said with a sigh. "Well, it was still the right thing to do. Here." She held out a piece of paper. "That's my new address and phone. You can contact me if you need to. I've come this far, I'll testify if it helps. There's not much left to keep under cover." She lowered her voice to a husky whisper. "Well, maybe the fact that I actually gave him the blowjob. That detail hasn't come out yet." Her smile had a hint of a tease in it.

Mac took the paper. He felt like shit the way this worked out, even though there had been no other choice. They should have done better at keeping the details under wraps. It hadn't taken much work for the press to dig out Sinclair's whole story and jump on him…her. "You did do the right thing. If we get this guy, it will be because of you. You should give yourself a lot of credit."

"Hey," she said. "Maybe when this is over, I'll write a memoir and get rich. *I knew the Dagger Killer.*" She stood and looked up at Mac. "So how's the world treating you, honey? Because you look like crap."

"Nothing a few hours of sleep and catching Anderson wouldn't fix. I'm fine."

"Good." She headed for the door. "You can call me if you need a little sympathy, honey." She paused in the doorway to give the assembled detectives one long cool look. "Bye, guys. Don't do anything I wouldn't do."

"Whoo-ee," Hanson said as Lulu disappeared. "That's a guy?

Man, she makes a hot woman. If I didn't know better, I'd date her."

"She can do better than you," Mac told him.

"Like you?" Terrance teased. "She sounds like she's after you. Better watch out, or people will think you're its boyfriend."

"Yeah, Mac," Johansson put in. "What's with that anyway? You getting a little light? I was down at the courthouse yesterday testifying, and there's a bailiff there swears you're queer and shacked up with some boy toy."

"Oh, yeah?" Mac kept his voice quiet, but his stomach rolled. *Now what?*

"I told him where he could put that bullshit," Johansson said. "I mean, ain't no fucking queers in this squad room."

"Okay." *Drop it, please drop it.*

"Thing is," Johansson continued, "This guy claims you said it yourself in court, right in front of him."

"I never told anyone I was shacked up with a boy toy," Mac said desperately.

"Hey, now," Oliver said from behind him. "Is this crap finding Anderson for us? Because if it's not, I have some fun assignments for you." He held out a couple of paper slips to Johansson and Terrance. "Your next hallucinating witnesses. Go forth and interrogate, and bring me back some kind of solid clue."

The two men grumbled, but grabbed the slips and made their way out. Hanson headed back to his computer. Mac held out for a few minutes after they were gone, shuffling the papers on his desk, and then made his way to the washroom. *Walk, don't run.* Once through the door, he plunged forward and just made it to a stall before his stomach tried to turn itself inside out. The bitter dregs of coffee tasted worse coming back up than they had going down. Thank God he hadn't eaten anything recently. The dry heaves were subsiding when Oliver's voice said from outside the stall, "Are you okay?"

"I'm fine," Mac said, as clearly as possible.

"Bullshit," Oliver told him. "Open the door."

Mac sighed and unlatched the door. Oliver peered in at him, and Mac met his eyes painfully.

"Jesus," Oliver said. "You look like death warmed over. You can't go back out there."

"I'm fine. Just something I ate."

"Right. And I'm Queen Mary. Listen, I'll get you an assignment, send you out to an interview for a bit. Can you get your act together before you come back?"

"Yeah, sure," Mac agreed. "That would be good."

Oliver scanned through the remaining slips in his hand. "Here. An elderly woman in Rosedale. Can't be too tough. She thinks Anderson is living in the vacant house next door."

"Got it." Mac took the paper and stuffed it in his pocket. He went to the sink, wetted a paper towel, and wiped his mouth. Oliver was still watching him silently. "What are you going to say," Mac had to ask, "if they bring up the subject of my boyfriend again out there?"

"I don't know. Depends." Oliver gave him a questioning look. "What do you want me to say?"

Mac just shook his head.

"Yeah, that's what I thought," Oliver said, but his voice was not unkind. "Get the hell out of here and bring me Anderson's head on a platter. Then no one will care who you fuck."

Tony had stopped answering the buzzer for the apartment door. Likewise the landline. So maybe it wasn't a surprise when Mac's voice on his cell Friday evening was a little exasperated. "Hey, you want to let me up?"

"Sure!" Tony hurried over to push the release. "Sorry. You were right, the press found us."

"It's quiet down here now," Mac told him. "I'll be up in a second."

Tony waited for his knock before opening the door, and closed it quickly behind him. Mac had him wrapped in a hug before he could step back. "God, that's good," his deep voice said against Tony's neck. After a moment he eased off and looked into the apartment. "Where's Ben?"

"Playing Wii in the spare room. I put the small TV in there." Tony took a first good look at Mac and whistled softly. "Okay, this time you've gone right over the top on the hit-by-a-bus look."

"Anderson's in the wind somewhere. And the rumors about me are starting to circulate."

"Ouch," Tony said sympathetically. "Okay, hot water, food, and sleep. In what order?"

"I need a shower to be human."

"Shower first while I make food then. Except…you don't have any clean clothes here anymore. I'll try to dig up some underwear and a shirt that you might be able to wear. Leave the door unlocked and I'll toss them in."

"You're amazing," Mac said fervently. "Too bad I'm too tired to show you how amazing."

"Small-boy-in-the-other-room alert," Tony said, smiling. "Go get in the water."

The sound of the water running was a homey background, Tony decided, as he piled chicken salad on a plate with big slabs of bread and slices of apple. Ben wandered into the kitchen.

"I thought we had dinner," he said.

"We did, sport," Tony told him. "But Mac's here and he needs food."

"We haven't seen him for three days," Ben said plaintively.

"I know." *Boy, do I know.* "I told you, when he's busy with work, we won't see him as much."

"He should live here. Then we could see him every time he has to go to bed."

"When he's really busy, he doesn't even go to bed," Tony told the boy. He put the food on the table and added a glass of water. If he was any judge, Mac was probably so caffeinated right now his eyeballs were vibrating. And he had noticed Ben got quieter when he pulled anything alcoholic out of the fridge, so no beer. Ben boosted himself up into his chair and waited expectantly.

After a few minutes Mac appeared, Tony's Hawaiian shirt almost fully buttoned over his wrinkled slacks. Tony wished he had x-ray vision, because the stretchiest underwear he had found was a thong. Odds were, it was only just keeping Mac covered. When he raised his eyes, the wicked grin on Mac's face told him that Mac had guessed the direction of his thoughts.

"Here," Tony said tartly. "Stop looking at me like that and sit down and eat."

"Looking at you like what, Tony?" Ben asked as Mac followed orders and took a big bite of bread.

"Like I want to kiss him," Mac said with admirable nonchalance, taking another bite.

"Do you?" Ben asked. "Want to kiss him?"

"Right now I want to eat." Mac looked up at Tony, and his eyes were serious.

*Yes,* Tony wanted to shout. *Yes, say it now.* He kept his mouth shut. It still had to be Mac's call.

Mac turned to Ben. "Sometimes I want to kiss him, though."

"Really? Like a boyfriend?"

"Exactly like a boyfriend," Mac agreed, and upended his water glass like he hadn't drunk in days. Tony grabbed the pitcher and poured a refill. Mac's eyes met his again. Tony tried to put everything he was feeling into that look. *I love you. You're doing this right. This is a good thing.*

Mac turned to Ben. "Would you mind if I was Tony's boyfriend?"

"Do I get to choose?"

"Not exactly," Mac said, "But if you don't like it, we'll keep the boyfriend stuff away from you until you get used to it."

"I guess it's okay. Except kissing is kind of gross."

Tony glanced at his lover and knew the same thought was going through both their minds. *Just wait a few years.*

"But Tony's gay. Don't you have to be gay to be a boyfriend?"

"I'm gay too," Mac said. "So that works."

Ben nodded, thinking about it. Mac pretended to eat, and watched him. "That's good," Ben said eventually. "'Cause then you could move in here and it would be like a family, sort of."

"Whoa, partner," Mac said. "Let's not get ahead of ourselves. Tony and I are just boyfriends. We're not living together."

"But you could," Ben said eagerly. "You could have the spare room. I could put the Wii in my room. It would be great! And Anna could be here a lot, and I'll teach her to play Wii, because when we bought it she said she didn't know how, but I could teach her."

Tony laughed. "Give Mac a break," he said, feeling so light he thought he might float right up off the floor. "He needs to eat and sleep. We'll talk about other stuff later. And it's just about your bedtime, sport. Go get ready."

Ben wiggled down off his chair. "Okay." He looked at Mac. "I'm glad you're here," he said, and ran out.

"And turn off the TV!" Tony called after him.

He listened for a moment, until the distant bleeping was silenced, then turned to Mac and smiled. "That was very nice. I'm proud of you, babe."

"It went better than I thought," Mac admitted, applying himself to his food for real. "Almost too well. He'll have us married by tomorrow morning."

*And that would be a bad thing?* Tony stomped on his euphoria. *Give the man time.* "I need to go read to him and tuck him in. There's an apple pie on the counter for dessert. You should take the bed; that couch was never made for someone your size, and there's no bed in the spare room."

He left Mac to his food and his thoughts, and went to corral a hyperactive six-year-old. If the reporters were really getting over their interest in Ben, he needed to get the kid out to a playground. The boy was much too physical to stay cooped up indoors. The therapist said he wasn't talking about anything serious with her yet, but he'd been even more agitated after the appointment. Tony had brought him home, thinking about picking up swim trunks and going to the pool, but there had been reporters on the doorstep again. As if Ben's life wasn't complicated enough right now.

It took four books and one glass of water before Ben's eyes finally closed. Tony hovered over him for a minute, marveling at how young a sleeping child looked, how angelic. It was the eyelashes, he decided, and the lax hands. Awake, Ben was a great kid, but he didn't make you think of angels.

In the bedroom, his other man was also stretched out on the bed under the covers, eyes closed. But when Tony would have taken the baby monitor and quietly retreated to give him space, Mac opened his eyes and held out his hand.

"Come stay with me," Mac said softly. "I need you."

Tony melted. "Of course." Locking the door, shedding jeans and T-shirt, he climbed into bed with his briefs on. Mac flipped the covers open for him.

"God, you look more sinful in those than naked," he murmured. "And me too tired to do anything about it."

Tony chuckled. "So how does my other underwear fit you?"

"Like covering a banana with a Band-Aid. I took it off to sleep."

"If you're my boyfriend," Tony said contentedly, pulling up the sheet, "Then you can bring some of your stuff back over here. Because nothing I wear is going to fit you. And much as I like your banana, there are times you'll want it covered."

"Mm," Mac agreed drowsily. He blinked, rolled on his side

to look at Tony, and made an obvious effort to focus. "So, I should have asked, how was your day? How did...hey, Ben had his appointment with his therapist, didn't he? How did that go?"

Tony pulled himself back from sleepy contentment. It was good Mac wanted to know about Ben, even if his timing sucked. He bit his lip. "Hard to say. I like Dr. Kelman. She was good with him, not pushing too hard and really just letting him say what he wanted to. But he was extremely quiet. Even when I stepped out to give them privacy, she told me he didn't say anything much. She has some toys, dolls, puppets, things like that. She says he may act stuff out that way if he's not ready to talk about it. But... it's gonna be slow. He's not the kind of kid to just dump his problems on an adult and trust them to take care of it."

"I guess he hasn't had an adult he could count on for that."

Tony's stomach lurched. "Guess not."

Mac must have caught his tone, because he brushed his fingers over Tony's cheek. "I didn't mean you, babe. He trusts you. You know that. But when you weren't around he had Sandy. And it looks like she was pretty unreliable."

"Mm."

"Hey. Like you said, it takes time. You're doing the right thing for him. And for me." Mac brushed a kiss on Tony's shoulder. "You're definitely doing the right thing for me. And, and...God, I was going to say something." He kissed Tony again, lips drifting over Tony's collarbone.

Tony couldn't help arching a little closer. "Something about Ben? Or about your mouth and my skin?"

"You. Me. We should talk about Ben and yeah, skin is nice, but..." Mac gave a jaw-cracking yawn. "I need to talk to you, but I can't think."

"Don't think." Tony rolled over to spoon his back up against that warm muscled bulk. "Go to sleep now, think later. Ben and I will both still be here tomorrow." Mac put an arm around him and pulled him in, and was asleep between one breath and the next.

Tony lay awake for a long time, dreaming, wishing, hoping. That was an enormous step Mac had taken with Ben tonight. Tony wished he was certain it was deliberate and not the result of being too tired to care anymore. He hoped Mac wouldn't have regrets in the morning. The hardest thing about coming out, he reflected, was that it was irrevocable. You couldn't put the genie back in the bottle, or in the closet. But the first confession was the hardest, and Mac had done it, with Oliver and with Ben. He would have to trust him for the rest.

He woke in the early morning hours to feel Mac shaking in the bed next to him. He switched on the light and looked over. Mac's eyes were still closed, his face twisted in some unpleasant emotion, his muscles twitching in inhibited fight-or-flight. A nightmare. It was hardly the first. Tony grabbed Mac's shoulder and shook him. "Mac. Baby. Wake up, you're dreaming."

Mac came to with a startled gasp and a wrench that broke him free of Tony's hand as he sat up. Tony lay down and waited patiently for Mac to come back to himself. They had learned to deal with each other's nightmares this past year. Occasionally, Mac would give him some clue about the content of his dreams, but usually he shied away from the subject. Tony had learned not to pry.

After a few minutes, Mac dropped back onto the pillows. He rubbed a hand across his face and blew out a breath. "Shit. Haven't had that one for a while. I'm sorry I woke you."

"'S okay," Tony said. "Want to talk about it?"

"No, just…are you awake enough to talk about other stuff. Because I'm not getting back to sleep soon."

"Sure." Tony rolled more comfortably on his side, where he could see Mac's face in the green glow of the clock. The big man lay flat on the pillows, staring up at the ceiling. "Something particular?" No one ever had to do much to encourage Tony to talk.

"How did you come out?" Mac asked.

*Oh, that kind of particular.* "Well I didn't do it all at once. It's kind of a process. I figured out I was gay by the time I was thirteen, but I didn't tell anyone else. The first person I came out to was my best friend, Ashley. She went by Ash, 'cause there were about a hundred Ashleys in our school. Anyway, we'd been friends forever, since before middle school. When we were fifteen, Ash was bugging me about some dance, teasing, you know. Like, who would you take if you could choose anyone at all in the whole school? And I finally told her I would take this guy in my PE class, with the big shoulders and the perfect butt, and the hair on his chest. She was kind of upset, which surprised me because she was more militant for gay rights than I was at the time. It took me a while to figure out that she thought we were becoming a couple. I loved her to death, but not that way, while she was getting romantic about me."

"Was she okay with it?" Mac asked.

"Eventually," Tony told him. "Things were a little strained for a while. It took about six months, until she fell for this hockey player. Then I became just her old friend Tony again. After that she was great. In fact, she was the one who blackmailed me into taking my boyfriend to the senior prom. We doubled with her and her latest boyfriend, who was a pretty cool guy."

"So you were out at school?"

"Gradually," Tony said. "At first I was terrified. There was this guy, one year ahead of me. He was out, proud and as flaming as it comes; pink hair, eyeliner, in-your-face gay. Now I can't believe how brave the guy was, but at the time I just wished he'd shut up. I was so scared I'd bring down the kind of shit he got dumped on him, and I was scared I'd turn out to be like him. I wasn't in the least attracted to fem guys, and I didn't want to be one." Tony laughed. "I used to secretly watch the most macho guys in the school and then I'd practice in front of a mirror walking and moving like them."

"You're not fem," Mac said softly.

"I'm fine with who I am," Tony told him. "Now, anyway. Back then I was pretty freaking scared. But I got up the nerve to talk to another closet case in tenth grade, and we kind of dated, and then in eleventh I had a real boyfriend. By senior year, people just kind of figured it out. I got harassed some, beat up twice, but mostly people just stayed away if it freaked them out. And we went to the prom and danced with each other, both for the fun of it and as a kind of fuck-you to the guys who'd been on our backs all year. Ash and some of the other students hung with us and made it safe, and I had a great time."

"I went to prom with a girl," Mac said. "I was a perfect gentleman, picked a girl who was probably a virgin. I'm sure she was mostly glad I didn't want to do more than kiss her on the front steps and leave. I had a lousy time, spent most of it trying not to look too hard at all the guys in their tuxes."

Tony leaned over and kissed his nose. "Poor baby. Except it means you were still available for me."

"So," Mac said after a minute, "How did you tell your family?"

"That was harder," Tony admitted. "My sister caught me on the phone with my boyfriend when she came home from college for Christmas my junior year. She just asked me, was that a girl or a boy, and I told her. It turned out she'd suspected it for a long time. She was cool. My parents, I waited until I graduated. I could have told my mother any time but she couldn't keep a secret from my dad. So once I had my college acceptance and my summer job, and my dorm room reserved, I real subtly waited until the next mealtime. Then when my mom asked wasn't I seeing any nice girl that weekend, and I said no, but I was dating a rather bad boy. My dad practically choked on his soup."

"Was he angry?"

"More pained, uncomfortable," Tony recalled. "My mother was mostly upset that there wouldn't be grandchildren, and she worried that I'd get beat up or something."

"Which had already happened."

"Yeah, well, I didn't tell her that. It took a month or two of wistful hints about nice girls and marriage and babies, before she began asking what nice boys I'd met. My dad just wanted the whole thing to go away. Still does. He shudders visibly when I use the word boyfriend, and then changes the subject. But he didn't reject me or anything. He just doesn't want to know about my personal life."

"So they are okay with it?"

"Basically. If we ever come out all the way, I want you to meet them. My mom and my sister will like you, my dad will have conniption fits trying not to imagine you fucking my ass."

Mac choked. "Maybe I should stay away from him."

"Won't arise for a while. They stay down in Florida and don't come back up here anymore. They did the snowbird thing for a couple of years, but now they're firmly planted in the orange state, home of alligators and flying roaches. We'll have to go down there to visit."

"Your mom should be pleased about Ben," Mac suggested.

"True," Tony realized. "I haven't talked to her for a couple of weeks, with all this mess, but you're right. She's going to have a grandchild at last. She'll be happy, even if he's not her flesh and blood. She may even make my dad bring her up here when she hears the news."

"And Ben will have second grandparents," Mac said.

"Yep." Tony wiggled in closer. "Family, complicated, but nice."

"Not always," Mac muttered.

"You never talk about your family," Tony prodded gently.

"No," Mac said. "I don't. So how about at work? Were you out from the start?"

*Hands off the touchy subjects, huh.* "Yes. That was a hard decision. I know I lost some job offers by being up front about my sexual orientation. But I didn't want to ever be in a position where I could be outed at the wrong moment."

"I can understand that," Mac said bitterly.

Tony could tell by the tone that they were getting close to what was bothering Mac. "Was it bad at work today?" he asked softly.

"It was…I don't know. Sinclair came in, in full Lulu mode, and flirted with me, which didn't help. Rumors were being repeated, from the courthouse. I kept thinking, I should just say it, you know. Just put it out there and say yes, I'm gay, and what freaking business is it of yours. But I couldn't make myself do it. I kept trying to change the subject, without actually lying about it. I ended up throwing up in the john. Oliver rescued me by sending me out on all these witness follow-ups. One of which may have been a real lead, but anyway it kept me away from the rest of the guys most of the day. But I have to go in again tomorrow."

"Okay," Tony said. Mac had no business sounding like a scared kid. Except Tony remembered how it felt when the stories began to make the rounds at school. Mac was going through the same shit, just twenty years later. "So let's look at this out in the open. What are the bad things that can happen? No one's going to shoot you, right?"

"Hopefully not." Mac's voice was a little annoyed.

"Beat you up, wreck your stuff?"

"Probably not. There are some who might mess with my cases to give me a hard time."

"Well that's just pathetic. If they're willing to spoil a homicide case to get back at you."

"It's odd how homophobic a lot of cops are," Mac said. "I heard it all the time in uniform, calling guys fairies and saying you shouldn't break up a gay fight too fast because maybe one of them will do the world a favor and off the other one."

"Jesus," Tony said. "That's worse than high school."

"It's a lot like high school. Bullies and the in crowd, and how bad it is to find yourself outside the blue line. Except in this case, when you call for 'officer needs assistance,' you may get someone who decides to sit on his ass and let you take care of yourself in a firefight."

Tony shook his head. He had thought Mac was being a little

wimpy about the whole thing. Sometimes he'd fantasized about accidentally-on-purpose just blowing the door off their closet. But maybe there was something real for Mac to be afraid of; maybe he was just being realistic. "So being out could be life-threatening for a cop?"

"I don't know," Mac said. "You hear stuff. Minnesota isn't too bad, especially here in the city, but if you're a gay cop in small town Texas, you'd better plan to spend your life in the closet if you want to survive."

"Things have to change," Tony said fiercely. "I'm sorry, but that's not acceptable. When Ben and Anna grow up, gay kids shouldn't have to hide." He pushed up on one elbow to look down at Mac and meet his eyes. "That's part of why you're putting yourself out there," he told his lover urgently. "It's not just for us, right now. It's because every gay man and lesbian that comes out makes someone realize we're out there, just regular people. All kinds of regular people. Maybe knowing you will make some other cop break up that fight sooner, or listen more sympathetically to a gay witness. Because if Jared MacLean is gay, then it's not such a freaky thing after all."

"Or maybe they'll just decide I'm a freak."

"Some will," Tony had to admit. "But some won't. What about Oliver? You said he helped you out?"

"Yeah. He's hanging in with me so far."

"Good," Tony told him firmly. "What are you most afraid of tomorrow?"

After a moment, Mac said, "I walk in the door and the faggot comments start, and the rest of the guys won't work with me, and I get fired."

"Um, is that likely?" Tony was no longer sure he had a grasp on the reality of the police department.

Mac sighed deeply. "The comments, yeah, some. Most of the team will still work with me, but they won't like it. A couple will treat me like I have the plague. I won't get fired, but Severs will start washing his hands after he touches me, which he'll do as little as possible."

"Can you survive that?"

"I don't know," Mac admitted. "I just don't know."

Tony lay down flat again and snuggled in against Mac's shoulder. "I wish I could help. Hey, I could start insulting you, help you get used to it and grow a thicker skin. I could call you fudge-packer and cock-sucker."

Mac growled. "Cut it out. Anyway from you they sound like invitations."

Tony snickered. "Boy-lover, ass-fucker."

Mac stopped his mouth with a kiss.

Tony sighed contentedly when Mac finally let him go. "I love you, you know that," he told his man.

"Yeah." Mac pulled him into a warm hold, their bodies touching from shoulder to thigh, skin on skin. Mac's breath fanned over his cheek.

Tony was almost asleep when Mac said in his ear, "That nightmare…"

Tony fought himself back up to awareness to say, "Tell me."

"I'm at the station, and everyone's looking at me. And they start calling me a faggot, and saying I'm sick and perverted. And then Anna's there, but they pull her away from me. They tell her they're going to put her in a nice normal family. And they're taking her away. And I try to go after her, but I'm cuffed to something and I can't break loose. Anna's crying but she won't look at me and she walks away with them."

"Oh, babe." Tony kissed his shoulder. "You're a great dad and Anna loves you. She won't care that you're gay, and no one can take her away from you. Hell, they gave me Ben and I'm not even related to him. Anna is yours."

Mac breathed a sigh into his hair. "Yeah. I know. But it helps to hear you say it."

Tony slid back into sleep.

CHAPTER 14

Mac imagined that conversations stopped when he walked back into the station around nine the next morning. When he got to Homicide, he knew it was no longer his imagination. Only a couple of people were at their desks. The rest were out tracking leads or working the gang-related killing that had hit their desks yesterday. But those who were there paused just a moment to look at him, then got very busy with something. Mac shrugged. No Loes, no Terrance, it could be worse.

He sat at his desk to write up his last two calls. He had already come in really early that morning, grabbed the first two messages on the stack, and headed out before the rest of the team arrived. But both sightings had been simple mistakes, people with only a vague resemblance to Anderson, and with solid ID.

Unlike yesterday. The lady in Roseville had actually been right. Someone was squatting in the empty house next door. It wasn't Anderson, unfortunately, but a background check had revealed that the man had outstanding warrants for burglary and assault, and Mac had picked the guy up. It had taken a while to process him, but Mac hadn't begrudged the time at that point. It felt like the only productive thing he had done in days.

He was finishing his notes when Captain Severs appeared momentarily at the door of his office.

"MacLean," he snapped. "In my office, now."

Mac rose slowly, straightened the papers on his desk, and headed that way. Before he reached the office door, Oliver appeared.

"Hey, Mac," he called. "Got a live one for us."

Mac shook his head and pointed. "Captain wants me."

"About?"

Mac shrugged one shoulder. Nothing good, he suspected.

Oliver peered at him, then strode ahead to pull open the captain's door. "Well, let's get it over with so we can move on this."

Mac hesitated, then followed him into Severs' office and closed the door. The captain looked up from his seat with a frown.

"Oliver, this doesn't concern you."

"My partner," Oliver said, leaning casually on the wall beside the door. "My case. And I need him, so go for it."

Severs hesitated, and then turned to Mac. "I've had a complaint of unprofessional conduct."

Mac just shook his head, wondering what was coming.

"The complaint states that you are a homosexual and you engaged in sexual activities with the witness, Walter Sinclair, in a way that could jeopardize our whole investigation." He stared coldly at Mac.

Mac sputtered. "I've seen Walter Sinclair all of three times. Once with Loes present, once with Oliver, and one time with half the squad watching. I've barely shaken hands with the man."

"Good." Severs appeared to relax drastically. "I thought it had to be a mistake. I mean, of all the people on my team, you're obviously not queer."

"No," Mac heard himself say. "That part is right. I'm gay. I just never had any kind of relationship with Walter Sinclair." He stopped abruptly and fought the inclination to put his hands over his mouth. After all these years, why was he suddenly losing control over what he said? *Although the last time his mouth got that far out of control, he'd asked Tony to marry him. Maybe his mouth was smarter than he thought.*

He watched as Severs' face went red. The man coughed, then sputtered, "And why wasn't I informed of this?"

"Because it was really no one's business but my own. What I do on my own time, as long as it's legal, has no bearing on my work. For all you know, Loes could be keeping a harem, but that's his business."

"It's not a joke," Severs snapped. "This could affect the whole department."

"I know it's not a joke. It's my personal life, and it has no influence on my work. What I do at home should have no place in the department."

Severs stared at him, the color in his face deepening. "You can't...don't tell me what has a place in my department. How long...?"

Mac kept his face bland. "Since I was twelve, actually." *Ask for TMI, get TMI.* Severs looked about ready to burst, the veins in his forehead standing out against his flushed skin.

"Are we done here?" Oliver put in from his place by the door. "Because we've got work to do. Mac told you the complaint's bullshit. He has witnesses. So can we get out of here?"

"You!" Severs turned his glare on the other detective. "You knew about this!"

"Yeah, so?" Oliver took a step forward. "Look, I like girls. I *really* like girls. But if Mac doesn't, so what? More for the rest of us. He does the job, better than most of the clowns out there. Why should I care who he goes home to?"

"It looks bad for the department!"

"The only thing that looks bad," Oliver said, "is you inviting a discrimination complaint. Are we done?"

Severs turned angrily back to Mac. "You better toe the line," he snarled. "I'll be watching you and I don't want to hear any more complaints about you. You understand me?"

*Then stop listening to Loes.* Mac didn't say it. There was a difference between a smart mouth and a smart man, and he wanted to keep this job. He gave the captain a nod and exited gratefully out the door Oliver had pulled open.

They walked through the squad room and into the hallway before Mac realized the muffled sound behind him was Oliver trying not to laugh. In the elevator, the older man leaned against the wall, chortling. "God, Mac, did you see his face? Man, I owe you money for that. What would you call that color? Chartreuse?"

Mac was caught between laughing and hyperventilating. "Puce?" he offered.

"Yeah, that sounds right," Oliver took a deep breath. "I thought he was going to stroke out."

Mac sobered. "Listen man, thanks…"

"Hey." Oliver punched him in the arm, maybe a little harder than necessary. "You're my partner. I've got your back, you've got mine. Not backside, mind you, but your back, yeah."

Mac choked and relaxed. If Oliver was up to joking about it, they were going to be okay.

"So," Oliver said, as they got off the elevator, "Let's go see what Ramsey has. She says it's really hot. She's probably chewed her fingernails to the elbow waiting for us."

They parked the Taurus behind Ramsey's unmarked car on a run-down suburban street. The houses were two-story single-family units, although in that neighborhood Mac bet most of them had multiple tenants. They were mainly covered in wood siding, in pale shades of paint, some weathered and some better-maintained. The yards were dusty and brown with the heat. Only the occasional patch of flowers showed a meager attempt at watering. The house where Ramsey stood on the steps fit right in with the rest, maybe a little neater than the average.

"What've you got?" Oliver asked as they approached.

"I think Anderson was here, just a couple of days ago," Ramsey reported, suppressed excitement in her voice. "We got the call from a Mrs. Linda Lo, that she had rented a room to a man that fit his appearance. There's an elderly woman home right now who is probably the mother or grandmother. I'd swear she recognizes the photo, but she has very little English. She won't let me in until Linda gets home, which I think will be soon."

"Should we get out of sight?" Mac suggested, "If Anderson

might come back."

"Both the phone call and the grandmother seemed certain he's long gone," Ramsey said.

"Even so," Oliver decided. "You stay here, you don't look threatening. Mac and I will take a walk. Call my cell as soon as the daughter gets home."

It was only five minutes of waiting down the block before Ramsey's call came through. They returned to the house to find her talking on the steps with a middle-aged Asian woman. Linda Lo was tiny, barely up to Ramsey's shoulder. She looked tired and rumpled in pale blue scrubs and white shoes. Ramsey introduced the two men. Mrs. Lo shook hands, her grip firm for someone so small.

"Will you please come in," she said, clearly but with a strong accent. They followed her into the house. An even tinier elderly woman smiled and nodded to them as they entered. Mrs. Lo put her bag on the counter and took down a kettle. "Would you like to have tea?" she asked. "I need tea after my work."

"Could we just ask you," Oliver said impatiently, pulling out the photo, "Is this the man you rented a room to?"

Mrs. Lo glanced at it. "Yes, that is the man. Same as on TV."

"Is there any chance he will come back here?" Oliver asked urgently.

"No," Mrs. Lo said certainly. "He is gone. Three days gone."

Mac and Oliver looked at each other. So close, but not enough.

"Mrs. Lo," Mac said more gently. "Could we see the room he rented?"

"Yes," she agreed with a sigh. "Downstairs. I will show you."

She put the kettle on the stove and led the way down a flight of stairs. At the bottom, four doors were arranged in a square. She pointed at each in turn. "Furnace room, bathroom, was Mr. Trahn's room, and that one, was this man in the picture."

"Mrs. Lo," Mac said formally. "Do you give us permission to

go in that room and search it, check for fingerprints, and collect evidence?"

"Yes," she said. "Go in, see what is there."

Mac turned to Oliver. "Good enough?" Neither of them wanted any risk of illegal search issues, which could invalidate evidence.

"Did you have a rental agreement with this man?" Oliver asked. "Anything written down on paper?"

"No," she said. "Only we said that he pays me on Fridays each week. But not yesterday, because he is gone. He did not pay. Not his room anymore."

"And you own this house?"

"Yes. It is mine."

"Good enough," Oliver said. "Her permission should be good." He pulled out his phone. "I'll get a crime scene team down here and start working. You and Ramsey talk to the two ladies, see if you can find out anything useful."

"Fingerprints would be nice," Mac told him.

"Oh, yeah. First thing on my list."

Upstairs, Mac agreed to a nice cup of tea and followed Mrs. Lo to the table. She passed out small, translucent, handleless cups of steaming green tea to all four of them. Mac cradled his between his palms, feeling like a giant between the two tiny women. Across the table, Ramsey took a small sip and nodded at him, agreeing that he would start the questioning. He made a little scribbling gesture with one hand to encourage her to take notes.

"Mrs. Lo," he said. "When you rented a room to this man, what name did he give you?"

"He had driver's license that said Mr. Leonard Johnson."

"Johnson?" Mac repeated. *Another top-ten Minnesota surname.* But that first name made it more likely this was the right man, not just another case of mistaken identity. "A Minnesota driver's license?"

"Yes."

"Did you see a car?"

"He had a blue car," she said. "Dark blue, not old, not new. It was clean. I look because a man who keeps his car clean inside will keep my room clean."

"Did you notice anything else about the car?" Mac asked. "Any stickers on the bumper, any dents, things hanging from the mirror?"

"No, just a car," she said.

"Do you know where the man worked?"

"Not the name of the place. But he worked with Mr. Trahn who was living here. Mr. Trahn knows I have a room empty, and he says this man works with him and needs a place to stay. So I rent him the other room."

"Where is Mr. Trahn now?" Mac asked.

"His brother in Duluth says there is better work there," she told him. "So he left to go to Duluth. One week now."

Mac made a mental note to get Trahn's full name and try to track him down. Finding Anderson's new workplace could open up plenty of leads.

"When did you first meet Johnson?" he went on.

"Three weeks," Mrs. Lo said. "He pays for the room, one hundred fifty dollars every week."

"He paid cash?"

"Yes, cash."

Mac sighed. Well, a check would have been a miracle. "Exactly when did he leave?"

"It was Tuesday, in the evening," she told him. "I am getting ready for work. I have the night shift at the hospital. I hear him downstairs in the room, shouting. He is never loud before but now he is shouting and banging."

The grandmother was nodding like she followed the conversation, and now she leaned forward and said, "Focking weetniss!" She pounded the table with her small fist, almost gleefully. "Focking weetniss." She added a rapid phrase to her daughter in another language.

Mrs. Lo nodded. "My mother says he is crazy," she told them. "He breaks things and was shouting this, you excuse my language, 'fucking witness,' so loud."

"Then what?" Mac asked.

"I go upstairs to the bedroom with my mother, because he sounds crazy. I hear the front door so I look out the window. This man, he takes some bags to his car and then he drives away. After awhile I go down and look at the room. He has broken the TV and the wall. But his things, they are all gone."

"But you didn't call the police?"

"No," she said quietly. "The renting rooms, you understand, it is not...I do not keep all the correct papers. And also, I am worried he might come back. He still has keys for the door. I wait three days. I see his picture on TV and I wait until I know he will not come back, and then I call."

"You did the right thing," Mac encouraged her. No point in getting angry over the delay. If he was a hundred pound woman, and worried that a raging Leonard Anderson might come back, he might have been reluctant to call too.

"Did you change the lock on the front door?" Ramsey leaned forward to ask.

"No." Mrs. Lo looked startled. "I did not think of this."

"I can call someone for you," Ramsey offered. "We'll get that lock changed. You'll feel safer."

"Thank you," Mrs. Lo said gratefully. "Yes, I would like that."

Mac settled in for more questions; what was Anderson's schedule, did he ever have anyone over, did he bring home take-out food from any particular restaurant, did he talk about himself at all, did he go out in the evenings, and so on. Part-way through, Ramsey went to the door to let in the technicians, who disappeared down the stairs. Mac reined in his desire to follow them and continued his questions. They didn't get much new information. Anderson had kept to himself, and Mrs. Lo was not a nosy landlady. Knowing that Anderson liked Arby's would not help them much.

After a while, Oliver appeared at the top of the cellar stairs, his face alight. "We got a match," he said. "Not official, but there's prints all over down there and a fool could see that they match the ones from Brand." He waved the print card he'd been comparing jubilantly.

*Yes!* Mac could feel the wide grin on his face to match Ramsey's. They had the right man! All this effort wasn't just a wild goose chase. And now they could add murder counts to the warrant and justify any action they needed to take. He hadn't realized the weight of uncertainty until it dropped off.

"Mrs. Lo has been very helpful," Mac told Oliver in return, "But we don't have any clues to where Anderson is living or working now."

Oliver shrugged. "We'll keep plugging. There's not much down in that room, although we should get DNA for sure, to firm up the ID. There's even blood, where it looks like he put his hand through the wall. When you're done, I'd like Mrs. Lo to come down and tell us if anything left in the room is Anderson's rather than hers."

"Now, if you like," Mac offered.

As they followed Mrs. Lo toward the stairs, Ramsey asked Mac quietly, "The thing with him yelling about a witness. Should we call Sinclair and warn her…him? Do you think Anderson might go after him?"

"Maybe," Mac agreed. "It would be stupid, but if he's angry enough…I'll call Sinclair. He's staying with friends right now, which should make him harder to find. But at the same time, now that he doesn't have a hundred cameras following his every move, he's more vulnerable. I wonder…it might be worth putting a decoy in Sinclair's apartment, in case Anderson does try to make a move on him." He thought about it. Worth proposing. It was only today that the media feeding frenzy had been noticeably winding down. Anderson might have been waiting for the opportunity. Mac decided he would spend a little time looking at the film of Sinclair's public appearances and talking to his neighbors, see if Anderson had been sniffing around.

At least they now had some actual physical evidence to work with. Who knew, maybe the techs would find a pay stub or gas receipt in Anderson's room. Something they could use to track the bastard. Although Oliver had said there wasn't much. Mac couldn't resist heading down after Oliver and Mrs. Lo to see the room himself. They were making progress, but it always seemed to be two steps forward and one step back.

Mac followed Ramsey into the Homicide squad room, mentally planning their next priorities. Locating Trahn and finding out where Anderson had been working was at the top of his list. A decoy at Sinclair's was appealing. He was energized by the knowledge that they were on the right track. A drawling voice from behind him made him turn around.

"Well look what the cat dragged in," Loes said, leaning against the wall in a pose designed to look casual but strung tight as wire. "It's Minnesota's own faggot detective. How about it, Mackie? Did you bring us back a bone in your mouth?"

Mac sighed and took a firm rein on his temper. "Give it a rest, Loes."

The room was still, everyone watching. Mac couldn't gauge how much support Loes had from the other team members.

"You're a disgrace," Loes hissed. "How can you just walk in, like you deserve to be here?"

"Come on," Ramsey said to Loes. "Just lay off. We have new evidence here. You need to let us work."

"And how did you get that new evidence, Mackie?" Loes

added, pushing off the wall and taking a step forward. "Did you fuck another transvestite for it?"

"Jesus," Mac muttered. He turned away, toward his desk.

Behind him, Loes' voice became more shrill. "I found out who your boy toy is." Mac looked back. "It's that fag teacher from Roosevelt, Tony Hart, isn't it? How is he, Mackie? You like the girly ones, huh? Does he come home from school and put on a little plaid skirt and bend over for you?"

Mac didn't remember moving, but the next thing he knew Loes was pinned up against the wall with Mac's arm across his throat. Loes' eyes bugged out in surprise. Mac leaned on his arm a little, drawing a choking noise from Loes.

"You can say what you like about me," Mac said slowly and coldly. "I don't give a shit. But you keep your filthy mind and your filthy mouth off Tony." He leaned harder, relishing the moment when distain edged into fear in Loes' eyes.

"What the hell is going on here?" Severs' voice shouted from behind him.

Mac dropped his arm and stepped back. Loes slumped against the wall, drawing in a harsh breath. He raised one hand to his throat.

"Well?" Severs demanded.

"We had a little disagreement," Mac said. "I think we have it straight now." He stared at Loes hard, although he was starting to shake inside. *I assaulted another officer.* It was nothing big, probably not even a bruise, but Loes could make something out of it. Loes glared back but said nothing.

"I can't have my officers fighting in the squad room," Severs said angrily. "MacLean, you're out of here. Take a day's suspension. In fact, I don't want to see your face around here until Monday. And then I'll expect an apology to Detective Loes. I won't have this kind of behavior from you."

Ramsey began to protest, but Mac put a hand on her arm. Now was not the time to contradict Severs.

"Yes, sir," he said. "Can I take ten minutes to brief Detective Ramsey on my case, which is getting hot?" *And which you are pulling me off of at the wrong moment.* It was his own fault, for losing his temper. *Fool!*

"Ten minutes," Severs agreed reluctantly. "And then I want you gone. Don't make me write this up officially." He stomped back to his office.

"That's not fair," Ramsey whispered as she followed Mac to his desk. "If Loes talked that way about someone's girlfriend, half the squad would help rough him up."

"Doesn't matter," Mac said. He glanced around. Most of the other detectives had gone back to work and were carefully not looking at him or Loes. A couple of people had gone to Loes, ostensibly to check him out. Loes was making a big production of feeling his neck. Mac shook his head in disgust. The man wasn't hurt. Mac could have done damage if he had wanted to. Fortunately he'd been smart enough to avoid that. *Not smart enough to keep your hands off the bastard in the first place.* He took up the papers from his desk.

"So you really are gay?" Ramsey said quietly.

"Yeah, really."

"Okay," she said. "So what do you want me to do next on Anderson?"

Mac concentrated on showing her the papers; a few more tips to follow, others that were his "definite whack-jobs" pile, not to bother with. They needed to set Detective Hanson tracking down Trahn, and while they were at it, do a new search under the name Leonard Johnson. Ramsey nodded and made notes. Finally he shrugged. "That's as far as I've planned it. The rest will depend on whether you find anything from that. Oliver will figure it out when he gets here. Will you call me...?" He shouldn't ask her.

"Sure," she said immediately. "I'll keep you informed. Oliver will be pissed that you're not here."

"Tell him it was my own stupid fault."

"Are you worried that Loes might make trouble for you?"

"A little," Mac admitted. "Not much I can do now. Maybe he'll be too nervous to push me."

"What do you mean?"

"Well," Mac glared across the room at Loes until the man ducked his head and looked away. "Think about the straight boy and the fag in a dark parking lot. Who are you betting on this time?"

Ramsey snorted. "I guess. He doesn't have to meet you head on to make a complaint, though."

"No." Mac shrugged and pulled out his car keys. "I'll be thinking of you suckers while I'm sleeping in on Sunday morning." *Not.* "Good luck." He headed out, not looking at Loes again.

CHAPTER 15

Mac pulled up outside his own apartment and climbed the steps to his door. The excessive heat was finally slacking off, and the enclosed stairwell was not the sweatbox it had been. His apartment was waiting for him, cluttered and dusty. He put away his gun and ran a finger over the counter. A clear line followed his fingertip; he had rarely been there, and then only to crash and sleep. He couldn't remember the last time he had cleaned or shopped, or done anything for this space.

He wandered to the window, looking out. The third-floor view had been his only consolation for this space. *Tony's new apartment was on the third floor.*

The shower was cramped, the water lukewarm, the towel stiff and thin. He looked in the small mirror, shaving carefully. The wall was three feet behind his head, painted plywood. *I hate this place.*

Clean, shaved, dressed, he stood irresolute in the kitchen area. He could eat…something, and crash. *You should think.* So, think.

He thought better when he was moving. He had a car, such as it was, and a tank of gas. He headed out.

After a while of driving aimlessly, he realized he was cruising past the downtown bars in hope of spotting Anderson. Futile, except as a way of postponing other issues. He drove down to the river and found one of his favorite pull-out spots on a bank overlooking the water. In the late summer sun, the Mississippi wound its lazy way, wide and brown, through Mac's city. And it was his city, he realized. He was settled here.

He liked Minneapolis. Arriving here from Chicago, on his way to points west, he had thought it flat and dull. But in the process of earning enough money to fix his ailing car, he had become interested in the people. He'd noted the odd mix of dark-haired small Hmong and Vietnamese among the big blond descendents of hardy Norwegian and Swedish pioneers. There were a lot of

Nordic types in Minnesota. Probably because they were the only ones whose ancestors were willing to face winters so cold they could freeze your ass to an outhouse seat. There were few of the Hispanics so common in Chicago, and a small black population. But it seemed to work. People were polite and friendly without being in your face. When he'd gotten his car back on the road, he had somehow hung around this city, where no one honked their horns, or rode an inch off your back bumper, and people actually let you merge ahead of them on a busy freeway.

The first winter had been a revelation, even to a native Chicagoan. But by spring he had passed his police entrance exam and been accepted into training. He felt the native pride at surviving the winter's snow and wind. The city greened and then heated, so fast that residents warned you not to blink during spring or you would miss it. The river changed from solid ice, to floating bergs, then fast and frothy with run-off, and lazy with summer heat. He thought it had character that the big lake in Chicago never showed. And if the city was flat, well it was also green, and around every corner was another lake, or pond, or stream. And so he stayed.

He knew this place now. Knew the skyway system that crisscrossed the downtown streets a story overhead, knew which silver building-block art museum was which, knew when the forty thousand students at the university would be crossing the streets, making driving slow and avoiding fatalities by the grace of God. He could find a good restaurant, or a good bar, or a park with miles of trail to run. He had made a life here. So now he had to decide what that life would become.

He was out of the closet at work with a vengeance now. Not just the fact of being gay, but Tony's name, their relationship. Nothing to hide or protect there anymore. He would either survive it with his job intact, or not, but he wasn't telling anything but the truth now.

*The truth is I want to be with Tony.* And with Ben? Because there was a catch. They were a package now; Tony came with a six-year-old boy attached. What he and Tony could have from here on out would be different from the intense sexual world they had made of the little apartment this past year.

But from the first, it had never been just about sex, with Tony. And Ben was great. Mac had always liked kids. He had thought about the fun he would have teaching Anna to play baseball soon. And with a boy, maybe they'd play football too, and hockey; he understood boys better than girls, he thought. He had no illusions about the work involved in raising kids. But surely he and Tony together could have more fun at it and do a better job than either one alone. And as far as sex went, there was that shower...

*So what's holding you back?* Anna, he realized, just Anna. Because if he did this, if he went to Tony and said, "I want to be with you, make a home with you and Ben," then he had to tell Anna he was gay. Somehow that was far more daunting than any of his other confessions had been. Mac had always been a hero in Anna's eyes. The thought of losing that took his breath.

And he would be taking Anna away from Brenda. Maybe not right away, but eventually it had to happen. Brenda just didn't have it in her to be flexible. He had cursed Anderson for taking Ben's mother. Did he have the right to chase away the only mother his own child had really known, just for his selfish pleasure?

Mac realized he had to see Anna, had to talk to her. Not to ask her whether she would choose him or Brenda. That was the most unfair question you could ask a child: do you like Mommy or Daddy better? But he could talk to her, ask other questions. Surely there would be some way to tell if he had to give up Tony, as he had willingly given up so much else, to keep Anna happy. He would do it, but this time he didn't feel willing. He started the car.

Brenda's house was small, but nice and excruciatingly well kept. It was clean and safe. Anna knew this neighborhood, knew this house as the only home she could remember. Mac parked on the street and just looked at the place for a while, before getting out of the car. Brenda opened the door for him when he rang the bell, her face surprised.

"Jared, I wasn't expecting you."

"I know," he said, keeping his voice apologetic. He usually tried to give her advance warning. "Is Anna available?"

"She's just finishing a snack. But actually," Brenda stepped out onto the porch with him and pulled the door closed behind her. "I wanted to have a talk with you."

Mac nodded cautiously. "About?"

"Anna's school next year. I know your plan is for her to start public kindergarten. I've thought and prayed about it, and I really think she would be better, safer, in a church school. My church only has the preschool, but there are others. I've been asking around. There are good schools close by, where she would be with her own kind, and taught in a godly way."

Mac winced. Fortunately there was a simple answer. "I can't afford it. Preschool has been a stretch as it is." He had paid for that much, knowing that Brenda needed a break from childcare during the day. But he had been looking forward to the relief of stopping those payments.

"I would be willing to pay some of it out of my own money," Brenda offered. "Some of them are not so expensive, only three thousand or so. I can do it, to keep Anna safe and happy."

Mac sighed. Brenda loved Anna. He knew that. He didn't need this reminder right now, that it wasn't just the money that made her take care of his small girl. "Why do you think she wouldn't be happy in public school?" he asked.

Brenda lowered her voice. "Some of the things she says, when she's been around other children. She says people don't have to go to church. She uses bad language. Do you know what she came up with the other day? She said homosexual men were nice! Can you believe that? 'Gay men are nice people,' that child told me. I don't know where she's getting this stuff. Are you sure that boy Ben you let her play with is a good child? Because she tells me 'Ben says this' and 'Ben says that' and some of it is not acceptable at all."

"Ben is fine," Mac said shortly. "And some homosexuals *are* nice. Some are bad, some are amazing, some are athletic, dumpy, artistic, petty, smart, deluded, successful, kind. They're just people."

"But not God-fearing," Brenda insisted. "They can't be that."

"Sometimes too much," Mac said bitterly. "Never mind. We won't agree on this."

"I know your job puts you out among all sorts of people. But a small child doesn't need to be exposed to it."

"You're the one who told her about fornicators," Mac pointed out.

Brenda's face flushed red. "You're right. I got down on my knees and asked God's forgiveness for that. I was just so worried, with these women getting killed, just because they can't live a godly life, and I said too much in front of the child."

*You didn't ask* my *forgiveness.* Mac let it pass. "Right now, I'd like to take Anna out for a couple of hours. I'll give her dinner. We'll talk about school…next week." By then he would have burned his bridges, one way or another.

"We need to do it soon, though. Some of those places already have a wait list. But all right. I'll get Anna."

Mac braced himself for his daughter's usual explosion out the door, but this time she exited demurely and just smiled at him. "Hi, Daddy."

He took her hand as they started down the steps. "No hug?" he asked her.

Anna glanced back at the house. "It's not ladylike. I've been extra good for days and days now, and Aunt Brenda is happier."

"Well, maybe I can get that hug when Aunt Brenda can't see us," he suggested. "Because I like it."

"Okay," Anna agreed, a sparkle in her eyes. They got in the car, and before fastening her seatbelt across the booster, Anna wrapped him in a stranglehold. Mac hugged her back.

"I missed you, princess."

"Missed you too, Daddy."

He let Anna set their course and they ended up at her favorite park. The summer heat had finally backed off, and it was warm and breezy. Mac sat on a bench and watched Anna play for a bit, but she soon came back and sat beside him.

"Done already?"

"It's better with someone else, like Cindy or Ben."

There was an opening to what he wanted to know. "You like Ben?"

"Oh, yes," Anna said. "He's the best boy I know. Cindy's brother Michael is always telling us we're just dumb girls and we can't do stuff. But Ben helps me do lots of stuff. He never says I'm just a girl."

"Um." Mac wasn't sure if this was good or not. "You know there are things Ben does that you're not ready for."

"Yes, 'cause he's bigger 'n me. But I'm growing fast."

"So you are." Mac thought about how to ask his questions. "Is Aunt Brenda really happier now?"

"I think so." Anna put her finger on her chin and thought. Mac's heart twisted. *How did she have Mai's gesture down pat, when she never saw it?* His daughter smiled at him. "Sometimes Aunt Brenda gets mad and sad, but if I'm gooder than good it helps. And she did extra church stuff."

"Do you miss your mom?" he asked. "Or does Aunt Brenda feel like a mom?"

"She's not quite a mom. When I was little once I asked if she was going to be my mom one day and she said no, not ever. But she's my aunt, which is almost as good."

"I've been thinking," Mac said slowly, "About moving in with Tony and Ben, and sharing their apartment. The new place is pretty big. They have an extra room."

"Oh yes, Daddy!" Anna's eyes were bright. "Your apartment is all small and stinky. Ben's place is awesome, and they have two TVs and lots of books. I want to go back there soon."

"The thing is, Aunt Brenda doesn't like Tony and Ben much. She thinks we shouldn't visit them so often."

"She should know them. They're so nice. If Aunt Brenda came with us to see them, she would know they're nice."

"Um, that's one of the things it's hard to change Aunt Brenda's mind about," Mac hedged. "Like not letting me in the house, even though I'm nice."

"Is it in her Bible?" Anna asked. "That she shouldn't like Ben and Tony? Because I think her Bible stinks sometimes. But she gets really mad if I say that."

"I'll bet," Mac murmured. "Yes, Anna, it's a Bible thing. And I don't know whether I should stay with Tony and Ben, if it makes Aunt Brenda mad at us."

"I think we don't have to tell Aunt Brenda. I think we should see Ben and Tony lots and not tell."

Mac sighed. Obviously he was teaching his child dishonesty from the depths of his closet. And he still couldn't decide.

"If Aunt Brenda decided to go away for a while and you had to stay with me and Tony, would you be really sad?"

"I don't want Aunt Brenda to go," Anna said slowly. "She's my Auntie."

"What if I had to go away for a while?"

Anna grabbed him around the waist and pressed her face into his stomach. "You can't go!" she said fiercely. "You're my daddy and you can't go. You have to stay with me always."

Mac stroked her hair. "Don't worry, princess. I just said if. I'm not going anywhere, just trying to figure something out."

Anna looked up at him without releasing her tight hold. "I could stay with you and Ben and Tony forever, if you wouldn't go away."

Mac kissed her hair. "I'll remember that," he said. "Okay, I think it's time for dinner. Where would you like to go eat?"

"You're not leaving?" Anna insisted.

"I will never leave you," Mac told her firmly. "I swear."

"Cross your heart and hope to die?"

"Cross my heart," he agreed.

Anna nodded. "Then I want to go to Taco John's and have lots and lots of potato cakes."

Tony was surprised to hear Mac downstairs on the intercom shortly after dinner that evening. Usually when a case was hot the way this one was, he was lucky to see the man every two days for a few hours of dead-to-the-world sleep and a hurried sandwich. He opened the door to Mac's knock. Mac hefted a big plastic bag and looked at him enquiringly. Tony couldn't hold back a smile. *Mac's home.*

Ben looked up from the TV and was across the room in a second.

"Mac!" he said. "I lost a tooth. Look."

Mac dutifully inspected the resulting gap and, with a wry look at Tony, inquired what the tooth fairy paid for teeth these days.

"Jimmy Peters gets a whole dollar," Ben reported. "Paco and Ramon only get a quarter, 'cause their mom says the tooth fairy doesn't bring as much in big families. But we're a small family so I think I should get a dollar."

"We'll see," Tony told him. "Only the tooth fairy knows the going rate. Put it under your pillow and you'll find out in the morning."

Mac allowed himself to be coaxed into a computer game match. Tony washed dishes, enjoying the background murmur of voices, Ben's high squeals of glee interspersed with Mac's low rumble. Bedtime was easier than usual, with the impending tooth fairy visit, although the boy coaxed a book from each adult before consenting to have the light out. Tony finally left the dim room, light filtering softly through the baseball nightlight, and pulled the door shut. The baby monitor was in the bedroom. He switched it on and carried it to the couch. Mac was already sprawled on one end, and Tony sank down next to him with a yawn.

"I know why kids have so much energy," Tony said. "They're like little vampires and they suck it out of their parents." He had done very little he could put a finger on all day, and yet he was wiped.

"How is Ben?" Mac asked.

"Pretty good," Tony told him. "The loose tooth was a good distraction, until it came out. I was wondering if we could borrow Anna again tomorrow, for company. Maybe go to a park or something."

"We'll all go."

Tony looked at Mac. "Aren't you working?"

"No," Mac said unrevealingly, but something in his tone made Tony look more closely.

"Spill it."

"I got suspended," Mac admitted. "Just until Monday."

"For what?" Tony asked indignantly.

"I pinned Loes up against a wall." Mac's voice was an odd mixture of chagrin and satisfaction. "And Severs saw me do it."

"Do I want to know what Loes did to deserve it?"

"No." There was no compromise in that statement.

"Okay. But that sucks, when you're finally making headway on the case."

Mac sat up, looking excited. "Real progress today. We found a room Anderson had rented and got prints. He's the guy. No doubt at all now."

"That's great!" Tony agreed. He knew it had gnawed at Mac not to be certain.

"But we still have to catch him," Mac said more soberly. "And I have to stay home and twiddle my thumbs."

"I can think of more interesting things for your thumbs to be doing," Tony offered. Mac clearly needed cheering up.

That made him smile. "I'll bet you can." He reached out and hugged Tony in close, but it was cuddling, not seduction. Tony went with the mood, leaning in, rubbing his cheek against Mac's shoulder. He drifted a little, too content to think about turning on the TV or getting up in search of activity.

"So tell me, Tony," Mac said very quietly. "You're smart. Why am I such a fucking coward about telling Anna the truth? I told Severs, for God's sake. Why can't I say it to Anna?"

That was easy, at least. "Because she matters to you. Her opinion matters, more than anyone else's. And because, my love, down in here," Tony tapped Mac's flat gut, "You still are not okay with being gay."

"I think I'm past that," Mac said a little huffily.

"No way," Tony told him, not raising his head from that muscled shoulder. "You wouldn't have trouble confessing this to her if you didn't think that it was a *confession*, that you're admitting something wrong. Whatever your head may tell you, down in your gut you still think of gay as *less than*. Less than normal, less than perfect, less than straight."

Mac was silent for a while. Then he said plaintively, "What do I do?"

"You live your life. You hang around people who think gay is as normal as a different hair color. You work with those kids at the center and see how much they need people to tell them they're okay, and believe it. You remind yourself of how ignorant your critics are. You let me show you the upside to being gay, as often as possible." He turned his face in and nipped at Mac's neck lightly.

Mac laughed. "And that will work?"

"Couldn't hurt." Tony pulled back a little to look at Mac. "Look, I'm no expert. I still have moments when I make an effort to pass, because it's easier. I'm still working on figuring out when it's necessary to take a stand and when it's not a good idea. But two things I am sure of: I'm gay, not going to change, ever.

And I'm okay. Not perfect, but I'm a good person, and so are you. And being gay is not just the sex, it's everything else that we have too. So it can't be wrong."

"There is nothing wrong with you," Mac told him intensely.

"Exactly." Tony stood up, grabbed the monitor with one hand and turned to Mac. "So now we need to work on confidence-building."

"Um," Mac stood. "Do I want to know?"

"Trust me," Tony purred, "And follow directions." *Ten steps to the bedroom, lock the door behind them, make sure a robe is on the hook for midnight child emergencies.* He turned to look at Mac, standing by the bed. "Strip," he ordered.

Mac raised an eyebrow at him, but began to comply slowly. Tony smiled as Mac began to draw it out a little, remembering that striptease Mac did for him in the stuffy little apartment. There was something incredibly sweet about a man moving that far out of his comfort zone to please you. Eventually, Mac was naked. Tony looked at him in the mellow light of the bedroom lamp.

Tony had always liked a big man, with a work-toned body. Mac lifted and ran, but he wasn't really ripped. He didn't have the time or the obsession. His shoulders were broad from the size of his frame, his biceps curved but not cut, his belly flat partly from muscle and partly because the man forgot to eat half the time. Strong legs, tight ass, light dusting of dark hair that thickened in all the right places. And then the bonus, which was hardening slowly as Mac watched Tony watching him. *Oh, yes.*

"Lie down on the bed," Tony ordered. "On your back." When Mac did so, he added, "Reach up over your head and grab the headboard bars."

"You having fun giving orders?" Mac asked, as he obeyed. Tony breathed hard as the pose arched Mac's ribcage away from his belly and curved his arms into an artwork of biceps and triceps.

"Yeah," Tony told him. "Neither of us has to always be the

one controlling things. We can take turns. Tonight I'm in charge."

Mac's cock bobbed and lengthened, and Tony laughed. "I see you like that." He pulled his shirt over his head, but left his jeans on. Climbing on the bed, he straddled Mac's thighs, pinning his legs to the bed. Tony traced a light finger over the flat belly and the arch of ribcage. Leaning forward, he let the rough seam of his jeans brush across Mac's sensitive shaft. And again, harder. Mac breathed in. Tony leaned down and kissed him, tonguing his mouth open. Mac met him at first, but then relaxed and gave way to the invasion of Tony's lips and teeth and tongue. Tony licked fast and deep and then pulled back.

Mac began to let go with a hand, and Tony closed his fist around the wide wrist. "Keep it there until I say let go," he growled. With some lovers he would have used scarf ties, but with Mac they had both learned that restraint was an immediate turn-off. It was sweet to let each other take control, but only as long as it remained a choice. Tony had memories of duct tape on his own wrists, so he knew where his hang-ups came from. Tony wondered if someday his close-mouthed lover would bring up an incident from his own past to explain why being restrained made Mac panic.

Mac obediently closed his hands on the bars again. Tony kissed the man's fist. "Good boy." He moved his mouth down that big body laid out for his pleasure, licking, biting. He nuzzled into one hairy pit, inhaling the tang of sweat and Mac. *So good.* He took a nipple in his mouth, rolling it, pulling up until he drew a small sound from Mac, then biting lightly. Mac groaned.

Tony's jeans were becoming really uncomfortable. He unbuttoned and unzipped, but didn't push them down. Sliding his hips, he let the metal teeth of his open zipper and the harsh edge of denim slide over Mac's cock.

"Careful," Mac whispered, but as he said it he was trying to open his legs and push upward into the friction. Tony pressed a little harder, closing his thighs to keep Mac pinned. He dug his fingers into the hard mounds of Mac's pecs, and rammed his ass down against Mac, who whimpered, "Jesus, Tony!" Tony laughed softly and did it again, lighter and faster, and then again, turning pressure to motion. Mac bucked up against him.

Tony slid down the bed and climbed off, walking around to where Mac could see him well. He stripped off his jeans slowly then slid his briefs down, a millimeter at a time. He knew Mac really liked him partially dressed, but for what he was planning he wanted his legs free. He kicked the fabric off his feet and stood, eyeing Mac and stroking himself slowly. Not that he needed to get harder, but he loved the heat in Mac's eyes as he watched. A slick drop of pre-come coated his finger; he walked to the bed and wiped it on Mac's mouth. Mac licked at his finger and then nipped the tip.

Tony shook his head. "No biting." He swung himself astride Mac's chest and leaned up, tracing over the arched arms and taut neck with the tip of his cock, leaving slick wet trails on Mac's skin. Pushing forward, he slid into Mac's hair. The feel of soft strands, wrapping and tugging at his sensitive head, made him moan. Mac turned to look at him, and the rough stubble of his cheek scraped Tony's shaft.

Tony grabbed those cheeks between his palms. "Open for me." And there was heat and wetness and Mac's talented tongue ready for him as he slid between Mac's lips. Tony flexed his hips, riding Mac's mouth, just giving him half thrusts. "Don't let your hands go," he cautioned, seeing Mac's arms flex. "Lie there and take me." Mac sucked deep, cheek muscles working. Mac's tongue stroked him. He could feel the man's throat working to relax, to take him deeper. It was so good, so hot, Tony didn't want it to stop, but he had plans.

He pulled out, sliding his wet length down over Mac's body. Reaching in the drawer, he pulled out the lube. As he reached Mac's hips, he drizzled a fat slick glob of lube over Mac's huge cock, and then slid his own through it too. They rubbed together in the cool liquid, and then he closed his hands around them both, thrusting into his grip. Mac panted and pushed too, driving them together.

Tony pulled out of his own hand and rose up on his knees,

straddling Mac's hips. Underneath himself, he redirected Mac, keeping a tight grip on the slippery steel shaft. He slowly guided the lube-slick tip of his lover's dick to his ass. He teased himself with silk-skinned pressure, circling his hole, gliding the tip up his crack and down. He drew a moan from Mac as he slipped that big cock into position and then shifted off again. Mac was breathing in short, shallow pants, and a steady seep of pre-cum trickled over Tony's fingers.

But Tony wanted more too. He felt empty, aching, needing to be filled. Slowly, inch by inch, he lowered himself down, taking Mac inside him. Skin on skin, so big, so hard, Mac stretched him just right. He loved that pressure, that burn, as his body struggled to open up for his lover.

Mac bucked under him and Tony moved up and away. "Uh-uh," he said. "You just lie still and take it." Mac eased down, shaking, and Tony resumed his descent. His body trembled as he forced it open, slow and steady, not backing off, until he was impaled on Mac's thick cock. For a moment he sat, looking at Mac. Those dark brown eyes were wide and eager, Mac's face was flushed, lips wet. Tony rose a little and pushed down. Mac moaned. Tony waited, and then did it again.

"Oh, God," Mac begged, "Come on, Tony. Move your hot ass."

Tony laughed. "You'll take what I give you." He waited, moved again. He drew lines across Mac's tight chest with his fingernails, flicking at his nipples as he clenched rhythmically around Mac's cock. But the heat was clawing its way through his body, tightening his thighs, filling his ass. He didn't want it that slow either. He began to move more, flexing his hips at first and then rising higher and harder, driving himself down on Mac. Suddenly he wanted his lover's hands on his hips. "Let go of the headboard now," he ordered, "And help me."

Mac's big warm palms gripped him tightly. Mac's body drove up into him, pounding, spreading him. Tony spared a hand for his own slick throbbing length, twisting and pulling. His pre-cum dripped on Mac's flat stomach. Mac's eyes were locked on his.

Mac's muscles strained, quivering, as he bucked upward.

Tony heard his own voice panting, incoherent grunts of sound. Mac's thrusts touched him everywhere inside, filled all the places that begged for it. Tony wanted to say something, but he was past the point of words. He gasped and bowed backward, feeling his mouth drop open, his eyes flutter halfway shut. Then heat and need came together like fire spilling out of him. He shot streams of white across Mac's chest and face. Mac groaned and arched his back. Mac's fingers dug into Tony's hips, pinning Tony tight against him. Through his own spasms, Tony felt the rush of heat inside as Mac came long and hard.

He fell forward on Mac's chest, gasping, and felt those muscular arms wrap around him. Mac's thighs pressed up against his ass. Tony laughed shakily. "You feel so damned good." Mac's softening cock slipped out of him and he shuddered with the aftershocks. "Oh, God."

Mac kissed him softly, butterfly kisses on his skin. "You can prove to me it's not bad to be gay anytime, babe."

For a while they just lay breathing hard, stuck together with sweat and cum. Slowly Mac's whole body softened under him. Eventually Tony reached in the drawer for the wipes then sighed. "We need a shower."

"Yep," Mac agreed with a wicked grin.

"Oh no," Tony said. "Just a shower. I'm wrecked. In a good way."

Mac kissed him again, deep and slow. "Just a shower," he agreed.

CHAPTER 16

Mac woke with Leonard Anderson on his mind. They knew who the man was, knew what he had done, they just needed to find him. Mac needed to think it through again. He started to roll out of bed then froze as someone whimpered in his ear. Tony.

Mac suddenly remembered that first time. Waking up in Tony's apartment, half panicked. Looking at a man beside him in the bed and wondering what the hell he was doing. Feeling like something inside him had changed. *He'd had no fucking clue how much.*

Mac held still and Tony's breathing evened out again into soft, even sleep. Mac squinted at the clock. Six AM. For Mac, with a case hanging over his shoulder, getting back to sleep was not going to be an option. But Tony had been up three times in the night with Ben, trying to get the boy back to sleep after nightmares. And that didn't include their joint post-shower venture to try and find a small lost tooth under a sleeping child's big pillow, with the child still on top of it. Tony had had to ask Mac for help, and then offered to buy him a fairy wand for his trouble. Mac smiled, remembering. Yeah, his life had changed.

Mac tried to slide out from under Tony's leg without disturbing him. Tony opened his eyes enough to squint at him. "Going to work?"

"No. I'm on suspension, remember. I thought I'd go run. You should go back to sleep."

"Mph. Have fun." Tony was asleep again between one breath and the next. Mac looked down at him, messy dark hair on the pillow, cheeks a little more hollow than they should be, long lashes curved over fair skin. Tony's lips opened slightly as his breathing deepened. *Mine.* Mac was surprised by the wave of possessiveness that swept through him. He bent and brushed his lips over Tony's soft black hair.

*See you in a bit, sleepyhead.*

Mac pulled on shorts and a T-shirt from his bag in the adults' bathroom, moving as silently as he could. When he let himself out of the building, the cool of the morning was a pleasant surprise. The sun was just coming up, gilding the street with early light. A small breeze lifted the dusty leaves on the trees and whispered cool across Mac's bare legs.

He stretched a little, feeling the tightness in his hamstrings from days of neglect. Then he set out, dropping into a comfortable mile-eating pace. He had the early Sunday streets almost to himself. He let his body find the groove and turned his thoughts to the job.

The more he thought about it, the more he wondered if Anderson wasn't still going to go after Sinclair. He tried to get into the man's mind. Sometimes he could do that, anticipate what a criminal was going to do, how they would think.

*You figure you're safe. You've killed four women, maybe more, but there's nothing to lead back to you. And then you're watching TV and there's your face, your name, everything. The whole world knows about you. Everyone will be watching out for you, coming after you. What do you do?*

If you are smart, you dye your hair, grow a mustache, get out of town and start new somewhere else. But if you're Leonard Anderson?

*You're mad. You're fucking furious. There's a witness. You'll never be safe as long as there's a witness. All those women done right, neat and posed and dead like they should be. But you missed with one. Missed with that Sinclair freak. And you'll never be safe until you take care of that mistake.*

Or something like that.

Mac shook his head and picked up the pace a little. He could be wrong. But the way Anderson put his fist through the wall at the idea of a witness, something about the contrast between the tidy posed murder scenes and Sinclair's description of the frenzied attack, suggested to Mac that this guy wasn't as cool as he wanted to be. The existence of a witness was not just a threat, it was an affront, a flaw in Anderson's tidy crimes. Logical or not, Mac suspected that Anderson wouldn't be content with just melting away into the woodwork, no matter how much smarter that would be. He'd want to fix his mistake.

As he began looping back toward Tony's building, Mac ran through it again. It still seemed right. Just a hunch, but Mac's case clearance rate showed the value of his hunches. He slowed to a walk for the last couple of blocks and pulled out his cell phone.

Oliver was up already and on his way in. "Which you would be too, if you hadn't taken it into your stupid head to lay a hand on Loes," his partner snarled at Mac. "In front of Severs, yet. What the fuck were you thinking? Never mind, clearly there was no thinking involved. You stupid git, I need you in here."

"Sorry," Mac said contritely. "I shouldn't have let him get to me. It was dumb."

"No kidding." Oliver's voice picked up a tinge of curiosity. "What did he say anyway? I've heard several versions."

"Doesn't matter," Mac said dismissively. He could only hope the gossip would die down soon. "Any breaks in the case?"

"Nothing good. We got through to the FBI profiler. She's not coming out here, since we have a solid suspect, but she tried to give us some insight. Not much use, frankly. She thinks we're missing a body, between the mess the guy made of Simmons' feet and the neat stab wound on Kowalski. And she doesn't think he's gonna stop until we stop him."

"I don't suppose she had any genius ideas about that?"

"Nothing she would commit to. I tell you, by the time she was done saying 'usually' and 'in most but not all cases' and 'although they can be unpredictable' I quit listening. Lots of weasel words so if she's wrong about anything, it won't come back on her."

"Listen, then, I've been thinking about Anderson. And the more I try to think like him, the more I think he might still make a move on Sinclair despite the obvious risks. We know he was mad about the witness. Sinclair's name, picture, stuff about him, is all available. The TV reporters have been parading the story of the transvestite who identified the dagger killer non-stop." It was Minnesota after all. Murder wasn't an everyday occurrence, and this one had enough color and twists to keep it front page news. "Anderson's ex-boss described him as a pretty smart guy. I just get the feeling he may be searching, hunting Sinclair down, to finish the job he started."

"You get the feeling."

"Yes." When Oliver was silent, Mac added, "You could run it by the professional profiler."

"If I want to hear her say 'maybe' one more time."

Mac was prepared to try to back up his hunch, but Oliver sighed. "Knowing you, you're probably right. You get into the mind of a killer better than anyone I know." He paused. "Which is kind of creepy for a guy I spend a lot of time alone with."

"Quit moaning and tell me if you're going to use my plan."

"Of course I'm going to use it. Because frankly, we haven't turned up anything better. I take it you have suggestions?"

Mac spent ten more minutes on the phone with Oliver. They hashed out a scheme to use Sinclair's apartment and a look-alike as a decoy, with plenty of well-concealed back-up surveillance. They also agreed on a significant increase in manpower to beef up the watch on Sinclair's new location. Hanson would see if anyone seemed to be searching for Sinclair's address information online. It grated on Mac not to be able to go in and be in on the manhunt, but at least Oliver was taking his advice. Which, considering the number of guys that would be tied up in this, was worth a lot.

"Have I said how glad I am that you're smart enough to listen to me?" he asked in closing, because a guy couldn't say *thank you for believing in me, even when there's no reason why you should.*

"Have I said how glad I'll be when you get your shit together and get back in here to do your share?" Oliver retorted. Mac figured that stood for *you're welcome.*

He put the phone back in his pocket and finished his workout by running full out up the stairs up to Tony's place.

Tony and Ben were up, although not dressed, and toasting

bread in the kitchen.

"Here's Mac," Tony drawled. "Trust the man to show up once all the food prep is done. Do you think we should give him any eggs and toast, or shall we send him out to hunt his own breakfast?"

Ben giggled. "I think he could maybe have some eggs."

"Thanks, kid." Mac reached out and snagged the fresh toast off Tony's plate. "Mm. That's good."

Tony smacked him. "That was mine. Go shower and I'll make you some of your own."

Mac shook his head. He managed to steal a sip of coffee too, and jumped back out of range. "I need to go home," he said. "I need to pack some more clothes and some other stuff."

"Will we see you later?"

Mac hated the hesitant look in Tony's eyes, the one that carefully didn't expect too much. Deliberately, he cupped Tony's jaw with one hand and kissed him. "Absolutely. In fact, I thought maybe once I get cleaned up, I would go pick up Anna. If I have to take a day off, I'm d…darned-well going to have some fun. We could go out, maybe find a good playground. It's cool enough to really enjoy being outdoors this morning."

Ben eyed them, head on one side. Mac kissed Tony again, lightly, then dropped his hand to turn to the boy. "What do you think, Ben? Would you like that?"

Ben's eyes lit up without hesitation. "Yeah. With Anna. That'd be fun."

Tony's eyes were bright too. "Sounds good. Minnehaha Park? Maybe about ten?"

Mac winked at Ben. "Be there or be square." He was whistling as he let himself out of the apartment. So he wasn't on the team tracking down Anderson. He'd done his share. And now he was going to enjoy a day with his family. It was time to find out who Jared MacLean was, when he wasn't being a cop. Time to add some well-roundedness to his life.

Oliver called as he was driving back to his apartment. "Well, your hunch is looking good, but maybe too late."

"What do you mean?"

"We got Sinclair's permission to set up a decoy in his apartment, but when we got there the place had been trashed. Knife holes punched in the walls even. No one saw or heard anything, but it had to be Anderson. It looked like maybe he stayed there in the apartment all night Friday. There was food and stuff in the sink that Sinclair says wasn't his. I guess Anderson either decided Sinclair wasn't coming back or he got scared off sometime yesterday. We just missed him."

"Shit." Mac tried to think it through. "Did you ask Sinclair if he left any forwarding address with anyone? If Anderson tries to track him down."

"Yeah. He said post office and one neighbor, and he warned both that reporters might try to trick them out of the information. But we'll follow up. The guy he's staying with is an old friend, so there are links Anderson could trace. I've asked the cops in St. Cloud where he's staying to help coordinate the stake-out of his friend's house. They got kind of territorial about our guys taking over, and they do know the layout better than we do."

"But they're keeping a low profile."

"I did point out that the goal was to catch Anderson, not just scare him off.  Without letting him kill Sinclair, of course."

"We could leak Sinclair's location," Oliver added.

"Would he agree to that?" Mac had already dumped the guy in deep shit. He wasn't going to deliberately make it worse without Sinclair's okay.

"Maybe. But if we make it too easy and the reporters swarm all over again, it will become a mess. Hanson said he was able to search online and guess about five possible locations where Sinclair had friends, and St. Cloud was one of them. If Anderson is as obsessed and smart as we're thinking, he may not need a hint."

That felt right to Mac too. If the man had made up his mind to eliminate the witness, he wouldn't give up easily. "If he got scared off and didn't realize Sinclair wasn't just out for the night he might still go back to Sinclair's apartment."

"Yeah. We're going ahead with the decoy. But if he knows Sinclair is gone, it's a toss-up where he'll head next. Could be St. Cloud, could be he's stalking another victim, maybe he'll be smart enough to get the hell out of town. Who the fuck knows? We're still following tips, trying to figure out where the hell he's been living the last few days. I'm worried about another victim. The profiler says he may be decompensating, seeing the hunt closing in. The next woman he goes after may be at random and not fit the pattern anymore."

Mac couldn't believe they'd come so close. It was his fault. If he hadn't gotten so screwed up with the mess with Loes, he might have looked for Anderson at Sinclair's sooner. "You'll let me know if…"

"I'll call you if we make any progress." Oliver hesitated and then asked, "How are you doing?"

"I'm…good." Mac was surprised to realize it was true. "Other than kicking myself for not getting onto Sinclair's place sooner."

"You and me both. Right, I'll call you later. I might cruise up to St. Cloud myself, if nothing else pops."

"Have fun." Mac hung up his phone and forcibly wrenched his mind out of work mode. Nothing he could do now. Oliver was more than capable. And Mac had enough waiting on his personal plate. Because after he cleaned up and packed some more stuff, he was going to go get Anna and tell her he was gay. *God help him.*

Minnehaha Park was perhaps Tony's favorite place to go in summer. He had heard it called the secret heart of Minneapolis. There were paths and trails and a playground, but there was also plenty of space and untamed woods, and the rippling thread of the creek running through it all. On a Sunday morning, when many people were in church, even the playground was fairly deserted. A few other families were taking advantage of the beautiful day, but Ben and Anna had plenty of room to play without waiting to take turns.

The children had spent time on the climber and the swings, and were now occupied with some game of sticks and leaves on the fringes of the play area. Tony was glad to see Ben playing and relaxed with Anna. He had been odd that morning, tense and jumpy at times.

When he first woke up, Ben had been pleased by the dollar the tooth fairy left him. The kid didn't realize how close he came to not getting it. Tony needed to find a way to tell him not to put the tooth so far under his pillow next time. It made it hard for the tooth fairy to get it out. He had almost given up last night, until Mac, watching over his shoulder, had carefully lifted sleeping boy and pillow together, enough for Tony to reach under.

But something had spooked Ben that morning after Mac was gone. There had been some kind of change while Tony was in the bathroom getting dressed. By the time Tony came out, drying his hair with a towel, Ben was watchful and subdued. And he wouldn't talk about it. He had been so quiet after breakfast, Tony had checked for phone messages from grandparents or child services, and even taken a quick look around for more reporters. He couldn't find anything.

Ben had stayed moody in the car, and wasn't his usual enthusiastic self even when Mac and Anna met them at the park. Now Ben seemed to be finally acting normally again. Tony put this new what-ever-it-was on his list of things to follow up with Ben.

Mac finished helping the kids and came over to Tony, having supplied Princess Anna with enough sticks for whatever she was building. He dropped with a grunt onto the bench beside Tony. Speaking of someone who'd been acting moody and uncommunicative. Tony sneaked a sideways glance at his lover. Mac's posture was finally more relaxed too. Playing with Anna was always good for him.

"What are the kids up to?" Tony asked.

"I don't know," Mac said. "Having fun." He sat up, tension seeping back into him. "I told Anna in the car."

"Told her what?" Tony asked cautiously.

"Everything. Well, almost. I told her I was thinking about moving in with you and Ben, because I love you. I didn't actually say the word."

"Gay?"

"Yeah, that one." Mac sighed. "I will. I mean, it should be obvious but she is only five. I just…a step at a time, you know."

"So can I kiss you in front of her yet or not?" Tony asked, holding back irritation as Mac automatically glanced around to see if they were overheard.

"Not yet. Today. I will lay it out for her today."

"She may not care about the gay part, as much as she may care about being jealous," Tony suggested. "You've been all hers for her whole life. She may not like sharing you with us."

"The first thing she asked was if she could live with me all the time too, if Ben was," Mac admitted.

"What did you say?"

"I said she could definitely sleep over sometimes, and we would talk about it." Mac shook his head. "It's all happening so fast. I haven't figured it all out yet."

"We don't have to do everything at once. You could keep your place for a while, go slow."

"I don't want to," Mac said emphatically. "I want to be with you, and Ben."

"And Anna?"

"Yes," Mac admitted. "My fantasies are the same as yours, all four of us in one place, as a family. But I don't know how many changes the kids should have at once, or what's fair for Anna. Brenda's the closest to a mom that she has; how can I take that away from her? And if Brenda walks away, then I'm sticking you with extra childcare."

Tony smiled. "Don't worry about that part. I've stuck myself with childcare pretty effectively already. Two's not that much harder than one, especially since she is starting kindergarten."

"But if she gets sick, or if her schedule is different, or…"

"Hey." Tony punched his arm lightly. "Stop borrowing trouble. Yes, we'll need to line up babysitters and figure out schedules, but we can make it work, I promise. If you want to. But you'd better be sure. Because if we make those two brother and sister, and you change your mind about staying, it's gonna hurt to rip them apart."

"What if *you* change your mind?"

"I'm yours," Tony said, looking into Mac's brown eyes. "All the way, whatever happens. And I love Anna already. I want this so badly it hurts, but only if you're ready."

For a moment Tony thought it might happen; Mac might kiss him in public. But he had to settle for the look in Mac's eyes. "I'll talk to Anna some more."

"And Brenda," Tony said. *That would be the big one.*

Mac sighed. "God, I don't want to."

"Do you want me to meet with her?" Tony asked tentatively. "Do you think if she met me and Ben…"

"No." Mac said emphatically. "She's seen me almost daily for five years and I still don't get past the threshold. She just doesn't work that way. There's no compromise in her."

Tony searched for something to offer, but a wisp of movement caught his eye. He turned a little and saw a dark stream of smoke rising from somewhere beyond the trees. "Hey, Mac," he said. "What do you think? Looks a little much for a barbeque fire?"

Mac turned to look too. For a moment as they sat watching the column of smoke almost died away, but then it rose again, darker and thicker. The other adults around the playground were starting to notice too. Mac got up.

"I'd better go check on it. You've got the kids."

"Go," Tony said. He glanced over at Ben and Anna. "They're fine."

Mac headed off down the path. Tony watched him go speculatively. After a moment Anna came over and stood beside him.

"Did Daddy go to look at the smoke?"

"Yep." Tony slipped an arm around her. "He'll find out what it is and then come back. He can call the firemen on his phone if he needs help."

Anna's nose wrinkled. "It smells bad."

"Sure does." It smelled like burning rubber or plastic, even at a distance. One mother called her daughter off the climber and headed for the parking area. The smoke was getting thicker and blacker as it climbed, but it didn't seem to be spreading. Although up higher where the wind caught it, the plume was widening out and blowing towards them. Mac would surely call if there was any danger. Still, Tony turned to locate Ben just in case.

At first, he wasn't concerned that he couldn't spot Ben. The boy was like quicksilver, never where you left him just moments ago. Still, that green T-shirt should have been obvious. Tony stood up to scan the playground more carefully. Then with growing anxiety, he did a careful look around the fringes of the play area. The stick structures the children had been erecting stood abandoned.

"Anna," he said, careful to keep his voice calm, "Did you see where Ben went?"

"No," she said. "There was a man, and Ben said I should go stay with you, so I did."

Tony's heart began thumping in his chest. "There was a man where, sweetheart?"

"Over there." Anna pointed. "By the edge of the woods."

"Did Ben go to the man?" *Surely not. How many times have we gone over the never-go-with-strangers rule? Unless he knew the man.*

"I think so. I think they went in the woods."

Tony bit back a word unfit for small ears and looked frantically around. He could call Mac back, but it would take time...

"Come on." He led Anna over to a heavyset lady whose two toddlers were playing in the sandbox.

"Excuse me," he said urgently. "Could you watch my little girl for just a moment? Her brother wandered off into the woods and I need to run after him. I won't be a moment."

"Um, sure," the woman said. "If it's not too long."

"Stay here," Tony said urgently, pushing Anna down onto the bench. "Don't move from this spot until Mac comes back, promise me."

"I promise." Anna's voice was thin and a little scared, but Tony didn't have time to reassure her.

"Good girl. Stay there." He lit out at a run across the grass, pulling his phone out as he ran. But Mac's went straight to voice mail. *He must be using it. Damn!*

"Go back to the playground, *now!*" he said after the beep. "Anna's sitting alone with some lady by the sandbox. She says Ben wandered off with a stranger. I'm going after him into the woods." He hung up and pocketed his phone.

The air was cooler under the trees, the ground thick with ferns and weeds. There was no path where Anna had pointed, but a trail of broken stems suggested someone had been through here recently. Tony ran, ducking the occasional poplar branch as the trail wound through the trees. A few hundred yards in, he heard voices, and recognized Ben's tones. One more burst of speed and he saw his boy ahead, one wrist in the grip of a tall man.

"Hey!" Tony shouted. "Ben! Get back here!"

Ben turned to look at him, and began struggling to get free. The man pulled him along, almost lifting him off the ground by his arm. But Tony was much faster, unencumbered, and he caught up to them. The man whirled to meet him. He yanked Ben back against his body and wrapped his free hand around the boy's neck. For a moment they stood panting, looking at each other. Suddenly it occurred to Tony why the man looked familiar.

"Anderson!" he said, realizing only a moment too late what a mistake that might be.

Anderson glared at him, breathing hard. "Fuck. Shit," he growled. He glanced around, as if looking for an escape, and then stared back at Tony. "Go back where you came from or I'll strangle the brat."

"Let the boy go," Tony said, trying to control his voice, "And we'll let you go. I won't even tell anyone I saw you."

"Liar," the man said bitterly. "You'll have the cops after me in minutes." He shook Ben roughly, one hand white on the boy's arm, the other tight against his neck. "Throw away your cell phone, now."

Tony pulled out his phone and tossed it into the weeds. "Let the boy go," he repeated. "He's no threat to you."

"He's a witness," Anderson said angrily. "They're all after me because of the fucking witnesses. I have to get rid of them! Him and that goddamned blond cross-dressing freak."

"But Ben's not a witness," Tony said urgently. "The boy didn't see anything. It was all the others. And not just Sinclair. People saw you in the bars, and one of the girls you attacked survived. A bunch of other people saw you, but not the boy. He doesn't know anything about you."

Anderson's hand on Ben's neck loosened a little, but eventually he said, "Doesn't matter. I have to do him now. And you too." He let go of Ben's throat to lean over, reaching toward his boot. *The knife!* Tony lunged forward, slamming into Anderson and taking all three of them to the ground. He focused on the hand holding Ben's wrist, slamming his fists into the man's forearm. Ben wriggled and twisted, and was free.

"Run!" Tony shouted. "Get to Mac!" He scrambled the other way. Anderson grabbed his foot and Tony kicked free, losing a shoe. Tony struggled up to one knee and stood, but Anderson was on him from behind, grabbing at his arm and punching his back. Tony staggered. Out of the corner of his eye he saw Ben sprinting away. *Good boy!*

For a second Tony got free and he ran in the direction away from Ben. Surely Anderson would chase the bigger threat. Tony plunged through the undergrowth, hearing the heavy footsteps behind him. Anderson's hand brushed the back of his shirt. Tony grabbed a tree, doing a slingshot reversal that made Anderson overrun him. Tony took off again, this time trying to head back toward the playground. For a few moments he kept ahead, dodging trees, but the missing shoe and the difference in height gave Anderson a longer stride. As Tony swerved left, he felt a hard thump between his shoulder blades. He stumbled, tried to recover. Then Anderson grabbed him. Both the man's hands wrapped around Tony's throat. Tony choked and gasped for air as Anderson's fingers closed on him.

Mac tracked the source of the smoke down the road from the playground. He cursed under his breath. If he had to be off duty, at least it was supposed to be a chance to have a nice day out. He planned to spend the time finding out what it was like to really be a family man. And instead of relaxing with Tony, he was breathing toxic fumes and probably going to have to arrest some drunk for dropping a cigarette in a trashcan.

The source of the smoke was out of sight around a bend in the access road. When he got there, he found a pile of garbage, soaked in gasoline and set ablaze inside a big old tire, which was smoldering too. The smoke was thick and harsh, making Mac cough as he approached. The smell of the gas was sharp. It wasn't that big a fire, but once a tire starts burning it's a bitch to put it out. Mac circled it as he pulled out his phone to call the fire department. This didn't look like an accident. More like deliberate vandalism. With the summer so hot and dry, the last thing they needed was for the park to be set ablaze.

It was a minute after he hung up with the fire department before he realized he had voice mail from Tony, another minute to hear the message. Then he ran for the playground as hard as he could.

Anna sat on a bench by the sandbox, next to a large blond woman. Her frightened gaze snapped to him as he ran up.

"Where's Tony?" Mac asked urgently.

"He told me to stay with this lady," Anna said thinly, "And he…" She broke off as Ben tore out of the woods toward them.

"He's killing Tony!" Ben shouted as he got near. "He's going to kill Tony!"

"Who is?" Mac asked, grabbing the boy by the arms. "What happened?"

"There's a man in there," Ben said, pointing back the way he had come. "He had my arm and he wouldn't let go." The boy held out a wrist marked with red bruising in evidence. "And then Tony came and he hit him and he's chasing Tony, and he's going to kill him."

*Who? Why?* No time for details. "Tony is fighting with someone?" Mac verified.

Ben nodded tearfully. "Tony made him let me go and he told me to run. And now the man's gonna kill him!"

Mac glanced around frantically. *No better solution than what Tony did.* He turned to the woman beside them, listening with wide eyes.

"Would you watch the children, just for a moment?" he asked. "Call 911 and tell them someone is hurt here at the park. Okay?"

"I…um…" but she was nodding, so he would take that as a yes.

Mac turned to the kids. "You two sit here, stay together, and don't move from this bench until Tony or I come for you. Is that absolutely clear?"

Two squeaks of agreement meant he had scared them, but there was no time for reassurances. He ran full out across the grass, calling 911 himself as he went. He called in an assault in progress and hung up on the follow-up questions. He wanted his hands free. Ben was too scared for this to be nothing.

The trail through the weeds underneath the green poplar canopy was visible and Mac followed it. He heard nothing at first. Surely if men were fighting he should hear the sounds. *But if they were done fighting? If Tony was hurt, or dead, and his attacker gone...?* Mac struggled to run faster. Then off to his right he heard a shrill scream. He had seen Tony in bad pain and never heard a sound like that from him. *What would you have to do to Tony to make him scream?* Mac plunged toward the sound.

Tony scrabbled at the strong hands around his neck, trying to dislodge them. His throat was on fire. *You're not helpless! What would Mary Liu do?* Tony stomped backwards hard. His sneaker slid off a leather shoe, but Anderson grunted and his fingers loosened enough for Tony to grab one tortured wheeze of air before they closed again. Tony twisted and kicked, aiming for shins or knees behind him, but he was too close against Anderson's body to get much force. His vision was tunneling in and there were sparkles floating in the darkness.

Tony clawed with his hands at the fingers gripping his throat. *Not enough fingernails to draw blood with.* Fumbling, he managed to work under the tip of one of Anderson's fingers and lever it up. Anderson whined and tightened his grip. Tony could feel his own pulse pounding in his temples, and a dark rushing sound grew louder in his ears. He got his second hand into position and forced the finger back sharply. There was a crack, like a twig breaking. Anderson screamed, a shrill keening sound incongruous with the size of the man, and suddenly Tony was free.

He dropped to his knees, gasping, and forced himself to roll away, even though his vision was still fuzzy. He wanted to lie there and breathe, but he struggled to get his legs under him. There was a thump beside him and he saw Anderson's shoe. Frantically, Tony jerked aside, and the next kick grazed his hip instead of breaking ribs. Tony turned the motion into a roll and came up against something hard.

*A tree.* Then the something hard moved a little and Tony was looking at familiar denim.

"Freeze!" Mac's voice ordered above him, colder and sharper than Tony had ever heard it. "Don't move or I'll blow a hole in your head! Freeze, right there. Hands above your head!"

"He broke my finger!" Anderson whined. Tony twisted to look at him. The man's hands weren't on his head, but he wasn't moving.

"Get your hands above your head or I'll put a hole in your skull," Mac ordered. "Now! Get 'em up."

Slowly, Anderson raised his hands and put them on his head.

"Close enough. Now stay real still," Mac ordered. "I'd love to kill you, if you give me any excuse. So stand there and don't move."

For a long moment, no one moved. The only sound was Tony's harsh, wheezing breath as he struggled to regain control.

Then Mac said, "Tony, talk to me. I need to know how bad you're hurt. If you need help, I'm going to shoot this guy and help you." His voice was shaking.

*Jesus.* Tony tried to say something and managed only a hoarse croak. He reached up and patted Mac's leg three times. Slowly he forced himself into a sitting position. "Wait!" Mac said urgently. "Don't stand up between this guy and my gun. Get out of the line first."

Tony crawled aside and used a handy poplar to pull himself up to his feet. Mac had a small gun out, aimed at Anderson. The range was short, and the way Mac held the gun suggested complete competence. No wonder Anderson wasn't trying to get away.

Mac glanced at him out of the corner of his eye without taking his gaze off Anderson. "Are you okay, Tony?"

Tony gave him a thumbs-up gesture.

"Can you make it back to the playground?"

Tony repeated the gesture.

"You're sure?" Mac said. "Because if you pass out or fall over on your way back, it won't do either of us any good."

Tony waved optimistically.

"Okay," Mac said. "The playground's that way." He pointed behind him with his free hand, without turning. "I called 911 before I caught up with you. Officers should be coming. I don't have cuffs with me, so I'm just going to stand here and point my gun at this guy until backup gets here, unless he makes me shoot him."

"You can't do that!" Anderson said.

"Sure I can," Mac said. "You move, and I'll spare the state the cost of your trial." He added, "Go on, Tony. I left the kids with the same lady you parked Anna with. She probably thinks we're nuts. Go take care of them for me. When the other cops arrive, try to tell them that I'm the one with the gun out, so they don't escalate things."

Tony nodded and headed back toward the playground. It seemed much farther the second time. In fact, he wondered if he was somehow going the wrong way. Once, he had to step aside and grab a tree trunk as his stomach heaved. He brought up nothing but bile, but the acid stung his sore throat, making him choke and gasp. It was several minutes before he could move on.

Finally he spotted the sunlight ahead and stepped out into the play area. A black-and-white was just pulling up into the parking lot. The officers jumped out, looked around, and then went over to the seated adults. Tony walked slowly towards them, and after a moment they headed his way.

"Did you call us?" the first officer asked as he approached.

Tony nodded, with a shrug to say close enough. He waited until the man was close and then rasped, "In woods, there." He pointed. "My friend, cop, has gun on Anderson, killer." He hoped the words were intelligible.

"You what?" The man reached out and lifted Tony's chin to take a look at his neck. "Jesus, what happened to you?"

"Anderson," Tony repeated, as best he could. "Dagger killer.

Cop has him, there."

"Anderson?" The second cop reached them. "The guy they're looking for? He's in there?" His hand drifted toward his holster.

"Yes." Tony said. "My friend, cop." *Please don't shoot Mac.* "Has gun on Anderson. No cuffs."

"You're here with a cop, who's holding Anderson back in there?" the first officer verified.

Tony nodded rapidly.

"And the guy who has a gun is the cop," the man repeated.

Another big nod.

"Okay," the man said. "Look, you stay right here. We'll have other units responding in a minute. They'll help you. We're going to go in there."

"Don't shoot cop," Tony rasped, just to be sure.

"We'll be careful," the man said. "Just stay here." He and his partner drew their weapons and headed into the woods.

Tony sighed. He would have to trust Mac to handle the situation. He made his way across the grass to the playground. Ben and Anna were wriggling around on the bench beside the plump lady, but Mac must have put the fear of God into them, because neither one moved until he came right up to them.

Then suddenly he had two children wrapped around his legs. Tony staggered and lowered himself to the bench. Ben was babbling about how scared he had been, Anna was asking where her daddy was, and the fat lady had questions of her own. Tony hugged the kids close and didn't even try to answer anyone. He was dizzy, and his throat felt like he had swallowed ground glass. A second black-and-white pulled into the parking lot and Tony could hear other sirens approaching. There would be official questions soon enough. He closed his eyes and savored how good it was to have oxygen available whenever you wanted it.

Mac aimed his back-up gun at Anderson's head and breathed

evenly. He wanted to blow this man away. For Sandy and Terri, Nicole and Cindy; for Emily's fears, and for the scar on Sinclair's hand, and most of all for Ben's loss and the marks on Tony's neck. It would be so easy. Killed trying to escape. He glared at Anderson, daring him to try something, but the man stood motionless.

Mac had seen Tony on the ground, and a man standing over him, kicking him. The kick had rolled Tony toward Mac, and in one leap he had reached Tony's side, grabbing for the ankle holster he wore as his back-up piece off duty. The snub-nose .38 wasn't big, but plenty for this. He'd aimed straight at the assailant's head and yelled, "Freeze!"

It was only after the man stood still, one hand cradled in the other, and looked at him, that he realized who they had here.

*Anderson!*

Now Mac stared at the man, as the sound of Tony's footsteps faded in the distance. All that time and effort chasing the man, and here he was. It didn't make much sense. Ben said the man had him by the arm before Tony arrived. That meant Anderson had grabbed Ben, but how, and why? Mac decided he didn't want to know just now. He watched the man and just breathed.

"My hand hurts," Anderson whined. "I have to put it down."

"Don't move or you'll find out a bullet hurts worse," Mac told him.

"This is some kind of mistake," Anderson said. "I don't even know that man. I've never seen him before."

"Pity you tried to kill him then." Mac was tired of this. "Shut up and listen. Leonard Anderson, you are under arrest. You have the right to remain silent." *Not that it will do you any good, since the physical evidence will nail you cold.* "If you do not remain silent, anything you say can and will be used against you in a court of law. You have the right to an attorney, and to have that attorney present during questioning. If you cannot afford an attorney, one will be appointed for you." *Hopefully a brand new PD who doesn't know anything.* "Do you understand these rights as I have explained them to you?"

"There's been a mistake," Anderson insisted.

*Yeah, yours.* "Do you understand these rights as I have explained them to you?"

"I guess so," Anderson muttered. "Can I put my hands down now?"

"Don't fucking move," Mac snapped.

Eventually he heard the sound of someone approaching. Mac called out, "Minneapolis police officer! If you're not police officers, stay back!"

"MPD uniformed officers," came the reply. "We are approaching slowly. Please stay calm."

"Don't get between this man and my gun," Mac said. "If he moves, I'm going to shoot him." That was for Anderson's benefit, so he wouldn't get any ideas. "My ID is in my right back pocket. Come over slowly and check it out." From the corner of his eye he could see one uniformed cop approaching, gun out but not aimed. He could hear another behind him. He kept his eyes fixed on Anderson as a hand tugged at his pocket and worked his ID loose.

"Detective MacLean," the man behind him acknowledged. "What would you like us to do, sir?"

"Get a pair of cuffs on this man," Mac said. "I'm off duty. Search him well. He's been known to use a knife."

Anderson's eyes were flicking wildly back and forth as one of the officers approached him, but he didn't run or fight as his wrists were handcuffed behind him. He whined and whimpered at the handling, but stood still.

When Anderson was secured, Mac took a deep breath and holstered his own weapon. The officers were doing a body search. Mac watched, making sure they were thorough. No slip-ups now.

"Sheath in his boot," the man reported, "But no knife in it. ID for Leonard Johnson."

"That's his alias," Mac confirmed.

"I'm hurt," Anderson complained. "I need a doctor. You can't keep these handcuffs on me. My hand is broken!"

"Don't take them off," Mac said, when one officer glanced at him. "Even if he says his hand is falling off. He's wanted for four murders, and if he gets loose you'll be writing parking tickets forever." He pulled out his phone. "Is a paramedic unit coming?" he asked the officer as he flipped the phone open and speed dialed.

"Yes," the officer said. "There was an injury call."

"Good." Mac held up a finger to say wait and turned his attention to the phone. "Hey, partner."

"You sound chipper for someone on suspension," Oliver's voice said.

"I have a present for you," Mac told him. "Where are you?"

"Home. We're stalled out looking for Anderson or Johnson or whoever he's being now. Severs sent everyone who was on overtime off the clock."

"Well, if you want Anderson, you could come down to the playground at Minnehaha Park."

"If I what?" Oliver's voice sharpened. "You found him?"

"Found, caught, and cuffed. I'm here with the family. You could bring him in."

"Give me fifteen minutes," Oliver said eagerly. "I'll be there." Then he paused. "Is anyone hurt?"

"He had his hands around Tony's neck," Mac said, "But I think Tony's okay. I'll meet you in the parking lot." He hung up and turned to the two officers, directing one of them to bring Anderson along and the other to stay put, to guide a search team who would look for the knife in case it fell out during the scuffle.

As they approached the playground, he saw three black-and-whites and a paramedic van parked. Officers ran toward them, and finally enough other people were watching Anderson that he could look away from the man. He spotted Tony and the children on a bench, and then he ran.

Anna jostled Tony, leaping toward Mac as he approached, and Tony's eyes opened. Mac scooped his daughter up in one arm and found himself on his knees in front of Tony. He reached out to tilt his lover's chin up. The marks of Anderson's hands were purple and red around Tony's throat, with a hint of puffy swelling.

"Are you breathing okay?" he asked urgently.

Tony nodded and Mac's heart finally began to slow down.

Anna muttered from where her face was buried in his neck, "Tony got hurt."

"Yes, he did, princess," Mac told her, "But he's going to be fine. We're going to go over to the paramedic van there and let them look at Tony and make sure."

Tony shrugged, but he got up slowly. Ben was clinging to his hand, face white and shocky. Mac lifted Anna to his hip as he stood and shepherded his small family over to the paramedics. They were tending to Anderson's hand, but when they saw Tony approaching, the woman came toward them.

"Ouch," she said, looking at Tony. "Come on over here and let's get a look at that."

"Get Anderson out of there first," Mac said coldly. "I don't want him near us."

The paramedic glanced at him, but something in his expression must have convinced her, because she went and arranged for her partner to take Anderson around the side of the truck. Mac put out a hand and guided Tony to sit on the rear bumper. Ben sat beside him. Mac guessed it was a measure of the small boy's distress that he didn't seem interested in the truck.

The paramedic busied herself checking Tony. She listened to his chest, slipped an oxygen sensor on his finger, and eventually watched him take a cautious sip of bottled water. "Well, you seem to be able to breathe and swallow, which are the essentials," she said eventually. "Oxygen level is normal. But you really should be seen. There are a lot of small bones in the larynx that can be damaged, and swelling can increase over the first twenty-four hours."

Tony shook his head, with a nod towards the children. Mac interpreted that as, *"Don't scare the kids."*

"Maybe you should go in," he suggested. "Just to be safe."

Another head shake.

"All right," the paramedic said. "Use ice, ibuprophen, maybe the kids' liquid version or grind up the pills. Sip cold liquids at first, soft food if you're doing okay with liquids. Watch for any increasing difficulty breathing or swallowing, or a cough or dizziness, shortness of breath."

Tony nodded. He guided her attention to Ben's wrist. She spent a moment feeling and flexing it, and then smiled at Ben.

"That's just going to be a spectacular bruise," she told him. "Wait 'till you see all the colors it can turn."

Ben said, "Okay," in a thin voice. Tony pulled the boy in against him roughly for a moment.

"You two are going to match," Mac told Ben, reaching to help Tony to his feet. Tony probably didn't need the help, but Mac wanted the contact. What he really wanted was to wrap his arms around all of them and never let go, but they were in public. Then he thought, *to hell with it,* and pulled them in close, with Anna squeezed between him and Tony, and Ben tight against their sides. For a moment they melded together, and he breathed into Tony's hair. Then he stepped back again.

"How is the prisoner?" he asked the paramedic.

"A dislocated finger," she said. "It went back in place when we were checking him. My partner's bandaging it."

"So he doesn't need the emergency room?"

"I don't think so. A doctor should look at it eventually, though."

"Hey, partner," Oliver said from behind him. "Trust you to find the excitement. Where's Anderson?"

Mac turned. "Behind the ambulance," he said, pointing with his free hand. "Tony dislocated his finger for him."

"Couldn't happen to a nicer guy," Oliver told Tony. He leaned closer to look at Tony's bruises. "I'd say you'll be able to prove self-defense there. Are you all right?"

Tony nodded gingerly.

"If you take charge of Anderson," Mac suggested, "And get a team down to search the woods, I'll get statements from my team here."

"You don't want to bring him in yourself?" Oliver asked.

"Don't want my hands on him," Mac said, biting back the rest, *I might kill him,* due to the presence of little ears. Oliver looked like he got the subtext.

"Okay, I've got him," Oliver said. "What are we searching for?"

"The knife. I left a man out there to indicate the area. I'd use a metal detector. Anderson was wearing the sheath but it was empty."

"I thin' he had it," Tony said, talking softly in the top of his mouth. "He 'eached down." Tony bent and swept his hand toward his leg in explanation. "M' phone's out there too."

"We'll look for it," Oliver agreed.

"Will you find my mom's necklace too?" Ben piped up.

They all turned to stare at him. "What necklace?" Mac asked.

"He had my mom's necklace. The one she always wore, with the charms. He showed it to me. He said I could have it, but he lied."

"You're sure it was your mom's?" Mac asked gently.

"Yes." Ben rubbed his eyes. "It had a cross from her first communion, and a silver little baby shoe from when I was born and her wedding ring, and it was her best thing. He said I could have it."

"We'll look for it, son," Oliver said. Tony squeezed Ben's shoulder.

"I'll take the gang home and get statements," Mac said, "And then meet you in interrogation...except shit, I mean shoot, I'm not supposed to be around the department until tomorrow."

Tony tapped his arm. "Take us in to office for state'ents," he suggested. "Excuse an' distraction." He nodded at Ben, looking pale and distressed.

"You sure?" Mac asked. "You should probably lie down and put ice on your neck."

"Ice, yes," Tony hissed painfully. "No' lie down."

Mac nodded reluctantly. He couldn't deny that he wanted to see the case come together, and this would provide a great reason to buck his suspension. And Tony knew Ben best. If he thought this was a good idea...and it would be ideal to have someone other than himself witness those statements. "Okay," he told Oliver. "I guess I'll see you back there."

It felt odd, entering the station with Tony and the kids. The officer on the desk gave him a startled look as he led them in and up the stairs, but said nothing. At the door to Homicide, he hesitated and then pushed it open. A glance around the room showed no sign of Loes, for which he was grateful. Most of his usual team was missing, but Ramsey was at her desk and she glanced up, and immediately came over.

"Hey, Ramsey," he said. "I need to get some statements recorded. Can you give me a hand?"

"Sure," she said, "But...this is Anna, isn't it?"

"Anna, Ben," Mac said, pointing, "And my friend, Tony. We had a little encounter with Anderson."

"You what?" She frowned. "I heard there was chatter that someone spotted him just now."

"That was us. Oliver's bringing him in."

"No shit!" she exclaimed. "I mean, that's great!"

"Yeah," Mac agreed. It was, of course it was. But it had come so close to being a disaster. And it was all his fault. He'd thought about Anderson coming after the witness. But he'd failed to remember that at that first press conference, the one that got Anderson so mad, Sinclair's name wasn't yet out there. It was Ben the press had latched onto then. It was Ben that Mac had failed to protect. And when this was done, he'd have to admit that to Tony.

Mac shook off the thought. For now, he needed to finish this thing, and get his family safely home. "I figured we'd better get the statements on record, in case Severs wants to do a press conference or something."

Ramsey smiled broadly. "He just might." Then she hesitated, eyeing Tony's bruises. "Has your...friend seen a doctor?"

"Paramedic," Mac said. "At the scene. He could use an icepack, though."

"I'll get it," Detective Drummond volunteered, getting up from his desk. "You really got Anderson?"

"Signed, sealed, and soon to be delivered," Mac told him. "Tony stopped him with his neck, and I bagged him."

"All right!" The man slapped Tony's shoulder in passing. "Good job."

They arranged for an interrogation room, and Mac installed Tony in one corner, writing out his own statement on the laptop. Tony typed one-handed, holding the ice to his neck, and watching Anna color with a few broken crayons scrounged up from somewhere by Ramsey.

Then Mac sat on the other side of the room, with Ben close beside him. "You run the recorder," he said to Ramsey, "And jump in if there are questions you want to ask. I didn't want this to be too much in the family."

"Okay." She looked over at Tony. "Do we have permission

from his guardian to record this?"

"Yes," Tony whispered. Ramsey switched on the recorder.

"Detective Jared MacLean," Mac said for the record, "Present with Detective Linda Ramsey, juvenile Ben Serrano, and his guardian Anthony Hart." He added location, date and time and then turned to Ben.

"Okay, son, tell me about the first time you saw the man in the woods." Mac heard Tony's fingers pause on the keys as he also waited for Ben's answer.

"He was in the trees," Ben said softly. "He held up the necklace."

"How did you know what it was?" Mac asked. "Those trees are fifty feet from the play area."

"He phoned me."

"He what?" Tony exclaimed sharply from his corner, and then winced and pressed the ice to his neck, glaring at Mac. The message was obvious: *ask him about that!* Mac nodded to him.

"When did he call you?"

Ben glanced at Tony, and then back at Mac. "This morning," he said. "At the apartment. After you left to get Anna and Tony was in the shower."

Mac winced. *Which makes it obvious I spent the night.* He mentally kicked himself. That was so not the issue here.

"You answered the phone?"

"I always answer if my mom's too busy or…"

*Or too drunk.* "And what did you hear?"

"It was a man," Ben said. "He asked, 'Are you Ben Serrano?' and I said yes, and he told me he'd found a thing of my mom's that she would want me to have, and he described the necklace."

"But you didn't tell Tony or me about it?"

"He said not to," Ben explained tearfully. "He said he would throw it away if I told any grownups! He said he didn't want to get in any trouble, but he would give it to me if I came alone."

"Came alone where?"

"He wanted me to come downstairs for it. But I said I couldn't just leave the apartment, so I said he could give it to me at the park."

Tony covered his face with his hand for a moment. Mac shot him a look of sympathy. You safeguard your kids every minute and they tell a murderer where to find them.

"So you told him where we would be?" Mac asked gently.

"Yes. He said he would wait somewhere for me, and give me the necklace, and to keep my eyes open. I told him I would wear my green shirt, so he'd know who I was."

"So then you saw him…?"

"At the park," Ben said. "I was watching and watching. And then after there was the smoke I saw him in the trees, and he held up the necklace. I saw it sparkle, and I knew what it was. So I sent Anna to stay safe with Tony and I went to get the necklace."

"You didn't tell Anna what you were doing?"

"No, 'cause she would want to come with and I was scared the man would be mad."

"Okay," Mac said. "So you went to the man…"

"I asked him to give me the necklace," Ben said with a sniff, "But he said we had to go further into the trees out of sight, and then he would let me look at it and if I could prove it was my mom's, I could have it."

"And you went with him?"

"Yes," Ben said slowly. He paused, and then burst out, "I knew it was a bad thing to do, 'cause Tony says never go anywhere with strangers, but he had my mom's best necklace with the ring my dad gave her, and I wanted it!"

"Then what?" Mac asked, as calmly as he could.

"We went a bit, and then he took hold of my arm. I asked for the necklace, and he kept saying just a bit more, and just a bit more, and I was getting mad."

"And then?"

"Then Tony was there," Ben said. "He was running and he yelled to get away from the man. I tried but he wouldn't let go. He grabbed my neck too, but I wiggled and Tony hit him and we all fell over. Then he let go and Tony said to run back to you so I did."

"So you did. Did you run straight back?"

"Fast as fast. 'Cause he was fighting with Tony and he was much bigger and I was so scared. But you're bigger 'n him and I knew you would help, and you're a cop and all."

"Did the man hurt you?" Mac asked.

"Just my arm," Ben said rubbing it. "But he hurt Tony and it's all my fault!" He burst into tears. Tony hurried over and put his arms around the boy, and whispered, "S'okay. 'M okay. No' yr fault."

Mac patted Ben's thin shoulders. "Tony's right," he said. "You shouldn't have gone with the man, but what happened after that was not your fault. He's a bad man and we're all really glad we caught him. You helped by running so quickly to get me."

"Really?" Ben turned a tear-stained face toward him.

"Absolutely," Mac assured him. "If you hadn't run so straight and fast, he might have gotten away." *He might have killed Tony.* Mac still didn't want to think about that. "You did the best you could, and it all came out all right."

"I'm sorry," Ben said. "I'm really sorry!"

"I know," Mac told him gently. "You were trying to do the right thing. But next time an adult tries to talk to you alone like that, you tell Tony or me, all right? You let us handle it."

Ben nodded and wiped his eyes with the back of his hand.

"Did the man ever talk to you before that one phone call?"

Ben straightened up and thought about it. "I don't think so," he said. "I answered the phone once and the person was asking questions but it was a lady and I hung up. I never talked to that man before."

Tony whispered, "Had some hang-up calls when I ans'd, Sat'day. Thought was repor'ers."

"Okay," Mac said. "If I think of other questions, I'll ask them later. Ramsey?"

She leaned forward and asked, "Did you recognize the man in the woods? Had you seen him before?"

"I don't think so," Ben said slowly. "He looked like somebody, but I don't remember who."

"I showed Ben the ID sketch when we first produced it," Mac said. "Maybe that was where you saw him before, Ben?"

Ben thought about it and shrugged.

"Did you see the necklace clearly?" Ramsey added. "Are you sure it was your mom's?"

"I think so. But he was going to show me for real and he never did."

Mac nodded and switched off the recorder. "I think that's enough for today."

"I still want the necklace," Ben said. "Please?"

"If we find it," Mac said, "Then eventually it will be yours, but for a while the police will have to keep it for evidence. I promise, we'll get it back to you if we can."

"Okay." Ben looked tired and subdued, leaning against Tony's shoulder.

Mac turned to Tony. "Are you done with your statement?"

Tony shook his head and held up five fingers.

"All right." Mac reached for Ben's hand. "Ben, Anna, why don't I show you where I work and we'll give Tony a little peace to finish his writing.

He led the children out into the bullpen and over to his desk. Ramsey tagged along behind. The room had filled with cops as word of the arrest must have filtered out. Johansson waved to him and came over. "I hear you struck gold, you lucky bastard," he said. "Terrance got sent out to direct some kind of search. Oliver is processing Anderson downstairs. I went and looked. You got the guy all right. Prints are an initial match."

"That's good," Mac said. Every piece of confirmation slid a weight off him. He felt oddly empty. "These are my kids, Anna and Ben. Anna, you've met Detective Johansson before."

"At the picnic," Anna remembered. "When Tony and Ben didn't come with us."

"Right," Mac said, wincing.

Ramsey said helpfully, "Hart helped catch Anderson. He's writing a statement."

Johansson looked surprised, but closed his mouth on whatever comment had come to mind. A slap on the back staggered Mac and he turned. "Hey, way to go," Hanson said. "I was in the neighborhood and thought I'd drop in and get the real scoop for myself. Met Oliver downstairs."

Mac nodded, wondering how processing was going with the stream of gawkers that seemed to have been passing through.

"I heard you stumbled across the guy at a park," Hanson continued, fishing for details.

"Something like that," Mac agreed. "I'll get my report in soon, and I'm sure the whole task force will get to round up the final details."

"I want in on the interrogation," Hanson said, "But I bet you and Oliver don't need the help."

"Probably not." There were still details they wanted. Not just the burning question of why strangle and stab blond women, but also whether that was Sandy's necklace, and if he took trophies from the other women, and where he kept them, and whether they had missed any early victims before his pattern was set. Interrogation was a formality as far as winning this case, he hoped, but he still wanted to confront the man.

There was a loud voice from across the room. "Someone want to explain to me what's going on here?" Severs strode into the room. "I was enjoying the first nice Sunday I've had in a while when I got a call to come in." He glared across the room at Mac. "And then I find you here, MacLean. You're suspended. Get your ass out of here."

"I brought the *children* along," Mac said, emphasizing the word to try to rein in the language in the pit, "to get a statement from Ben here, about how he helped catch Leonard Anderson."

"He what?" Severs marched over and glared down at the boy clinging to Mac's hand, and then stared at Mac. "Start from the beginning, MacLean."

"Anderson came after Ben for some reason. Probably because he thought Ben was a witness against him. Tony stopped Anderson, Ben came and got me, and I arrested Anderson."

"He's in custody?" Severs said.

"Downstairs. Oliver's booking him."

"So that's why the crowd. All right, that's good. That's very good." Severs suddenly looked much brighter. "Has the press been notified?"

"Not yet. But it's sure to leak momentarily."

"I'll call them," Severs said, standing straighter and reaching up to smooth his hair. "Set up a press conference, let them know that the department has come through for the people of Minneapolis." He frowned. "If someone had told me the details, I could have brought a proper suit. I don't consider that message Oliver left adequate at all."

Mac shrugged, since saying anything would be worse. At least Severs would enjoy doing this press conference himself, which would let Mac off the hook.

Oliver came through the door behind them. "Hey," he called. "Delivered, searched, and booked." He came over to Mac. "You want to start the interrogation now, or do you need to run your family home first?"

"MacLean isn't doing any interrogation," Severs said, with a glare at both of them. "He's still on suspension, and he's leaving." He stomped off to his office.

"What hair got up his butt?" Oliver asked. "You'd think he'd be jumping for joy."

"Your fault," Mac told him. "You didn't warn him to bring in a suit, so now he's going to have to do a press conference in his weekend clothes or else go home for one. How could you be so thoughtless?"

"Jesus." Oliver ran a hand over his hair. "So what do you say?" he asked. "You want to sit in on the interrogation anyway? Or I guess we could use the prisoner's injured hand as an excuse to wait until tomorrow morning."

Mac thought about it for a moment, and then shook his head. Sure he wanted to be in on this, but not enough to buck Severs for it. Anderson was caught. Everything else was gravy. And his own personal life needed some urgent attention. "Take Ramsey in with you," he suggested. "She heard Ben's statement, and Anderson might talk differently in front of a woman. It's not like we need a confession. If he doesn't give you much, we'll tackle him again on Monday. I'm going home."

"Okay," Oliver agreed. "Your call."

Mac collected Anna from where one of the detectives was distracting her by using pencils to play pick-up-sticks, and led the children toward the hallway. Tony came out, carrying the laptop, and met him halfway.

"Finished?" Mac asked.

Tony nodded.

"Give it to Ramsey to read and print," Mac suggested. "But you can sign it tomorrow and I'll e-mail mine in. We're out of here."

CHAPTER 17

As they walked in the door of the new apartment, it felt like home to Mac for the first time. He sent the kids to wash their hands and pulled Tony into their bathroom. He was holding it together. He was damned impressed with himself.

"Okay," he said, "Come here and let me see those hands. I noticed the scrapes." Tony's hands were abraded from the scrambling falls in the woods. Mac held them under the tap, washing gently with soap until the grazes came clean. Nothing was deep. No worse than a fall off a bicycle. "Anywhere else?"

Tony raised his shirt and pushed down his jeans to bare a bruise on one hip. It didn't look too bad.

"Now you're just looking for sympathy," Mac said. He knelt and kissed Tony's flat abdomen, just above the mark, smiling at the hitch in Tony's breath. Mac closed his eyes and pressed his cheek against the warm smooth skin. This was his lover, life and body and breath, and he was not letting him go. It took a moment to realize that his face was wet and Tony was holding him up, stroking his hair.

"Holy God, babe," he breathed, staring into the darkness behind his eyelids. "I want to lock you safely in a closet somewhere."

"No closets," Tony rasped.

Mac laughed, halfway to a sob, and hugged him tight, arms locked around those slim hips. "I'm sorry," he whispered against that soft skin. "So sorry, Tony. That was my fault. I thought Anderson might come after someone. I just didn't think about Ben. All that manpower covering Sinclair and I didn't protect Ben."

"Shh." Tony's hands soothed him. "Hush. It's not your fault. We're fine."

"I should have thought…" He pressed his wet eyes against

Tony until his vision dissolved into sparkles. Black and lights and nothingness in front of him. *He was supposed to be so good at his job, and he had almost failed.*

"'S okay," Tony murmured. "'S okay."

After a long moment Mac stood up and rubbed his face. "Sorry, sorry. Didn't mean to do that. I'm always unloading on you."

"Any time," Tony said breathily. "Lets me know you're mine."

"Oh, yeah," Mac agreed. He puffed a breath. He straightened. "Okay, kids to deal with."

Ben and Anna were sitting at the kitchen table, looking a little lost. Mac pushed Tony into a chair beside them and opened the refrigerator. "Not much here," he said. "How about mac and cheese?"

"Yes, please," Anna said, brightening. It was her favorite. Mac bustled about making lunch, talking about inconsequential things, like how they needed more milk, and whether cooked carrots would be good. Slowly the children lost their frozen look and began talking back more easily. Mac set Tony to making a shopping list, with suggestions from the peanut gallery. Judging by Ben's choices, Sandy had fed the boy out of packages and junk food. Or maybe he just wished she had.

By the time they had eaten, everyone was more relaxed. Mac had hidden his relief at seeing Tony able to eat a little cooled macaroni and mashed carrots. Ben barely nibbled at first, but there must be a secret kid-pleasing ingredient in Kraft Dinner, because he quickly started digging in. Ah, the wonders of salt and fat and macaroni.

Mac put the dishes in the sink and got his family moved to the living room, the kids between him and Tony on the couch.

"Okay," he said. "We all need to talk, except Tony who's going to write on this pad because if he strains his throat I'm going to be angry with him." He reached over and set pad, pencil, and a glass of ice chips in front of Tony.

"So." He cleared his throat. *Maybe start with the easier thing first.* "Ben. You know you broke a rule by going with that man and not telling anyone, right?"

Tony looked at Mac, startled, and shook his head, but Ben nodded. Mac hoped he knew what he was doing here.

"Okay. Well, there are consequences for breaking rules. You aren't responsible for all the other things that happened, only for that one rule. No going off with strangers. That was the only thing you did wrong." That was the message he was trying to get across, and he saw Tony's frown clear as he got the picture. "So I think you should have no Wii for three days, as a consequence. Does that sound fair?"

"I guess."

"He could maybe play when he's teaching me, though," Anna said hopefully, patting Ben's knee.

"Nope," Mac said. "Break a rule, have a consequence. No playing for three days. You can wait a little for your lessons." He smiled at them. "You two are pretty tough and independent kids, but you need to tell an adult when you have problems with other adults, all right?" He hoped the artificial consequence in this case would distract Ben from the actual consequences of his actions. Getting someone you love hurt is a severe lesson. *And not one I needed to learn again.* With an effort he didn't take another look at Tony's neck. He'd seen Ben glancing surreptitiously at Tony's bruises too, and looking devastated. Enough was enough.

"Now the other thing I need to talk about is us, this family. We are a family now, for sure." He was warmed to see the eager look on both small faces. They might be jealous later, probably would be, but for now the idea was obviously popular. Tony was watching him. Must be tough on his verbal lover to be forcibly silenced. Mac would have to do the best he could.

"I love Tony, and he loves me, and we both love both of you," he said, plain and simple. "We want to be together, and we're going to make it work. But you're both old enough to know it won't be as easy as a regular family, with a mom and a dad."

"Because you and Tony can't get married," Ben said.

"Partly that," Mac agreed. "And because some people don't like gay men raising children." He glanced at Anna when he said the word, but she didn't react. Either the shoe hadn't dropped, or she had already assimilated the idea and moved on. It was tricky to know how much to say. "I would like to be able to tell you that what other people think isn't your problem," he said. "But sometimes it will be."

"Some people will be fine with it," Tony rasped.

Mac frowned mock-sternly at him and nodded at the paper. "Write it, babe." He looked back at the kids. "Tony's right. Lots of people will just be happy that you each have two dads instead of one. People like Detective Ramsey, or Oliver, or Tony's friends. They know family is good, in any shape or form. But a few people won't be happy." He sighed. "Unfortunately, some of those people will be your other family."

"Aunt Brenda doesn't like gay people," Anna said sadly. "I don't think she knows any."

*She knows one.* Mac wasn't quite ready to tackle Brenda yet. "Right," he said. "And Ben, your grandparents didn't want Tony to raise you, partly because they love you and want to raise you themselves," *At least I hope so.* "But partly because he's gay and they didn't think that was good for you."

Ben grabbed Tony's hand. "But they can't make me go away, right?" he said anxiously. "I get to stay with Tony and you?"

"That's right," Mac reassured him, as Tony put an arm around him. "The judge knew you would be happiest with Tony, and he's your guardian now. But your grandparents will want to visit with you, and they may say mean things about gay people. I hope they won't. I hope they can just have fun with you, and we'll all get along. But you need to not get mad if they say something ignorant. If something bothers you, tell me or Tony, and we'll talk to them."

"Maybe when they get to know Tony they'll see how nice he is," Anna suggested optimistically, "And then they'll like him."

*I'm not holding my breath.* "Maybe. I hope so," Mac agreed. "And then there's Aunt Brenda." And there he stuck for a moment.

"We don't have to tell her," Anna suggested. "Like with McDonalds."

Mac shook his head. "It can't work that way, princess. It's one thing to not tell your aunt if I give you fast food for dinner. If she doesn't ask, there's no harm in not mentioning it to her. But if you live here with me and Tony and Ben, she needs to know that. She needs to know where you are and who you're with, and that you're safe." He looked at Anna. "Not telling her only works if you live there at her house, like you have been, and just sometimes visit with me here. Then what Tony and I do can still be none of her business." *There, give her the chance to choose Brenda without thinking she's hurting your feelings.* Still, Mac was relieved when her pert little face wrinkled up in anger.

"No way, Daddy! I want to live with you! I don't want to just visit!"

"Okay, Anna," he said. "I just wanted to give you a choice. Because if you live with us, and Aunt Brenda gets really mad, she may not let you come home with her at all. You may not get to ever see her."

Anna looked sad. "Like she doesn't let you in the house because you're a forminator?"

"Yeah, like that."

"If I live with you," Anna asked, "Am I a forminator?"

"Um, no. Remember I told you that's an adult thing. But, um, she just might be mad enough to not want us around at all, because she thinks being gay is worse than being a, um, forminator."

"You could tell her Tony's a girl," Anna suggested.

"Except that's not true," Mac said. "That's not the right way to handle things. We don't lie to Aunt Brenda." *We just don't tell her all of the truth sometimes.* Jesus, it was hard to find a moral balance between Brenda's intolerance and a child's black-and-white view of the world. He clutched at a straw to avoid the whole lying issue. "Even if Tony really was a girl, unless we were married, Aunt Brenda still wouldn't like it. She's still mad because I lived with your mom before we got married."

"Mac," said Ben. "What's a forminator?"

Mac threw a harried look at Tony, who shook his head and opened his hand at Mac. Tony's mouth twitched upward in a small smile as he touched his throat. *Yeah, now you don't want to talk. Thanks, babe.*

"Okay," Mac said. "So the real word is fornicator, and it means two adults who love each other and live together but aren't married. Some people like Aunt Brenda think that's bad."

"But Tony says they won't *let* you and him get married," Ben pointed out.

"Right." Mac blew an exasperated breath. "May I just say that religion and logic don't always go together, and then we can move on." Ben nodded, but Mac caught his lips shaping the word fornicator, as if memorizing. From Tony's bright eyes, he had caught it too.

"And you're no help, Tony," Mac told him. Tony touched his throat again and gave him an innocent look.

"So now I have to talk to Aunt Brenda," Mac told Anna. "The question is when. You could go back and stay with her tonight, at least. I could wait to talk to her till the morning."

"No. I'm staying here, like Ben does." Anna folded her arms and set her chin, reminding Mac forcibly of her mother. He had never budged Mai from that position either.

"Okay. Then I'll talk to her today."

"Will she let me have my things?" Anna asked. "My dolls, and my stuffies, and my clothes?"

"I hope so." *I paid for those, after all.* Not that that would matter if Brenda was adamant.

"Maybe I should tell her about living here and the new 'partment and all my own self," Anna offered.

"Thanks, princess," Mac said, "But this is a grown-up conversation." He looked down at her. "Will it make you very sad if you can't stay with Aunt Brenda anymore?"

"Some," Anna said pensively. "I love her, but staying with her and being good all the time is really hard. I don't do it right much anymore."

Mac hugged her. "Well you do it just fine with me. I was really proud of the way you listened to Tony and me this morning, and did what we asked, when you were probably curious and scared. That was very important."

"I wanted to go see the smoke," Anna said, "But I didn't."

*Thank God. Anna wandering off to see the fire would have been the last straw.*

"It was just a pile of garbage burning," Mac told her. "Smelly and not very interesting."

Anna nodded. "So where am I going to sleep? 'Cause there's not enough beds. There's two beds and four people."

Tony raised an eyebrow at Mac, glee in his eyes, waiting to hear him explain this one. Fortunately Anna was pretty sheltered and wouldn't put two and two together yet.

"Tony and I will share his bed, because it's big," he said blandly. "We'll have to get you a bed for your room, where the TV is now."

"That's my room?" Anna wiggled down and ran to look in with new eyes. "Can I keep the TV?"

"No way!" Ben retorted. "That's my TV!" He headed for the playroom on her heels.

Mac kicked Tony's ankle as he went past, although secretly he was glad Tony could chortle like that. He remembered himself sometime in the past saying, "How hard can it be to raise a child?" Probably before Anna actually hit the ground. Man, he'd been a moron in his younger days.

❖ ❖ ❖

Mac looked at Brenda's house, gathering his courage. The place was the tidiest on the block, white siding and grey roof with a postage-stamp yard. The grass was cut and flowers bloomed along the walk. There were blue curtains in the windows and a pot of marigolds by the door. He thought Anna had been happy here.

Mac walked up and rang the doorbell. Brenda opened it with her usual caution, and looked past him.

"Where's Anna?" she asked.

"She's with a friend. I need to talk to you."

"About her school?" Brenda said. "Yes, we need to move quickly on that." She hesitated, and then pulled open the door. "You could maybe come in, just this once. I have papers to show you."

Mac followed her into the house. It figured. He'd come to drop the boom on her and she was finally being human to him.

The interior matched the outside of the house; neat, clean, and a little Spartan. Brenda led him over to the kitchen table and they sat down. She opened a small folder of papers. "I have it here," she began.

Mac put his hand on the pile. "Wait, Brenda. Before you start, you should know that I've moved into a bigger apartment, and I want…I'm *going* to have Anna spending a lot more time with me, including nights."

"But your work. What will you do if you have to go in to work at night?"

"I'm sharing the apartment with a friend," Mac said. "We'll be able to make sure someone is watching Anna."

"A friend," Brenda said slowly. Her lip curled. "What kind of friend? Another one of your loose women?"

"No. Actually another man, and his six-year-old boy."

"Well I won't have it," Brenda said sharply. "I don't know this man. He could be anyone. He might be a pervert. How can you leave Anna alone with a strange man?"

"He's not a stranger," Mac said. "He's my best friend. He's a teacher, and he's great with kids. And Anna is good friends with his son Ben."

"Ben!" Brenda exclaimed. "That's the boy she talks about, that told her all sorts of nasty things. You can't let her live with them!"

"She's living with me," Mac said flatly. "And with them. But you can decide how often she stays with you, especially in the summer when there's no school."

"What about school? Are you going to send her to a safe Christian place like we talked about?"

"I don't know," Mac hedged. "Right now I'm busy moving into the apartment. I'll think about her school later."

"But you won't, will you?" Brenda said. "She'll end up in the public school, learning who knows what, exposed to all kinds of bad influences. I've put five years into raising that child, Jared MacLean, and I won't have it."

"You've done a great job with her," Mac said, gentling his voice. "She's an amazing child, and I couldn't have raised her this far without you. But I want more time with Anna and that's final. I want her to live with me and eat meals with me. I want to read her bedtime stories and hear about her day. You wouldn't let me share that with you here, so I've found a place elsewhere."

"You can't afford it," Brenda hissed.

"I will have to cut back on what I pay you, once she isn't here so much," Mac admitted, "But I'll give you the full payments for another few months, because of the short notice, until you find something else."

Brenda shoved herself to her feet. "What else am I going to find?" she demanded. "I'm forty-eight years old. What work am I going to do?"

"I don't know." Mac couldn't believe he was feeling so guilty, but he hadn't thought about Brenda's finances in this. Even a few months was more than he could really afford, but he did owe her a lot. Surely she could line up some kind of job.

"Maybe I could change things," Brenda offered. "Maybe you could come inside here sometimes and be with Anna. It was a long time ago that you sinned with Mai. If you've been God-fearing since then, maybe that's enough."

Suddenly Mac was tired of beating around the bush, trying to pretend to live by Brenda's standards.

"I'll never fit your definition of God-fearing, Brenda. I'm gay."

"You're what?"

"I'm gay," he repeated. Those words were getting easier.

"You can't be," Brenda whispered. "You were married. You have a child."

"I'm in love with another man," Mac told her, taking a bitter satisfaction in the way her face paled. "I sleep with him."

For a long moment the older woman just stood there staring at him. Her mouth worked, but no sound came out. Then suddenly she stepped back violently. "You filth!" she hissed. "You pervert! Get out! Get out of my house!" Her voice escalated to a shriek. "How dare you come in here like a normal man and say that filth to me. Get out!"

"I'm going," Mac said, heading for the door. He turned. "But Anna is my child and she's staying with me. I would like her to be able to still see you. She loves you and none of this is her fault."

"Does she want to come back and live with me for good?" Brenda demanded.

"Not for good. Just to visit."

"You're lying," Brenda said. "I've taught her, I've shown her how it should be. She goes to church with me. She would never stay in a house where…that kind of thing happens."

"She's just a child," Mac said tiredly. "She has no clue what sex even is. But she knows Tony and I love each other and she's happy with us."

"That's the thanks I get. All these years, treating her like my own flesh and blood." Brenda paced back and forth, and then stopped, fingers white on the edge of the table. She glared at Mac. "But she's just like her mother. No morals. Like her mother and like you, Jared MacLean."

"Yes, she is like Mai," Mac said. "Strong, and loving, and stubborn, and good. And she loves you too. And you can go on seeing her, if you are willing to share her with Tony and me, and treat our situation with respect."

"Never," she said bitterly. "Never! If Anna wants to live in a house of perversion and sin, then she's no child of mine. I'll pray for her soul, night and day, but I won't have her here. And you can keep your filthy money, too. Now get out!"

Mac stepped out the door, and turned again, but the door slammed in his face. "I'll send someone for Anna's things," he muttered. *That went well. Smooth, MacLean.* He hoped Brenda wouldn't be mad enough to destroy Anna's possessions before he could collect them.

*You just had to do that, rub her nose in it.* But he couldn't help a small feeling of satisfaction. All these years, he'd had to take her lectures and her preaching. And now he could flat out tell her the truth and not care. He was worse than she'd ever imagined, *and he didn't care.* He hadn't realized how much he resented her attitude, and the necessity that tied him to her, until it was gone. He headed back home feeling better than he had ever expected about making the break with Brenda.

Sunday evening was edging into the early hours of Monday morning before Mac finally made his way to the bedroom. Tony was sprawled across his own side of the bed, face down, under the light sheet. Mac sat on the edge of the bed to set his alarm.

"Work in the mornin'?" Tony mumbled without looking up.

"Yep," Mac said. "Case meeting bright and early." He had spent a long time on the phone with Oliver off and on through the day. Anderson had talked at first. Apparently he had latched on to the idea that Ben was one of the prime witnesses against him from news stories. All that human interest crap about the "brave young boy the only witness to a brutal killer" that KVOL had come up with. Then they made it easy for Anderson to track Ben down by identifying the adult with him as "courageous teacher Anthony Hart who survived his own close encounter with a killer just last year." Add Tony's listed phone number and some rudimentary computer skills, and Ben had been wide open. One of Mac's tasks today had been to convince the phone company that Tony needed a new unlisted number right now.

But when they had confronted Anderson with the necklace, found at the scene, he had apparently clammed up completely. They hadn't been able to find out yet where the man had been living, and he refused to answer anything else, even though he had yet to request his lawyer. The profiler thought Anderson had probably taken souvenirs from each of his victims, and was protecting his treasures with his silence. His car had been located a few miles down the road in the park, but had yielded no new clues.

They had also found the knife in the woods. Mac had been pleased to hear about it, but there had been a tiny clutch in his gut as he realized that only luck had kept the weapon out of Anderson's hands when he fought Tony. With a weapon, even a small one like that dagger, things might have turned out very differently.

Eventually, Oliver had taken Anderson back to his cell. They would try interrogating him again in the morning, with Mac adding his efforts. Anderson's arraignment was also upcoming, and would doubtless be a media event. Even without the DNA results yet, there was plenty of physical evidence to lock in the case. Mac wasn't worried about Anderson getting turned loose. But he dreaded the renewed publicity.

Severs had been a pig in clover at his press conference. He preened in front of the cameras, dressed in a suit he had apparently sent some underling to pick up for him. He had touted the effectiveness of his department without once using

Mac's name. Mac was just as glad. But he wondered a little what his boss would be like at their next meeting.

He sighed. Life wasn't perfect. Loes would be back in the office on Monday, with a legitimate reason for an official complaint if he chose. Even without a complaint, Mac expected a very mixed reception from his co-workers. Loes would doubtless spread venom where he could.

He had fucked up the situation with Brenda as thoroughly as was humanly possible. Not that there had been a good way to do that, but Mac was sure he'd found one of the worse ones. He would have to find someone else to send for Anna's things. Maybe Ramsey would do it for him.

Anna had been subdued at dinner, and insisted on praying a long time at bedtime. Then her sleep had been troubled. Only now, after two glasses of water, one trip to the bathroom, and another hour that Mac spent going in and out of her room, had she finally drifted off into a deeper sleep. Mac shot a glance at the new monitor on his side of the bed. The rustling and breathing had quieted at last.

Ben had had one nightmare too, and Tony's boneless pose looked like deep fatigue. Both kids were undoubtedly upset. Mac wondered how regular parents made it through times like this. Although, even regular parents probably didn't have many times like this. The weight of responsibility was suddenly heavy. Anna was all his now.

Well, his and Tony's. He looked over at the man beside him and slowly slid the sheet down. Because there were good things about this arrangement too. Really good things. And not just knowing Tony was in this parenting thing with him. Not just having this man at his side.

Call him superficial, but it was amazing to just look over and see that fine curve of muscle and skin, the line from shoulder down Tony's back to the hollow of his ass. There the graceful arc of light off lean biceps, gaining a little added muscle as Tony had joined Mac with his weights now and then. He loved the angle of hip, and the deep divot of dimple in that fine ass, inviting his tongue. He leaned over and placed a kiss in the spot, brushing soft skin with the stubble of his unshaved face.

"Mmm," Tony whispered sleepily. "Hi, there."

"Hi, babe," Mac breathed, continuing a gentle exploration of the body laid out for his tasting. Lean muscled legs, feathered with dark hair, and those narrow arched feet. Tony moved a little under his mouth, spreading his legs. Mac was on his way back up one warm thigh when a whimpering cry interrupted them.

"Yours or mine?" Tony rasped.

Mac glanced over at the monitors. Ben's glowed steadily; Anna's had a row of lights dancing in time to the sound. He sighed. "Mine. I'll go see what she needs. You wait here and hold that thought."

He shut off the monitor, grabbed his robe from the hook on the door and made his way to Anna's room. His daughter sat up in her sleeping bag, face flushed and distressed. Mac lowered himself to sit beside her. Her new bed was on order, but for now this arrangement of sofa cushions and sleeping bag was the best they could do.

"What's up, princess?" he asked softly.

"I had a dream," she said, snuggling up beside him. "I dreamed that you and Tony were locked up in a room and I had to go live with this strange old woman, and she made oatmeal."

"Yuck," Mac said lightly. "Oatmeal."

"I wasn't scared of the oatmeal," Anna said reproachfully.

"I know," Mac agreed. "Tony and I aren't going anywhere, except home and work and all the regular things. We'll be here in the morning and then your bed will come, and Tony will take you shopping." *Although Tony doesn't know it yet.* Mac ruthlessly sacrificed Tony's morning to Anna's enjoyment.

"Daddy," Anna said. "Are you sure God won't strike down you and Tony, like Aunt Brenda says?"

"Yes, baby, I'm sure." He hugged her. "Remember Jesus told us to all love one another. And Jesus came after all those older parts of the Bible." He felt like a hypocrite, but he needed to explain in terms Anna was used to. "There are lots of other gay couples out there, being happy and raising kids. We'll have to meet some of them." *Another task for Tony. Surely there must be some website to help gay parents link up. He knew he'd seen stories in Lavender Magazine about gay parenting.* "God doesn't strike any of us down."

"So Jesus thinks it's okay for you to be gay?"

"Yes," Mac said ruthlessly. "Those older guys in the Bible didn't like it, but Jesus never said anything bad about it and He should know."

"I guess," Anna murmured, getting sleepy again. "What church will we go to, Daddy?"

Mac blinked. "Do you want to go to church, baby?"

"Well, the sermons are boring, and the minister yells a lot, but I really like the Sunday School lady and we got juice and cookies."

Mac was relieved. He was better with cookies than sermons. "How about we wait for a few weeks, and then if you decide you want to go to church, we'll find one that will be happy to have us." There must be some. He'd heard there were some churches out there that were welcoming and inclusive. Hell, the Basilica downtown hung a rainbow banner from the bell tower for Pride week.

"Okay," Anna said. "And Tony 'n Ben can come."

"If they want to."

"Mm." Anna was limp against him. Mac lowered her to the bed, but left the cover loose. Maybe if she wasn't so warm she would sleep better. He kissed her forehead.

"Sleep well, princess."

She murmured a little, smiled, and slid a hand under her cheek. Mac watched for a few minutes until he was sure she was down, then made his way back to his room.

Robe off, door locked, monitor back on, and he slid into the bed. He kissed Tony's shoulder. Unfortunately, that wasn't a purr of pleasure he got in return. That was definitely a snore. Mac rose up on his elbow to look over Tony's shoulder at his face. Eyes closed, mouth relaxed, and yes, snoring softly. *Damn.*

Mac eased back down. He wasn't about to wake the man. He stretched his length out on the bed and pulled the lax sleeping body gently against him. Tony's hair tickled his chin, one thigh pressed against his, and that fine rounded ass cradled his hardness. He slid an arm over and pulled them closer together. Tony murmured and wiggled in without waking. It was torture, but it was sweet.

This time last year, he was solitary, successful in his job but cut off from everything else. He saw his daughter a few times a week, and never got to kiss her good night. His version of being gay was a frantic weekend out of town, anonymous sex in hotel rooms with men whose appearance he couldn't even remember and whose names he never knew. He had never spent the whole night with a man. He had never made love with the goal of pleasing someone else more than pleasuring himself.

He pulled the covers up over the two of them. His life might be more complicated now. He might face flack from all sides in the morning. But he had a life, not just an existence. It was difficult, but it was real, and it was good.

He pressed in against Tony, moving a little, deliberately letting the heat and the want rise unfulfilled. He wouldn't get to relieve that want tonight. Eventually he would have to sleep. But there would be the morning, and showers, and tomorrow night, and the next day. He kissed Tony's hair lightly. This was so much more than he could have imagined only a year ago. Still sleeping, Tony's hand closed on his own. Mac wove their fingers together, and closed his eyes and breathed. And lived.

# About the Author

KAJE HARPER grew up in Montreal and spent her teen years writing, filling binders with stories about what guys like Starsky and Hutch really did on their days off. (In a sheltered-fourteen-year-old PG-rated romantic sense.) Serious authorship got sidetracked by ventures into psychology, teaching, and a biomedical career. And the challenges of raising children. When Kaje took up writing again it was just for fun. Hours of fun. Lots of hours of fun. The stories began piling up, and her husband suggested it was time to try to publish one. Kaje currently lives in Minnesota with a creative teenager, a crazy little omnivorous white dog, and a remarkably patient spouse.

If you're a GLBT and questioning student heading off to university, should know that there are resources on campus for you. Here's just a sample:

US Local GLBT college campus organizations
        http://dv-8.com/resources/us/local/campus.html
GLBT Scholarship Resources
        http://tinyurl.com/6fx9v6
Syracuse University
        http://lgbt.syr.edu/
Texas A&M
        http://glbt.tamu.edu/
Tulane University
        http://www.oma.tulane.edu/LGBT/Default.htm
University of Alaska
        http://www.uaf.edu/agla/
University of California, Davis
        http://lgbtrc.ucdavis.edu/
University of California, San Francisco
        http://lgbt.ucsf.edu/
University of Colorado
        http://www.colorado.edu/glbtrc/
University of Florida
        http://www.dso.ufl.edu/multicultural/lgbt/
University of Hawai'i, Mānoa
        http://manoa.hawaii.edu/lgbt/
University of Utah
        http://www.sa.utah.edu/lgbt/
University of Virginia
        http://www.virginia.edu/deanofstudents/lgbt/
Vanderbilt University
        http://www.vanderbilt.edu/lgbtqi/

CPSIA information can be obtained at www.ICGtesting.com
Printed in the USA
241107LV00001B/8/P